Fatal Attraction

Gorgeous, Armed, and Dangerous - Book 8

Elisabeth Garner, K.M. Ringer

Paperback ISBN:

Ebook ISBN-13:

Credit to Books by E M Garner for book cover, formatting, and headshot.

Credit to Gail Delaney and Kimberly Ringer for editing services.

Contents

Also by Elisabeth Garner

The "Love Prevails" Series

(Contemporary Romance)

Even Angels Fall

Even Hearts Struggle

Even Hope Returns

The "Gorgeous, Armed, and Dangerous" Series

(Suspense Mafia Romance)

Not Just Another Pretty Face

Pretty Little Picture

Pretty (in)Significant

Pretty Much Screwed

Locked and Loaded

Loaded Question

Loaded Vengeance

Loaded Secrets

Fatal Attraction

Fatal Consequences - Release Date Late 2026

Final Fate - Release Date 2027

Destination Unknown – a Gorgeous, Armed, and Dangerous Novella

Paranormal Romance Standalones

Lady Lilac – A Deadly Garden Coalition Novella

Forbidden Flame – A Burn Me Down Novella

Dedication/Acknowledgements

Mom, Dad, Matt, and Em - My pillars. My anchors. My ports in a storm. Thank you for always having my back.

To Abi, Nik, Al, Rad, Arzez, and Arafel - Thank you for giving me a place to escape, rest, heal, and recharge so I could write this. You were a lifeline I didn't know I needed.

Kim – Thank you for "dragging" me into this mafia world with you. Enjoy your Wolf.

My girls - I wouldn't be here without you. I'm grateful for your puppies, our pool noodles, and floating doors.

My ARC/Street team and readers - I cannot put into words how much your feral love, encouragement, and support mean to me... Not without writing another book.

Auntie 'Nette - Thank you for being an amazing aunt and role model. Your fierce strength and love helped shape me.

To everyone clambering for a certain character to get their comeuppance - I delivered, as promised.

"All magic comes with a price."
- Rumpelstiltskin, Once Upon A Time

Content Considerations

Fatal Attraction is a mafia suspense romance. That being said, there are dark elements in this book, including but not limited to physical, gun, and knife violence, blood, and gore, on page death, loss of a family member, PTSD and trauma-based flashbacks, anxiety, toxic family, mention of parent death, mention of and conversations about infertility, adoption, and strong language.

There is a young child who is a significant character in this book. Nothing bad happens to her. Ever.

Note from the Author

The Rodriguez family is another mafia family in the Chicago Syndicate and is a creation of K.M. Ringer, who has given her permission for me to use within this story.

If you would like to read more about this family, as well as the Dallas and San Augustine families, please head over to www.kmringer.com for her Chicago Syndicate books.

Chapter One

Two years ago.

Dante

"Jesus, is it too much to ask for you to leave me some fucking hot water?"

I chuckled and shook my head as I took a sip of my coffee. This was at least the second time my sister had made this complaint this month. "Get up earlier or take a shorter shower."

We lived in a two-bedroom apartment in an older building about ten minutes from the Agosti compound. It was close enough to rush in for an emergency, but far enough to be able to disengage from the job. Not that it ever really happened. In this line of work, there really wasn't 'clocking out'. The Job never stopped.

My fingers moved on autopilot as I swiped through my phone with one hand, the other clutching a mug that was big enough to double as a murder weapon. I'd sent my usual morning message to Sabrina, but she hadn't replied yet.

Noting the time, she was definitely awake, possibly already at the range, but more likely still curled up in bed, poring over some report or ledger. My thoughts shifted to how she'd been yesterday morning, kneeling at the foot of my bed. Her dark hair cascading over her shoulders, chin up, focus locked on me as if daring me to make the first move. I had to shift in my chair as part of me reacted to the memory.

Why hasn't she texted back yet?

I was still as obsessed with Sabrina as I was the night I met her three years ago. It was my first time attending the Agosti's annual Christmas party. I'd been sent outside to collect the ladies for dinner, and she was standing there, talking with Lianne. Normally, I would have called for them from the door, but they were laughing so hard, I walked to be heard. I scuffed my shoe on the stone surface, and the next thing I knew, Sabrina had whirled around and was holding a knife to my throat. Lianne shook her head and started laughing even harder. Between the fire in Sabrina's stunning brown eyes, her gorgeous body, and her obvious lethal skills, I was hooked.

She was the only woman I'd ever met who could run a boardroom, shoot a man between the eyes at fifty yards, and then crawl naked into my arms with a need so sharp it cut me open every time.

God, I love her so damn much.

Talia emerged from the bathroom and removed the shower bonnet from her hair, releasing the micro-braids from their confines. "You got plans today, or are you just gonna stare a hole through your phone?"

I shrugged as I set down my mug. "Sabrina's got a thing at noon, and I thought about stopping by the house afterward. Then, I'm covering for Connor tonight. You?"

She rolled her eyes and worked on making herself an omelet. "I'm taking Lynette to another meeting with some hedge fund asshole. He was such a pain in the ass last time. Why do they all assume she's uneducated? She's a Don's wife, for fuck's sake. I swear, if I have to listen to one more guy try to mansplain municipal bonds, I'll..."

I glanced over as she trailed off and shrugged. "Shoot him?"

Talia snorted. "Tempting, but unless he threatens Lynette, I have to keep my gun and bullets to myself."

My phone buzzed, and my heart skipped a beat when I looked at the screen.

Kitten: < Morning, Wolf. You really put me through my paces yesterday. I can't remember the last time I woke up this sore. >

I grinned. She'd been in a hell of a bad mood yesterday, and I'd spent half the day coaxing her out of it. Not that I minded. Sabrina's moods were like Chicago weather—unpredictable, sometimes violent, and always character-building.

The truth was, I loved her best when she was fighting for every inch of ground. She lived her entire life like that, white-knuckled and raw. Constantly at war with the expectations that came from being Don Ceaser Rodriguez's golden heir. Even when we were alone, even when I had her gasping and undone in my hands, part of her was always watching, always bracing for the next blow.

It had taken months for her to admit that she needed anything from me, and nearly a year before she actually asked for it. I remembered the first time she finally let go, the first time she let me take the reins all the way. Sabrina had arranged for us to use one of the Rodriguez safe houses for a night, wanting us to have as much privacy as possible for two people deeply entrenched in the mafia.

"I trust you, Wolf. Make me yours."

I was never stupid enough to think it was just sex. That wasn't how it worked for either of us. For her, it was about being able to trust someone enough to peel away all the layers of the mafia badass she had to be during the day and be vulnerable and open enough to let someone take care of her. For me, it was about control—being the one who could protect her from everything, even herself. Especially herself.

Talia dropped a plate in front of me, pulling me from my thoughts again. It was loaded up with more eggs than I'd ever admit to eating. She slid into the chair across from me, a coffee mug cradled between her palms, and raised an eyebrow. "You okay?"

“I’m fine.” Something had been off in Sabrina's texts all week.

My sister narrowed her eyes, studying me as if she was trying to decide if I actually believed what I was saying. After a moment, she took a slow sip of coffee. "You know she'd walk through fire for you, right?"

"I know." My phone buzzed again.

Kitten: < You at the apartment or the compound? >

Wolf: < Apartment. >

Kitten: < Stay there. I’ll be there in 20. >

A tense breath came out. It wasn’t relief, but it wasn’t concern, either. "She'll be here in twenty."

Talia's eyebrows shot up. "Here? I thought you were meeting her later?"

"Change of plans. You know how this life is." I shrugged and then started shoveling food into my mouth, not wanting to waste the delicious breakfast my sister made for me.

"Great," she muttered, gathering her coffee mug and phone. "Guess I'll make myself scarce."

Guild washed over me. "Tal, you don't have to—"

"Yeah, I do." She tossed the dishtowel at me. "Last time you two had a 'talk' in this apartment, I found a knife stuck in the drywall. Before that, the place smelled of leather, lube, and sex for days. There are things I never want to see or hear."

A smirk tugged at the corner of my mouth as I recalled the memory. "That was different. Also, you have time to at least finish breakfast before heading out."

Talia rolled her eyes and picked up her phone. "Whatever. “

Eighteen minutes later, three quick, hard knocks thudded on the door. It was Sabrina's signature. Talia sighed. “Don’t burn the place down, please. Text me when the coast is clear." She grabbed her jacket and slipped out the fire escape with practiced ease.

“I’ll do my best.” Standing, I walked over and opened the door. Sabrina stood there with a can of pineapple juice, condensation beading on the metal. Her eyes were dark, wide, and utterly unbreakable.

"Brought you something." She pressed the cold can into my palm.

"Thoughtful." I stepped aside to let her in. "Usually I'm the one bringing you these."

She smiled, a brief flash of teeth, then pulled me in by the lapels and kissed me like she was staking a claim. "I'm leaving. Today. Right now, actually."

I blinked at her in confusion as I set down the can before I dropped it. "What?"

A tense breath rushed out. "I'm on my way to the airport. Shit hit the fan, and I have to take care of some things."

Fear rocked through me as I processed the information.

What? No. She can't leave. I have plans. We have plans.

"When will you be back?"

Her gaze darted between my eyes. "Wolf, this one is gonna be a long one. I'll be gone for over a year, maybe longer."

"Kitten..." I wrapped her in my arms. We knew someday there would be family business that would separate us. It was the one thing being loyal to two separate Dons in Chicago made inevitable. Our Dons were allies. Hell, they were best friends, which made this much easier. Regardless, business was still business.

She broke the silence first. "I won't be able to call for a while."

My hands tightened on her waist. "I figured."

Sabrina pulled back and looked up at me, eyes narrowed. "You're not going to ask about it?"

I shook my head. "It's Rodriguez business. Not my place."

She softened, just a little. "If it was your business, I'd tell you."

"Would you?" I teased, and she punched my shoulder, just hard enough to hurt.

"Yes, you asshole."

In an attempt to have one last moment with her, we moved to the kitchen. I poured Sabrina a coffee, adding a healthy splash of her favorite caramel creamer, and she smiled after taking the first sip, perched on the edge of the counter, boot heels thumping the cabinet below.

"You're really going to be gone for a *year*?"

She didn't answer for a second, but then shrugged. "Maybe more. It depends on how everything plays out."

My heart dropped. "A year is a long time, Kitten."

Sabrina set down her mug, not taking her eyes off it. "I know."

I watched her fingers, the way she slid them around the rim of the cup and the edge of the handle. She looked as apprehensive about this as I felt. "You could say no."

She let out a humorless laugh. "Not really."

"You *could*."

The woman I loved looked up, a deadly serious expression on her face. "No, Dante, I can't. If I don't go, a lot of people will die. That's not something I can walk away from." She paused, studying me. "You understand that, right?"

I hated how much I did. "Yeah."

She slid off the counter and stepped close enough that I could smell the vanilla and orange from her shampoo. "I'm coming back to you," she whispered, as if saying it aloud made it true. "That's not negotiable either."

I cupped her face and kissed her hard, desperate to press my love into her. She melted against me, hands gripping my shirt tight.

This was more than a kiss. It was a goodbye... One that burned.

Eventually, Sabrina broke away, eyes wet with unshed tears. "Rod's going with me."

That helped a little, and I nodded. "He's good. He'll keep you safe."

She rolled her eyes. "*I'll* keep me safe. Rod's just there to carry the bags and look intimidating."

I smiled, then kissed her again, slower this time. "I want you to come back with no new holes."

Sabrina reached up and touched my face, her thumb tracing along my jaw. "I will. Unless you find someone better."

"Impossible." There was never going to be anyone else for me. She was my one and only. She was my forever.

"I need you to be good for me and not get hurt, either." She looked up at me, her expression so vulnerable I almost looked away.

"Kitten, I'm always careful. You know that."

She narrowed her eyes at me. "Seriously, this is important, Dante."

"Yeah, but so are you."

She pressed her forehead to mine, eyes shut. "I love you. I love you so fucking much. Please never forget that. No matter what you hear. No matter what happens. Remember that I love you to the very core of my soul. You are the only one who can quiet my mind."

"I love you too." I took a shaky breath. "Come home to me."

There was a quick nod as she let go. But as Sabrina headed for the door, she looked back over her shoulder, and for a second I saw the part of her that needed me more than air.

I stared at the door for a long time after she pulled it closed behind her, already counting the seconds, the minutes, the hours, the days until she'd come home to me.

Chapter Two

A Year and a Half Later

Sabrina

On the drive back to Havana after a tense, but potentially productive meeting with a tobacco farm owner, my thoughts kept going back to the way he flinched whenever *La Muerta Rubí* cartel was mentioned, how he steered conversation away from local security, and how his smile faded whenever we passed the perimeter of the property. Something was coming, something *bad*, and I needed to figure out what it was before all hell broke loose.

Rodrigo eventually broke the silence. "Did you notice the black SUV two kilometers outside the farm?"

"I noticed on the way out." I kept my voice at a whisper, not wanting to draw the driver's attention to our conversation.

He nodded slowly, his focus never leaving the window. "They're expecting us to run. Or try to make contact."

I let out a deep sigh. The same thought had also crossed my mind. "Tonight's meeting is likely a setup."

"Probably."

As the countryside rolled by, each kilometer brought us closer to the city and whatever waited for us in the gilded cage of the Hotel Nacional. Our dinner was going to be with the man who actually owned and ran the cigar business. The farm owner couldn't approve the purchase of his farm, so we had to have yet another meeting.

All to keep La Muerta Rubí cartel from taking over all of Cuba.

Another sigh came out. There was a reason my uncle sent me here. I finished deals and got shit done. I just hoped I could seal *this* deal without too much bloodshed.

Rod shifted and leaned in a little closer to me. "If it gets ugly, you know what to do." I gave him a pointed look as if he had forgotten who he was talking to, but all he did was shrug. "If they want to make a point, you know it'll be public. You're a Rodriguez. They'll want to break you in front of an audience."

Arching an eyebrow, I smirked. "But they don't know who I am here. They think I'm just your little meek wife. Hell, Orlando doesn't even know who I really am."

My partner narrowed his eyes at me. "Not the point, boss."

He was right, and I knew it. Letting out a sigh, I glanced at the duffel bag by his feet, knowing the firepower we'd brought with us. "Do we have enough to fight our way out?"

His laugh was dry. "If we don't, Zee will send flowers."

That brought an involuntary smile to my lips. Zara Leveer, my right hand still back in Chicago, had a knack for knowing when and where to send backup, or at least a timely condolence bouquet. *Jezu*, I missed them. I missed them almost as much as Dante.

We reached the hotel as the sun dipped into the horizon in a beautiful orange and yellow cascade, and as much as I wanted to enjoy the view, it wasn't why we were here. Linking arms with Rod, he escorted me into the lobby crowded with Americans, Russians, and a few locals. Miguel handled check-in for us and then handed us our key with a smile.

"Your suite is on the top floor with the best view." He gave a small bow. "Enjoy."

Once inside the room, we immediately dove into our investigation for surveillance bugs. It wasn't a matter of *if* they were present, but *where* they were hidden. In a matter of minutes, we found three in the different light fixtures, one under the phone, and a fourth in the toilet tank, of all places. Rod and I collected them with an efficiency that would have made Zee proud, stashing them in a glass of water on the balcony. We weren't leaving anything to chance. Not here. Not now.

He grinned, the first genuine smile of the day. "Either they're getting lazy, they want us to know we're being watched, or we're better at this than they are." He took a step toward me, resting a hand on my shoulder. "Rest while you can, Boss. Tonight's going to be long."

I wanted to fight him, but Rod was right. Dinners here were a long, drawn-out social affair. Even if everything went perfectly, it was going to be a late night. "Fine." Despite the stunning view, I pulled the curtains almost entirely, plunging the room into darkness, save for the sliver of light peeking through the drapery, and then plopped onto the bed. The exhaustion of the past year and a half on the run weighed heavily, and I hoped we were almost done. I wanted to go home. I wanted the other part of my life back.

Rod didn't sit. He never did, not unless he deemed it safe enough for him to get some sleep, and even then, I swore the man still had one eye open.

I laid back, shoes still on, and stared at the ceiling before closing my eyes, counting the seconds until night fell and the game began.

I never fell asleep, but simply rested as best as I could. Part of me pretended Rod was actually Dante and that he would crawl onto the bed and hold me tight, reminding me that everything was going to be okay. A few tears gathered as I thought about how I missed that man like nothing else. Sure, Rod and I played the part of a loving couple in public, but it was all for show. No one could hold a candle to my Wolf. He was the only man who could turn my brain off. The only man I would ever submit to.

Tío promised me he'd let Dante know I was safe. And while I was grateful, I wanted more. I wanted to talk to him for a few moments. I wanted to be anywhere but here for five minutes.

My gut swam with unease as I wrestled with the fact that tonight was going to be a shitshow. I knew it, and all I wanted was a moment of comfort and reassurance. The best I could do was surrender to the memory of Dante. His sharp brown eyes, which were so dark they were almost black. The way he was solid muscle from head to toe.

I could almost feel the pressure of his full lips as he kissed down my neck. I could envision the way his gaze transformed from gentle to commanding an instant before he'd back me against the wall and remind his Kitten exactly where she belonged.

Rod cleared his throat, pulling me out of my fantasy. "We should start getting ready."

Glancing at my phone, I saw that an hour had passed. "You're probably right." I pulled myself out of bed and changed into a simple black dress for dinner. Not because there was a need to impress, but because I wanted to remind myself that I held the power here. Not Rod, not Orlando, not *La Muerta Rubí*. Me. Control was an illusion, and even if the evening went off without a hitch, I liked wielding as much control as possible. Even if it was *just* in the clothes I wore.

Rod changed into a grey suit, strapping holsters to both his chest and ankle. The obvious one silently announced *I'm here to kill for her*. The message was not lost on me, nor on the two men who met us in the hotel lobby. Each dressed in a dark grey suit and the stereotypical aviators to hide where they were looking, and they nodded their heads in silent greeting as we all stood there, waiting for Miguel.

Miguel appeared at seven on the dot, leading us down a marbled hallway to the restaurant terrace, which overlooked the expanse of the city. The room was more crowded than I had expected, but there was an eerie calm hum of conversation throughout the room as we walked through. It put me on edge. *Am I just being paranoid?*

Our host for the evening sat at the end of a long table, looking every bit Havana's unofficial ruler and collector of debts, both financial and mortal. Señor Ernesto Damas was younger than I'd expected, maybe late thirties, with the kind of dark and handsome features that would make dark romance readers swoon. It had no effect on me. His gaze lifted to meet ours, and a smirk tugged at the corner of his mouth, as if he found the whole spectacle amusing.

"Maria." He stood and reached out a hand. "It is a pleasure. I've heard rumors of your beauty, but words fail to describe your radiance."

I'm sure you have.

Keeping up the façade that I was positively affected by the compliment, I let him kiss my knuckles, then took my seat to his right. Rod settled in beside me, back to the wall, eyes watching beyond the table. I didn't miss the way that a few men at the table glanced at him, then immediately looked away, as if staring too long would invite death.

Initially, the dinner played out like a well-rehearsed play. Food appeared, empty dishes vanished, and more food appeared. Laughter echoed against the pillars and the hard-tiled floors, and drinks flowed freely. I answered questions about the vision for the farm and the quality and export quotas, all while evading the fact that I knew *La Muerta Rubí* was behind much of our production issues in South America.

The whole night was going well, but I knew better than to take it at face value. There were too many men with their hands close to their guns, and then there was the small talk. It felt like Damas was stalling for time. Like he was waiting for something.

But what?

Halfway through the third course, a man at the far end of the table, who hadn't said much all evening, stood and raised a glass. "A toast! To our guests and to new beginnings."

I raised my glass, but the wine never reached my lips as I faked the sip. He gave me the fakest sincere smile as walked over and stopped between Damas and me, bending down between us. "To be honest, I'm surprised you came here yourself, Señorita Rodriguez."

The words were whispered, but I heard them as if they had been shouted.

How and when did my cover get blown?

I set my glass down smoothly, pulling on every ounce of training I had in me to continue selling the rouse. "As flattering as that is, *señor*, I'm afraid you're mistaken. My name is Maria Castro."

A wide, predatory grin spread across his face as he leaned closer to me. "We have friends in Chicago, *señorita*. Don Vaux sends his regards."

Time slowed to a crawl as my mind raced through the potential connections., and several people shifted closer to us, as if a silent order had been issued.

Suddenly, the table jerked as Rod flipped it up, sending bottles and dishes into the air and scattering across the floor. I dove left as the first shot rang out, glass from one of the lights hanging over the table exploding above my head, and Rod immediately returned fire.

People screamed and ducked under tables as I pulled my gun, looking for the man who had outed my identity. Damas was gone, vanished into the kitchen with two of his guards on either side of him. The rest of the terrace dissolved into chaos — guns drawn, knives out, blood spraying across the pristine white linens.

I scrambled to the veranda's edge as I saw one of the guards take aim at Rod. Lifting my gun, I pulled the trigger, and the man dropped immediately as pain bloomed in my abdomen. Looking down, the black fabric became darker and wet, and much too fast.

Rod appeared at my side, crouching over me. "Fuck. You're hit."

"No shit, *cabrone.*"

He practically growled as he grabbed one of the napkins that had slid across the floor and stuffed it against the wound. "He's gonna be so pissed at me."

Who?

"Let's get you out of here, boss." As he pulled me to sit up, I bit back a groan as pain lanced through me. "I got you. Can you walk?"

I rolled my eyes. "Since I was eight months old."

Miguel appeared in our path, his suit dark with blood as he lifted his gun to Rod's head. A sinister smile appeared on his lips. "Should have stayed in Chicago, señorita."

Rod didn't hesitate, shooting Miguel in the throat before lifting me and shoving me past the man as he fell to the ground. "Let's go!"

The next few minutes were a blur as pain wracked through me with each terrified stride I took away from the restaurant. Adrenaline kept me going. That, along with the echo of continuing gunfire. I lost my shoes somewhere, and the temperature change from warm marble to cool concrete hardly registered. It didn't matter. I had to keep moving if I wanted to stay alive.

More gunshots rang through the air, and pain shot through my right shoulder. "Fuck!"

Rod lifted me up when I stumbled, half-carrying me as we continued to rush down the hall. "Stay with me. Just around the corner. We're almost there."

We ducked into a service alley, and Rod propped me against a dumpster and checked the wound again. "You'll need a hospital, but not here. They'll find you."

I gripped his wrist, trying to focus on his face. "Rod, you're hit too."

He looked down, as if noticing for the first time. His shirt was soaked with dark patches along his ribs and shoulder. His skin was already the wrong color. "Doesn't matter."

For a long moment, I looked at him. No words, no fake comfort. Just the unbreakable bond of two people who had worked together for years. "You're gonna make it."

"Liar." He pressed a gun into my hand, his backup piece, right as two guards from the restaurant walked into the alley. Standing, he spun around, guns raised high, and was steady as a sniper as he fired. The others returned fire, but Rod didn't bother ducking for cover. He walked straight toward them, pulling the trigger with each step.

The first man into the alley went down with a bullet to the chest. The next two fired wildly, and each hit Rod took made his body shudder, but he kept moving forward somehow and kept shooting until he was the only one standing.

As silence fell, he turned, smiled at me, and took a few steps before crumbling onto the pavement. I winced and gasped through the pain as I crawled and dragged myself toward him, listening to his ragged, wet breaths. "You got them," I whispered when I pulled his head into my lap. "You did it."

"Good." He let out a wet rattle of breath before looking at me and saying, "Get home, marry Dante, and love fiercely, boss."

Then he was gone.

I staggered through the city, every step sending a fresh wave of agony through me. Blood trickled down my side and my arm, and my stomach burned like someone was branding me from the inside. I kept to the shadows, moving along the dark side of buildings, ducking into alleys where *la policia* never patrolled and the only law was don't get caught.

Just a little further.

Another few blocks was all I had to go before reaching somewhere I could at least get patched up. Claudia lived on the second floor of a crumbling building, just far enough from the tourist belt to be invisible. She was a contact from my trip a few years ago in Cuba, a university professor moonlighting as a document forger, but what I valued most was her ability to make things disappear. People, evidence, debt — it didn't really matter. If you needed a ghost, Claudia could make one for you, and for the right price, she wouldn't ask why.

I made it to her stoop, collapsing against the door as I knocked twice. "Claudia, it's me. Open up!" When she did, I slumped into the hallway, panting with exhaustion and relief as my heated skin made contact with the cool tile.

She swore under her breath as she grabbed my arm and pulled me inside before closing and locking the door. "Bathroom, now." The order was low and sharp as she guided me with a firm grip. I barely made it into the room before falling again, watching my blood smear on the smooth tiled floor.

Claudia knelt beside me, her hands quick and clinical as she tore more of my ruined dress to inspect my wounds. "You're an idiot. And a lucky one at that."

"Rod's dead." The whispered words tasted rotten in my mouth, and I forced myself to swallow down the pain of his loss.

Her hands froze, and she looked at me for a long moment before giving a curt nod. "He was a good man, but you knew he was always going to die for you."

That didn't make me feel any better. "He never should have." Her fingers pressed against the wound in my shoulder, and I hissed. "He should never have had to." My eyes snapped to hers. "How am I going to get him home? I just... I left him... in the alley." I closed my eyes, fighting tears. The tile was cold against my cheek as I laid on my side, and for a second I wanted to let the world go quiet.

Claudia slapped me, not hard, but enough to pull me back to the present. "Stay awake. I'm not cleaning up your corpse."

"But Rod—"

“Enough,” she cut me off and let out a tense breath. “We are going to keep your ass alive so we can get you home. Thank God the bullet isn’t stuck in here.” She poured cheap vodka over my wound, and I nearly blacked out from the stinging pain. When I came back, Claudia was stitching the torn flesh with the focus of a surgeon and the compassion of a hangman. After knotting off the end, she locked eyes with me. “We’ll get him home, *Mija*. Now, who did this?"

"*La Muerta Rubí.*" I panted the words out through the pain. "Rod bought me time."

She shook her head. "He didn’t buy you time. He bought you one last chance. Don’t waste it getting all sentimental on me."

When I could stand without passing out, she led me down a narrow stairwell to the cellar. The air was thick with the smell of mildew and the damp metallic tang of old blood. There were three cinderblock walls, a steel door, and shelves stacked with canned beans, pickled vegetables, and a scattering of bottles of illegal Cuban rum. I don’t know why, but it amused me that Claudia’s cellar pantry doubled as a panic room.

At least I won’t starve if I’m stuck down here.

She made a nest for me in the corner, fussing over layering old blankets and ratty towels. Once I was settled, Claudia set a bottle of water at my side, then handed me a burner phone. I immediately called the secure line at home, which was hard since my head was spinning from all the pain and movement.

“*Mija.*”

I was never so relieved to hear my Uncle Ceaser’s voice.

“Rod’s dead.” My voice was weak to my own ears and faded to a whisper. “Need to take... flight...”

“*Mija*?”

My phone slipped from my hand as everything went numb, and my head fell to the floor. Claudia barely caught me, and in the recesses of my mind, I heard her talking quickly before everything went black.

Chapter Three

Dante

My calves ached, and my tense neck and muscles screamed in protest. I'd been on a razor's edge with everything going on. Shit was hitting the fan, and the house was still in chaos when the security footage Ryan miraculously snagged revealed that Liam had been the one to kill George. I'd never seen so many pissed-off people in my entire life. None of us were okay. Not one bit. We all were coming apart at the seams, held together by pure will and caffeine.

The pain of losing George hit us all hard. Harder than I thought possible.

I didn't cry. Not openly, not where anyone could see. Almost none of us did. We all had jobs to do - mainly that of keeping Lynette safe and alive.

As expected, everyone looked to her for guidance. She had been part of the family long before George became Don and knew the business and her husband's wishes best. Lukas was around, but seeing as he lived in Colorado almost exclusively now, flying back and forth made things more difficult.

Then team restructuring happened.

Lianne had stepped up to be Lynette's right hand. And while she was doing a phenomenal job, her hands shook a little sometimes when she passed out the daily briefs. Even Lukas, who previously had been untouchable, was unraveling a bit. Every trip back and forth left him more brittle, and less able to hide the haunted look in his eyes.

Even the toughest faces among us were drawn and wary, as if our entire foundation had shifted overnight. Which it had.

We wanted a ghost to come back to life.

But George would never walk through those doors again. We would never hear his low, rumbling laugh at a well-phrased joke. We'd never hear praise for a job well done. All we were left with were the lessons he'd pressed into us: no patience for excuses, the demand for precision, and bone-deep loyalty to the Agostis.

That was likely why I couldn't sleep. Even with a house full of trained operatives, I kept an overly vigilant eye on everything. I started second-guessing everything, triple-checking the simplest details, demanding updates at all hours, demanding more from myself even when there was nothing left to give.

All of this was made worse by not having Sabrina nearby. I stretched my neck, hoping to relieve some of the tension there, and checked my phone for the millionth time. No new messages. No missed calls. The screen only showed my last, unsent draft to Sabrina "Kitten" Rodriguez. I closed my eyes and saw her clear as day in my mind. The way her smooth, dark hair was always just out of place after I kissed her, the tiny crinkle of concentration between her brows when she read reports, the sharp intensity of her eyes when she issued orders to her men.

The only information I had was from Don Rodriguez, her uncle, reiterating that her condition was stable and she was safe. In desperation, I'd even gone to Lynette, hoping her close relationship with the man would get more information, but he'd told her the same thing. Sabrina was alive.

Alive. That was the bare minimum, wasn't it? It was supposed to be a relief, but it felt like a taunt. I was alive. I was here. But I was also in limbo, and no one was telling me why. I needed answers. I *needed* to hear her voice. I'd memorized the cadence of her speech, the deliberate way she spat out a syllable if she was angry, the drag and lilt of certain words when she was being clever or cruel. Her voice would tell me everything I needed to know.

"That's it."

Connor spun around and met my gaze. I'd been wandering mindlessly through the house and had found myself in the crew kitchen in the basement. "What's it?"

Shaking my head, I looked at him, my decision made. "I'm heading out. I'll be back in a few hours."

He narrowed his eyes at me. "Haven't you been up all night?"

"Yeah, and?" The words came out bitter and sharp. I was tired of getting shut down.

Connor held up his hands, either in self-defense or because I was acting like a feral animal. "I am not the enemy here. I'm just saying you look like shit and could do with some sleep."

"Couldn't we all?" I stomped out and headed for the garage.

Thirty-five minutes later, I pulled through the main iron gates of Don Rodriguez's compound and parked in front of the white stucco Spanish-style home. I used to love the dark wood windows and door frames, as they led to where the love of my life lived, but today they felt like barriers keeping me away from the truth.

Getting out of the SUV and striding up the steps, Cobra met me at the door, cutting me off as I headed straight for Don Rodriguez's office.

"Dante. Hold up. Don's busy." The man was dressed in a pair of jeans and a light grey V-neck long-sleeve shirt, and his hair was dark and looked as if he had been running his hands through it for hours.

I glared at him. "I don't care."

He put his hand on my chest to stop me, but I knocked it away. Cobra gripped my shirt and pulled hard enough that it would have ripped had I fought it. "Fucking stop, will you?" When I complied, he took a deep breath. "There hasn't been any new information."

"Well, *he* can tell me that. He can also give me a lot fucking more information than the fact she's alive. I need something good to hold onto. You know what hell we're living in right now." My throat tightened slightly as the thought Sabrina could be anything other than okay flickered at the edges of my mind. *No. She's fine. He just needs to fucking talk to me.*

Understanding shone in his eyes for a moment, and he dipped his head lower. "Look, you have all the team's condolences, and Don Rodriguez will be at the late Don Agosti's funeral, but you can't just storm in here like a man possessed. People get shot for that shit."

I was about to ask if he was going to stop me when Don Rodriguez appeared in the doorway to his office. "It's okay, Cobra. Dante, come on in."

Shoving the man's hands off me, I turned and walked into what should have been one of the most intimidating rooms in the city.

Don Rodriguez's office was a blend of the old-world and modern. The wooden desk was built by his great grandpa while he still lived in Cuba, but once it was moved here, glass was added to the top to protect the wood from damage. On the floor was a rug that anyone associated with the Rodriguez's knew the history of. The last two Dons had both died and bled out here. One from an ambush, the other from the man falling due to old age, hitting his head, and slowly fading off into the afterlife.

Please don't let me die here.

Don Rodriguez circled the desk. When our eyes met, I knew he felt much of the same loss I was. Hell, the grief in his eyes matched that of Lynette's too closely. It made sense considering how close the families had been for decades.

“I need to know more than that she’s alive.” The words tumbled out fast, hurt, and without hesitation.

He regarded me for a long second, then stubbed his cigar out in a silver tray. “That’s not how this works, Dante.”

I straightened, refusing to flinch. “She’s out there somewhere, completely off the grid, and I’m supposed to pretend it’s all going to plan? I haven’t slept in three days. Sure, it’s been from more than this, but...” I ran my hand over my hair and turned to kick a piece of lint on the floor. “Fuck, Ceaser, you know I love her. I need to hear her voice. I need to know...”

He gestured to the leather chair across from him, the motion as much command as invitation. “Sit. You’re making my carpet nervous.”

I sat, but didn’t relax as I met his gaze, unblinking. “If you don’t want me to keep asking, give me a reason to stop.”

Ceaser finally sighed, and the composed façade slipped for the briefest moment. “She’s in the wind for good reason. You of all people should understand the necessity of secrecy and discretion.”

I shook my head, jaw tight. “Don’t give me the company line. Give me facts. It’s been over a year and a half since I’ve heard her voice... Seen her face. With George...” I swallowed my anger for the briefest moment. “I need my arms around her. I recognize that can’t happen. Sabrina has a job to do. I respect that, but—”

“The pain is all on the surface.”

You get it. “Yes, sir.”

A faint smile crept onto his lips. “I’ll see what I can do. But only if you can tell me right now that you’ll follow my orders when the time comes.”

I hesitated, and that was answer enough.

“Thought so.” Ceaser reached for a fresh cigar. “You’re dismissed.”

I pushed away from the desk, fighting the urge to scream. “I’ll be waiting.”

"Wouldn't have it any other way."

Ceaser flicking his lighter was the only sound as I strode out of the room and out of the house.

Chapter Four

Sabrina

A loud series of muffled bangs on a door woke me with a start. It was immediately followed by Claudia spewing curses in Spanish at whoever was demanding entrance to search for me. I also caught the rhythmic tapping of her foot over the cellar door. It was a warning to stay silent.

"Where is she?"

I could practically hear Claudia's eye roll. "I don't know. I haven't seen Señorita Rodriguez since last year."

God bless this woman.

I heard them tearing her home apart. Glass shattered on the floor. Drawers were pulled and tossed onto the ground. I sagged into the blankets in the corner, feeling horrible that it was my fault her place was being destroyed. Another fifteen minutes passed before they finally left, and Claudia climbed down into my hiding place.

"I'm so sorry, Claudia, but thank you."

She shrugged and let out a long, weary sigh. "You've gotten me out of trouble a time or five. It's the least I can do. Besides, I owe Don Rodriguez my loyalty. He's ensured my sons have prosperous lives in America. They are happy boys with wives and children of their own because of him."

I nodded as she fussed over me again, checking my bandages, handing me more pain medication, food, and antibiotics. That was how my uncle worked. He took care of the people who helped take care of him. "You talked to *Tio*?"

"*Si*. You're to stay here until Zee calls. Do not answer the door. Do not answer the phone unless it's one of them. If I'm not here, do *not* go upstairs at all." Sabrina let out a shaky breath. "We both know they will come and look for you again."

I nodded. "I know, and thank you."

Claudia looked down at me, mouth pressed in a hard line. "You have to pull through. If I find out you died in my cellar, I will bring you back and kill you again myself."

"Fair enough."

After she left, I lay there, shivering, trying not to think about every possible thing that could go wrong between not and when Zee contacted me. At some point, I dozed off. When I woke, the light under the cellar door was faint and milky. Someone was moving upstairs—slow, deliberate steps, two pairs of them. I held my breath, hand gripping the burner phone as if I could squeeze it into a weapon. The footsteps moved through the kitchen, paused over the trapdoor, then retreated.

I exhaled, pain knotting my insides. *Please be gone.*

Hours passed, and my phone rang at dawn, a single vibration. Zee's number. I answered.

"Do not speak. At twenty-one hundred, a tan hatchback will stop at the corner of your street. Get in. There will be a package in the back seat. Take it. Inside are clothes and an envelope. Follow the instructions."

The line immediately went dead, I clutched the phone to my chest, and let out a shaky sigh of relief. Hiding out in this cold, damp, dark cellar was almost over. *I just have to make it through the rest of the day.* When Claudia came back some time later, she brought more meds, a bag of chips, and a plastic-wrapped sandwich.

"You're lucky you're pretty," she said, inspecting the stitches. "Otherwise, I would have sold you to the highest bidder."

I raised my eyebrows in intrigue. "There's already a price on my head?"

Claudia huffed out a laugh and nodded. "Of course. Half the city wants you dead. The other half wants you out. I'd say you have about twelve hours before they come back here, looking for you again."

"Good. I only need eight."

"Perfect."

The rest of the day crawled by. I slept, woke, and slept again. My dreams were an endless loop of gunfire, running, pain, and Rod's face, serene and resigned in death. When the time finally came for me to leave, Claudia dressed me in a loose linen shirt and battered jeans from her closet. She tucked a forged passport into my pocket and walked me to the curb.

"Don't waste Rod's gift."

The car pulled up on schedule, and the driver never looked at me, just unlocked the doors and kept his eyes on the road. After glancing around, relieved to see no one along the narrow street, I slid into the back. As promised, there was a small duffel bag and an envelope. I quickly read the note, which spelled out where and how to find Zee at the airport, as well as that I should check underneath the seat of the car. Reaching between my legs, I had to feel around a bit before finding a small pistol.

Thank you, Zee.

Despite being armed again, I didn't relax on the way to the airport. My gaze kept going to the driver, who was sweating bullets and gripping the wheel tight. However Zee got him to ignore me, it was clearly done through intimidation, and I hoped it lasted until I was far from here.

The vehicle stopped at a small cafe a few kilometers down the road, making my anxiety spike. This wasn't part of the plan. Then Zee slipped into the back seat with me. I opened my mouth, but they shook their head once. A silent order to keep my mouth shut.

What happened now?

They leaned forward and gave the man directions to continue down the road until they told him to stop. We rode in silence for a good fifteen minutes, and it was all I could do to maintain my mask of indifference.

"*Deténgase aquí.*"

The man jumped at Zee's barked command and immediately pulled over.

When I looked around, there was nothing but open road in front of us and the ocean to our left. *Why are we stopping here?*

Zee jumped out of the vehicle, walked around to the driver's side, opened the door, pulled out their gun, and shot the man in the head. Letting out a deep sigh when he slumped over in his seat, they holstered their guns and looked at me. "Change of plans. The airport is too hot. They're watching the planes."

I nodded, a little stunned, and not by what had just happened. "Okay, so now what?"

"Grab the bag; we've got a walk to take."

Gritting my teeth, I eased out of the back seat, jammed the gun into my waistband, and slung the bag over my shoulder. "If you wanted to take a moonlit walk on the beach, you could have just asked."

Zee rolled their eyes, but I didn't miss the amused smirk that flickered across their lips. "Let's go, smartass."

It wasn't long before I spotted a short pier with a small, dark skiff floating alongside. *Please don't tell me I have to walk farther.* The pain in my side and shoulder throbbed more with each step I took. "Is this our ride?"

They nodded. "Yep. We're heading to the island safe house."

A ghost of a smile appeared on my face. "Man, I haven't been there in forever. Dad took me once when I was a teen. Mom loved that place."

"Well, I love staying alive, so let's keep moving."

It took longer than I liked, but after we settled onto the boat, Zee took their hat off, and my eyes went wide. "You cut your hair!"

They smiled, eyes bright. "Well, yeah. It's hot and humid here. Wasn't sure how long we'd be holed up, so figured I needed to find a way to stay cool while working on my tan."

"Yeah, 'cause you need to work on your tan." Chuckling hurt, but it was nice to joke with them again. A tan. Zee had the darkest skin of anyone I knew. Their bright hazel eyes caught the moonlight and sparkled with amusement. Being female-presenting meant they often had to do twice as much to prove themselves a bit more in our line of work, but they had more than proven themself to Uncle Ceaser and had been working for our family for over fifteen years.

An hour later, a small cay materialized from the darkness.

Gracias a Dios. Everything hurt beyond the point of ignoring. The last round of pain meds wore off long ago, and I didn't have any more with me. Aside from that, the hike along the beach, and the bumping and swaying of the boat as it skimmed the water, I was exhausted. Narrowing my eyes, I didn't recognize the place.

Wait. That's not where the safe house is.

Zee clocked my confusion as they helped me out of the boat and onto the dock. "This is a pit stop for the night."

Once on the sand, they helped me out of the boat. It was a slow process, but I followed them toward the silhouette of a house perched above the shore, moonlight illuminating everything in a dull, blue-white glow. I focused on that as I walked, trying to ignore how every breath and step shot a sharp burst of pain through me.

Almost there.

The house was set on weathered stilts, with battered white paint peeling in strips. The front door was still the same cheery yellow, even if faded a bit. Inside was blanketed in complete darkness until Zee flicked on a lamp and gold light filled the room. There were no family photos, no personal effects, just a battered couch, a rusted ceiling fan, and a small round table with two chairs that had seen too many storms. Zee thoroughly checked the doors, the windows, and every lock. Only when they were satisfied did they gesture towards the couch from where I leaned on the wall.

"Sit. Let me see."

I slumped down, the world tilting as stabbing pain temporarily overwhelmed me. Zee knelt, scanning my face, my shoulder, and where Claudia stitched me up. There was no hiding their grimace. "They got you good." Zee leaned back and looked me in the eye. "I believe the deal we made was you coming back with no new holes."

I gave them a halfhearted shrug. "Listen, I bobbed and weaved the best I could, okay?"

They pulled a first-aid kit from their bag. "Claudia did a pretty good job, but you tore the stitches. Now hold still while I fix it."

Again? I let out a tense breath. "Can you at least buy a girl a drink before rearranging her guts?"

Zee rolled their eyes and pulled a bottle of vodka from their bag, followed by a bottle of pain relievers. "Pick your poison."

A wicked smirk spread across my face as I took both. "You *do* love me."

"Obviously."

After I was medicated, they cleaned the wound, restitched what I'd torn, and changed the dressing with the steady, competent hands of someone who'd patched bullet holes far too many times. The entire time, I tried not to think about Rod or the way grief pulsed through me with each heartbeat.

I can mourn him later. I need to honor his sacrifice by staying alive.

When Zee finished, they handed me a bottle of water. "You need to drink more than vodka, or I'll get my ass kicked. We're sleeping here tonight and will head to the safe house in the morning."

I wanted to protest, but the words wouldn't come. I was too exhausted. Zee tossed a blanket over me, found a battered chair, and cut the light before they settled in near the door, pistol in their lap. The message was clear. They'd watch so I could sleep.

For the first time since Rod fell, I let my body relax in an attempt to actually get some sleep. I drifted in and out, and my dreams flickered from seeing Rod's calm eyes, feeling Claudia's skilled hands, tasting the tang of gunpowder, and eventually hearing Dante's voice in my head telling me to sleep. At some point, rain started pattering against the metal roof, and the soothing sound reminded me of nights when I was a child, safe in my uncle's house.

Early dawn light filtered through the slats of the wooden blinds, waking me. Zee was already up, boiling water on the stove. They poured two mugs and set one on the table for me, moving carefully, as if the floorboards creaking would make too much noise, but I caught the edge of concern in the way they watched me drink.

"We leave in ten. You have fresh clothes in your bag. Go change." They sat down and checked the wounds on my shoulder, side, and thigh. "Stitches look good. You'll make it. Guess you'll have to see Dante's annoying face again after all."

I gave her a playful glare. "Watch it. I love that man."

There was a soft smile on their lips as they nodded. "I know. If it's any consolation, he's been harassing Ceaser for updates. He even showed up at the compound and nearly beat up Cobra before Ceaser pulled him into his office. He gave Dante enough to keep him off edge, but that man is *worried* about you. Now get dressed so we can get the hell out of here."

As much as I tried to move quickly, my muscles screamed in protest as I peeled off the clothes Claudia had given me and pulled on a pair of loose-fitting linen pants and a black tank top. Between the running, the tension from the pain, and everything I'd been through over the past several days, I wanted a tranquilizer and the world's longest nap.

Maybe when we get to the safe house.

When I emerged, Zee nodded, grabbed my bag, and led us out of the house. I took as deep of a breath as I dared as I stepped outside, allowing myself a moment to smile. There was nothing like the clean, crisp scent of the air after a good rain.

As we pulled away from the cay, I watched the house fade into the mist. We were safe for now, but the city still simmered behind us, and I felt a shadow reaching out relentlessly. I leaned back. "Our farms were the only real competition for *La Muerta Rubí* in Cuba, so I understood why they set their sights on us, but why also in South America?"

Zee let out a sigh as they expertly navigated the boat across the water. "We got word a few weeks back while you were still in Guatemala that they are trying to expand their reach. Partnered with another one of the cartels. *La Serpiente Azul*."

I tipped my head back. "Rod and I put a pretty large dent in their militia in Guatemala about eight months back. That was quite a fight. Dante would have loved it. We used every explosive we could get our hands on."

They laughed. "That he would have."

"Do you think Uncle Ceaser would let me talk to him for a few minutes?" A tear slipped down my cheek as the longing hit hard. I knew it was mostly from exhaustion, but I really wanted my Wolf's arms around me.

Zee gave me a look that clearly said, *What do you think*?

"Yeah. I know. No contact until I'm better. Likely until the heat dies down."

They chuckled and shook their head. "We are in the Caribbean, Sabrina. It's always hot."

"Fuck you, Zee."

"Fuck you, too." Still laughing, their bright eyes met mine. "Damn, I've missed you."

The sky brightened, pale orange through the clouds. I pressed my hand to my side, wincing at the pain, and let the wind whip through my hair. Somewhere ahead, my temporary home waited. But right now, survival was enough.

Chapter Five

Several Months Later

Sabrina

I glanced around the safe house that had been my home for the past several months and let out a deep sigh. Anyone else would have probably loved being stowed away in the heart of the Caribbean, but I was over it. The ocean views no longer brought me any solace. I was pissed, heartbroken, and homesick.

Zee had been a literal lifesaver and hadn't left my side while I mourned Rod and then Claudia's deaths, healed from all my physical wounds, rebuilt my strength, and generally missed my old life.

There were days I wondered if my Uncle Ceaser had forgotten about us. But that was stress, boredom, and exhaustion talking. I knew he hadn't. The steady and discreet stream of supplies showed me that. There were also the infrequent messages and brief conversations we had on the burner phone he'd sent.

It didn't make me miss home any less.

I sat on one of the porch swings on the back veranda, staring out over the ocean, willing the warm ocean breeze and the sound of the waves to soothe my restless soul when the phone in my pocket rang. There were only two people who had this number.

Please let it be him.

Letting out a deep breath, I answered it. "*Buena.*"

"*Mija*, how are you?"

Relief washed over me, and I grinned at the nickname and the familiar, warm voice of my uncle. "*Tio*! I'm okay. What's up?"

He let out a heavy sigh. "There's been a change of plans."

The smile disappeared from my face, and I immediately stood up and headed inside toward Zee's room. "How quickly do we need to move?"

"That depends on whether you're ready to take on a new assignment."

Adrenaline shot through me as I considered his words. *Already?* It seemed fast, but I'd been feeling great for a couple weeks now. There wasn't any reason for me *not* to move on. "I'm good to go, and Zee can confirm it. Where, what, and when, *Tio*?"

"A protection detail much closer to home."

I nearly dropped my phone. That was the last thing I'd been expecting. "Has it cooled off enough for that to work?"

He let out a tense breath. It was all I needed to confirm the trail was still hot. "I'll send the arrangements within the hour, *Mija*. Be ready. Stay safe. *Te amo.*"

The call ended, and I hugged the phone to my chest.

I love you, too.

Chapter Six

Present Day

Dante

This was not going at all how I'd imagined it, not that I ever *wanted* to see Lianne and Lynette in the same room as Liam and his idiot associates.

It was currently both better and worse than any scenario I'd thought of. Liam, who had tried to surprise us with a visit, was standing in the middle of the foyer with two of his guys, and had at least six guns trained on him. He'd brought Chloe, his beautiful two-and-a-half-year-old daughter, who had been whisked away to the kitchen by Jess to see Lynette and Ben almost immediately upon arrival.

Adair had just taken out William, a man who had apparently double-crossed her back when she lived in a safe house in Indiana. Lianne gave her blessing, but it still wasn't every day someone was executed in the middle of the foyer.

Now Nolan, Liam's second, was running his mouth with misogynistic bullshit about who should and shouldn't be Don.

"You're in over your head, Lianne. You need—"

Narrowing her eyes, she squeezed the trigger, and his shoulder was thrown back at the same time a concussive bang filled the foyer. "That's *Don Agosti* to you."

Even though I'd been expecting Lianne to pull the trigger, I still blinked at the intense volume. With all the solid surfaces in the enclosed space of the foyer, there was nowhere for the percussive sound to go. My attention snapped to Adair and Peter as he grabbed her hips and pulled her closer to him. I could tell he was a split-second from pulling her out of here, not that I blamed him. It was no secret they had gotten attached over the past several months while he helped protect her in hiding, and if it had been me, I'd be doing the exact same thing.

Nolan's eyes went wide in shock as he clutched his shoulder, blood seeping between his fingers. "What the fuck is wrong with you?"

Lianne glared at Liam's second in command. "I'm sorry, did you want to die instead?"

Movement in the corner of my eye caught my attention as Avery walked from the foyer into the kitchen, and Ryan immediately entered, looking the most pissed I'd seen him in months. He held a small, lidded jar half-full of a clear liquid. And rolling around the bottom was something small, round, and *very* familiar looking. "I think Don Agosti is more than justified in killing both of you, especially since I found this."

Please tell me that's not what I think it is.

Lianne kept her gun and attention on the two men still standing in front of her. "Because of *what*, Ryan?"

He walked closer to her, making sure to stay well out of the range of her gun. "Remember that earpiece we gave Avery a few weeks ago when she was covering Poppy?"

Our Don nodded, tightened her grip on the gun, but still didn't take her eyes off where it was trained. "Yes?"

Ryan let out a tense breath. "Well, we found one in Chloe's things. In the ear of her stuffed bunny, to be precise."

Sounds of disgust and low growls of anger filled the room, and I thought Gage was going to jump Liam and beat the shit out of him. The truth was, we all wanted to. Lianne's direct order not to take Liam out was the only thing keeping that man alive.

None of us liked following that order, but our Don had her reasons, and we respected her.

Lianne's entire posture stiffened, and her eyes narrowed on her brother. "You did *what* to your daughter?"

Please end this. This man had hurt the family in too many ways. It needed to end.

Liam turned and glared at Nolan. "What did you do to her bunny?"

"Followed your wife's orders."

"But her bunny? You fucking idiot!" Liam looked outraged, and if I was reading his reaction correctly, he didn't seem as pissed about the earpiece, but more because Nolan messed with his daughter's stuffed animal.

What the hell is going on here? I was desperately trying not to jump to the wrong conclusion.

"Excuse me?" Lynette, having rejoined us in the foyer, suddenly stepped forward, glaring death at her oldest son. "You wired your sweet baby girl to eavesdrop on us? You actually made *her* a pawn in your sick, twisted game?" She shook her head, eyes narrowed, looking absolutely disgusted. "Your father and your uncle are both rolling in their graves right now. I hope you're pleased with yourself."

Adair suddenly stood up straighter, pulled her gun from her holster again, lifted it, and then nodded after Peter whispered something into her ear.

My eyes went wide as I glanced from her to Peter to Liam and back to her. *What is she planning?*

Liam spun back around, cowering in Lynette's presence. "It-it's not like that, Momma. You have to—"

The Agosti matriarch cut him off as she slapped him across the face, the sound echoing off the paneled walls as his head snapped to the side from the impact. She then crossed her arms over her chest, let out a disappointed huff, and glared at the man in front of her. "I don't have to do a damn thing, *son*. What else could *possibly* be happening here right now?"

The sharp tone mixed with her frigid posture had me fearing for *my* life, and I wasn't the one staring at the business end of a gun. Adair tsk-ed as she took a slow, measured breath. Peter tightened his hold on her hips, eyes wide. From the pissed-off, determined expression on her face, I wasn't sure if Liam was going to live much longer. She'd already killed William a few minutes ago.

Liam committed a similar crime... and worse. He's earned his death several times over.

"You won't give us information we're entitled to. Why should we share ours?"

Lianne sneered at Nolan's shitty comment. "Oh, I'm more than happy to give you what you're *entitled* to, you insufferable pain in the ass."

"Me too." I watched Adair pull the trigger, but heard two shots go off in an impossibly quick succession.

The back of Nolan's skull exploded, and brain matter, blood, and other fluids splattered onto the wall and tiled floor as Liam let out a pained shout, clutching the side of his head, blood seeping through his fingers.

That had to be Lianne's shot. If there was anyone who could make a bullet skim the side of his skull but not immediately kill him, it was her.

As she let out an angry breath and stepped forward, Lianne pressed the barrel of her gun to his forehead. "Start talking or you're next."

None of us moved. It wasn't as though we'd never seen Lianne shoot, but we had never seen her hold a gun to someone's head.

"Why didn't you kill me? Afraid to pull the trigger?"

The cool, calm rage simmering in my Don's blue-grey eyes matched that of Lukas, who had taken a step closer toward his twin sister, his gun at the ready. "As much as it pains me to admit, I'm with our fuck-up of a brother on this one, Li. Why *is* he still alive?"

"Paperwork."

Confused glances were exchanged all over the room, and Lukas took another step toward Lianne. "*What* paperwork?"

She narrowed her eyes in disgust. "This asshole signed a contract between previous Agosti and Vaux Dons, with the late Don Supreme witnessing. Now, I may not be the one who broke the contract, but I *am* the Agosti Don, which now makes this my problem. I need to read through the damn thing and then arrange a meeting with Don Dallas to discuss the finer details to make sure killing *brother dearest* doesn't immediately put us in the middle of another fucking war." Lianne growled out the words as she pressed the gun more firmly against Liam's head, forcing it to tip back. "Are you going to continue to run your mouth and be a problem, or have I fucking made my point?"

I'd never seen Liam so pale in my entire life. His eyes never left Lianne. "Cr-Crystal clear, Li—Lianne." He swallowed hard again. "Don Agosti."

"Good." She glanced at her twin brother as she holstered her gun. "He stays alive... for now. Get him the fuck out of my sight before I change my mind."

Without another word, Lukas and Connor quickly removed Liam from the foyer, practically dragging him across the tile. Her attention didn't waver from the trio until they were physically out of her sight. Only then did Ryan walk to Lianne's side. "How would you like us to take care of this?" He gestured to the bleeding corpses on the ground.

Letting out a sigh, she glanced down and furrowed her brow. "Leave the bodies and Liam's car somewhere Susan will find them."

He nodded. "Any message to be left with them?"

Lianne's eyes went cold and hard before she shifted her attention to him. "Tell her to do her own fucking dirty work." With that, she turned and left the foyer.

Lynette let out a deep sigh. "Well, that escalated quickly." She looked over at Gage. "Come with me. I'm going to talk with Lianne, and I don't want us interrupted."

He gave her a quick nod. "Yes, ma'am."

As they followed in Lianne's wake, Avery walked back into the foyer and glanced around the space. "Ben, Jess, and Chloe are upstairs in Liam's old room. I told them to stay put until otherwise directed by Lianne or Lynette."

Ryan and Regina looked at each other and had a silent conversation. After a moment, she nodded and left, making her way down the hall as Ryan turned toward us. "Peter, please take Adair to her room. Dante and Avery, take the bodies outside and put them near the car. We need to search and strip it before returning it. Talia, I need you to help me and Regina clean up in here as quickly as possible."

I looked at Peter, who held Adair tight in his arms, and all I could feel was pride and concern for her. She'd held herself admirably today. Facing the people responsible for ruining her life could not have been easy. I watched them as they made their way past us and down the hall to their room. "She going to be okay?"

Avery let out a deep sigh and nodded. "Yeah... she will be. That woman has too much fight in her." She cleared her throat and faced me. "So, which poor, unfortunate soul are we hauling out of here first?"

It didn't take long for us to bag up the bodies and move them outside. Talia had already pulled out Chloe's car seat and was in the process of going over the vehicle with a fine-tooth comb. By the time the SUV had been cleared, loaded up, and was ready to leave, Connor had joined me outside, keys in hand. "I'll be following you and bringing us back. You ready to roll?"

Chapter Seven

Sabrina

The plane's tires touched down, and a nervous yet excited breath rushed out as we rolled along the runway. The familiar and welcoming city skyline I saw in the distance before landing brought tears to my eyes. It had been a long time since I'd been in Chicago. Since I'd been *home*.

Will I get to see Dante? Mom? Tio? What is this assignment?

We'd left the safe house in the dead of night, taking off and landing at two other airports before this. During the long travel day, Zee and I had discussed our theories about where I could be working. They had also made me sleep, so I would be ready for anything when we finally stepped off the plane.

"You okay?"

I glanced at my bodyguard, who studiously observed me, and nodded. "Yeah. Just a lot, you know?"

Zee gave me an understanding smile. "It's good to be back."

A tense chuckle came out as I turned back toward the window and tried to keep my emotions contained. "That it is."

As soon as the plane was off the main runway, I took my American phone out, powered it up, and a message immediately popped up.

Tío: < Welcome home. >

I rolled my eyes but smirked, not at all surprised Uncle Ceaser knew I had landed.

S: < Thank you. Do I get to know how Z and I are getting out of here, or are we hitchhiking? ;) >

Tío: < Look for Raine. >

He sent his best enforcer? I was immediately on edge, hoping there weren't going to be any problems. *Uncle Ceaser just wants me safe.* But beyond being his niece, I was also the heir to his throne. There were extra precautions he was always going to take with me, regardless of the amount of danger I was in. One of which included the private jet taxiing off the runway and directly into one of the airport's small, private hangars.

My heart raced with excitement and nerves when I spotted a familiar-looking dark grey SUV with windows tinted black as night, parked along the white metal wall. It was another slice of home I'd desperately missed. The lack of people in sight also reminded me how serious the situation was, even when the worst of the danger was over twelve-hundred miles away.

Yes, I had my gun, and yes, I trusted my uncle and our crew, but with everything I'd been through in the past two years, there was no relaxing in this situation. A quick glance to my right made me smirk with pride. Zee had her gun out and ready. Ally territory or not, they also weren't leaving anything to chance.

As per protocol, we sat tight until the hangar doors were completely closed. Only then did Anders Raine step out of the SUV and walk toward the plane. Seeing the short, black-brown hair and scruffy beard of my uncle's number one enforcer put a smile on my face. That man was a force to be reckoned with, and I loved him like a brother. I was grateful for his presence in our lives.

Once the door was open, the co-pilot looked over. "You two are free to deplane now."

Nodding, Zee and I stood. I shrugged on my backpack and glanced at them. "You want to lead out?"

A smirk appeared on their face before they shook their head. "What is this, amateur hour? Raine would have my ass if I let you out first."

That same man smirked as I finally made my way down the airstairs, meeting me at the bottom. "Ms. Rodriguez."

I rolled my eyes before breaking all protocol and giving him a quick hug. "You can fuck right off with that *Ms. Rodriguez* bullshit."

He chuckled and roughly patted my back. "I can't tell you how good it is to see you."

A deep sigh came out as I stood tall again, noting the dark circles under his eyes. "Don't I know it."

Raine glanced around before gesturing to the SUV. "We need to get moving."

Right. The job. There would be time to catch up later. *I hope.* I nodded as he escorted me to the vehicle. But nothing could have prepared me for who was waiting inside when he opened the door.

"Hello, *Mija.*"

Tears flooded my eyes as I dove into the SUV and hugged my uncle. "*Tio*!" *Holy shit. He came to pick me up!*

Uncle Ceaser held me tight until the luggage was tossed in the back and Raine and Zee slid into the front seats. Only then did I sit up and stare at his face, taking in every familiar wrinkle and scar, noting a few new ones... and how tired and older he looked.

The past two years had been hard on him.

"*Mija*, I cannot tell you how good it is to have you here and in one piece."

Zee let out a tense breath. "I did my best, sir."

"And I appreciate it."

I shook my head. "They're still a little mad that I broke my promise of not coming home with new holes. Now *technically* I haven't, but..." I trailed off. *Thanks to Rod, Claudia, and Zee.*

Pain flickered in my uncle's eyes. "Rod made it home. Thanks to Claudia. We made sure her remains made it to her boys, too."

Tears flooded my eyes as I nodded. "Good. I'm glad." I hated that two of our best people had to die to keep me alive. We all knew the cost of this life, but that never made it hurt less when we lost someone.

"She made sure I knew how important it was that it happened."

Wiping my face, I cleared my throat. "Speaking of important, what protection assignment was important enough to bring me home... and now?"

"Don Agosti's second called in a favor."

My eyes went wide. *The Agostis never ask for help, least of all Liam.* "I'm going to be working for another Don? Is that... legal?" It was well-established that we assisted our allies, but this assignment felt far more significant than simply being an ally.

He nodded. "Yes, it's completely legal. I signed off on it."

I took a deep breath and let it out slowly. "What do Uncle George and Liam need help with?"

"All I told Lynette when she called with the request was that I would send one of my most trusted people. You will report directly to Don Agosti for details after I drop you off."

Wait. Don Agosti and not Uncle George? What the hell am I getting into? "Hold on." My thoughts riffled through my mental Agosti family roster. I pulled my hair down from the messy bun I'd been rocking for travel day and ran my fingers through it, hoping to make myself look a bit more presentable. "I thought Liam was second."

Uncle Ceaser shook his head. "Not anymore." We sat in tense silence for a moment as he clenched his jaw. "There's no easy way to say this, *Mija.* George was killed several months ago. After Liam was unofficially blamed for the death, significant restructuring happened. Lianne is now the Don, Lynette is her second, Liam is estranged, and his daughter Chloe is going to be your charge."

I stared at him in disbelief. *Holy shit.* For the second time, tears flooded my eyes. "Uncle George is dead?" He nodded and gave my hand a squeeze as I breathed through the shock. That man was like another uncle to me. I glared at my Tío. "Why the hell didn't you tell me before?"

"That would be my fault."

Zee's confession hit me like a freight train. "What?"

They glanced over their shoulder, nodding. "You were in such a rough spot after losing Rod and Claudia that I couldn't tell you one more bad thing." Tears filled their eyes. "You're so strong, but I didn't want to break you by telling about his death."

I sucked in a breath and let it out slowly, blinking back tears of my own. "Well, while I don't agree with your decision, what's done is done, and now I know." I took a moment to shove my feelings down before looking at Uncle Ceaser again. "Wait, did you say *Lianne* is Don?" He nodded again. "Holy shit." All I could do was stare at him for a moment as I processed, not really registering anything as Raine drove.

What all happened that she's in charge now?

The Agostis were more than allies; they were our chosen extended family. Lianne and I grew up together, running around each other's houses and yards, harassing her brothers, even going to the range together once we were older. We celebrated birthdays and holidays together.

Wait. Birthdays. Babies. Chloe!

My attention snapped to my uncle's face. "Is Liam's wife still alive?"

The corner of his lip twitched before he nodded. "Yes, but with recent events and information, Chloe will be kept under Lynette's roof."

I nodded in return. Susan had always come across as controlling, despite her attempts to pretend she was flexible. *How is she going to take her daughter being kept from her? This is going to be interesting.*

The rest of the drive was quiet, giving me a little time to process all the information I'd been given. It wasn't until we turned onto a familiar street that I snapped back. *We're almost here.* My heart rate took off at seeing the familiar property: the dark metal gate, the sandstone fence, and the two-story brick house. It had been almost two years since I'd been here. And they had no idea I was showing up right now.

I had to swallow down more emotions when we rolled past the gate and I watched Talia walk up to the vehicle. *Fuck, I miss her.*

Uncle Ceaser rolled down his window. "Hello, Ms. Wilson."

Talia's eyebrows went up slightly, but otherwise, she kept a professional, calm expression on her face. "Don Rodriguez, how can we help you?"

He gave her a polite smile. "I'm here to speak with Lynette, and I have Ms. Rodriguez here as well, who needs to see Don Agosti."

Talia's focus snapped to me, and she froze momentarily in shock before looking at him again, a huge smile on her face. "Of course, sir." She gestured where we could park and grabbed her phone as soon as our vehicle stopped.

Tío rolled up the window and glanced at me. "Ready?"

I let out a steadying breath before narrowing my eyes at my uncle. "Is Dante here?"

He nodded.

My Wolf!

Hope, fear, frustration, and anger all surged up inside me. "Should I even bother reconnecting, or are we going to be separated again?"

There was no holding back my bitterness. My heart broke when I had to leave Dante for my last assignment, and then it shattered when everything went to shit and I got hurt and had to go even deeper into hiding. I wasn't sure for a while if I was ever going to see him again. The mere thought of him, his voice, his touch, his *love* was the only thing that pulled me through some of my darkest days.

Dante and I had started conversations with my uncle and Don Agosti about next steps that needed to be taken before we eventually got married. He wanted to propose, but not until he had permission and blessings from both Dons. Which didn't happen before I had to leave.

My uncle's shoulders dropped as he reached over and took my hand. "You know the risks of mixing love and business."

I clenched my jaw and swallowed hard. "That didn't answer my question, *Tío*."

He gave my hand a gentle squeeze. "I won't stand in the way of your happiness, *Mija*. If he is your forever, chase it. Take it. I want nothing more than to see joy on your face."

"Then give him your blessing and let me stay." I was pushing it with my demands, but I didn't care. *Am I even still answering to him after my meeting with Lianne?*

A tense breath flared his nostrils. "You have my blessing, *Mija*, fully and completely. I already gave Dante my blessing. And I'd happily let you stay if this assignment was mine to run, but it's not." He paused for a moment. "We both have meetings to get to that will provide more information on what happens next."

I nodded, took a deep breath, and shoved every last feeling down as best as I could. I was a professional. A mafia heiress about to walk into a meeting with another Don. Regardless of personal history, there was protocol and our family reputation to uphold. "I serve Don Rodriguez with honor and grace."

"And such honor and grace you have, *Mija*." He reached over, hugged me tight, and gave me a long kiss on my forehead before he let go. "I'm so glad to have you home. Now go. We have work to do."

I had barely stepped out of the SUV when Talia pulled me into a tight hug. "Not that I'm not ecstatic as fuck to see you, but what in the hell are you doing here?"

"Protection detail as per Lynette's request."

Talia's eyes were wide as she leaned back. "Are you here for Chloe?"

I let out a deep breath and nodded. "As much as I *really* want to chat with you, I need to see Don Agosti. I was told to go to her office directly."

Talia nodded and stood tall again. "Right. Sorry. This way." She gestured to the open garage door. "I apologize for the use of the side entrance, but we're still cleaning up the main foyer."

Uncle Ceaser and I didn't even bat an eye, though I was curious as hell about what happened.

As I rounded the back of the SUV, Zee handed me my suitcase and bag before squeezing my shoulder. "I'll leave you to it. Be good."

It was then it finally clicked that they weren't going to be at my side. After months of seeing no one else but them, I was now walking away. "I—"

"I'll be in touch. You're not rid of me *that* easily." They glanced up at the house and then back at me, smiling. "If you're going to be safe anywhere without me up your ass, it would be here."

I blinked back tears and swallowed down the sudden surge of emotions. "Finally. I'll be able to brush my teeth without you breathing down my neck."

"Bitch."

"Right back at you. See you soon." I grabbed the handle of my suitcase and followed Talia into the garage. The second we stepped inside, the sharp smell of bleach hit me, and I saw an unfamiliar black woman and an unfamiliar Hispanic-looking man with enormous muscles scrubbing the floor in the foyer.

It's only been two years. How many new people are on staff now?

My uncle cleared his throat. "Is Lynette in her office?"

As Talia turned to answer him, Lynette breezed into the hallway. "Ceaser, you didn't have to make a personal visit." Her focus shifted to me, and an excited and stunned expression appeared on her face. "Sabrina?" She looked at my uncle and then back to me. "I... I'm so pleased and honored to see you. Are you…" Lynette returned her attention to Ceasar. "Is she here for Chloe?" He nodded, and then my honorary aunt stared at him for a moment, as if studying his face. "I see. We need to talk."

"Yes, we do."

Lynette glanced at Talia. "If you'll excuse us. Lianne is expecting Sabrina."

"Yes, ma'am." She held back for a moment as the two 'grown-ups' walked away before glancing around and stepping close. "Does Dante know you're here?"

I shook my head. "No, but to be fair, I barely know I'm here."

She furrowed her brow. "What do you mean?"

I gestured to my suitcase as we walked. "I literally came straight from the airport. Uncle Ceaser flew me in, personally picked me up, and told me where we were going as he brought me here."

"Oh, shit." Talia looked at a closed office door. "Do you want me to say anything to Dante?"

I shook my head again. "Not until I know exactly what Don Agosti needs. I don't want to get anyone's hopes up."

"That's fair." She nodded and then knocked on the door, opening it and poking her head in. "Don Rodriguez's… helper is here to see you." Talia nodded and then turned to look at me again, grinning as she wrapped her arms around me, and I hugged her back. "Lianne's ready for you. Welcome home."

Chapter Eight

Sabrina

As I entered the room, Lianne glanced up, and a stunned smile appeared on her face. "Sabrina?" Before I could react, she raced around the desk and wrapped me in a tight hug. "Holy shit, am I glad to see you."

"Me too!" After a moment, she stepped back, and it was then I noticed the grief and stress all over her face. The light, spirited woman I grew up with was still there, but there was a heaviness in her eyes. One I saw in my uncle's eyes quite regularly. "So, you're Don now. Congratulations?"

She huffed out a tight laugh and shook her head. "Yeah... Thanks. It's been *quite* the adventure."

I glanced around and opened and shut my mouth a couple times before finally cobbling my thoughts together. "I... What... How am I supposed to address you now?"

Lianne stared at me for a moment before chuckling. "I'm still very much Lianne. I only use the title during official meetings... or when people are being complete dumbasses."

There's the Lianne I know and love. When she glanced to the side, I couldn't miss the small splatter of red on her cheek. "Would a dumbass be the reason there's blood on the right side of your face?"

Her jaw tensed for a moment before she went back behind her desk, opened a cabinet, and looked at a small mirror. "Apparently. Fucking hell." She opened a first-aid kit, pulled out an alcohol wipe, and removed the offending life essence from her skin with a snarl. “Thank you for telling me. I didn’t think I’d gotten any idiot on my face earlier.”

I shrugged. “Girl code, ma’am.”

Her attention snapped to me, mild annoyance in her eyes. “Ma’am? *Really*? We were practically raised together, Sabrina. I swear to God...” She shook her head as she trailed off.

A nervous laugh came out. “Sorry. It’s this office. Anyone behind the desk gets a ma’am or sir.”

Lianne looked down at the furniture piece in question and then sighed. “Fair enough.” She studied me curiously. “Not that I’m unhappy to see you, but *why* are you here?”

“Uncle Ceaser said your mom needed help.” I narrowed my eyes, trying to piece this together. “I thought you were expecting me.”

She let out another deep sigh and sat in her chair, gesturing to the one next to me. “Yes, but no. All Mom said was that Uncle Ceaser was helping us out with security coverage for Chloe. I didn’t know *you* were going to be showing up. How much do you know about the situation?"

I related what little had been relayed on the way from the airport, and then Lianne filled me in on more of the events of the past six months. My jaw was on the ground by the end. “*La hostia.*” *Holy shit.* I thought I'd been living in hell and chaos.

She leaned back in her chair and nodded. “Yeah. You’re telling me.”

We sat in silence for a moment. Lianne was clearly lost in her thoughts, staring down and to her right, working through something. My thoughts went to the cleanup crew in the foyer and the blood on her face. *How long ago did she take out someone before we rolled in?*

After a minute or two passed, she sat up straight again, meeting my gaze. “Would you like to meet Chloe now? That is, are you ready to dive in, or do you need a minute to settle?”

I let out a nervous breath. "About that. Can I ask how long you project you'll need me around? And where am I staying for the duration?"

Lianne sighed heavily, as if the weight of the world was on her shoulders. "I don't have a definitive timeline for you. I need my niece safe until this whole fucking mess my brother made is cleaned up... and then after... whatever *after* looks like." She glanced to her right before looking at me again. "You'll eventually stay in Liam's old room, but that's not an option tonight, and maybe not tomorrow, depending on how Chloe acclimates to being here." There was another pause as she glanced at the opposite wall, lost in thought again. "I want to offer you a guest room, but..."

"But Dante and I were practically engaged before I had to leave town?"

Lianne nodded. "No, but yes. It's not that, though. I don't have a guest room to offer. I can't believe I'm saying this, but the house is full."

My eyes went wide. "Can I get a quick rundown of who all is staying here?" *And why is the house full?*

She let out a deep sigh. "Well, in the hallway behind me, Dante and Talia share a room when the need arises, then there's Gage and his girlfriend Sunny, then Nash, Poppy, and Avery, and then Jess and Connor. The two guest rooms in the same hall as the lounge currently house Ryan and his fiance Ellen, and then Adair and Peter. Upstairs is full with Mom, me and Ben, Lukas and Quinn, and *Liam*. The guest room up there has been converted into an office for when we have to put the otters in lockdown protocol."

My brain swirled with the influx of names and information. "Wait, wait, wait. When did Gage *and* Ryan get partners? And who's Adair? And who or what are the otters?"

Lianne chuckled as she leaned back again. "Damn, I forgot how much has happened in the last couple of years... and that it's *only* been a couple of years. The boys found their perfect matches within the last six months or so... and Adair." She paused again before locking her eyes on mine. "I'll fill you in on her later. That's quite a story, and one I'm still getting information on." Another laugh came out. "The otters are all significant others to my crew. Jess named them on a whim, and it stuck."

I couldn't stop a grin from appearing on my face. "Would that make me an otter?"

She stopped and stared at me for a moment. "Again, yes, but no. While you're with Dante, you also outrank most of the people in this house. You and I are in a league of our own."

"That we are." I nodded slowly, taking in all the new information. One of the names popped back into my brain. "You mentioned someone named Poppy. Is that Gage's sister? Why would she be staying here?"

"She's dating Nash. He's one of Lukas's guys... had been working undercover for the Barlowes. Another long story for another day." Lianne scoffed and shook her head. "I swear we need an onboarding binder or tutorial on why three-quarters of our crew is staying on property."

"How about we come back to my purpose for being here? When am I meeting Chloe, and where am I staying tonight?"

Lianne pursed her lips as she picked up her phone and tapped the screen a few times, likely checking messages. "Liam is out of the infirmary and upstairs with Chloe and Lukas now. Avery is also upstairs. I say we give Chloe a little more time with her father, not that he gave me the same consideration." The last line was grumbled through clenched teeth.

As much as I wanted to hug the woman I'd practically grown up with, she was a Don... and currently my boss? There was protocol to maintain. Seeing her shoulders drop slightly as she let out a shaky sigh, my reserve broke, and I moved to give her that hug. "I know I'm breaking a lot of rules, but right now I don't give a shit. Right now I'm just a cousin hugging her cousin, who's having a really rough day. I'm sorry I had to miss your wedding. I'm sorry everything went sideways with your brother. I'm sorry you lost your dad. I'm sorry I'm only showing up now." Tears welled up in my eyes as she wrapped her arms around me and hugged me back, just as tight. "But I'm here, and I'm not going anywhere unless you order me to... and even then I'll still have your back."

"Thank you." The hoarse, whispered words brought tears to my eyes as I heard a fraction of her pain.

We stayed like that until she tapped my arm twice, signaling to me that she was done. I stood again and let out a deep breath as I wiped my eyes. "So, I know I'm here on assignment, but I'm afraid I need to make some requests."

Lianne's eyebrows raised. "Okay?"

I let out a tense breath. "Not sure what you know, or if Uncle Ceaser told you, but while on assignment in Central America, I caught some lead and have been in hiding while recovering. Now, while I am very much recovered and fully capable of protecting and taking care of Chloe, I need to keep strengthening my shoulder. Zee and I made a lot of progress, but I have to keep up with my physical therapy so I'm not a liability. That, and I could use some range time. The safe house didn't exactly have a place for me to keep those skills as sharp as I'd like."

She nodded, only letting a brief flicker of anger and sympathy cross her face before glancing to the side, writing something on a sticky note. "I'll tell Doc to expect you. And I'm not sure when we'll be able to get you to the range, but we do have a single stall downstairs you're welcome to use in the meantime." Lianne looked up at me again. "Do you need a gun?"

"I came in packing." I turned, pulled my sweater to the side, and showed my holster. "I will need a gun safe or locker, though."

A small smile appeared on her face as she made another note. "That, we can easily do. Anything else?"

Pride filled me at her efficiency. "Would it be okay for me to stash my things in Talia and Dante's room for now? At least until we know more about... all of this?"

Lianne grabbed her phone, grinning even more after reading something. "Yeah. You have an hour. Make it count, but then be ready to dive into the deep end."

Who was she texting? "Yes, ma'am."

Something told me I was going to find more than just a place to store my suitcase when I opened that door.

Chapter Nine

Dante

Connor and I were almost back to the house when my phone buzzed.

Talia: < Can you pretty please grab my chapstick from our room and bring it to me when you get back. >

I furrowed my brow at the request. It wasn't like my sister not to have it on her person.

Dante: < Where are you now? >

Talia: < Upstairs with the otters. Gage assigned. >

Talia: < Please? My extra tube is in my desk drawer. >

Dante: < Of course. >

I let out a sigh. "Sisters."

Connor glanced my way. "She hitting you up for something?"

"Chapstick. There are worse things."

He nodded. "That there are." He narrowed his eyes as we rolled up the Agosti driveway. "What in the hell happened while we were gone?"

Nothing could have prepared me for the sight of two of Don Rodriguez's crew: Anders Raine, his enforcer, and Zara Leveer, Sabrina's main bodyguard, standing next to a dark grey SUV, chatting with Jess.

Wait.

Zara had flown out to join Sabrina on assignment months ago.

Why are they here?

My heart raced with excitement and apprehension as my thoughts wildly oscillated between Sabrina potentially being here or dead. Shaking my head, I immediately pushed the thoughts away as best as I could. Someone would have told me if something bad had happened.

No news is good news.

After Connor cut the engine, we both hopped out of the vehicle and walked up to the trio. Jess immediately locked her focus on us. "Everything go well?"

I nodded. "Textbook."

She let out a small smile. "Good. Did you get Talia's message?"

How does Jess know? Something felt off here. "Yeah. I'm taking care of it now." Shaking my head, I hurried inside to the on-property room Tal and I shared when shit was a little too chaotic at work. I'd barely opened the desk drawer when there was a knock on the door. *Now what?* "Be right there." I spotted and grabbed the light pink tube and had barely turned around when the door opened. "Tal, I said..." My words trailed off as I stood frozen, unable to process the woman actually standing in the doorway.

What? There's no way this is real.

My heart stuttered in my chest as I reminded myself how to breathe. It couldn't be her. Yet there she was, with those unmistakable dark eyes that had haunted my dreams for the past two years. Her long brown-black hair I'd spent hours running my fingers through. The full peach lips that I'd memorized the feel of.

"Hi, Dante." Her voice cracked as a sob escaped and tears welled in her eyes.

"Sabrina?" As much as I wanted to run forward and wrap my arms around her, I was having a hard time believing she was actually here. It was as if my loneliness had manifested a vision of her to hold me together. *Have I finally lost my mind?* Before I could react, she launched herself across the room and into my arms. Orange and vanilla filled my nose as I breathed deeply. "Holy shit, you're really here."

She let out a chuckle and sniffled. "I really am."

I leaned back, looking into her deep brown eyes, still trying to convince myself the love of my life was in front of me. "Who else knows?"

"Uncle Ceaser, Lianne, Lynette, and Talia."

My eyes almost popped out of my head. *That little shit!* "My sister knew and didn't fucking tell me?"

Sabrina reached up and held my face in her hands. "Only because she was at the gate when Uncle Ceaser and I rolled in. Also, I asked her not to say anything until I knew how long I was going to be here. I—"

My lips cut off her words as I couldn't hold back anymore. I had to kiss her. The last two years without her had worn me down more than I'd ever admit to, and I missed her more than I thought was physically possible. My heart came back online the second our lips touched, and I never wanted to let her go ever again.

She broke off the kiss. "Dante..." My name came out as a breathy moan as I trailed open-mouthed kisses down her neck and held her as close to me as I could.

"Hmm?" I didn't want to stop. I needed to touch every inch of her. Refresh my memory of her scent, taste, and how she felt in my arms. She'd been gone for far too long, and I wasn't going to waste a second of being able to hold her.

"I'm not going anywhere."

I stopped kissing her long enough to lean back again and look her in the eyes. "What do you mean?"

The smile that appeared lit up her face made my heart skip another beat. It was the most beautiful thing I'd seen in years. I didn't care if it was corny; I loved everything about this woman.

"I'm going to be working here... and living here."

All I could do was stare at her in disbelief. "How?"

"Chloe."

Is this because of Lynette's call to Don Rodriguez yesterday? "*You're* the favor she called in? How did you get here so fast?"

Sabrina shrugged and let out a soft chuckle. "Apparently. And I got a call last night and left a couple hours later. I literally got off a plane less than an hour ago. Trust me, I grilled Uncle Ceaser and Lianne about this and us when I got here."

My eyes went wide. "You *grilled* them?"

"Yeah, I needed answers. I didn't want to get my hopes up only to have them shattered."

That's my woman. I hugged her tight to my chest, running my fingers through the ends of her hair. "I missed you so damn much, Kitten."

"I missed you, too. God, did I miss you." She melted into me, and we just stood there for a while, soaking in the fact we were in the same place. After a moment, Sabrina let out a half-laugh. "How fucking insane and awesome is it that Lianne is a Don? I love and hate it for her."

The random topic shift didn't even faze me. Sabrina was here. In my arms. "She's been through hell, but is making her way through it with more grace than I thought possible. Lianne is growing into a truly fierce and awe-inspiring leader."

The woman in my arms leaned back and looked up. "I hear you've been pretty impressive, too."

"What are you talking about? And how did you hear *anything* about me?"

She chuckled, giving me another quick kiss. "Zee *may* have mentioned how you helped the Don Supreme with a certain Vaux problem."

Absently, I dropped my hand to where the scar would forever remain on my thigh. "Yeah, that was quite an interesting mission." A nervous laugh came out. "By the way, watching Avery and Maloy work together? Terrifying."

Sabrina snickered. "Well, Maloy is terrifying all by himself, but Avery? I know she's a badass in the interrogation room, but I've never seen her on a mission."

I stared her in the eyes, wide-eyed. "Kitten, seriously. Avery skipped in glee to help me blow the place up, and when they were inside? I definitely heard some devious chuckling. Hell, there was even an obnoxious bow from Avery. It was wild. Don't believe me? Ask Connor. Oh, and rumor has it that while at the hospital covering Backnoff, Maloy gave out hugs. I don't know to whom, or what was going on, but Maloy and hugs just don't go in the same sentence."

She stared at me for a moment in disbelief. "Desiree must be making him soft. Well, as soft as he can be. Hugs or not, that man will never be anything less than terrifying." Sabrina let out a sigh and snuggled up against my chest.

Again, I rested my head on top of hers, absorbing how amazing it was to hold her in my arms. "I still don't know if I'm dreaming, but if I am, don't wake me up."

She pinched my side and then smacked my ass. "You seem to be awake."

"Kitten..."

Keeping her head on my chest, she looked up at me, warmth, lust, and love in her eyes as she toyed with the bottom edge of my shirt. "Yes, Wolf?"

As I picked her up, swung her around, and sat on the bed, Sabrina wrapped her legs around my waist. Pulling her close, I couldn't help the growl that rolled through my chest as I captured her lips with mine. "Fuck, you are going to be the death of me."

Chapter Ten

Sabrina

I hated how fast the hour flew by and let out a small whine. "I need to get back to Lianne's office. She was kind enough to give me some time with you, but I don't want to push her generosity."

"I'll take any and all time I can get with you." Dante kissed me again before sitting up. "Fuck. I'm just glad you're here. Safe. Alive."

"Me, too."

Once we left his room, he insisted on walking me to Lianne's office, never letting go of my hand. The physical contact was comforting, but it also made me nervous. I gave his hand a squeeze and then glanced up. "Aren't you worried?"

He arched his eyebrow. "About what? It wasn't a secret we were together before you had to take off."

I let out a tense breath. "No, but I don't know the rules here. There's new management, so to speak. The last thing I want to do is piss off a Don."

"You won't do that by holding hands." Lynette rounded the corner, giving me a wide smile. "Hello, my dear."

Tears pricked at the corners of my eyes at the sight of my honorary aunt walking toward me. "Hi, Auntie 'Nette."

The woman's smile grew wider, and she pulled me in for a hug. "Sabrina, I'm sorry I didn't properly greet you before."

I leaned into her embrace for a moment before standing straight again. "It's been a more than eventful day for all of us. Something was bound to slip through the cracks."

"Fair enough." My Auntie 'Nette smiled broadly. "I am delighted to see you here again, *and* with your Dante."

Grinning, I reached over and gave his hand a squeeze. "Same."

She smiled again. "Are you two heading to Lianne's office?"

"We are."

"Fantastic. So am I." When we got to the door, Lynette stopped and looked up at Dante. "I need just Sabrina for this next part, but you're about to get an assignment. In the meantime, make sure we aren't interrupted unless there is a legitimate emergency."

Dante gave her a quick nod. "Yes, ma'am."

"Thank you, my dear." She opened the door and walked in, and I followed behind her.

Lianne's head popped up as we entered, and she immediately stood. "How's Adair? That was a lot earlier."

Who is this Adair? And is she talking about whatever happened in the foyer?

Lynette let out a tense breath. "She's in Peter's capable care. Last I saw, ice cream was being scooped." The woman paused. "She wants to talk to him again."

Lianne's shoulders dropped slightly as she let out a deep sigh. "I had a feeling she would. And after everything she's been through, Liam *will* sit there and listen to anything and everything she wants to unload on him."

Lynette let out a sigh, but it was Lianne's low chuckle that pulled my attention back to her face.

"Can I ask what's so funny?"

Lianne gestured to the chairs in front of her desk. "You might want to sit for this."

My eyebrows went up. "Oh?"

She nodded. "Yeah. That long story I talked about earlier? Well, it's story time." After I settled into the nearest chair, she continued. "Do you remember when Victoria Vaux disappeared?"

Now it was my turn to nod. It had been a chaotic manhunt, with multiple Mafia families searching for her. "Of course. Uncle Ceaser and I helped look for her."

Lianne glanced up at her mother and narrowed her eyes. "Wait. Was he actually searching, or was he throwing people off certain trails?"

Now it was Lynette who smirked. "I can't speak to what Ceaser did while we were searching for my almost daughter-in-law."

There was far more going on here than I had information for. *Why would my uncle throw anyone off a trail?*

"Anyway." Lianne redirected her attention to me. "My mom, for extremely good reasons, hid Victoria from everyone... and did so until about two weeks ago. Victoria is now going by Adair, and she is currently living with us."

My eyes went wide in shock. "Holy shit. Wait... Does Susan know?"

A sour expression appeared on Lianne's face as she pursed her lips. "We speculate she does, if Liam's appearance today is any indication. My brother doesn't actually care that Lukas and I just had our birthdays. Especially when his opening line, after bitching, was asking about *her*."

I nodded. "That explains Adair, but what was so funny?"

Lianne chuckled as a genuine smile appeared on her face. "He has no idea the powerhouse woman she's turned into. Hell, I barely know. I can't wait to be a fly on the wall when she unleashes on that man." She paused for a moment. "Is Dante nearby?"

"Right outside the door, per Auntie 'Nette's insistence." I turned to the woman in reference. "Can I still call you that, when appropriate?"

The way Lynette's face lit up as if I'd given her the greatest gift as she stood and squeezed my hand. "Yes. Honestly, I'd prefer it." She walked to the door and opened it. "Lianne would like a word."

Dante looked slightly nervous as he stepped into the office. "What can I do for you, Lianne?"

She sat up straight in her chair. "I'm putting you on Liam duty. Aside from Avery, you're one of the few people who physically intimidate him and could take him down without a problem."

The man's face was almost unreadable, but I caught the flicker of determination in his eyes as he nodded. "Thank you, ma'am. Any specific instructions about keeping him in line?"

Lianne narrowed her blue-grey eyes slightly as she glanced to the side for a moment, clearly deliberating something. "Do what you need to keep everyone safe, but don't kill him."

Dante nodded again. "Noted. When do I start?"

Lynette cleared her throat, but when I looked at her, the woman's focus was on Lianne. "How about Dante and I iron out those details while you take Sabrina upstairs to meet her charge?"

Lianne smirked as she stood and walked out from behind her desk. "Works for me." She looked at me. "You ready for more chaos?"

I snickered. "I've just spent months healing, being bored off my ass, and with only Zee for *intellectual* company. While the scenery was great, I prefer being useful."

"Perfect. Let's do this."

After we left her office, Lianne led me through the sparkling clean foyer that still smelled faintly of bleach, through the kitchen, but stopped at the bottom of the dark wooden staircase, letting out a heavy sigh as she gripped the banister.

When she didn't move for a moment, I shifted to her side. "Everything okay?"

Lianne nodded. "I just needed to remind myself of something." After a few more seconds, she took a deep breath, rolled her shoulders back, and headed upstairs.

It was something I'd seen my uncle and some of his team do before heading out to take care of an assignment. The same serious, determined expression in her eyes. The weight on her shoulders. The face of a leader.

When we turned the corner, another familiar person stood outside the door to Liam's room. A tall woman with pale white skin, short black hair, and laser-sharp blue eyes. "Avery?"

She turned her head, blinked several times, and looked at Lianne, who gave a quick nod. The next thing I knew, I was wrapped in the tightest hug. "Holy shit, it is good to see you. Not that I want you gone, but why in the hell are you here?"

I'm going to get this question a lot. "For Chloe."

Avery released me and looked from me to Lianne, and then recognition hit. "Your mom's favor." Her attention snapped back to me. "Please tell me you've talked to Dante."

There was no keeping the smile off my face. "Oh yeah. He is extraordinarily glad I'm here."

The woman chuckled. "As he should be."

Lianne cleared her throat. "Who's in there with Chloe?"

Avery stood a little taller, falling back into 'business mode.' "Lukas, Liam, and Regina."

I nodded. "One for Liam, one for Chloe?"

Avery shrugged. "More like one to keep Lukas from killing Liam, one for Chloe."

Lianne pressed her lips together and fought a smile. "Fair enough. Time to make some introductions."

Avery nodded before pushing open the door and poking her head inside. "We have two visitors for Miss Chloe." She stepped back and pushed the door open the rest of the way, gesturing inside. "The room is yours."

I stepped into a place I'd never seen before, immediately torn between wanting to smirk at Lukas and Liam's stunned reactions at seeing me, wanting to punch Liam for his actions, and wanting to ignore all the adults and sit on the floor to chat with Chloe. I didn't miss the heavy bandaging on Liam's ear, or that he was uncharacteristically dressed in a plain black T-shirt and sweats. Any other time I'd seen that man, he was always in a button-down shirt and dress pants, if not a full suit.

Was it his blood on Lianne's face?

Both men were sitting on the floor. An adorable little girl with blond hair, whom I could only assume was Chloe, was sitting in Liam's lap, and a beautiful yet formidable-looking black woman was perched on the edge of a chair, holding several books and toys in her lap.

"Lukas, Liam, I'd like to introduce you to who will be looking after Chloe."

Lukas's face lit up with a huge smile when his eyes met mine. "Sabrina! You're a sight for sore eyes. When did you roll in?"

I gave a casual shrug. "Maybe three hours ago. Apparently, my presence was needed."

Liam's posture stiffened as I maintained hard eye contact with him, and it pleased me. *You should fear me.*

"Sabrina, this is Regina, my personal shadow."

The stunning and intimidating black woman smiled and nodded at me. "Pleasure to meet you."

Lianne gestured to me. "This is Sabrina, a very close family friend."

After nodding politely greeting her, I crouched down and waved at the adorable little blond girl sitting in Liam's lap. "Hi, Chloe. I'm Sabrina."

She gave me a timid wave and then looked up at Liam. "Dada, stranger?"

Liam swallowed hard and looked at Lianne with a flurry of emotions racing through his eyes before kissing the top of his daughter's head. "It's okay, sweetheart, she's not a stranger. Ms. Sabrina works with Auntie Li and has known us for a very long time." He cleared his throat. "She's going to help me take care of you. You should show her your stuffed bunny."

Nodding, Chloe hopped off his lap and ran over to Lukas, grabbing a stuffed purple bunny from his lap, and showed it to me. "Bunny got a boo-boo. 'Geena fix-t it."

I noted the tape wrapped around the end of the ear and nodded. "Regina did an excellent job. Did you already kiss it to make Bunny feel better?"

The little girl gasped and immediately kissed where the repair had been made. "You kiss Bunny, too?"

"Of course." I gently took the precious stuffed animal and kissed the ear. "There. Now she's perfect."

Chloe nodded and walked back to her dad, where she plopped in his lap.

I cleared my throat and glanced up at Lianne. "Don Agosti," I didn't fail to notice the slight flinch from Liam. "When possible, I will need to talk with Liam to get more details and some perspective on the entire scope of Chloe's care. Schedules, routines, favorite things, to name a few."

Lianne nodded, but there was no missing how she clenched her jaw. "You can absolutely talk to him, but it won't be alone."

"I have absolutely no problem with that, ma'am."

Regina cleared her throat softly. "I'm happy to stick around."

Lianne's face softened a bit as she looked at the little girl. "Chloe, would you like a snack?"

Her short blond hair bounced as Chloe jumped up. "Nack! Cookie? Pease?"

Lukas chuckled as he stood, taking his niece's tiny hand in his. "Okay, sweetie. Let's see if Uncle Ben has something fun for us in the kitchen."

Once they were out of the room, Liam looked from Regina to me, and I clocked fear in that man's eyes.

"I won't bite if you don't. We're on the same page here."

He narrowed his eyes at me, issuing a silent challenge. "Are we?"

I crossed my arms over my chest and stared at the man. "Yes. I'm here to make sure your daughter stays safe and well-cared for. As her dad, I assume that's your goal as well."

Chapter Eleven

Dante

I let out a tense breath as Sabrina and Lianne walked out of the room.

"I spoke with Ceaser earlier, when he rolled in with Sabrina."

My attention snapped back to Lynette. "Okay?" *I thought we were going to talk about Liam.*

She gave me a warm smile. "Apparently during the brief ride from the airport to here, Sabrina gave him quite the earful about her relationship with you. Before I go on, know that neither of us wants to get in your way. I know there discussions regarding alliance ramifications started with George and Ceaser before her mission, particularly for after a future proposal."

Shock shot through me. This was not where I'd expected the conversation to go. "Yes, ma'am. Mr. Agosti told me he needed to have a conversation with Don Rodriguez before giving me a final answer. Sabrina flew out for her assignment two days later."

Lynette cleared her throat, and a slightly uncomfortable expression flickered in her eyes. "I informed my dear husband that the fact he didn't immediately tell you to go out and marry that woman was one of the stupidest things he'd ever done."

My eyes went wide with shock. "Ma'am?"

She let out a deep sigh and sank into her chair. "It's no secret that I worked closely with my husband while he was Don. It was not advertised *just* how much I knew about the goings-on, but that was on purpose. He and I were a team. We kept each other balanced. Focused. On target. We called each other out when we were being ridiculous, and we defended each other with every fiber of our beings. There weren't many arguments between us, but this was one of them." Her focus never left my eyes. "I'd like to let you know, formally and officially, that you two have every blessing and permission to continue your relationship however you see fit."

Again, this was not how I thought this conversation was going to go. "I... Thank you, ma'am. But what about the loyalties we've sworn to separate Dons?"

Lynette nodded. "Shortly after your visit to the Rodriguez compound after my George's passing, Ceaser and I had a *long* discussion. He admitted he had given you his blessing to become family." Lynette's voice was full of resolve and exhaustion. "For the foreseeable future, Sabrina is under our roof and under our protection. There were reasons she had to lie low and stay no-contact in Cuba, and there are reasons she is in this house now."

I narrowed my eyes, not daring to jump to any conclusions. "What are you saying?"

My boss smirked ever so slightly. "You temporarily work for the same Don, so there are no issues. Once everything settles with Liam and Susan, we will reevaluate, if needed." Lynette reached out and gave my arm a gentle squeeze. "I want to make it abundantly clear that I'm not separating you and Sabrina unless there are *extremely* extenuating circumstances."

"Thank you, Lynette. I appreciate it."

She nodded. "Of course. Some view love as a liability and a weakness, and while there may be some truth to it, I see it as a strength and driving force. It is an invaluable part of life that needs to be protected, respected, and nurtured. We are better off having it in our lives."

"Yes, ma'am. I couldn't have said it better myself." I took a deep breath and let it out slowly. "You mentioned wanting to iron out some details about my assignment with Liam?"

A tight smile appeared on her face. It looked pained, not that I blamed her. I couldn't even begin to imagine having to view your own child as a threat. "Yes. Unless he's in a holding cell or Avery's office, you're to be no more than two feet away from him at all times. He makes any indication he's going to do something he shouldn't, you take him down."

I blinked in surprise. "Ma'am, Lianne gave direct orders not to kill him. Are your orders different?"

Lynette shook her head. "No. I meant 'take down' in the tackle and restrain sense. Then Lianne can decide the appropriate consequences and repercussions."

That made more sense. "I can do that."

A genuine smile crept onto her face. "I know you can. Now, this evening and through the night, Avery and Lukas will be on Liam and Chloe duty. Tomorrow starts yet another round of settling into a new normal. Let's try to salvage what's left of today and then get a good night's sleep tonight so we can make the best of it, shall we?"

I nodded. "Yes, ma'am. And thank you... about Sabrina."

Her face softened as she nodded. "Of course, my dear. Everyone deserves more than a scrap of happiness in this life. If I can ensure any chance of it happening, I will."

I left Lynette's office full of relief. There were going to be no more lengthy debates about my loyalty, no veiled threats about distancing myself from Sabrina, and no bureaucratic games between Dons. It was as if a boulder had been lifted off my chest, but the sheer amount of hope rushing through me made my pulse jittery. I rubbed a hand over my face as I made my way down the hall and headed straight for my room.

Once inside, I paused two steps in, taking stock of the place as if I'd never seen it before. My clothes were in some semblance of order, but the bed looked like a war zone—sheets tangled, one pillow on the floor, a half-zipped up hoodie hanging off the nightstand. I imagined Sabrina curled up in my bed and realized it was past time to change my sheets. Suddenly frustrated with myself, I yanked off the bedding, wadded it up, and went about remaking the bed.

Halfway through tucking the sheet, the latch behind me clicked, and I spun around, expecting Sabrina, but laying eyes on Talia instead. She leaned against the door frame, arms crossed, and mischief sparkling in her eyes. "I'm going to stay at the apartment tonight."

I stopped and glanced over my shoulder. "What? Why?"

My sister walked over, picked up the dropped pillow and handed it to me, then began smoothing out the top sheet with practiced efficiency. "The love of your life waltzes back into your life today, and you think I'm going to be anywhere near this room? Absolutely not." She tried to mask her concern with levity, but her movements were tight and too precise.

Although her concerns were valid, there were bigger factors at play. I tossed the blanket onto the bed and turned to face her. "I need you safe, Tal. Did you forget everything that happened today? That Lianne had me leave two dead bodies in Liam's car as a message for Susan?"

Talia's bravado slipped. She let out a deep sigh and shook her head, jaw clenched. "I'm more than aware there could be retribution. I was thinking of asking Avery to join me, but she's working."

I wanted to reclaim every inch of the woman I loved. Hold her close. Hear her heartbeat. Feel her breath on my skin. Run my fingers through her long hair. I needed to remind myself of every tiny detail about Sabrina that had gone out of focus.

As much as I needed all that, I also needed to know my sister was safe.

There was a reason George and then Lynette and Lianne did their best to ensure Talia and I were on separate assignments. Yes, we worked well together, but after everything that happened with

Ryan and Ross, and then Lianne and Lukas, unless shit was hitting the fan, siblings didn't go out together.

"Tal, please stay."

A half-smile that was part exasperation, part challenge played on her lips. She crossed her arms, bracing herself as if she already anticipated my rebuttal. "Seriously, Dante? I thought for sure you two would want—hell, *need*—some privacy." She arched an eyebrow theatrically, pausing to let the word dangle between us. "You know, so you could... do the things you so obviously want to do. It's not like anyone here is going to judge you, but—"

I cut her off with a sharp glare and a wave of my hand, an unusual heat crawling up my neck. I didn't want to be talking about my sex life with my sister. "It's complicated, okay? There's too much on the line right now. Regardless of Sabrina being here, I need to know you're safe."

For a second, I saw the flash of hurt in Talia's eyes that quickly shifted to understanding. She didn't look away but instead, squared her shoulders and took a step closer. "Dante, I know you're on edge. And I get it. You're worried. We're all worried. But I can handle myself. I'm not some fragile thing you have to keep under glass."

A deep sigh came out. "I know. You're right. I'm sorry if I'm coming off like an overprotective asshole, but I won't apologize for wanting to keep my only sister safe."

She grinned at that. "Thank you. How about as a compromise I see if Nash is also working the overnight, and if he is, I'll crash in Avery's bed." Talia paused, glancing between the two beds in the room. "Seriously, I love you and Sabrina with everything in my heart, but I want more than six feet of air between us tonight."

A chuckle came out. "Nash will be working."

Talia chuckled. "Well, I'd better go chat with Avery then. If anyone will understand my plight, it will be her."

"Plight?" I shot her a half-hearted glare. "Dramatic much?"

She popped her hands onto her hips. "Oh, so you would be *absolutely* fine if I had a boyfriend and brought him here after not seeing him for two years and had all of us sleep in the same room?"

I opened my mouth to protest, but stopped short when I imagined some faceless, overconfident guy barging into my space, having his hands all over my sister. The idea put a pit in my stomach and, despite everything, I couldn't blame her for wanting distance. "Fair enough." The words were muttered as I conceded the point with a nod.

The tension between us eased, and Talia's posture softened as she stepped forward and wrapped her arms around me in a fierce, quick hug. It was over before I could return it, but it left me feeling lighter, as if some of the weight I carried had been transferred, even if just for a moment.

She held me in her gaze as she stepped away, mischief returning to her voice. "You know, you could stand to loosen up, Dante. Maybe enjoy yourself. It's not every day you get a reunion like this."

"Enjoy myself?" I echoed, snickering. "Have you met me?"

My sister grinned. "I have a time or two. That's why I'm saying it." With a final squeeze to my forearm, she pivoted and sauntered out of the room, calling over her shoulder, "Don't do anything I wouldn't do! And lock the door, for everyone's sake!"

I love my sister. I love my sister. I love my sister.

I waited until her footsteps faded down the hall before letting out a slow breath. The room was quiet again. I sat down on the edge of the bed, running a hand through my hair, and let my thoughts drift to Sabrina. The curve of her mouth, the way her eyes brightened when she thought no one was looking, and the feeling of her hand in mine.

For the past two years she was over a thousand miles away, and now she was a few rooms away. For the first time in a long while, I let myself believe that maybe, just maybe, we would have a shot at something resembling normalcy.

I finished making the bed, moving with more purpose than before. I straightened each wrinkle, double-checked the corners, and fluffed the pillows until the room looked almost inviting. I couldn't control the chaos outside these walls, but this? *This* I could make perfect for my Kitten.

Chapter Twelve

Lianne

I was finishing some paperwork for Ryan and trying not to think about how Susan was going to react to our message when there was a knock on the door. It wasn't a specific pattern, so I was intrigued about who was visiting me. "Come in?"

I glanced up as Tori opened the door and took two steps into my office, holding something in her hands. "Is now a bad time?"

A smile spread across my face as I shook my head. "Nope. Come on in."

She walked up to my desk and handed me a few sheets of paper. "Ryan made a copy of my contract for you. I'm surprised you didn't already have one."

A deep sigh came out as I took them from her, eager to see what in the hell Dad had signed. "I'm sure there's a copy somewhere, but considering I didn't even know there was a contract until you mentioned it earlier, this is much faster."

Tori narrowed her eyes at me slightly. "Your mom didn't say anything to you about it?"

I glanced up again and shook my head. "No, but there hasn't been much of a chance to talk about it... or you."

She let out a tight laugh. "No, I suppose not. Do you want me to stay and answer any questions, or do you want to study it on your own and then talk?"

It's like she's never been away. "I'm sure you'd rather spend time with Peter, especially with everything that happened today." It was then it hit me that this was the first time Tori and I were talking since earlier when she had her grand reveal to Liam before we killed Nolan and William. *How is it still the same day?* "How *are* you doing, by the way? That was fucking insane earlier."

Tori flopped into the chair across from me and let out a deep sigh as she shook her head. "There were so many things that happened today... I never thought I was going to get closure. And I've done my best not to let the anger consume me, but seeing them, *all three of them*, right there? And acting like the self-righteous assholes I knew them to be?" She let out a low whistle before looking me in the eye. "There was no stopping me. I'm sorry if I overstepped with Nolan."

I couldn't help the grin that appeared on my face. "Overstepped? Tori, you were a fucking badass who did *exactly* what needed to happen. Trust me, after hearing you lay out the shit they pulled, if you hadn't pulled the trigger, I would have." Another image popped into my head. One that filled me with pride. "By the way, loved seeing you with a certain ring on your finger and an Agosti special in your hand."

Another nervous laugh bubbled out as she played with the mentioned ring still on her finger. "Yeah. I still can't believe your mom gave those to me. I thought they'd be a nice touch."

"Oh, they were. I didn't miss Liam's reaction." *Fucking asshole.* It had been spectacular to see him thrown off his game for once in his rage-inducing life.

She smirked. "Yeah. I knew the second he clocked it. And then his reaction to Derek's name."

Thank God she brought it up! "Yeah... and the fact you and Derek were *married*? Talk about a mic-drop moment. Shit." I leaned forward, rested my elbows on the desk, and tried not to look too eager for information. "Can I ask about it? We don't have to talk about him if it's too much. I don't want to add any more to an already overwhelming day."

A sad smile tugged at the corner of her mouth as she glanced down and fidgeted with the simple gold band on her left hand. "I'll tell you this much tonight. It wasn't legal, seeing as we couldn't file paperwork, being in hiding and all, but it didn't make it any less real to us." Tori's smile widened when she raised her chin to look at me again, and tears glistened in her eyes. "I think he's resting easier knowing I avenged his death."

"Well, that's one person." I let out a deep sigh, wrestling with my own struggle for revenge. "I'm sorry you don't have him anymore."

There was sadness in her eyes, but also peace as she nodded. "Me too, but I'm pretty sure he hand-picked Peter to have my back."

I had definitely noticed how close they were upon their arrival from Colorado, and every moment since. How protective he was of her. How she almost always stayed close to him. It was everything Liam never was with her. *It's how he should have been.* "Peter is a really great guy."

She swallowed hard and blinked back the lingering tears. "He really is." Suddenly, she shifted, pulled her phone out, and then smirked at the screen. "Speaking of, he's checking in."

I arched an eyebrow as intrigue captured me. "Does he know where you are?"

"Oh yeah. But like you, he's also worried about another post-chaos crash." Tori snickered. "He's questioning the lasting power of good ice cream."

I glanced at my phone, not at all surprised to see a few texts waiting for me. "Ben's gently poking at me, too. Maybe we should put the guys, and ourselves, out of misery and let this day fucking end."

She cleared her throat. "Li?"

"Yeah?"

"So, I know I told you and Lukas I was good with being called Tori, but after," she gestured around the room, "everything that's happened since I've come home, I'd rather just go by Adair."

I stood up, walked over to her, and pulled her into a hug. It made sense that she wanted to be Adair and not Tori. Tori was the one who had been constantly running for her life. Tori had to hide. Adair was moving forward and living. She was sharper, smarter, a version of herself that was born swinging. I couldn't help but respect the hell out of that. "Then you're Adair. You don't have to explain it to anyone."

"Thank you." A deep sigh came out. "I know there is no need to explain it, and I know Tori is a significant part of me, but that's also not who I am anymore. I'm not the same person I was then."

I leaned back and rubbed her shoulders. "I feel that in my bones. None of us are the same as we were before *he* decided to abandon us."

She met my eyes with a gentle, almost maternal resignation that was so much older than either of us had the right to be. "No, we aren't, but I can see it now, Li. We're all better off for it in some twisted way." There was no self-pity in her gaze, only the acute awareness of the life she'd had before and the unapologetic acceptance of where she was now. I watched as she flexed her hands, the pale scar on her thumb catching the light—one more trace of the past that would never really fade.

For a moment she was the excited and determined woman I remembered from training sessions... the woman who joined me in the backyard, eating ice cream, giggling about some silly thing we had seen that day... the woman who was so excited to be part of this family. I was so damn proud of her.

"We had to be stronger than we wanted. I used to think that I would never feel safe or happy... that I would never stop looking over my shoulder, but I don't think that's true anymore." Adair glanced away for a moment before continuing. "I think we're going to blaze a trail of our own, settle the score, build the most amazing future, and have the 'happily ever after' we both very much deserve."

Her optimism was contagious, and my chest ached a little less. "The only thing I ever wanted was to be seen for me. Not my family name. Not the businesses. Not the first female Don. Just Lianne." It was the first time I'd said those words out loud to anyone aside from Ben. As much as I felt like I should have been embarrassed by the admission, I wasn't.

Adair didn't even blink. "You are already so much more than *just* Lianne now. You are a kickass woman running a multimillion-dollar business."

A deep sigh came out. "It's still the Agosti name, though." I never wanted this business, but I would be damned before abandoning my family.

She gave me a sad smile, understanding in her eyes. "Yes. You weren't able to outrun that, but you can do so much now, and on your terms. Hell, you already have. There is shit you've made happen that would have taken your father or even Liam twice or three times the amount of time to achieve. You're bold. Smart as hell. And you don't take shit from anyone."

"That's true enough, but I—"

"You have a say in this part of your life." Adair wrinkled her nose as she smiled and gave my hand a squeeze. "You are doing so well. Please believe me. It was a long time ago, but I spent a *lot* of time in meetings with Uncle Kobe and Mr. Agosti, and even one or two with Don Dallas. You are running this show like a seasoned professional and look damn good doing it."

I took a deep breath, and it escaped as a shaky laugh. "Well, thank you." My phone vibrated on the desk behind me, and I let out a long breath. "The boys are getting anxious. Let's put them out of their misery."

"Sounds good." She stood up. "Good night, Li."

"Good night, Adair."

We walked out of my office together, and as she turned right to head toward her room, I headed left for mine, making my way through the foyer before slowly climbing the stairs. When I opened the door to my bedroom, Ben was lying there with a notebook in his hand. I swallowed hard as his warm eyes, shining bright with love, met mine. This was my safe place. *He* was my safe place.

I stripped on the way to the bed, not caring I was down to my bra and underwear, and climbed in next to him. After wrapping my arms around his chest and resting my head on his shoulder, he shifted and pulled me close, pressing a kiss to the top of my head.

"I love you."

A smile tugged at the corner of my mouth as I leaned into his hold. "I love you, too."

The day had been a lot, and as I listened to his heartbeat, I found my body slowly relaxing. As much as I wanted to give in to the exhaustion, I needed this time with Ben. He was my anchor in this chaos.

Chapter Thirteen

Sabrina

I was trying to make peace with the fact that Liam was staying with Chloe in his old room tonight. Knowing how much of an ass he was, I didn't trust him. Regina had set up a little toddler bed for her in the corner, and Lynette made sure Bunny and a couple of the softest blankets in the house ended up there as well.

Liam was hesitant as he went through the motions of getting his daughter ready for bed, no doubt from being watched. Avery was already posted up by the door, arms folded, pretending to be casual about watching Chloe's every step. Lukas was stationed just outside the room, fiddling with his phone, but glanced up every few seconds, making it clear that any move toward the stairs by Liam would be intercepted and not end well for him.

I offered to stay in case Chloe needed something.

"Absolutely not." Lukas looked at me as if I'd offered to sleep outside in the cold.

For a second, I thought about pushing it. Chloe was my assignment. My charge. My responsibility. When I glanced at Avery for backup, she subtly shook her head, a silent plea for me not to turn this into a power struggle. It was hard for me to relinquish power to someone else. I was used to running the show and calling the shots. "Okay."

Instead of immediately going downstairs, I hovered in the hallway, listening to Liam read Chloe a bedtime story. I tried to tell myself they would be fine, that no one here would let him hurt a hair on his daughter's head, but I couldn't shake the nagging urge to help.

Lukas took my hand and squeezed it. "She's fine. They're just reading. Avery and I are here for the night. You should get some sleep." When I narrowed my eyes, he let out a deep sigh. "Seriously, Sabrina, we are good." I'm sure he meant it as an informal order, but there was something else in his tone. It was like he had also spent a few too many nights on the wrong side of a locked door.

I nodded. "But—"

"You just flew in. I know Lianne gave you some time earlier, but Avery and I have this. Trust me. If we need you, we *will* get you up here." He let out a tense breath. "Please enjoy one night of relative peace. Tomorrow is going to be a lot."

"Okay. Have a good night." Finally accepting I was not in charge, I headed downstairs, letting out a tense breath once on the main level again. *Now what?*

As I made my way down the staircase, past the framed family photos on the wall, I thought of a time long since passed. Liam, Lianne, and Lukas playing in the yard. School pictures. Family photos of a time when the twins' life hadn't been so complicated. There were also a few more recent photos unknown to me, and I drank in the memories vicariously, loving every moment of joy frozen in time.

Needing some water, I walked into the kitchen, opened the fridge, and stared at the contents, hoping I'd find answers. Of course, there was no cleanly written plan for world peace hidden among the lunch meats, cheese, leftovers, and cookie batter that I'd seen Ben working on with Chloe earlier.

Oatmeal chocolate chip with coconut shreds in it.

Oh, I can't wait for those to get baked off.

I giggled when Chloe had eaten more of the coconut than she'd put in the bowl, but I wasn't the only one. Ben and Lukas had smiles on their faces, too. For all the chaos, bloodshed, and tension the day held, I was grateful there had been a light moment in the evening.

I grabbed a bottle of water and shut the fridge, but not before I took a spoonful of the batter and ate it raw. I didn't know whether Ben would be mad about it. I hadn't spent any real time with him yet and didn't know how protective he was of his baking. All I really knew was that he made Li happy.

Twisting the cap off and taking a drink, I looked around. For the first time since arriving, I realized how strange it was to be in this house, not as a guest, but as someone who worked here. I had missed the Agostis, missed spending time with Dante, but being here now and under these circumstances was so wild and different. The intimacy of all our relationships had changed. It was there, but buried under layers of protocol, politics, and mutual rage of Liam.

Then there was the fact that I wasn't in charge, and was now answering to a different Don… with my uncle's blessing, all while still being sought after by *La Muerta Rubi*. I had been transferred from one safe house to another.

But now I have Dante.

For months I had been begging any deity in the universe to find a way to bring us back together. Being here now, with him, was absolutely wild and brought me so much joy and peace. It was going to be a delicate balancing act, but I was grateful for the challenge.

He and I had always kept things separate. Work was work. It was either Agosti business or Rodriguez's business, and we tried not to talk about it. Everything else was just us. Now that the division was gone, and every aspect of our lives were colliding in one very crowded space.

I found myself wandering toward Dante's room. As I rounded the corner of the hallway his room was in, I nearly crashed into Talia.

"Oh! I'm so sorry."

She let out a slight chuckle. "You're fine. This is actually convenient. I was just heading upstairs to talk to you and Avery."

What? "Why me?"

Talia grinned. "To make sure Avery's cool with me crashing in her bed so you and Dante don't have to pretend you don't want to do things to each other that would put me in therapy."

As much as I wanted to fight the 'accusation,' she wasn't wrong. "I assume mentioning I didn't want to kick you out of your bed wouldn't change your mind?"

She shook her head and chuckled. "Nope. Dante already tried to lie about how you two would behave." I opened my mouth to try to defend him, but Talia held up her hand. "I know you would try, and because I love you both, I want you to have as much privacy as you can. This house is a damn fishbowl on a good day."

I wrapped my arms around her shoulders and hugged hard. "Thank you, Talia."

She returned the gesture and let out a sigh. "You're welcome. I cannot tell you how grateful I was to see you roll in today. Dante would probably be pissed I'm telling you this, but he didn't handle the news of you getting hurt well at all, and it only got worse after that." She leaned back to look me in the eye. "I was worried about him more than you, if that tells you anything."

"Yeah..." I let out a tense breath. "Uncle Ceaser mentioned something about that when I demanded updates."

Talia chuckled. "You're probably one of three or four people who can demand anything out of him and live to tell the tale."

"And I try not to take too much advantage of it. Have a good night."

She squeezed my shoulder as she passed, and I looked towards Dante's door. A happy, giddy feeling filled me. *I get to be with my Wolf tonight. All night.* I didn't stop to knock, but just opened the door and walked in.

I heard the water running in the shower. As quietly as I could, I shut the bedroom door behind me and made my way to the bathroom, which was filled with steam. Inhaling, I took in the almond smell of his soap.

God, I missed this.

I could see the outline of his arms as he braced his hands against the tile, head bowed. The sound of water hitting his skin was rhythmic and soothing. I leaned against the sink, letting the steam soak into my hair and shirt, letting the warmth settle into my shoulders, letting go of the tension that had been my constant companion since I left the Caribbean.

Was that really only earlier today?

Eventually, the shower shut off, and Dante muttered something under his breath. The glass door swung open, and as he stepped out, dripping, he secured a towel around his hips. Maybe it was the water clinging to his skin or the fact I hadn't seen him like this in years, but fuck, he looked good. I slowly took in every inch of skin I could see, noting the new scars, specifically the one that ran from under the towel to his knee.

He caught sight of me when he looked up, and his whole face lit up with an unguarded smile. "You could have joined me, you know."

"You know as well as I do that I wouldn't have the self-control not to get on my knees before my Wolf." Biting the corner of my lip, I had to press my legs together to keep from doing it, anyway.

Dante ran a hand over his face as he took a slow, deep breath. "Damn, Kitten." His deep voice was a balm to my soul. He closed the distance, pressing me against the counter, hands bracketing my waist. I breathed him in as our foreheads touched.

Neither of us said anything for a long moment. There wasn't any need. The weight of the time we lost together hung between us. I wanted to kiss him, but I also noted the look in his eyes that showed me he had slipped into Dom mode. It was almost as if that would slow time down enough for us to stretch this moment out for hours.

"I missed you so damn much."

Dante pressed his lips to my forehead, keeping them there as he exhaled, slow and steady, grounding us there in that spot. His phone buzzed on the counter beside us, breaking the hold this moment had on us. He glanced at it, and then at me, a reluctant smile tugging at his mouth.

"Talia's asking if we had dinner."

I blinked several times as I tried to remember the last time I had eaten. "No, but I probably should." Food hadn't even cracked the top twenty-five things I'd been worried about today. "I hadn't even thought that far ahead. I figured I would eat whatever was available here." So much had been going on, I didn't even realize I was hungry.

Excitement lit up Dante's face. "You just got back into town... is there anything special you want to eat?"

A low chuckle came out as I realized, once again, that I wasn't hidden away on a remote island. "Running out to pick up food hasn't been an option for quite some time."

His smile split into a huge grin as he ran his hands down the sides of my arms. "Then take a minute to think about it." Then he reached over blindly and handed me his phone. "Look up whatever restaurants you want. We can go from there."

"I have a phone, Dante."

"And maybe I want the search history so I'll know what your new favorite foods are." He leaned in and kissed me. "Or maybe I just want to take care of my woman."

My heart raced at the intensity of his love and desire for me burning bright in his eyes.

Talia was so right. There's no way we could have behaved all night.

I glanced down at the phone and let out a groan. "I would kill for my mom's empanadas, but I don't know if I can touch base with her yet." Guilt and loneliness slammed into my chest. It was the first time I'd thought about my mom since landing. *Am I the worst daughter?*

Dante whined softly. "You *had* to tease me about that, didn't you, Kitten?"

I caressed the side of his face, wiping away a few lingering droplets of water. I loved beyond reason that he was standing in front of me. "Not intentionally. I'll talk to my uncle about seeing her... and we'll have her cooking again soon enough. But to answer your question, I haven't had a decent cheeseburger in well over a year."

The stunned expression that appeared on Dante's face was almost comical. "That feels like either the most heinous crime or a violation of the Geneva Convention."

There was no stopping the snicker that came out. "*Jesucristo.* Dramatic much?"

"Fuck, I've missed your swearing." He took my head in his hands and pulled me in for a hard kiss, that he turned up the heat to when he leaned in, teasing me with his tongue until my knees went weak. His passion was barely bridled, and I didn't realize how much I'd missed making him squirm. I could feel *just* how much he missed me as his hips pressed against mine.

"Feed me dinner and I'll let you tease and pull every swear in the book out of me later."

Dante let out a low, warning growl as he swept me up in his arms, lifting me as if I weighed nothing at all, and tossed me onto the bed. His hands pinned me on either side, caging me in with his body. The mattress gave way under his weight, the tension in those broad shoulders clear as he loomed over me, water still slowly making its way through the defined muscles of his chest and stomach. "You are *severely o*verestimating my self-control, Kitten."

I smirked and let out a hum. "Who said anything about me wanting you to stay in control?" I slid my fingers beneath the towel at his hips and tugged him closer, so his body pressed closer against mine and our faces were mere inches apart.

He chuckled, and I felt the low sound against my own chest. "You always play with fire, Kitten."

His pupils dilated just before he took my shirt and ripped it up and over my head. Underneath the bravado, I saw the way his jaw tensed, the way he was holding himself back, testing the fine line between restraint and surrender. Every muscle in his body vibrated with the effort not to ruin me, and to remind my body *exactly* who it belonged to.

Without warning, his hands moved, one tangling in my hair at the base of my neck, the other securing my hip with a tight grip as he rolled us over. He pressed his forehead to mine, his breath hot and uneven. "You are my—" His phone dinged, making me jump. "Fuck." He dragged out the word as he held me tight and caught his breath.

"Designated tone?"

He nodded. "Yeah."

I rolled off Dante and watched his face as he checked in. The frustration quickly morphed into irritation, relief, and then pure annoyance. *Who messaged him?*

"Talia will be in Avery's room tonight... and Avery is being a shit."

I couldn't help laughing. "Oh?"

Dante arched an eyebrow as he looked at me. "She asked if I remembered how to have sex, or if I needed a refresher course from someone who's gotten laid recently."

That woman is a delightful menace.

He let out a sigh as he tossed the phone back onto his bedside table. "We need to figure out dinner. I *have* to feed you before we get carried away. You're going to need it."

Don't tempt me with a good time. "I thought we were having burgers." A low chuckle came out as I leaned forward. "The last thing I want is for the Agostis to be accused of violating the Geneva Convention."

"We can't have that." Dante grinned as he got up and pulled on some clothes. "I need to introduce you to a local burger place we fell in love with. It's a crowd favorite. Do you want fries and a chocolate shake, too?"

Now I had to snicker. "Are you trying to get into my pants?"

"Obviously." He grinned and gave me a quick kiss. "But I need you to eat. Have you seriously not had anything since you arrived?"

I gave him a slight grimace and shook my head. "There wasn't exactly time. And the hour I had 'off' was spent with you. We're both to blame."

He narrowed his eyes at me, *not* pleased with my response. "Kitten, how are you going to have energy for me to remind you what you mean to me if you don't eat? That being said, are you allowed to leave the house so we can pick it up together?"

I paused and then shrugged. "I wasn't told I had to stay, but I don't think I should leave. It feels reckless and disrespectful, especially in the context of everything that happened today. And just because no one knows I'm back in town doesn't mean I want to play fast and loose with my safety. I *also* don't want to get off on the wrong foot with Lianne."

"She loves you; all the Agostis do."

I took Dante's hands in mine. "I'm not questioning their love for me. I'm taking into consideration the fact I'm lying low here for a bit as well as to keep Chloe safe."

Dante's eyes went wide as he realized what I hadn't directly said. "The threat isn't gone?"

I shook my head. "No. I've basically moved from one safe house to another. If I read between the lines correctly, Ceaser and Lynette exchanged favors."

He nodded. "So we keep you inside, away from prying eyes."

A deep sigh came out. "For now, yeah. Makes it convenient since the same applies to Chloe."

"Okay. I respect that." He held me close and then kissed me again before heading out. "I should be no more than twenty minutes. Make yourself at home. I love you, Kitten."

"I love you, too."

I twisted the lock on the door after Dante left, relishing the click. In Cuba, I'd quickly learned that privacy was a luxury, and one never guaranteed. Even here in a house full of people I trusted completely, with as much firepower as my own home, I wanted that small boundary. A locked door meant that I could breathe and let my guard down. At least a little.

Before changing, I straightened up the top of his dresser because the scattered mess put me on edge, opened my suitcase, and shook my head at the summer clothes I'd brought. Sure, there was another pair of jeans and one long-sleeved shirt, but I was going to need more clothes, and warmer ones at that. March in Chicago was wild when it came to weather, and I was not prepared for most of it with the wardrobe options present.

I'll have to talk to Tío and see what he can send over from my place.

The stretchy capris would be fine to sleep in tonight, as would my T-shirt, but I was going to need warmer things. Smirking, I opened the dresser closest to Dante's bed in search of a sweatshirt. I found one and slipped it over my head, giggling at how huge it was on me. I didn't care. It smelled like him and made me feel safe.

Still needing to kill at least another ten minutes, I settled onto the bed and took out my phone.

S: < Settled in as much as I can be for the moment, but I'm going to need a lot of stuff from my room. >

Tío: < Make a list and I'll have it delivered tomorrow. L said she'd cover anything you need. >

S: < Estimate on job length? >

Lianne had said until the Liam situation was resolved, but I knew from experience most Dons didn't keep prisoners long.

Tío: < Until it's done, Mija. >

Yeah, I should have expected that.

S: < Does my mom know the update? >

Tío: < We're having dinner together. I'll be filling her in then. >

Hope filled my chest. I missed my mama.

S: < Will the communication rules be changing? And what about visits? >

Tío: < You can talk to her, Raine, and Z, but that's it on this side. Let's see what the next few days bring before we add more. >

So no contact with any of Uncle Ceaser's team. Interesting.

S: < Do I need a burner for in-house communication here? Or can they have this number? >

It felt like overkill to have two phones, but since it had been bad enough to keep me in hiding, the question felt valid. Not to mention this was a Rodriguez phone, so technically it was up to my Don.

Tío: < They can have this number. >

Tío: < and yes, he can, too. >

S: < Thank you. >

After sending my uncle the list of what I hoped was still in my bedroom, I curled up on my side and relished being surrounded by everything Dante, shaking my head as drowsiness overtook me.

I'll just close my eyes for a minute.

The door rattling pulled me from my sleep, and I sat up with a start, reaching for the gun that wasn't on my hip.

Where is it?

As quickly as the adrenaline kicked in, I spotted my gun on the bedside table and lunged for it. As I wrapped my hand around the handle, flipped off the safety, and took aim at the door, Dante's voice registered, and I immediately let out a tense breath.

"I should have known she was going to lock up behind me."

"Do you think she'll be mad I made you late?"

That's Lianne. Wait. Late? How long have I been out?

He chuckled as the door opened. "Nah. You two pretty much think the other walks on water."

I hopped off the bed and rushed to the door. "Is everything okay?"

As Dante stepped in, Lianne was still in the hallway, looking guilty as she held a paper bag in one hand and a to-go cup in the other. "Yeah. Dante texted me before leaving... and I added to the order."

I grinned at how un-Don-like Lianne looked right now, standing there in leggings, a tank top, and an oversized cardigan, holding a bag of fast food. "It's apparently a house favorite. I would have been mad if he *hadn't* picked up something for you."

She smirked and took a sip of her drink. There was a spark of approval and understanding in her eyes as her attention flicked to the gun still in my hand. "Well, now that I know you two are good for the night, I'm going to try to pretend I'm not queen of this chaos for an hour. Good night."

"Night, Lianne."

I closed the door, locking it again, and turned to see Dante setting the food out on the desk. Flipping the safety back on, I went over to the dresser and put down my gun. I loved that neither of them had said anything about me about it. Technically, what I just did was a *major* faux pas, one I could and *should* have gotten into a lot of trouble for.

"I see you tidied up. I started to earlier, but..." He trailed off when our eyes locked. "I still can't believe you're here. I prayed the entire time I was driving to and from the restaurant that the universe wasn't pulling the biggest prank on me and that you'd still be here when I got back."

"You and me, both."

Dante gave me a look, the one that said he meant every word, that he would have burned the world down to get me back, if that's what it took. He separated our meals, passing the fries over with a little bow. "Kitten, I believe these are yours."

I arched an eyebrow. "You got the large for me, didn't you?"

A snicker popped out. "Obviously. Neither of us are good at sharing food."

I plucked a fry, savoring the perfect amount of crunchy softness as I settled onto one of the desk chairs. *Holy fuck, these are good.* Dante set up on the other side of the desk, like we were at a restaurant for two. It was such an entirely normal activity that I didn't know what to do without the high-tension, bullet-dodging civility I'd become accustomed to over the last two years.

"What are you thinking?"

I took a few more fries and popped them into my mouth, not daring to make eye contact. "What makes you think I was thinking anything?" I hated how immediately I went into self-preservation mode. *This is my Dante. My Wolf. The love of my life.* There was no reason to shield or hide parts of myself from him.

He tilted his head slightly. "Your eyes go a little unfocused when you're thinking of a lot of things at once. Not usually good, either."

I shrugged as a warm feeling spread in my chest at how well he knew me. "It's just... This is the safest I've felt in... fuck if I know. Even before I left, there was so much going on. The cartels, the shipments, the products." I was rambling and quickly took a bite of my burger to stop the torrent of words.

All coherent thoughts evaporated from my mind as flavors exploded in my mouth.

The char from the grill, the seasoned beef, the sweet bite of red onions, the juicy tomatoes, even the cheese was perfect. This burger was quite possibly one of the most amazing things I'd eaten in months, and the indecent noises I made were likely testing Dante's ability to keep his hands to himself. I wasn't trying to be obnoxious; the food really was that delicious. It could also have been because it felt like a million years since I'd had one, but I didn't care. I loved it.

After a moment, he nudged the milkshake over with a straw bent perfectly so that I hardly had to move to take a drink. "Thank you."

We ate in comfortable silence. Every few minutes, I'd catch Dante's eyes on me. There was an undercurrent of lust there, but mostly it was a softer, reverent, in-awe gaze that had heat rising to my cheeks. I wondered if he was counting the times he thought of this moment, when we would see each other again, and if he'd built it up in his mind to be something unattainable.

God knows I have.

"When I was away, I used to dream about this."

His lips lifted at the corners. "Me too. Only you were a little more... tropically dressed."

I couldn't help but chuckle as I took another sip of the milkshake. "What in the hell is that supposed to mean?"

"Meaning you were in much less clothing."

A low chuckle came out. *Yeah. That tracks.* "Let my food settle, and we can make that happen."

We finished eating, trading stories about who had the worst travel day. Dante's consisted of nearly hitting another truck because he was distracted by me changing in the back seat, while mine was definitely the asshole customs officer who all but strip-searched me for contraband.

As Dante stood to toss out the trash, I caught his hand, and for a long second, I held it, thumb tracing the scars on his knuckles. He didn't pull away, and when I lifted my gaze, my words were soft and quiet. "I don't care what happens next. This is enough. Just us. Right here."

His throat bobbed as he squeezed my hand back, and for once, Dante Wilson was at a loss for words. His eyes were bright as he nodded and pulled me up for a kiss, slow and steady. It was the kind that cemented that being with him was home more than any location could be.

Twelve hours ago, I had been on a plane, and now I was having dinner with the love of my life.

As the kiss ended, we sat back down, our hands still entwined. My focus darted around the room, finally landing on the remnants of our meal. The urge to clean it up and make it look like I was never here was overwhelming. *I don't have to do that here.* Regardless, I didn't want to leave a mess to deal with in the morning.

As I moved to start cleaning, Dante stopped me. "Please let me take care of you."

I wanted to fight him on it and insist I could help, but there was a need that shone through his words and actions. He needed this more than I needed to be self-sufficient. "Can I at least use the bathroom on my own?"

He narrowed his eyes at me in a harmless glare. "You're adorable, and I'm going to let that slide tonight."

"How chivalrous of you." I kissed him on the cheek. "I'm also going to jump in the shower real quick." My mind rolled over everything Zee and I had done to get here, and I wanted to rid myself of the last remnants from my time in Cuba. A wave of exhaustion flowed over me now that I had eaten and was actually relaxing. "Then I think it's time to sleep."

I took my time in the shower, letting the hot water, steam, and familiar scent of his soap wrap around me. While I let the conditioner sit on my hair, I tilted my face up, letting the water trace its way over my face and along the edges of my jaw where Dante had kissed me. My entire body was humming with a strange new energy, equal parts adrenaline and the kind of contentment I'd been dreaming about.

The tiny bathroom was heavily fogged by the time I finished, and when I wiped down the mirror so I could see my face, I looked tired, but not as haunted and strained as I had been earlier.

Being this 'high up' in a mafia family had its costs. Uncle Ceaser and I knew that all too well. He'd lost his wife and both of their children in a freak plane accident, and I'd lost my father when he took a bullet for Ceasar. Then I lost Rod and Claudia in Cuba when they both took countless bullets for me. My thoughts went to Lianne, as she now carried the weight of that loss, as well as the weight of following in her father's footsteps.

And one day will be me.

Losing loved ones was always going to hurt, but as with everyone else who had given their lives to protect us, it was our duty and honor to carry on and make them proud.

I brushed my teeth, using Dante's minty toothpaste because I could, and chuckled as I thought of all the times Zee and I had complained about the gross cinnamon flavor we'd been stuck with. My hair was surprisingly cooperative, considering the chaos it had been through today. I was tempted either to braid it or to coil it up into a bun, but I left it down as Dante loved running his fingers through my hair.

After putting my pajamas back on, I practically dove into his hoodie again and padded back into the bedroom, the bedside lamp casting a gentle light into the space. Dante was stretched out lengthwise on the bed, wearing a loose pair of dark grey joggers, his bare chest exposed. He was holding an ancient-looking crossword puzzle book and was attacking it with the same intensity he brought to everything else.

There was something about this combination—the hulking, dangerous body and the battered crossword, the way he furrowed his brow and chewed the end of his pencil—that made my heart skip a beat. This domestic version of Dante, so at ease in the half-dark, made me want things I'd not let myself think about the entire time I had been gone.

I hovered in the doorway a little longer, watching him. He must have sensed it, because he glanced up, met my gaze, and grinned as if he'd discovered the eighth wonder of the world. After he patted the empty spot beside him, I walked over and sank into the mattress, instantly enveloped by his warmth.

"Feeling better?" he asked, voice pitched low, like we were in some secret den.

"Better than better." Leaning against him, I had the perfect view of the current puzzle he was solving. "You still on the easy ones?"

"Only at night. I want to relax, not get my brain worked up."

"You know you're not sixty-five, right?" I couldn't help teasing him. "Or is this your stealthy way of showing off how many synonyms you know for 'murder'?"

He let out a slightly annoyed sigh before nuzzling my shoulder with his stubble. "Don't knock it. Keeps my mind sharp... and it's weirdly relaxing."

I furrowed my brow as I studied the puzzle grid again. "You spelled 'valedictorian' wrong."

He snorted. "No, I didn't."

"You did. There's no 'k.'"

Shaking his head, he tossed the book onto the side table and pulled me close. "There's something else I'd rather do."

I gave him an innocent look and arched an eyebrow at him. "Oh? And what would *that* be?"

He gently wrapped his hand around the base of my throat, squeezing just tight enough to show me he was the one in control. My heart raced, but not because I was scared. The action flipped a switch in my brain, and my core pulsed as he pulled me close. "Did my Kitten forget her manners?"

I couldn't help the whimper of submission that came out of me as I shook my head. "No, but she misses her Wolf and wants to remind him how much she loves him."

His breath faltered as he growled and then pressed his forehead to mine. "It's been far too long since I've heard those delicious words leave your lips."

"Then we'd better make up for lost time."

Chapter Fourteen

Dante

When I opened my eyes the next morning, I thought I'd dreamt of being with Sabrina the night before. Glancing around, I was definitely in my room, but when I looked down, she was snuggled against me under the covers.

When I shifted to kiss the side of her head, she let out a sleepy moan. "If I'm dreaming, don't wake me up."

I wrapped my arms tighter around the love of my life, savoring how her body felt pressed against mine. "Not dreaming, Kitten."

Her head popped up, those golden-brown eyes locking onto mine as a brilliant smile lit up her face. "I'm really here."

"You're really here."

She leaned in a little closer, kissing my chest. "I never want to leave this bed."

The honest comment made me chuckle. "As much as I'd love to make that happen, you and I both have very important jobs to get to."

Sabrina sat up with a start, turning and reaching for something. "Shit. What time is it?" When the light from her phone shone on her face, I watched the panic fade to relief. "It's just after six. Oh, thank God." She flipped the sheet back, and it was all I could do not to grab her hips and pull her back into bed before she sauntered over to her suitcase and bent over.

"Kitten, you aren't playing nice."

She glanced over confused at first, and then realization registered in her eyes. "It's not my fault we fucked until we passed out and I didn't have a chance to put my pajamas back on."

I arched an eyebrow at her as I smirked. "Isn't it, though?"

A deep sigh came out as Sabrina grabbed clothes and a bag of what I assumed were toiletries. "I'm going to take a quick shower before heading out. As much as I love smelling like you, showing up to work smelling like sex probably isn't a good idea. Besides, I don't know what time things start around here, and I really don't want to be late on my first day."

Her words were a bucket of ice water to my thoughts. I'd been so wrapped up in having her in my arms again, I'd temporarily forgotten *why*. She was here to protect and look after Chloe. I was now in charge of keeping Liam in line. "Right."

It wasn't long before we were both dressed and ready to head out. As I reached for the doorknob, Sabrina grabbed my wrist, stopped me.

"Dante, we have to talk about how we act once we walk through this door." She pinned me where I stood with a hard look. "I can't afford to screw this up. There is literally no room for error. Too many lives are on the line."

I nodded. Again, my woman wasn't wrong. "We are professionals. We've worked together before, Kitten. We can do it again."

Sabrina shook her head. "Dante, as much as I love you, that nickname *must* stay in the bedroom. And while we are professionals, we've never had to work in this close of proximity for this long. You *have* to stow your overprotective Dom side outside this room. I can't have you freaking out if someone gets in my face. That includes Liam, who will no doubt push limits at some point."

I clenched my fists, forcing every muscle in my forearm to relax as I took a calming breath. This was not a firefight in some back alley. This was the daily operation of a mafia household. She wasn't just my partner, not just the woman in my bed, but a future Don, and more dangerous than any rival ever dreamed of being. She was more than capable of handling herself.

Fine.

I tried to smile, but it felt like trying on a new suit that hadn't been tailored to fit. "You're right. There will be some adjustment. I promise to do my best, okay?"

She reached up, fingers strong and callused from years of weapons training, and cupped my jaw. I leaned into her touch, not breaking eye contact. I could see the gears turning behind her eyes, the calculations she was already running about every possible threat, every angle of vulnerability. Sabrina held my face still for a moment, as if memorizing it, then let out something between a sigh and a laugh. "I know it's going to take some time to adjust and settle in, but with you at my side again, we've got this."

Those words shouldn't have been enough. But they were. I let her pull me in for a kiss. The way our lips pressed together was a full, lingering promise that we were continuing to build our new normal. When my Kitten finally pulled away, she did it with a grin that was both business and trouble. "Let's get some breakfast."

We stepped out into the hallway; the shift from private to public was instantaneous. Sabrina stood tall, shoulders back, head on a swivel. I followed her, automatically staying a half-step behind her, both out of habit and out of unspoken deference. Around here, every gesture was a statement. I might be the muscle, but she was the chess player with a knife under the table.

Talia was already downstairs when Sabrina and I strolled into the crew kitchen. Her face brightened with a knowing smile that crinkled the corners of her eyes. "Good morning, cuties."

"Morning, Tal." The kitchen smelled of fresh coffee and cinnamon, and I was looking forward to a mug of it. Since no one else was in sight, I kissed the top of her head as I passed her, heading straight toward the coffeemaker.

"Did you sleep okay, Sabrina?"

Sabrina nodded, tucking a strand of hair behind her ear. "Once I got there, yeah."

My sister tilted her head to the side. "Have a hard time settling down?"

Sabrina and I shared a soft smirk as I handed her a mug of coffee, our fingers brushing. "Something like that."

Talia's attention jumped to me. She narrowed her eyes and shook her head, lips pursed. "I knew it. I *so* called it."

"Congratulations," I replied dryly, taking a long sip from my own mug.

We ate quickly, and by the time we made it upstairs, Lynette was in the kitchen drinking coffee with Ben while Ellen was filling two mugs.

"Good morning."

Lynette smiled brightly. "You two are up earlier than I expected."

Sabrina stood tall and proud. "I'm not one to dawdle, ma'am."

"You don't need to ma'am me in front of Ben and Ellen." Lynette cleared her throat, and a warm, loving smile appeared on her face as she gestured to the two people sitting at the table with her. "Sabrina, this is Ben, Lianne's husband and my amazing son-in-law, and Ellen, my soon-to-be daughter-in-law. Ben, Ellen, this is Sabrina Rodriguez. She is Chloe's new nanny and personal guard and will be here for the foreseeable future."

Ben sat up a little taller as a stunned expression appeared on his face. "Wait. Are *you* the favorite cousin I've heard so much about?" When Sabrina nodded, he stood and closed the distance between them. "It is fantastic finally meeting you. I have heard so many stories."

"I... Thank you?" I could tell by her guarded, polite smile that she was trying to read the man's intentions.

He started to reach for her, but then froze in place. "Can I hug you?"

With a chuckle, Sabrina nodded again, letting some of her professional mask slip. "I'd love that." After a warm embrace, she leaned back and regarded Ellen. "You're engaged to Ryan, right?"

"Yeah." The blond woman smiled and gestured to the plate in front of her. "I'm actually pulling some breakfast together for him. After everything that happened yesterday, I'm going to have to put food in front of his face to make sure he eats."

"And Lianne and I appreciate it."

Ellen glanced around, looking wary and a little nervous. "I also want to clear out of the kitchen before our guests come down."

I considered her phrasing and the shift in her demeanor. "Ryan's request?"

She looked at me and nodded. "Yeah."

As if on cue, Lukas's voice floated down from the stairwell, and Ellen's eyes went wide before she looked at Ben and Lynette. "I've been *advised* to work from home today. I'll be in Ryan's office or our room if you need me."

Seconds after she rushed from the room, Lukas strolled in the other entrance to the kitchen, holding a sleepy-looking Chloe. "Good morning, everyone. Chloe decided it was time for breakfast."

I grinned and waved at the tyke in his arms, pleased when she waved back.

"Dada seepy."

Lukas nodded and gave his niece a kiss on the cheek. "Yes, your daddy was still sleeping. Do you want pancakes?"

Her face lit up with an enormous smile. "Pease!"

Ben grinned. "I'd be happy to make some for you, sweetie. Give Uncle Lukas a hug so he can go take a nap."

"Night night Unca Lu!" She kissed his cheek and reached for Ben. "I help Ben Ben?"

He smiled at her and nodded. "Of course, you can help me, Chloe."

It was adorable watching Ben work with his niece to mix the batter. Sabrina had joined them at the long quartz-covered island, but only assisted or stepped in if actively asked, or to make sure Chloe didn't get hurt. I glanced to my left and caught Lynette watching the trio with a smile on her face. The Agosti matriarch had been through so much, I didn't take her joy for granted.

The beautiful moment was cut short by an angry voice. "Don't make me get your mother."

Lynette tensed up, her focus immediately going to the archway that led to the stairwell landing.

"Ma'am, would you like me to see if Avery needs a hand?" When she nodded, I ducked out of the kitchen and glanced up the stairs. Avery was standing at the top, glaring at Liam, who looked just as pissed.

"Do I need to bring up handcuffs?"

Liam's attention snapped to me, rage burning in his eyes. "In my own home?"

This again? "Don Agosti and her team have made it abundantly clear this *isn't* your home anymore. You are here and alive at the will of Don Agosti. Are you going to play nice so you can join your daughter for breakfast, or do we need to make *other* arrangements?"

I put my hands on my hips, one resting above my gun.

Several emotions flickered across Liam's face before he let out a tense breath. "I'd like to have breakfast with my daughter."

A smirk appeared on mine. "Glad you can see reason. Please don't make me scare Chloe by disciplining you." I looked at Avery. "I've got him. Go get some sleep."

When we walked into the kitchen, Chloe was sitting in her highchair looking grumpy. She had her arms crossed over her chest, her chin tucked low, and those blue eyes narrowed at the bunny on the tray in front of her. It looked like Ben had tried to patch the ear again with a bit more tape, but she did not look pleased with the results.

Sabrina, who had been watching from her place at the island, slid off her stool and came over, lowering herself to eye level with the kid. She didn't say anything at first, just studied the stuffed animal for a long moment. Chloe scowled harder, her little fists bunching up, but there was something almost hopeful in the way she glanced at Sabrina out of the corner of her eye.

"Bad day, Bunny?" Sabrina asked quietly, as if talking to the toy itself.

Chloe nodded, silent but emphatic.

Sabrina gently examined the bunny's sad ear. "We'll fix it." She flicked her eyes up at me and then at Ben as she moved to fetch something from a drawer. I realized she'd read the room and saw this seemingly tiny problem for what it was. This bunny was the whole world to a little girl still learning what was safe and what wasn't, and it was 'broken'.

Ben set down the whisk and came over with a roll of medical tape and a pack of smiley-face Band-Aids. "Emergency repairs," he joked, but kept his voice gentle.

Sabrina worked quickly, deft and sure, and soon the bunny's ear was wrapped in a neon bandage. She handed it back to Chloe, who hugged it close and gave the woman a grateful smile. It was a small thing, but so very significant.

I couldn't help but smile at how Sabrina was with her. Would she be like this with our children? I found myself half paying attention to Liam when he brought a small bowl of grapes over, half dreaming of the future I still might be able to have with my Kitten.

Shaking my head, I refocused on the situation before me. Liam towered over the breakfast table, struggling to pull a smile from his daughter. She slouched in her seat with her bunny clutched tight and her face scrunched in defiance, bottom lip trembling on the verge of a full-blown meltdown. When Ben slid a small plate of fruit in front of her, she didn't so much as glance at it. Instead, she locked eyes with her father and let out a guttural little wail—one both pitiful and impressively loud for someone her size.

"Chloe, please," Liam pleaded, his voice a mix of exasperation and real worry. "Just eat the grapes. For Daddy?"

The child's only answer was to launch a single grape onto the glossy kitchen floor. She watched it roll away and then turned her attention to Sabrina, searching for backup. Once again, Sabrina crouched down to Chloe's level, and I watched her study the little girl's face with an intensity and love that made my chest tighten. My Kitten had always been observant, but seeing her focus that skill on a child, the way she noted the set of Chloe's jaw, the dart of her glance, the white-knuckled grip on that battered bunny, it hit differently.

"What do you want, Chloe?" she asked in that quiet voice she used when disarming bombs or calming me after nightmares.

Chloe sniffled. "Appa ice."

Liam blinked, utterly lost. "Apple... ice?"

I caught Sabrina's suppressed smile. She'd always been good at decoding languages, which apparently included toddler ones.

"Apple slice," she translated, standing and walking over to the fruit bowl. With the easy confidence that made me fall for her years ago, she sliced a red apple into thin crescents, arranging them in a perfect fan. I recognized the careful gentleness in her hands—the same hands that could break a man's neck or caress my face with equal skill.

Chloe devoured the apple slice Sabrina held out to her, juice running down her chin, looking at my Kitten like she'd hung the moon. Then she beckoned her closer with a sticky finger. "More appa ice, pease."

"Of course, sweetheart." Sabrina smiled and handed her another slice.

Liam thanked her stiffly, watching their exchange as if it was written in a language he couldn't read. I knew that feeling. It was jealousy mixed with admiration. I'd experienced it the first time I saw Sabrina take down three armed men without breaking a sweat.

It didn't take long for the tiny tyke to finish her fruit and a few pancakes. When Sabrina offered to find crayons so they could color a picture, Chloe lit up so bright, I couldn't help but wonder what in the hell Liam and Susan did with her in their home. As they left for the breakfast nook, Chloe's tiny hand in Sabrina's deadly one, I caught myself wondering what our own child might look like. Would they have her eyes? My height? Her uncanny ability to read a room?

I shook the thought away. In our world, those dreams were dangerous luxuries.

Chapter Fifteen

Lianne

I avoided the kitchen like the plague during breakfast. As much as I wanted to see my niece, I didn't want to lay eyes on my brother. The fact I hadn't killed him the day before was a miracle. I wasn't sure divine intervention would happen two days in a row.

Settling into my leather desk chair, I took a moment to run my fingertips along the seam on the arm. Dad had always done the same thing.

I miss him.

With a heavy sigh, I reached for the center drawer of my desk. It clicked open with the same reluctance it always did, as if even the desk didn't want to let go of the secrets it hid away. I pushed aside a stack of blue sticky notes, my father's favorite signing pen, a small bag of sour gummy worms, and an extra set of headphones to get what I was looking for. My fingers hit the cool metal of a small tin box, and I let out a calming breath before I pulled it from its hiding place. Opening it, my focus zeroed in on the warped piece of lead that had killed my father.

Staring at it for a long moment, I picked it up and closed my fist around it, letting the jagged rim bite into my skin, focusing every ounce of anger, love, and guilt I had into the bullet. It felt heavier this morning, as if it knew the man responsible for shooting it was nearby.

I swear I'll avenge you, Dad. I'm working as fast as I can.

Lukas tried to fight me on keeping the bullet that killed our father, but my rage won out that day. I could still hear his words in my head.

"It's not going to bring him back, Li."

He didn't want the reminder to exist, let alone be in the house. Dad deserved to be remembered not by the hole his early departure had left, but the mark he left on our entire family, including its extended members. I needed the physical reminder of what my oldest brother did... whose side he was *really* on. What he stole from us.

As if Dad's absence wasn't more than enough.

After giving the metallic object one more squeeze, I put it back in its hiding spot in the drawer and let out a long breath as I closed it. There was work to do, and first on the list was reading the damn contract he'd signed.

It was then that a specifically patterned knock sounded on my office door.

Mom.

She always knocked the same way, and it made me smile. "Come in."

The door swung open, revealing my mother holding a plate and a mug. "Have you had breakfast, my dear?"

I pressed my lips together before responding. "No. I was waiting for the kitchen to clear out."

Mom arched her eyebrow as she walked in. "Didn't want to test your restraint around Liam?"

"Nope." I dropped my focus to the items in her hands. "You're not one to have breakfast on the go."

She placed the plate with a banana and a bagel with cream cheese on the desk. "You're right. This is for you."

I flicked my attention back to her face. "Where's Ben?" This morning had been one of the rare times he woke me up and was out the door first. I'd been hoping he would visit me. I needed one of his hugs.

"He made pancakes with Chloe and just headed upstairs to check on Quinn and the otters. He and Talia are smoothing things over with safety concerns and making sure everyone is settled in and has what they need."

A smile appeared on my face. *Classic Ben.* He was always taking care of us. Ellen, too. They were two of the best things that happened to me when I was a temp at the interior design office they worked at. Ben with his rolled-up sleeves, cute little grin, and tea-stained sketches. And Ellen with her impossibly organized desk and the way she'd slip me lemon pastries and whatever tips and tricks she could to make my day go smoother.

And look where I am now.

My attention dropped to the contract sitting in the middle of my desk. "Mom, do you have a minute?"

She immediately sat in the chair in front of my desk. "Of course."

I gestured to the paperwork. "What in the hell did Dad do to be forced into signing a blood debt contract?"

Mom rolled her eyes as she leaned back in the chair, crossing her legs and arms. "I wouldn't have let George get caught up in it or sign it if I had been around, but we are all young and dumb at some point in our lives."

Interesting deflection. "That didn't answer my question."

We stared at each other in tense silence before she let out a deep breath. "I can't recall."

I narrowed my eyes at my mom. "Can't or *won't*? You and Dad talked about *everything*. I know you know why he signed it."

Her fingers twitched ever so slightly, and her next breath was a half-second longer, and more controlled. Most people would have missed it, but I could read my mother extremely well. "I don't have all the details."

Liar. "But you know *something*."

Mom's mouth tightened as pain and sorrow flickered in her eyes before she shook her head. "Sharing that information won't change anything."

What? Realization hit. "It's really bad, isn't it?"

She nodded.

"It was so bad, you promised Dad you would never say."

She gave another single nod, and I sagged in my chair as a heavy sigh came out. "Okay. So, we have no idea why Dad signed it. Noted." I glanced down at the paperwork again. "I still have to talk to Dallas about how we handle the fact it was broken by both parties. All the original signing parties are dead, and there is no Vaux Don."

Mom cleared her throat. "I know you do. It's your responsibility as Don to make sure we don't unintentionally start a war."

My attention shifted to my closed office door, and I glared at it. "Someone else may have started it, but I'm going to end it." I barely had time to finish my own threat before another knock sounded at my door, a much softer, almost apologetic rap. I recognized the rhythm instantly, and the way my mom's posture softened told me she did too.

She rose, smoothing her hands over her shirt. "That'll be Ben. I'll let you two talk." Before leaving, she bent down and gave me a quick kiss on my hair before opening the door and heading out.

Ben poked his head in, his sandy hair rumpled like he'd been running his hand through it a million times before coming in here. I was both relieved to see him and concerned about what had him so worked up already.

"Hey, cutie. I was wondering when I was going to see you."

He came inside, shutting the door behind him, a file folder tucked under one arm and a mug in the other, but as soon as he saw my face, he crossed the room in two, set everything down on my desk, and wrapped me in a tight hug.

I let myself lean into the embrace for a moment, letting it soothe away some of my frustrations and re-ground me in the present. Ben was one of my anchors in this world. My port in a storm. A constant reminder that no matter how shitty things got, there was always hope for something good.

"Do you have a minute for me?"

I glanced up at the man I desperately loved. "For you? Always."

Ben snickered. "When something isn't blowing up at least."

A deep sigh came out as I looked up and half-glared at him. "Anyway... something tells me this visit is about more than just hugging me."

He glanced down at my desk. "I'll tell you if you eat some of your breakfast."

Now I actually glared at him. "Sit down, Benedict."

Ben held his hands up in surrender and moved to settle himself in one of the chairs in front of my desk. "Li, can you *please* eat something?"

I grabbed the bagel and took a bite. "Happy?"

"For now." He took a deep breath and let it out slowly. This wasn't the first or one hundredth time we'd had this 'argument', and it wasn't going to be our last. "So, I've been talking to Ellen, Blake, and Dayna more about taking that leave of absence."

This again? I already felt guilty for disrupting that office as often as I did when we kept Ben, Ellen, and Blake home for security reasons. "And?"

He leaned forward and tapped the folder he had placed on my desk. "It's official, effective today."

I stared at him in silent shock for several seconds. "What?"

"I'm officially on a leave of absence from the office until this Liam mess is over. Yesterday was insane, Lianne. You are my priority, and with everything going on, I don't want to be far from you. Are you one of the smartest women I know? Yes. Are you a badass capable of taking care of herself?" A mischievous twinkle appeared in his eyes. "With the exception of breakfast, yes. Do I still worry about you? All the damn time." He stood up and walked behind my desk again, kneeling next to me. "I need to know you're good, and being here is the only way I can do that."

I stared at him, slightly caught off guard by the abrupt timing of his decision. We had barely talked about it. "Ben, you don't have to—"

"I *want* to. You're my wife. The love of my life. The woman I will always protect." He squeezed my hands. "You don't have to do any of this alone, Li. I love you, and while this house is full of people who love, respect, and would do anything for you... *you* are my priority. Chloe is now also my priority."

A few stubborn tears gathered in the corners of my eyes at the wholesome and genuine declaration. "I love you, too, Ben." A deep sigh came out. "I've been working on delegating and letting people help me."

He brought my hands to his lips and kissed my knuckle, right above my wedding ring. "I know, and I'm so incredibly proud of you. Now, I know you were in the middle of something before I walked in. Please tell me you're going to take a break soon. I'd really like to spend a little more time with my wife."

A smirk tugged at the corner of my lips. "Yes. I need fifteen more minutes."

He held out his pinky. "Promise?"

I let out a sigh, smiling wider as I hooked mine around his. "Yeah. I promise."

Ben stood, leaned in, and held my face as he kissed me, letting his lips linger for a moment. "I love you, Lianne. Nothing will ever change that."

I narrowed my eyes at him in confusion at his sudden intensity. "I love you, too."

He kissed me again, leaning in until my chair had reclined as far as it would go, making my heart race a little. "You are the first winter snowflake. Beautiful, waited for, cherished, celebrated. There's only one, just like you, and you're mine."

It never failed to amaze me how my husband could take my breath away with a few words. "I... Well... You... You're my favorite handgun."

A chuckle came out as he looked at me curiously. "Oh, yeah?"

I nodded. "You're the one I always want at my side. The first thing I go for when I need backup. Dependable. Reliable. *Mine.*"

Ben's eyes twinkled as he leaned in once more and pressed his lips to mine. "Damn straight, I'm yours." He slowly returned my chair to its usual upright position. "Please try to keep it under a half hour."

"I pinky-promised fifteen minutes."

He chuckled and shook his head. "That's like a reader saying 'one more chapter.' We all know it's never going to happen."

After he left my office, I stared at the closed door for a moment. He was truly the best thing ever to happen to me. I let out a deep sigh and glanced at the contract in front of me.

Right. Back to figuring out how to get us out of this without someone dying.

~~~~

After I finished reading, which was exactly twenty-two minutes after Ben walked out of the office, I picked up my plate, left my office, and found him in the kitchen, working on his laptop.

A cheeky grin appeared on his face when he glanced up and locked eyes with me. "Told you it wasn't going to be fifteen minutes."

"Quiet, you." Sitting down next to him, I took a few minutes to finish eating and rested my head on his shoulder. He didn't say anything, but he didn't need to. We enjoyed each other's company with or without conversation.

As much as I would have loved to stay there longer, there was more work to be done. I stood, kissed the top of his head, and headed back to my office. I settled back in at my desk and stared at my phone. There was only one other person I could think of to help me solve this breach of contract.
~~~~

I don't need the boys for this.

Honestly, I didn't want the boys for this. Ryan and Gage loved to hover. Regina, too, at times, though she was far better at reading the room and knowing when to back off.

I took a deep breath, picked up my phone, and dialed.

"Don Agosti, this is a surprise. How are you?"

I was slightly surprised he answered so quickly. "I'm doing well, sir, all things considered. Thank you for asking." I let out a deep breath, forcing my nerves down. "How are Webber and Backnoff healing?"

"Slow but steady. Backnoff is still complaining about not being able to go out, but Beth is keeping him in line. God, I'm thankful for that woman." We both chuckled at that before he circled back around. "What can I do for you, Lianne?"

"Sir, do you have time to discuss an old contract both our fathers signed?" There was silence for a moment. Long enough I checked to see if the call had disconnected. It hadn't. "Don Dallas?"

He cleared his throat. "I don't often say this, but to which contract are you referring?"

How many contracts did Dad co-sign with the Dallas family? I glanced down at the paper. "It's a blood debt marriage contract between my dad and Callum Vaux, with your father as one of the witnesses." I gave him a few more details, including the date it was signed as well as the others who signed.

There was another pause. "Lianne, I'm sorry. I believe it exists, but I don't remember hearing about this particular contract. Can I call you back after looking through our files for our copy?"

I leaned back in my chair, gently turning side to side, somehow relieved even the Don Supreme was at a loss on this. "Until a couple days ago, I didn't know of it, either. I'd be happy to send a copy over with Gage if necessary."

"You could also send it electronically."

I shook my head, not that he could see me. "Not this one, sir."

"I respect that." Don Dallas cleared his throat. "I'll keep you apprised."

"Thank you, sir."

As I ended the call, the door in my office that connected to Ryan's opened, and he poked in his head. "Everything okay?"

I arched an eyebrow at him. "How long were you eavesdropping?"

The muscles along his jaw tightened momentarily. "Since I heard the words 'Don Dallas' leave your mouth."

I glanced at the door. *Wasn't it closed? How did he hear through it if it was closed?*

"Lianne?"

Blinking, I returned my attention to my favorite tech specialist. "What are your thoughts on the marriage contract?" When he didn't respond immediately, I rolled my eyes and pointed to the chair in front of me, silently telling him to join me. "Adair told me you helped her make copies. I know you read it. I want your thoughts."

Ryan glanced back into his office and then stepped into mine, closing the door behind him. "Part of me thinks she is better off for never having been with Liam, but then there is another part of me that thinks she could have stopped Liam from turning into what he did if she *had* married him."

"Glad I'm not the only one having that train of thought." There was another knock on my door, and I let out a tense breath. *Now what?* "Yes?"

It opened, and the tall and almost too serious man who guarded my mother was standing in the doorway. He glanced at Ryan and then back to me. "Is now a bad time?"

There was something about his behavior that sent up a red flag. *Something happened.* I shook my head. "No, Gage, come on in."

He hesitated for a moment and then fully stepped inside. There was worry and frustration in his eyes, like he'd been arguing with someone. "Susan sent a message."

My eyebrows shot up as I leaned forward. "Start talking."

"When Lukas and Connor removed Liam from the foyer yesterday and dragged him downstairs, one of the first things they did was take his phone. It's been in my possession ever since. This morning she called him twice and left a voicemail after the second call." He held out the phone. "Would you like to hear it?"

"Absolutely."

Gage walked up to my desk, tapped on the screen a few times, and then set the phone down in front of me. Seconds later, my sister-in-law's voice came from the speakers.

"What in the hell happened yesterday, Liam? You should have been home by now, but no, you're nowhere to be found and our two best men are dead? And for what? Did you confirm anything? Are you even alive at this point? You're about as useful as my sister right now. Ugh! Get your ass home... and with our daughter. I don't want to go through all that again."

The voicemail ended, and all I could do was stare at the phone.

There are men dead, and all you can do is bitch about getting information and shit talk Adair? Are you fucking kidding me? "Well someone woke up on the wrong side of the bed this morning." I glanced up at Gage. "Any other intel from that front?"

He shook his head. "Nothing yet, but we're monitoring."

"Okay." I expected him to turn and leave, but tilted my head to the side when he didn't move. "Is there anything else?"

"Lianne, I wanted to brief you on a change of plans regarding Sunny and Poppy." His hands were empty, but I didn't miss the way his fingers twitched.

What has him so worked up about his girlfriend and sister now? "What's going on there?"

He crossed his arms over his chest. "I'm not comfortable with Sunny and Poppy being here the same time Liam is. I trust the team implicitly, but not *him*."

The way Gage said my brother's name matched the frigid restraint usually reserved for his parents, which really showed just how far he had come from being Liam's 'yes man'. I lifted an eyebrow, waiting for him to get to his point.

"I'm taking them to Don San Augustine's. Today."

Interesting... but not completely unexpected. Wait.

I narrowed my eyes at him. "Are you paying this debt, or is this yet another thing I will have the honor of settling?" As much as I sympathized with wanting to keep people safe, sending them off to another Don's compound was not the first option in my play book. We had protocol for this kind of thing. Three different safe houses, for starters. While Vincent San Augustine was Sunny's father, and wouldn't or *shouldn't* have an issue safeguarding her, taking on Poppy to protect was another story. I didn't want additional debts to repay..

His throat bobbed nervously, not that I blamed him. I'm sure I look pissed. "Ma'am, I—"

I lifted a hand to cut him off. "Has he signed off on it?"

"Yes, ma'am." He let out a tense breath. "Poppy isn't thrilled, but she's promised both me and Nash she won't go AWOL on us and will stay at the compound. For the record, I told Don San Augustine that I would cover any additional expenses for Poppy's care... that it was my favor and not yours."

I nodded, grateful there was one less thing on my plate. Leaning forward, I folded my hands on the desk and tried to channel my father's calm way of discussing matters like this. "And how long do you anticipate keeping them there?"

Gage pressed his lips into a tight line. "At least until Liam is removed from this house."

My eyebrow twitched at how he phrased it, and I looked at Ryan. "I assume you're going to monitor the drop off?"

He nodded, but didn't look up from his phone. "In addition to the usual trackers, I have a dash cam on the SUV Nash is taking. The girls are loading up now."

He's watching cameras. Good. I returned my focus to Gage. "What of San Augustine's crew? Are they going to keep this quiet?" Regardless of this being Gage's debt, I didn't want extra trouble showing up at another Don's front door because of my crew.

"Don San Augustine said that he will have everyone on strict orders to keep it secret. His team won't talk. Lindholm is spending a bit of time over there with Haggarity, but as part of Dallas's team, we know she won't breathe a word, either. Everyone knows what's at stake."

I nodded. "Thank you, Gage. Let me know if anything changes."

"Yes, ma'am." He turned to leave, but then looked at me again. "Thank you."

I gave him a single nod before glancing down at the contract on my desk once more.

Ryan and I spent a few minutes discussing it when there was another knock as the door opened, this time my mother poking in her head. "Do you have a minute to chat?"

Ryan immediately stood and turned around. "Do you need me to leave?"

She shook her head. "No. It's about our hummingbird."

Chapter Sixteen

Dante

Liam had been sitting in the interrogation room for about a half hour when Lynette walked up to me. "Dante, just the person I need to talk to."

I stood up a little straighter. "How can I help you, ma'am?"

"Adair would like to have a conversation with Liam, and considering everything he's put her through, I happily agreed."

Is this why we moved him to the interrogation room? I nodded. "And the ground rules?"

A tight smile appeared on her face. "Liam will have at least one arm handcuffed to the table the entire time. Avery will be in there with you. Peter will walk in with Adair and stay at her side for the duration. Lukas and I will be in the observation room. A recording will be taken."

It all sounded completely reasonable. "And the ETA on this meeting?"

"In roughly fifteen minutes. Avery looked *far* too excited before leaving my office. Lukas, naturally, is worried and not particularly pleased with my decision."

I studied the Agosti second-in-command, who looked as cool and professional as she always did. Though, the woman was far too seasoned to let her true feelings show. "And you, ma'am?"

Amusement and something fear-inspiring twinkled in her eyes. "I expect *quite* the show, as should you. You know where to find me." Lynette walked into the observation room, pulling the door shut behind her.

Moments later, Lukas stepped out of the war room at the end of the hall and headed my way. Once within a few yards of me, he asked, "Has my mom briefed you?"

"Yeah." I nodded toward the door. "She just headed in to get ready for the show."

He let out a tense sigh. "I get why Adair wants to talk to him, but he doesn't deserve to be in the same room as her. Not after all the shit he put her through."

I understood some of his rage. Adair was like a sister to him. If someone had harmed a hair on Talia's head, I wouldn't want her anywhere near them, either. "That decision is well above my pay grade."

Lukas shook his head, a cross of amusement and frustration on his face. "It was above mine, too."

Ah, got outranked by Lianne and Lynnette.

It was then Avery strolled up, her leather roll of knives in hand, and a terrifying grin on her face. "Hello, gentlemen."

I gave her a confused look. "Gentlemen? You're in a good mood."

She snickered. "I get to bust out my throwing knives, *of course* I'm in a good mood." Avery stretched her neck, making it pop, before glancing at the door. "Do I need to restrain the guest of dishonor?"

"I'm sure you'll get more pleasure out of it than I will."

Her smile widened. "That I would. I'll get to it." She walked past me and opened the door. "Liam, you're about to be part of a conversation you don't deserve. Don't be an asshole. Or do. You're stuck with me either way."

After it shut behind her, Lukas coughed over his chuckle. "She is something else."

I nodded. "That she is. She's amazing, terrifying, and fucking brilliant at her job."

Lukas hummed in agreement. "No arguments here."

It wasn't long before Peter and Adair walked up, Adair with her head held high, and Peter with barely concealed unease all over his face. Lukas sighed as he looked at her, worry heavy in his eyes. "You don't have to talk to him, Adair. You don't owe him anything."

She gave him a soft smile, but there was no missing the determination as she rolled her shoulders back and stood taller. "I know, but this is for me, not him. There are so few moments in life when you have the opportunity for this kind of closure. I'm taking it and will extract everything out of it I can."

Lukas glanced over his shoulder at the door and let out another deep sigh before looking at her again. "I can't argue with that."

Peter gave Adair's arm a gentle squeeze. "You ready?"

She narrowed her eyes as she stared past me, presumably at the door. "Yeah. Let's do this."

I opened the heavy metal door and gestured for Adair and Peter to walk in first. Lukas gave me a worried look, his hand twitching toward his sidearm.

Placing my hand on his shoulder, I squeezed. "It will be fine."

He glared into the room and then let out a tense breath. "I don't care what Li said. If Liam even *thinks* about hurting Adair, you take him out."

Before I could remind him that her orders outranked his, he walked into the observation room. When I entered the interrogation room, Liam's focus was squarely on Adair. He was sitting too still, nearly emotionless. If I had to guess, he was working extra hard to school his facial expressions, though there was no hiding the swirl of emotions in his eyes.

After a moment, he cleared his throat. "I'm glad you're here."

She arched her eyebrow slightly as she looked him over. "Are you?"

Liam nodded. "While you may not believe me, I *am* relieved you're alive and well."

Adair snorted in derision as she rolled her eyes. "You're right. I *don't* believe you. You literally told Susan to kill me and then did nothing after she shot me." She let out a deep sigh and crossed her arms over her chest. "Why *did* you come here, Liam? None of us are stupid enough to believe it was to celebrate Lianne and Lukas's birthdays. You had enough information to figure out I was alive. Why the personal visit? You're not stupid enough to think your mother and sister would ever let you walk out of here after everything you've done to them. To me."

He sat quietly for a moment, his throat bobbing as he swallowed, and if I hadn't been entirely fixed on his reaction, I would have missed the flicker of sorrow in his eyes. If it was even genuine. Not that it mattered at this point. *Too little, too late, asshole.*

"I needed to see you one last time."

Adair glanced at Avery, giving her what looked like an '*are you buying any of this shit*?' look before returning her attention to him. "That doesn't sound dramatic or morbid at all. Are you dying?"

We could only hope.

Liam shook his head. "Despite all the guns pointed at me yesterday, no, I'm not."

"Pity."

All our eyes went a little wider at that comment. Liam's included.

"Victoria, please. I—"

"She's dead, remember? You and Susan killed her. You know my name."

Liam's eyes went wide, and he swallowed hard again. "I... Adair, I'm sorry. Please let me at least *try* to find a way to make this up to you."

She let out a low, humorless laugh that made even me uncomfortable. "Why should I? How in the hell could you possibly make up the seven years I lost because I had to be undercover and on the run to stay alive? How could you repair the damage *she* caused? You're still married to her, or have you forgotten that *tiny* detail,

Liam? You chose to marry the woman who wanted me dead. And for what? Some money? Did she cause you brain damage while you were dating? Though, maybe the brain damage was already there."

Avery snickered as she picked up one of her throwing knives, tossed it in the air, and caught it by the handle without looking. I couldn't help but smirk at the look of fear that crossed Liam's face. *This is why Lynette put her in here.*

Returning his attention to Adair, anger flared up in his eyes. "I had to marry the oldest Vaux daughter, and you know it. I didn't know you were alive."

Adair rolled her eyes. "Again, you certainly wasted no time assuming I died after *letting* her shoot me. Although my sister was smarter than you there. *She* knew the golden rule: no body, no proof. *She* kept looking for me, albeit with the intent to kill. *She* put in more effort than the man contracted to marry me. Though, you always liked her more than me, regardless of the agreement."

Peter reached out and gave her hand a squeeze, and she took a deep breath before nodding.

Liam's focus narrowed in on their hands as bitterness and anger filled his eyes as he leaned forward.

Avery sat up a little taller. "Is there a problem, Liam?"

His focus shifted up to Adair's face. "Are you *with him*?"

She tilted her head slightly as she stared at him. Her expression was too neutral. Too controlled. It was impressive as it was unnerving. "What are you talking about?"

He gestured angrily at them. "You and Peter. Are you two together?"

Adair's posture and expression didn't waver as she continued to stare at him. "Why do you care, and why does it matter? You moved on. You and your *wife* made it so I had to. Are you truly *that* much of a hypocrite to be upset that I might be with someone other than you?"

"No." Liam clenched his jaw as his eyes hardened.

Avery rolled her eyes and shook her head. "Liar."

He glared at her accusation. "I am not."

She flipped the knife she'd been playing with and threw it across the room, sinking it dead center on the board behind his head, making Liam flinch. "Me thinks someone protests too much."

The man half-growled as he shifted his attention back to the woman standing in front of him. "You signed a contract to marry *me*."

Adair narrowed her eyes at him. "And yet, you arranged for my death because I refused to break that contract and start a war. And why? So you could continue to fuck her behind my back?" A frustrated huff rushed from her lips. "Why are we having this conversation *again*? Nothing has changed, Liam. You don't get to judge how I made it through hell when *you're* the one who put me there." She went to step forward, but Peter's hand stopped her. After trying to shrug out of his grip, she turned and glared at him. "Let go."

He shook his head. "No. It's not going to change anything, Adair. He's still going to be an entitled dumbass regardless of what happens here. If his own family threatening his life hasn't changed his mind, you won't either. He's not worth your effort or time."

"You don't get to speak for her." Liam's words were hissed through his clenched teeth.

My attention snapped back to him, who looked even more pissed. A vein was bulging on his forehead now. *Please throw a clot.*

"Oh, my God. You spoke for me all the time when we were together. It never bothered you then, so what is your problem *now*? Also, I can defend myself without your assistance, and have been doing so for years, thank you very much." Adair glared at him before looking at Avery and gesturing to the throwing knives on the table. "Can I use those?"

Avery tipped her head to the side, glancing toward the two-way mirror and then back to Adair. "I'm going to have to ask why before giving an answer."

"I want to give a nonlethal demonstration."

The way Adair said it made me nervous. I knew everyone employed by the Agostis would honor Lianne's order to keep Liam alive, but Adair technically didn't have to follow those orders. She also wouldn't have the same consequences if she didn't.

Avery narrowed her eyes for a second and then nodded. "Fine, but I can revoke permission at any time. You know the rule."

"Fair… and I do."

With a flourish, Avery gestured to the table where nine knives lay in a perfect row on top of the black leather. "Then the table is yours, my esteemed lady."

Liam's focus had been bouncing between the two women with an intensity that amused me. "Adair, what are you doing?" The man's voice shook a little, betraying his genuine fear.

Interesting.

Shaking off Peter's hand, and ignoring Liam, she walked over and picked up the first knife, appraising the weight and shape of it with a smile. "These are amazing, Avery." Adair flipped and caught it effortlessly. "That's a gorgeous balance. I might need a set of these. I had some at one point, but they weren't nearly this nice."

Avery nodded, pride all over her face. "Alex and I will take you shopping whenever you want."

"Thanks." Taking a deep breath, Adair narrowed her eyes as she looked across the room, let the breath out, and threw the knife. When it flew past Liam's face and landed just off center with a satisfying *thunk*, a proud smirk crossed her face.

"What the fuck?" Liam glared at me, fear matching the outrage in his eyes. "Aren't you supposed to protect me or something?"

I gestured toward the knife-wielding woman. "What do you want me to do, stand in front of you and take the knife? Adair said it was going to be non-lethal. I believe her. Avery gave permission, as is her right, since they are her knives. No one in the observation room weighed in on the situation. Whether you believe it or not, Liam, you're not in mortal danger."

Avery chuckled. "Nicely thrown, Adair. You've been practicing."

She smiled proudly. "As often as I could."

"What are you doing, Adair?" Liam stared at her, eyes wide with fear as she picked up and flipped another knife in her hands.

"Making a demonstration, like I said. You see," she threw another knife and smiled as it sunk into the board right above the previous knife. "Knowing where your target is and how to hit it correctly are crucial in knife throwing... and life in general."

Liam flinched and was paler than he had been before. Avery had moved, so she was within arm's distance of Adair, poised to grab the woman if necessary. Peter's back was against the window. As much as I felt I *should* have backed up, I needed to stay close to Liam, also just in case I needed to grab him. I wasn't worried about getting hit. If Avery trusted Adair enough to hand over her personal weapons, I knew significant training had happened. Avery may be reckless at times, but she wasn't stupid.

Adair picked up another knife, her focus still locked in on Liam. "The same goes for your enemies. You have to know where they are and what it will take to hit them successfully." She threw this knife with too little force, and it bounced off the wall, hitting the ground with a loud metallic clang. "Hesitancy will only let them know someone was trying to make the hit, but that they didn't have the nerve to put in the required effort to make it count." She snatched another knife, again flipping it in her hand a few times before throwing it, this time significantly harder. It hit the board, but nowhere near the middle. "Now, too much force isn't the solution either. You're definitely going to hurt something, but is it the damage you wanted?"

I hadn't spent much time with Adair, but this display was impressive as fuck. There was no denying her skill and technique… or how intimidating she was right now.

And Liam picked Susan over her? What an idiot.

She reached back and grabbed another knife. "But what if everyone's been looking at the wrong target the entire time? What if the obvious one they've been keeping their eye on isn't the one they *should* be watching? What if it's a manipulative red herring?" Adair snarled as she threw the knife, sinking it into the wall just above Liam's head.

I swore her eyes lit up when he flinched again.

"Adair?" Avery reached out and wrapped her hand around the woman's wrist.

She let out a tense breath before turning to face the woman. "I'm done. I promised a non-lethal demonstration." Swallowing hard, Adair shifted her focus back to Liam, glaring at him angrily. "And unlike other people, I keep my word."

"I never—"

"I didn't ask, and I don't care anymore." She cut him off. "You've had years to do anything right, and yet," Adair gestured to the interrogation room, "here we are. You are sitting in handcuffs with a million regrets, no power, and a death sentence hanging over your head, and I am standing here trying very hard to crawl out of the shadows and live my best life with the family that worked tirelessly to keep me alive and well." She looked at Peter, who had returned to her side, and kissed him on the cheek. "I'm done here. We can go."

He nodded as a stunned expression took over his face. "Okay."

Adair faced Avery, who looked more than amused. "Thanks for letting me toss a few of those."

A proud smile appeared on her face. "It was my pleasure."

Chapter Seventeen

Sabrina

Chloe climbed into my lap with the casual entitlement of any child who was loved, bearing a heap of coloring books and a faded mesh bag bursting with crayons that had been snapped and worn down to nubs. I spread out the art supplies on the table, clearing enough space for both coloring and the inevitable snack disaster. She selected a unicorn page and immediately set to work, tongue poking out of the corner of her mouth in concentration as she colored neon orange on the mane, and bright green for the horn.

I watched her for a minute, quietly cataloguing details. The way she held the crayon with a kind of desperate passion, as if it could disappear at any moment. The way her eyes darted, tracking my approval whenever she made a color choice she suspected I would like. Occasionally, she would narrate her process.

"Dada no like bornge, but I do."

"Orange is a great color." I said. "It's the color of the sky right before the sun goes to bed."

She stared at the crayon for a moment before scribbling in the corner of the page, using the last inch of the crayon before presenting her artwork to me with a flourish. "For Bina."

I felt something in my chest loosen and shift. A warm, fuzzy feeling I had hidden away months, if not years ago. Clearing my throat, I shoved down the sudden influx of emotions. "Thank you,

Chloe." She smiled brightly, and I couldn't help returning it. "Does your mama read to you?"

Chloe shook her head, distracted, and kept coloring. "Mama busy. Dada busy." She put her crayon down before grabbing a book and looking up, eyes bright and hopeful. "Book, pease?"

The request caught me off guard in its simplicity. "Would you like that?"

She grinned as if I had granted some long-awaited wish. "Pease!" Almost immediately, she ran to her bag and returned with a battered copy of *Good Night Moon* and a squeezable pouch of applesauce. "Moon book!"

I read aloud, mustering my best dramatic voice, and supplied silly commentary. Chloe echoed the words, pointing to her favorite things on each page with sticky fingers. She patted my shoulder every time I got to a new page, urging me along, fully invested in the outcome.

When the book was finished, she wanted to read it again. So we did, this time with her 'reading' to me, reciting from memory, and improvising where the pages stuck together. Chloe would often glance up if she forgot something, worry in her eyes. It broke my heart how fragile she was. It made me want to march downstairs and teach Liam a lesson or two.

I made a mental list as we went through our morning: more books, crayons that could last more than a day, child-safe scissors, a few easy puzzles for hand-eye coordination, and more toys in general. The Agostis had the basics for short visits, but nothing that would hold her attention for more than a few minutes before she got bored or restless. I also wanted to see more whimsy and joy in her life. Bubbles, paint, dress up clothes and accessories, a tricycle, a toy kitchen, age-appropriate musical instruments. The works. This little girl deserved a world full of joy and love, not whatever bullshit version of parenting Liam and Susan had been half-assing.

I need to talk to Li or Auntie 'Nette.

After Chloe and I finished with the book, we played an improvised version of tag, running around the bedroom suite until Chloe collapsed on a mound of pillows.

"Legs tired, Bina."

I bet. "Should we rest them so we can race Uncle Ben or Uncle Lukas later?"

A tired smile appeared on her face as she nodded. "Yes! I fast!"

"Yes, you are." I scooped her up, carried her to the bed, and tucked her under a blanket. She fussed, but only until I started to rub her back. The way her entire body immediately relaxed nearly brought me to tears. *You and I aren't so different, little one.* After a deep sigh came out, Chloe curled up and shut her eyes, her thumb finding its way to her mouth.

I let her lie there for a few minutes, continuing to rub her back until I was sure she was all the way asleep. Only then did I quietly clean up the aftermath of our activities. Stray crayons, empty snack packets, the book with sticky pages, and every stuffed animal that had been scattered all over the place.

Once satisfied with the state of the room, I checked the time and figured I had an hour or so before she'd be up again, asking for more stories or to see one of her aunts or uncles. It was then that I messaged Talia.

Sabrina: < Can you watch Chloe's door for me? She's napping, and I need to take care of a few things... and talk to Lianne if she's available. >

Talia: < Of course! I'll be right up. >

After she made it to the suite, I went downstairs to roam the kitchen and pantry, doing what I always did when I was restless and in a new environment: take inventory of the supplies. I moved quietly, opening cabinets and refrigerator doors, trying not to be too loud. I'm sure it didn't matter, but it was ingrained within me to be as quiet as possible. Every time I found myself in a new place, it likely meant I was lying low. I huffed a laugh; I *was* lying low, but in a house that was in the middle of chaos all on its own. This time though, instead of watching over my shoulder for *La Muerta Rubi*, I was looking at what we had that was two-year-old appropriate.

From the meticulously labeled glass jars of spices and seasonings to the variety of pasta-making ingredients, it was obvious the Agostis valued quality. I checked for easy to grab snacks, bread, lunch meat, fruits and veggies that she could eat with her fingers.

Smiling, I pulled out a carton of cranberry juice, checked the seal, and poured it into a sippy cup, topping it off with water. I'd never met a kid who actually liked straight cranberry juice, but Chloe had guzzled hers with the manic energy of someone mainlining espresso. *It could be worse.*

I started prepping snacks and easy to assemble lunch items to make mealtime easier. I sliced up ripe strawberries, carrots, grapes, and apples, cubed sharp cheddar into toddler-safe pieces, and put a saucepan of water on the stove to make some mac and cheese. I'd learned long ago that tiny, colorful portions went a long way toward bribing a child to eat. There was a steady, calming rhythm to the chopping, peace in the careful arranging of everything into small, reusable food storage boxes. I felt bad using all the ones available and made a mental note to ask Lynette if more could be ordered.

As if summoned by my thoughts, she appeared next to me while I rinsed off the cutting board. My honorary aunt moved with the casual authority of someone who had never once questioned her right to be anywhere.

"Smart move pre-cutting and packaging the food."

I smiled at the compliment. "Grab and go makes life infinitely easier with little ones. They aren't known to be the most patient." A chuckle came out. "Big kids, too, sometimes."

Lynette hummed in agreement and glanced at me. "Would you be referring to my youngest?"

There was no hiding my grin as I dumped the box of elbow macaroni into the boiling water. "Does Lianne still hyper-focus on her work and forget to eat?"

"Yes, and it's only gotten worse since she became Don."

The heaviness of Lynette's tone made me look at her. "Oh?"

She nodded. "Ben, Jess, and I work together to make sure food ends up on her desk... and that she drinks more than coffee and tea all day."

I cleared my throat and gestured to the short stacks of 'Chloe snacks'. "If you order more containers like this, I'm happy to prep food snacks for Lianne."

With the way some of the tension left Lynette's shoulders, you would have thought I'd given her the solution to all her problems. "That would be lovely, my dear. And Ben and I will happily help you with that. You're here to make sure my beautiful grandbaby is safe and taken care of, not my children, too."

"Respectfully, Auntie 'Nette, making sure Chloe's aunts and uncles are taken care of will help me take care of her. Never underestimate the power of an adorable toddler handing over containers of food, asking that person to have a snack with her."

Understanding and pride filled her eyes. "You have a solution for everything, don't you?"

I let out a deep breath. "You don't survive this world for long without at least a half-dozen contingency plans."

Lynette nodded knowingly. "That you don't." Silence fell between us until the noodles were cooked and I was straining out the water. "Send me a list of all the foods you want to see here for Chloe. I'll combine it with mine before ordering the groceries."

"Like more mac and cheese?"

She laughed and nodded. "Yes. That little girl would eat her weight in pasta if you let her." Lynette shook her head as amusement sparkled in her eyes. "She'd also eat raw garlic if you let her."

Good to know.

After setting down the pan, I looked at her again. "And what about other requests I have for Chloe?"

The older woman tipped her head to the side and studied me curiously. "Like what, my dear?"

"Books, toys, games, that kind of thing."

A warm smile appeared on Lynette's face. "Send that, too. I know we weren't fully prepared to take Chloe full time when she and her father rolled in. We'll see who has the longer wish list for her." Lynette leaned against the counter as I finished making the mac and cheese. "What have you learned about my darling granddaughter so far?"

"She goes down easier if you read to her until she's almost asleep. She likes interactive books the best. The ones with flaps, textures, that sort of thing. She hates loud noises, but she's obsessed with those old-school stacking blocks." I grinned as I thought about the tower-building contest we had earlier. "She's also extremely bright."

Lynette arched an eyebrow as she continued to watch me. "Beyond the biased grandma standpoint?"

I nodded. "Yes. I noticed on day one she's always reading faces. She watches for reactions more than I've ever noticed with any child her age." I sighed as I leaned on the counter and faced Lynette. "You and I both know the level of trauma needed to make it so someone feels the need to read people to determine how to act around them."

The implication hung there in the silence. I didn't ask about Susan or Liam's involvement. I didn't need to. I knew the shape of absence when I saw it. It was also telling that Chloe hadn't asked about her mom, and had only asked once so far today if she would see her dad. That broke my heart. Partially because it was a sign that she went extended stretches of time without seeing them.

Lynette let out a deep sigh, one that spoke of disappointment and mild resentment. "You noticed that, too."

"Yes, ma'am." I stirred the mac and cheese absentmindedly. "Chloe needs stability. Routine, sure, but mostly people who don't disappear or lie to her."

She nodded, with an approving glint in her eyes. "Part of the reason she's here. I wanted her around us as much as I wanted us around her. She needs to be surrounded by a loving family." A soft chuckle came out. "If I'm being honest, her presence will add a little softness to the household in general... and keep Lianne and Lukas from becoming too hard and jaded. With all the stress, pain, and chaos that has enveloped us the past year and a half, we need a reminder of the good in the world. That the future isn't as bleak as it looks." She took a deep breath and let it out slowly. "I don't want to put that much pressure on a child, but..." she trailed off, glancing up in the direction of where her granddaughter was sleeping.

"But we live in a world where unfair things happen more often than they should."

We stared at each other, silently acknowledging the pain neither of us ever wanted the other living through.

After a moment, Lynette closed the distance between us and hugged me tight. "I'm so grateful you're here. Ceaser was absolutely spot on choosing you for this assignment."

I'd just finished my lunch when Quinn rushed in, face pinched in discomfort and immediately grabbed an apple from the bowl on the island and nibbled on it.

"Everything okay?" I eyed the redhead with concern.

Her attention snapped to me, and panic flickered in her blue eyes before she nodded. "My stomach is off. It's probably stress." She gestured around. "It's not exactly been calm or quiet around here lately."

A quick breath of relief rushed out. *Not an emergency... but what is it?* "From what I've heard, no, it has not."

Quinn studied me for a few seconds while she chewed on another bite of apple. "How long have you known the family?"

She doesn't know? "I was more or less raised with Lianne and Lukas. My uncle is best friends with Lynette."

Quinn nodded again. "Right. Lukas mentioned that. I..." She trailed off and rubbed her forehead. "I'm so tired of having a fuzzy brain. I swear I can't remember anything lately."

Perfect segue. I stepped closer to her, making sure to keep my voice down. "Are you *sure* you're feeling okay?"

The woman looked around, seeming relieved that no one was near. "Yes and no."

Her immediate matching of 'keep it secret' energy had me on high alert, and I was already brainstorming ways to help. "Do you need to see Doc?"

Quinn shook her head, a ghost of a smile teasing the corner of her mouth, confusing me slightly. "No. He and I have already chatted."

Interesting. "Okay. Is there anything I can do to help?"

Her eyes went wide with panic. "Please don't tell anyone about this."

Oh shit. "Even Lynette and the twins?"

She let out a tense chuckle. "Lukas already knows, considering..." Quinn trailed off, smirking and shaking her head. "I think Ellen is catching on, but she's too nice to call me out yet." Quinn grabbed my hand. "I'm not saying anything to anyone yet."

I mimed zipping my mouth shut, hoping I was reading between the lines correctly. "Not a word, I promise. I value and respect this family too much."

Quinn stared at me, almost as if in shock, and then nodded. "Thank you."

I leaned in closer, so our faces were inches apart. "But if you need *anything*, I'm quick, discrete, and can relate pretty much anything to Chloe if needed. Food, beverage, medicine, a cover story, just say the word. Chloe may be my main priority, but that doesn't mean I can't keep an eye on other people in this house."

Relief flooded her eyes again. "I appreciate it. Truly. Honestly, I'm almost glad for some of the chaos. It's making hiding away a little easier."

"I know we just met, but—"

"But Lynette, Lianne, and Lukas all trust you with that little girl's life. That tells me everything I need to know." Quinn gave me a tight hug. "I'm glad you're here and cannot wait to get to know you better."

The sudden show of affection caught me off guard, but I embraced and very much appreciated it.

Chapter Eighteen

Sabrina

By that night, I had been informed that Liam was going to sleep in a holding cell and Chloe and I were going to share the suite upstairs. He read her a couple books, and they cuddled a bit while I tidied up the mess we had made after dinner.

Her blue eyes were wide after Dante escorted Liam out of her room. "Bina go, too?"

I smiled and shook my head, rubbing the side of her arm. "No. I'm going to sleep in here with you."

The high-pitched squeal of joy she let out brought Lukas to the door, whose confusion melted into a huge smile when he saw her happy dance. When Chloe turned and saw who had walked in, she ran over to him. "Unca Lu, Bina seep wiff me!"

He chuckled as he scooped up the toddler and hugged her. "That's awesome, Chloe!"

"Tubby time?"

Lukas glanced at me. "Want an extra set of hands?"

"Absolutely." The joy on his face told me he needed this, too. *Lynette was right about Chloe's effect on him.*

Bath time was absolutely chaotic, and by the end, I wasn't sure if there was more water in the tub or on me and Lukas. And while his version of helping wasn't the most efficient, the smiles on both their faces were more than worth the extra cleanup.

Ben made an appearance while Lukas was helping Chloe put on her pajamas, and there was a sheepish smile on his face as he held up a couple books. "My moms dropped off a few things today, and I was wondering if I could read to Chloe?"

Lynette's words from earlier once again echoed in my head, and I nodded. "Of course. She's a huge fan of being read to and then reading the book to you. The sillier the voices, the better."

There was a happy squeal of, "Ben Ben!" and Lukas shook his head as he walked to where I was standing. "I don't know if I've ever seen Chloe smile this much, ever."

"Having people paying attention to you and doing fun things with you will do that." I let out a sigh as I watched Ben and Chloe snuggle on the big bed, books in hand.

Lukas sighed. "Well, she's not used to that. Not like this, at least."

"Oh?" I glanced over, more than mildly curious.

"Yeah. If Liam and Susan did what they talked about, Chloe had at least one nanny, if not more."

All of a sudden, everything made sense why Liam barely knew anything about his daughter's schedule or favorite foods.

And he calls himself a father.

It didn't matter how much mafia shit was going on, my dad and uncle always made time for their family. Dad could be on a mission for weeks at a time, but still made sure to call every night he could to tell me he loved me. He'd come home with some special treat, or make some of my favorite foods, or would even surprise me by picking me up at school. The nights he couldn't, Mom or Tia filled in, but I never once doubted my importance to them.

My phone buzzed, and I smiled when I glanced at the screen.

Speaking of important men.

Dante: < Can I see you at all tonight? >

Lukas bumped my shoulder. "You can take an hour or two off if you want."

My focus snapped to his face. "What?"

"I saw the text." He let out a tense breath. "I know your last assignment wasn't a walk in the park, but that man did *not* do well, especially after we learned you had been hurt."

My heart clenched as I nodded. "It was hard on all of us. Having to disconnect completely from all the important people in my life nearly broke *me*. It was only concentrating on the job at hand, getting everything straightened out, Zee not letting me stay down, and Uncle Ceaser's updates that made it possible to get through it."

Lukas studied my face for a long moment, and I didn't miss the understanding in his eyes. "But seriously, would you like to take a break to spend some time with him?"

Is he doing this because he feels bad? "I'm not looking for any favors, Lukas."

He shook his head again before nervously running his hand through his hair. "I know you're not. Honestly, my offering is just as much for me as it is for you. If it helps, think of it as me asking to spend time with my niece. I know she's with Ben and will be sleeping soon, but you're not the only one who's been missing someone. Li and I love that little girl so much... We've hated not being able to see her."

There was more to what he wasn't saying, but it wasn't the time or place to pry. If I needed to know, he'd tell me. "Okay. That does help, actually."

Lukas stepped closer. "Quinn also told me you two talked earlier. I'm grateful you've got her back."

"Of course." I smirked. "Girl code."

He chuckled. "Oh, I know all about that from Jess and Li. That is sacred and *not* to be trifled with."

"Nope. So, how long would you like to sit with your niece?"

A smirk crossed his face as he glanced at the bedroom door. "Maybe a couple hours? Or more if you need it. I have some reading to catch up on... might just sit next to her bed once Ben clears out."

"Okay."

I quickly and quietly made my way downstairs, smiling at how peaceful the house was. For all the busy-ness and hustle and bustle during the day, the contrast of seeing the place empty and silent was wild. It was then I realized I had never responded to Dante's message.

More fun to surprise him.

I hurried to his room, knocking on the door. Nothing could have prepared me for the view when he opened it. Dante was standing there, wearing nothing but a towel wrapped around his waist, and my mouth immediately went dry. The sight of his broad shoulders and muscular chest momentarily short-circuited my brain, and years of self-reliance and independence went up in a cloud of smoke. "Hi."

He pulled me into the room, closed the door, and pinned me against it, sliding his hands up my neck and into my hair, gripping ever so gently. "Hello, Kitten."

Every remaining coherent thought in my brain scattered as he kissed me. A whimper came out when he pulled away, and I tipped my head back, closing my eyes. I was re-acclimating myself to just how intoxicating this man's lips were.

"Eyes on me, love."

I had to force a breath in before I slowly opened my eyes again and took in the deep brown ones absolutely fixed on me.

"Good girl."

My knees went weak, and I would have been pissed by how strongly and immediately this man had full control over me, but this was Dante. *My* Dante. The love of my life. The man who would do anything to protect me.

He released his hold on my hair and wrapped his arms around me, holding me tight against his chest, his deep chuckle rumbling in his chest. "You still with me?"

I let out a shaky breath and nodded, appreciating how soft his skin felt under my fingertips as I traced the compass tattoo over his heart.

Dante kissed the top of my head. "I need to hear the words, Kitten."

My heart raced at the name, and a smile spread across my face as I lifted my head. "Yes, Dante."

"That's my girl." He captured my lips in a searing kiss that made me melt a little more. "What do you need?"

"You. Now."

"Done."

I barely registered the flick of his wrist before the towel fell in a heap on the floor. Dante's hands were confident as he pressed me back, pinning me against the cool wooden door. My breath stuttered at the sudden show of control. He claimed my wrists in one hand, raising them over my head, the positional leverage rendering me dizzy with lust while also rendering me nearly powerless, but I wasn't afraid. I had no reason to be.

I felt the hard length through the thin barrier of my leggings and shirt as he leaned against me. Dante could have torn my clothes off, and probably wanted to, but he took his time, teasing my skin as he stripped me piece by piece, his mouth tracing my skin as it became exposed. Any insecurity was overridden by the absolute certainty of his attention. When he paused and looked at me, his gaze was hungry, but reverent.

There was nothing gentle in the way he claimed me with his hands and mouth. It was hot, possessive, and had me craving more. My body responded without hesitation, arching into him. I didn't have time to think as he slid into me, but that was one of the things I loved most about Dante. He didn't ask what I wanted or needed. He didn't need to. We'd written the rules together a long time ago. These moments were some of the few times I didn't have to think...

didn't have to plan... didn't have to be in charge of something. I could temporarily let go of all my responsibilities and just *be.*

I trusted Dante with my life. He would never do anything to hurt me or make me uncomfortable.

"Check in, Kitten."

A pleased grin spread across my face as a moan slipped out. "Green, Wolf. Bright fucking green."

"Perfect." Dante practically growled his response as he thrust into me a little harder, pulling a moan from me.

When I wrapped one leg around his waist, he immediately released my wrists and slid his hands under my thighs, holding tight as he pounded into me, pushing me closer and closer to the edge. It didn't take long for my first orgasm to hit, and by the time we finally made it to the bed, I was glad he had a firm hold on me. My legs were so shaky, I wasn't sure I would have been able to walk.

Eventually we wore each other out, if only for the time being, and we lay in his bed, basking in how perfect we were together. As my thoughts finally returned to my brain, one came in much louder: I needed to get back upstairs. I had a job to do. Did I have to rush back? No, but I hated the thought of shirking my duties. I wasn't here to sleep with Dante; I was here to keep Chloe safe.

When I moved to sit up, Dante tightened his hold on my waist. "Where are you going?"

Letting out a sigh, I settled back onto my side and gave him a gentle kiss. "I have to get back to Chloe. Lukas was kind enough to offer to sit with her, but I don't want to push my luck by staying down here too long."

He clenched his jaw, and I could see the counter argument swirling in his eyes. After taking a deep breath and letting it out slowly, he finally nodded. "I respect that."

I gave him another kiss. "Thank you for not going full Dom on me."

"It's not my place to tell you how to do your job. I love and respect you too much." A low chuckle came out. "Also, I really don't want two mafia Dons pissed at me."

"Smart and handsome. Did I win the jackpot, or what?"

After another long hug, I slipped out of bed and headed into the shower. It wasn't long before Dante joined me, and eventually we were both clean, out, and dressed.

I melted into him, as I kissed him goodnight, his arms around me, steady and sure. "I love you, Kitten."

"I love you, too, Wolf." I gave him one more quick kiss before turning and heading out, keeping my eyes on him until the door finally broke my view. Sighing, I headed down the hall.

As I walked into the kitchen, Quinn was sitting at the island with a bowl of ice cream in front of her and a piece of toast with peanut butter on it in her left hand. She smirked when I stopped and stood next to her. "You look more relaxed than earlier."

"A hot shower does wonders."

Her smile widened as she gave me a knowing look. "Especially when *conserving water*?"

This is how she wants to play? I grinned, loving the banter. "Is the reason you're down here having a late-night snack because of *your* water conservation buddy?"

The woman chuckled. "I earned that. And yeah."

"I'm heading back up to Chloe. If Lukas is still in there, I'll send him your way."

"Thanks, Sabrina."

I quickly made my way upstairs and into what was now Chloe's room. The sight of Lukas slumped on the ground next to Chloe's bed had me reaching for my gun as I ran in and took a closer look. A shaky, relieved breath rushed out when I saw he and Chloe were fine. They were both fast asleep, sharing a pillow, her hand clutching his thumb.

As I holstered my sidearm, I smiled at the love and innocence in front of me. For all the bullshit and chaos swirling around this family and within this house, this moment reminded me why Lianne and my uncle worked as hard as they did. To protect their families. To make it so uncles and nieces could have story time and a cuddle. Not all that long ago, Uncle Ceaser had been the one sitting next to my bed, reading me to sleep.

It was in this moment that my assignment became so much more personal. While I didn't want Chloe to lose her father like I had, that was outside of my control. But I could ensure she knew she was safe, wanted, and above all else very much loved.

How long do I leave him there?

Confident Chloe was still safe, I headed out of the room to look for Quinn, only to run into her on the stairs. "Just the woman I needed to talk to."

She furrowed her brow in confusion. "Is everything okay?"

I couldn't help but grin. "Very much so. Lukas is passed out on the floor next to Chloe's bed, and I'm trying to figure out if I should leave him there or not."

Quinn smiled, and her eyes glistened with unshed tears. "I love that he gets more time with her. He needs that little girl as much as she needs us." She took a deep breath and cleared her throat. "Let me wake him up and talk to him."

She stepped into the room, and I waited outside. Moments later, she and a sleepy-looking Lukas walked out, hand in hand.

"Thank you."

I gave him a curious look. "For what?"

He let out a soft chuckle as he ran his free hand through his hair. "For tonight. I appreciated the time with Chloe."

I was so confused, not a feeling I was accustomed to. "You're allowed to hang out with your niece."

"While that may be true, you didn't hover, and you didn't make a big deal of me falling asleep on the floor."

Quinn tensed up slightly. "Sabrina isn't your dumbass brother. Unlike him, *she* understands the importance of quality uncle time."

I nodded proudly. "Quinn, you and I are going to be great friends."

Chapter Nineteen

Lianne

"Good morning, Li." A kiss was pressed to my forehead.

"Hmm?" I sleepily opened my eyes to see Ben crouched next to my side of the bed, completely dressed and giving me the most adorable smile. "Why are you up already? I wanted to snuggle."

His grin turned apologetic as he tucked some of my hair behind my ear. "I'm going to make sure the otter office is good to go. Yesterday we pretty much had everyone stay in their rooms while you all figured out the plan."

I nodded and let out a heavy sigh, once again feeling guilty about how many lives were being disrupted by our family drama. "I'm sorry, Ben."

He leaned in and cupped my face as he gave me a gentle kiss. "There's nothing to apologize for, Li. We all knew the risks of falling in love with people in this family. I have no regrets." There was no denying the love shining in his dark blue eyes.

"You're too good for me."

Ben shook his head. "No. We balance each other perfectly." He rubbed my cheek with his thumb. "Don't worry about stopping by the kitchen for breakfast. I'll bring something after I'm done in the office."

Leaning into his touch, I grinned. "Are you going to have breakfast with me?"

"Absolutely. There are few things I love more than spending time with you."

A smirk tugged at the corner of my mouth as I thought about everything Ben liked trying in my office when the world wasn't on fire. *Maybe he was right about the balance thing.*

With a final kiss, he stood up and walked out of our bedroom, and I rolled onto my back, letting out a deep sigh. As much as I wanted to stay in bed, there was too much to do.

I threw back my blanket and got out of bed, heading to my closet with renewed purpose. With Liam in the house, I felt the need to dress more professionally. Not that it proved anything, but knowing my unfortunate brother was in training sweats, me showing up looking polished and professional was going to set us apart even more. While I was fine wearing a suit, I drew the line at starting the day in heels. I could always put them on later if I wanted.

After dressing and putting on some makeup, I smirked as I grabbed my favorite lip stain. If there was anything I'd learned in the last year or two, albeit superficial, it was that lip stain was better for daily operations. Lasting wear aside, it didn't leave any evidence.

Shaking my head, I slid into my favorite work flats and headed out of my room, stopping short when I saw Avery posted outside the door to Liam's old room. *Why is she there?* "Is everything okay?"

Avery nodded. "Sabrina asked me to watch the door while she was showering, on the off-chance Chloe woke up before she got out of the bathroom."

Smart thinking. I nodded. "Thank you."

"Of course. We're a team here. I'm also going to talk to Ben about the new otter protocol once she's done. Two birds, one stone."

Nodding, I hurried downstairs and into my office, feeling calmer once the door was closed. When I reached for my mug and found it empty, I scowled at the ornate, antique liquor cabinet, secretly loathing that my mom told me I couldn't have a tea or coffee maker in here.

"You'd never leave your office, Lianne."

Not that she was wrong.

I was about to harass Regina into picking up a latte for me on her way from the gun range when my phone rang. Seeing whose name was on the screen, I sat up a little taller as I answered it. "Don Dallas, how can I help you?"

"Good morning, Don Agosti. I apologize for the early hour, but do you have a minute?"

I glanced at the clock. *It's not that early.* "Of course, sir."

He let out a breath. "I found my father's copy of the contract you asked about and have reviewed it."

I pulled open the drawer to my right and pulled out my copy as well as a blank piece of paper. "And your thoughts on it, sir?"

Dallas cleared his throat. "From how it reads, the Vaux family is the one who has breached the contract the fewest number of times. They are also the family calling for payment. The Agostis have to make this right."

I nodded. It was the same conclusion we'd come to here as well. "Without a Vaux Don, how do we proceed? I have the main offender in a holding cell right now. I don't want him there long term."

There was a pause. "Main offender? Are you referring to Liam?"

"Yes, sir." I clenched my jaw, trying to keep my tone calm and composed.

"I see." There was a pause. "May I ask *why* you're holding him in a cell?"

I balled up my hand not holding the phone and pushed my rage down. Not at Dallas, but at Liam. While I technically didn't have to say anything aside from 'it's Agosti business,' there wasn't any reason to hide the information. "He's a traitor, sir. One who intentionally put his daughter in the middle of a dangerous situation that had nothing to do with her. Among other things."

He let out a deep sigh. "I see. Is it safe to assume Ms. Victoria Vaux is still under your care?"

Hearing Adair's deadname made me shudder. "Yes, she is." *Why?*

"I need to have a meeting with both of you as soon as possible to discuss a possible resolution to this. How soon can this be arranged? I'm willing to come to you if it will expedite the process."

I blinked several times in shock. "I... That's very generous of you, sir. Can I call you back with a time after I confirm a few details?"

"Of course, Lianne. This is a high priority, but it's by no means an emergency. I would have been stunned if you had given me a response immediately."

The call ended, and I stared at my phone.

Holy shit.

I messaged Adair.

Lianne: < Are you free for a quick chat? Important but non-emergency. >

Her response was almost immediate.

Adair: < Yes. When and where? And should I come alone? >

I loved how well she was integrating back into this chaotic life. *Not that her life prior to this was so calm.*

Lianne: < Now. My office. Just you and me. >

Less than a minute later, she was walking into my office and closing the door behind her. "Is everything okay?"

I nodded and gestured to the chairs in front of my desk. "Yeah. I just got off the phone with Dallas about the contract. He wants an in-person meeting between the three of us."

Adair's eyebrows shot up. "He wants to meet with *me*? Why?"

I glanced at the contract on my desk. "Well, you signed it. You're the oldest living Vaux. It's your family that is owed retribution. Unfortunately, this continues to be your problem." I looked up at her again. "He wants to meet soon. Again, I'm guessing, but I think he was taken aback by the fact I'm holding Liam as a prisoner."

She frowned. "If *I'm* being honest, I hate that he's here at all, but I get it."

Same. "So, how soon do you want to meet with the Don Supreme?"

Adair looked at Ryan's door. "What about our shadows?"

I shrugged. "What about them? Dallas said he would come here." A smirk tugged at the corner of my mouth. "Also, I'm Don Agosti. That means I get to inform *them* when I'm having a meeting with another Don, especially an ally. My concern is *you.* This is your life and family we're going to be discussing."

She let out a deep sigh and leaned back in the leather chair. "Not today. Yesterday was a lot, and I'd like a day without complete chaos breaking out." A tight laugh came out. "Is that even possible?"

I leaned back in my chair and let out a tense breath of my own. "That's what I've been told. Mom and Gage keep insisting that this level of chaos is unprecedented and that I'm handling it beautifully." I rolled my eyes. "While I appreciate the vote of confidence, I'm getting pretty fucking tired."

"It has to get better at *some* point, right?"

"God, I hope so."

Adair's phone buzzed, and an adorable smirk appeared on her face as she glanced at the screen. "Apparently, my breakfast is ready."

My eyebrows went up. "Oh?"

She glanced up, smiling. "Peter headed to the kitchen when I came here. He's back in the room now."

I shot her an amused look. "You didn't want to chance going to the kitchen, either?"

My almost sister-in-law snort-laughed. "Oh, *hell* no."

Chapter Twenty

Dante

Despite not being able to share a bed with Sabrina, I slept like a log. *Fantastic sex will do that.* I chuckled and shook my head as I got dressed and geared up for the day. Downstairs, the crew kitchen was deserted except for a plate of eggs and roasted potatoes left under foil with my name written on it in marker in a very familiar block print.

Thank you, Talia.

I had the best little sister. I ate standing up, reading the police blotter on my phone while also replaying the previous night with Sabrina in a continuous highlight reel. We picked up right where we'd left off, and I loved every moment we shared.

After I finished my coffee and rinsed my mug, I headed for the medical area. The first room on the left was Doc's office, the second was a supply closet, and the last was the nicest of our holding rooms, complete with its reinforced door and security camera. It wasn't jail, exactly—more like a padded anxiety box with a cot, toilet, and not much else.

Liam should be thrilled to have that much, the fucking bastard.

Nash was parked outside the door, feet propped on a milk crate, reading a battered paperback—some detective novel with a woman's legs on the cover. His sidearm rested on his thigh, finger drumming the grip.

He glanced up, marked his page with one of Sunny's bookmarks, and gave me a sharp nod. "Morning, Dante."

I eyed the book, intrigued by the choice. "You stopping crime with that, or just trying to learn from the competition?"

Nash grinned, teeth white and perfect. "Little from column A, little from column B."

I noticed a sandwich wrapper, two empty energy drinks, and an untouched crossword puzzle. The man had taken his post seriously, as he always did. "Anything happen overnight?"

He shook his head. "Nope. Liam went to bed without a fuss. No need to knock him out." The man almost sounded disappointed. We all really wanted to take a swing at this man.

"Good." I clapped him on the shoulder. "Go get some sleep."

Nash chuckled as he stood up and collected his garbage. "Don't need to tell me twice."

I knocked twice on the door before unlocking and opening it. "Good morning, Liam."

The man glared at me from the cot he was sitting on. "What's so good about it?"

I returned the glare. "Well, you still have your life, though, depending who you ask, could be considered good."

Liam scowled and stood up so abruptly, the metal cot scraped against the floor and bumped against the wall. He made a show of rolling his shoulders, chin jutting out, as if every inch of bravado might erode the reality of the fact that I, not he, held the keys to his freedom. *Well, the limited and temporary freedom Lianne has granted him.* When I didn't step aside, he scoffed, squared his jaw, drew a deep, ostentatious breath, and then tried to shoulder through.

I'd been dealing with assholes like him since high school. I saw the little tensing, the split-second warning in his eyes, and braced myself as he barreled forward, all pent-up entitlement and too many years of being the biggest, most powerful guy in the room. I let him hit me, just enough to let him feel the impact, then caught him clean as my hand clamped around his bicep. He froze, surprised to discover in a flash of pain when I dug my thumb into the exact spot on his arm where every muscle is weak.

He tried to rip free, only managing to twist himself closer. There was a moment, hanging in the standoff, when I could see the storm of options play across his face. I leaned in, and his bravado whittled itself down to the slimmest edge of defiance. "Listen here, you little shit. Breakfast with your daughter *and* doing so without handcuffs are two luxuries that can be taken away at any moment. All I have to do is tell Lianne you're refusing to follow the rules. What's it going to be? I'm more than happy to lock your ass in here all day and bring meals and pictures of your daughter to you. No skin off my nose not to have to follow you around all day."

Liam glared at me for a long moment before letting out a tense breath. I could see the war in his eyes. This man had been *this close* to being Don and was used to giving directions, not being forced to follow them. *Play stupid games, win stupid prizes.*

"I'll behave."

"Good boy. Now, let's see if you can get through breakfast without disappointing your mother anymore."

I had my gun pressed against his lower back as we made our way upstairs and through the house. I holstered it only once we rounded the corner and were in sight of the kitchen. None of us wanted to scare Chloe unnecessarily.

The adorable Agosti toddler was already settled in her high chair next to the island, with Sabrina next to her. When we walked in, a huge smile lit up her face. "Dada!"

"Hey, sweetie." He wrapped her in a tight hug and kissed the top of her head. "Did you sleep okay?"

She nodded. "Yes! Bina read stories!" The small toddler kicked excitedly in her chair as she grabbed another piece of pancake and handed it to Liam. "Dada eat?"

"Of course." He grimaced slightly as he took the sticky piece and ate it. "Can I sit by you?"

"Pease!"

While he chatted with her about her bunny and helped her eat, Lukas plated and heated up some pancakes before sliding them in front of him.

"Say tank you, Dada."

Liam cleared his throat and looked up. "Thank you."

Lukas smirked. "You're welcome." He then leaned in close to Chloe. "And thank *you* for having such good manners."

She grinned widely. "Welcome!"

It was a miracle Chloe was this polite and well-mannered. *We all know it didn't come from Liam and Susan.*

Not too much later, Peter walked in and looked around, nodding at me and then wrinkling his nose slightly at Liam. "Good morning, everyone." He grabbed two bagels from a bag on the counter, popping them both open.

Lukas stepped closer to where he was standing. "How's Adair this morning?"

"She's okay, all things considered. Slept a lot better than I expected. She's with Lianne right now."

I studied Peter's face, noting the exhaustion and worry in his eyes. I also noticed Liam had gone completely still and was locked in on the conversation happening near him. *Your claim to her ended years ago. You don't get to be worried about her anymore.* When I cleared my throat, Lukas glanced my way, and I pointed at Liam.

He nodded before walking to the fridge and taking out the cream cheese, handing it to Peter. "I'll check in with her later."

"I'm sure she'd appreciate it."

Chloe regained her dad's attention, giving Peter and Lukas time to pull together food and Peter to leave without any more interaction with Liam.

I wasn't the only one locked in on Liam's behavior. Sabrina was splitting her time between the father-daughter duo. There was an intensity and feral protectiveness in her eyes that filled me with pride. *That's my Kitten.*

Chloe, who had been quietly constructing a pancake sandwich on her tray, despite her father's urging to stop playing with her food and just eat it, suddenly straightened in her chair as if struck by grand inspiration. With one determined slurp, she drained the last of her milk from the sippy cup before slamming it on the high chair tray with a comedic thunk, milk froth dribbling down her chin.

"I fin-isht!" She stretched the word out like a song before surveying the adults. "I see Gamma. Pease." Liam tried to reason with her, telling her he wanted to read her a story, but Chloe simply chanted, "Gamma! Gamma! Gamma!"

Sabrina, who had been quietly sipping coffee at the island, broke into a rare smile. "I'll take you, sweetie." She slid off her stool and set her cup down with the same controlled precision she used to rack a slide on a pistol. "Come on, let's wipe off your hands and go see what Grandma's up to."

Chloe squealed and wriggled, nearly toppling the high chair. Sabrina took the wet washcloth Ben handed her and wiped off as much of the sticky, syrup mess she could before unbuckling her in one swift motion. The little one immediately launched herself into Sabrina's arms, clutching her around the neck, an excited smile radiating all over her face.

The sight made my heart clench. I wanted that with Sabrina. As problematic and complicated as it was to have a family in the mafia world, George and Lynette Agosti had been a fantastic example of how it could be done.

Well, for the most part.

My attention shifted back to Liam, visibly annoyed at being upstaged, as he reached over and attempted to smooth Chloe's hair. "Hey, try to listen next time, okay, sweetheart?"

Chloe twisted away, ignoring him, and put her hands on Sabrina's face. "Gamma, pease!"

"We're going right now." Sabrina winked at me before heading out, and the toddler waved goodbye to her captive breakfast audience.

As the echoes of Chloe's chatter echoed in the foyer, Lukas collected the contents of the high chair tray and put them directly into the sink, and Liam slumped onto the island counter, his shoulders hunched in defeat.

Interesting.

It was then that Ben strolled into the kitchen. His eyes narrowed, and his steps slowed as he clocked who was in the room. It wasn't until we locked eyes that his shoulders relaxed slightly. "Morning, everyone."

Lukas, now pouring himself a second cup of coffee, acknowledged Ben with a nod. "Everything good with the otters?"

He smiled and nodded. "Oh yeah. They're back in their room, happily working away."

Lukas eyed his phone, scrolling through notifications as he compiled toast, peanut butter, and sliced apples on a plate with an artist's efficiency.

Ben looked at the spread and gave Lukas a curious look. "Is Quinn okay? I was surprised she wasn't in the office, too."

The question hung in the air as Lukas reached for the electric kettle, filled it, and set it on its base before answering. "Yeah. She was in bed on her laptop when I left, prepping for her call with Chelsea at nine. I told her I'd bring up breakfast for her."

Ben nodded. "She's more than welcome to join the otters after her call. I know Ellen and Blake would love the company. Does she want any coffee?"

Lukas shook his head. "No, she's back in her tea phase. Lianne introduced her to a new company, and I think they're working through the entire catalog." He shrugged, smiling as he poured hot water into a mug, stirring in honey from the communal jar. "Whatever puts a smile on both of their faces."

"Amen to that." Ben shared a brief grin with his brother-in-law before his focus flickered to the far side of the room, where Liam still sat hunched in defeat. The two men exchanged a tense glance, and I caught the tiniest twitch of a smirk at the corner of Ben's mouth when Liam looked away first.

Well done. I loved seeing his ego take another hit.

It was then Avery breezed into the room. "Good morning, gentlemen, Liam."

I hid my amusement at how the man bristled at the exclusion of being called a gentleman.

She walked to the fridge and pulled out one of Chloe's sippy cups. "There was a beverage request."

Lukas smirked. "That girl loves her juice."

Liam sat up with a scowl. "Don't give her too much. I don't want her to have a ton of sugar."

Avery stopped and turned to glare at him. "You know we cut it with water, right? You may be the only living father in this building, but that does not make you the nutritional expert."

"I'm on my way out. How about I deliver the cup while you continue to educate my brother?" Lukas held his hand out to Avery, who handed over the beverage.

"With pleasure."

If I had to guess, Lukas was done dealing with his brother for the time being and wanted to move on with his day. Not that I blamed him. I'm not sure how well I'd handle it if Talia turned against me. I bit down my smirk, and when I glanced at Ben, he was doing the same. As much as we all hated Liam's presence in this house, there was a significant amount of satisfaction in being able to take potshots at him.

Is this why Lianne is keeping him alive?

Avery leaned in close to Liam's face, making their faces mere inches apart. "Anything else you want to weigh in on and micromanage when it comes to your daughter? Did you want to approve of the books, toys, and activities Sabrina has on the docket? Or are you going to trust the decision-making skills of your mother, a Don, and another Don's heir?" The woman stared at him hard until he scoffed and looked away. "That's what I thought."

She walked to where I was standing and narrowed her eyes on my charge as he went back to sulking over his breakfast.

I bumped her shoulder against mine. "You good?"

Avery nodded before shifting her focus. "Ben, is that for Lianne?"

He glanced up. "Yeah. I promised earlier that I'd bring her food."

It wasn't a coincidence he, Lukas, and Peter were keeping their significant others out of the kitchen. If anything, it was for Liam's protection more than the ladies.

Liam scoffed. "Lianne is more than capable of making her own breakfast. I don't understand why everyone is catering to her."

Ben let out a sigh. "I like making breakfast for my wife and then eating it with her."

"This is why I should never have left. Everyone here has gone soft."

Ben set down the butter knife and looked up at his brother-in-law. "And yet you did. You made your decision, and these are some of the consequences. Deal with it."

Liam's eyebrows went up at the outburst. "I *am* dealing with it. I'm here now, aren't I?"

"Like a fucking blister. Also, you showed up completely uninvited and are only alive by the grace of the Agosti women living here."

I had to bite my tongue to keep from snickering. *Go Ben.*

"Excuse me?"

Ben now glared at Liam, and I didn't miss how his arms tensed up. "No one asked you to show up. You came here under the guise of wishing your siblings a happy birthday."

The oldest Agosti sibling snarled. "The *guise*? Are you insinuating I *lied*?"

"If the shoe fits, asshole."

Liam stood up. "Do you have a problem with me?"

Who doesn't? I took a step closer, readying myself to grab and tackle the idiot running his mouth.

"What was your first clue? Do you even *think* before you speak, or are you *so* arrogant that you think everything you say is gold? You hid a listening device in *your daughter's favorite toy.*" Ben let out a frustrated huff and gestured in the direction of the offices. "Look around, Liam. The only reason you're even alive is because Li told all of us not to kill you. Bitch about it all you want, but never forget that it's *my wife* and *your Don* who literally holds your fate in her hands, despite our *vehement* protests."

Liam shook his head and glared at Ben. "Dad never should have let Lianne work with that temp agency."

Avery's eyebrows went up in surprise, and hers weren't the only ones. *What the hell does he think he's going to accomplish by bringing that up?*

Ben stalked over and stood toe-to-toe in front of Liam, and the way they glowered at each other, I had a bad feeling this wasn't going to end well. "And what the fuck is *that* supposed to mean?"

"That if our father had kept Lianne home where she was safe, and made her do what she was told, she wouldn't have gotten into so many messes we had to clean—"

Liam's sentence was cut off when Ben's fist slammed into his mouth, making the man stumble backward a couple steps. "Just shut the fuck up for once, will you? You're such an arrogant piece of shit. Lianne's job was *not* the reason there were messes to clean up. *You* are."

After stumbling back a step, Liam wiped his face with the back of his hand. His eyebrows went up as he looked at the blood from his lip. He appeared genuinely stunned that Ben hit him. I knew Ben had been training with Connor, Avery, and Regina, and damn did it show. This hit was calculated, precise, and almost knocked Liam flat on his ass. *Well done.*

As Liam swung in retaliation at Ben, I started to move forward, but Avery stopped me. "Wait."

I pushed against her arm, glaring at her. "Are you insane?"

She shook her head, smirking. "No. Ben needs this. Hell, he *deserves* this."

The man easily blocked Liam's hit, rolling his eyes. "You think you're such tough shit. Fucking fight like it!"

There was a feral glint in his eyes and a ferocity to the tone of his voice I'd never seen or heard before, and it put me on edge. This was not the cheerful Ben I knew.

Liam made another jab that Ben easily redirected. "Seriously, Liam? *This* is your best? Some fucking mafia man you are. When was the last time you got your hands dirty and actually did your own dirty work? Do you remember *any* of your training?"

The man snarled. "You want to shit-talk. Fine. I never wanted to see my sister dating, let alone married to the son of a druggie whore. She deserves so much better than the likes of you. Your father should have taken you and Aaron out when he had the chance. Your stupid adoptive moms, too." Liam sneered. "But love made him weak and pathetic, just like you."

Ben went deathly still, and his eyes became devoid of any emotion. It lasted for a split second. Something feral and wild flickered across his face right before his fist slammed into Liam's jaw with an intensity I didn't think possible.

Liam once again stumbled back from the impact, but couldn't catch himself before Ben punched him again, this time knocking him to the ground.

"Shut your fucking mouth!"

He didn't give Liam a chance to stand up, but instead, tackled him and pinned him to the ground, making it rain punches. Most were to the head, but there were at least one or two to the throat.

Liam didn't have a chance to block most of the attacks, and I was equal parts terrified and impressed.

Lianne

Ben should have been here by now.

The man was punctual to a fault when it came to making sure I ate, and if he couldn't deliver it, he made sure someone else did. It was adorable, and I was grateful he was so invested in making sure I was taken care of.

And all I do is cause him headaches.

Noting the time, I decided to take the gamble that Liam was out of the kitchen and grab some coffee while looking for my husband. When I stepped out of my office, I heard giggles and laughter coming from my mom's office, and it put a smile on my face. We needed more of that kind of levity here. While I hated the circumstances that put Chloe in our house, I was beyond grateful for the extra time with my niece.

A growled roar from the opposite direction caught my attention and made my blood run cold. *Shit. That's Ben.* I took off running, and as I rounded the corner from the hallway to the foyer, I saw into the kitchen where Dante and Avery were tearing Liam and Ben away from each other.

What the fuck?

I raced into the kitchen, where Avery was actually struggling to restrain Ben, whose lip was bleeding.

"Take a fucking breath before you force me to take drastic measures. Do you really want Lianne to see you like this?

Ben gasped and immediately stopped struggling. "Shit. Li's gonna kill me."

Oh, hun. Never. "No. I'm not."

He jumped as he turned to face me, eyes wide. "Li, I—"

"Stop. You're fine." I shook my head and looked to my left, glaring at Liam, who had an impressive amount of blood running off his face. *Was that just from Ben? What the hell happened in here?* "Dante, take Liam to Avery's office. I'll be down in a minute." My focus stayed on my idiotic excuse of a brother as he was dragged out of the room. As soon as they were out of sight, I shifted my focus back to Ben. Avery's arms were still around his shoulders, ensuring he didn't follow.

His eyes were wild as they locked onto me. So many emotions flickered across his face. Anger. Disappointment. Frustration. Sadness. It broke my heart.

"Avery, let him go."

She glanced at me, furrowed her brows in concern, but then slowly released her hold. Ben stood stock-still, practically vibrating.

In a flash, I moved forward and wrapped him in a tight hug, not giving a damn if I got blood on me. "I love you, Benedict."

"But I—"

"And I'm so damn proud of you." I cut off his words. He was going to beat himself up for losing control, and I didn't want any of that. He did nothing wrong. Hell, I was impressed and even a little jealous.

"But Li—"

"No." I leaned back and lifted my chin to look into the blue eyes of the man I loved. "No buts. You did *nothing* wrong. The only reason Avery pulled you away is because the crew has strict orders not to kill him."

"I know I should have pulled him away faster, but—"

"*You* did nothing wrong either, Avery." I glanced to my left at the woman who could drop almost everyone in this house in a fight. "Thank you. I'll join you and Dante downstairs in a minute."

Once she left, Ben took a deep breath and leaned forward to rest his forehead on mine as he let it out slowly. "I expected him to try to get under my skin by saying shit about me, and even you to some extent, but..." His shoulders sagged. "But then he mentioned my dad and... taking Aaron and I out... and then Bernie and Charlie... and... I... something in me snapped." His head popped up, and the feral intensity in his eyes was jarring. "I was right back in that house protecting my little brother all over again. I'd never let anything happen to him... or you. Or anyone here."

Rage coursed through me as I took his face in my hands and pressed a gentle kiss to his lips, not not giving a damn if I got blood on me. Ben had worked through so many of the demons from his past, but that wild, protective side was never far away. "I will never get mad at you for defending and protecting your family. It's one of the many things I love about you."

He blinked away the tears gathering in the corners of his eyes and nodded. "Okay."

I needed to make sure Ben was okay before I dealt with Liam. "What do you need right now?"

Ben pulled me in for another hug, this one much tighter, and let out a tense breath. "This helps a lot, but I still need you to eat breakfast, and then I think I'm going to make mini cheesecakes. Maybe cookies, too."

He's better with a task.

My rage cooled ever so slightly. "Sounds perfect. I'm going to have a little chat with Dante and Avery, and I'll be back in a few to enjoy my breakfast with you. Okay?"

He nodded.

"Maybe call Aaron while I'm downstairs? Hearing his voice might help."

A tiny smile appeared on my husband's face as he stood straight again. "Yeah. I think that would. You're so smart. How did I get this lucky?"

"We were both lucky to find each other." After giving him another kiss, I forced myself to walk away and head downstairs, but not before stopping by my mom's office.

Chapter Twenty-One

Dante

Talia walked out of the gym, towel draped over her shoulder, eyes wide as I forcefully escorted Liam past it and toward the interrogation room. "Holy shit! What happened?"

"A fight. Can you bring a first-aid kit to Avery's office?"

"I... Of course."

Dragging Liam past the medical area, I yanked the heavy metal door of the interrogation room open, shoved him inside, and then onto the metal chair in the center of the room.

"What the fuck, Dante?"

I shook my head as I slapped one side of a pair of handcuffs to his right hand, and the other side to a solid metal loop on the table next to him. "You're a fucking idiot, that's what." I repeated the action on his left wrist with a second set of handcuffs and then took a step back, feeling confident the man was contained for the moment. "Don't do anything else stupid." Ignoring his angry response, I stepped outside the room and leaned against the door, letting out a tense breath. *Holy shit.* I was going to be replaying the calculated and feral way Ben went after Liam for a long time.

"Can you talk about what all that was about?"

I looked to my left, giving my sister a tight smile as she approached, pleased to see the first aid kit in her arms. *Not that the man deserves it.* "Liam ran his mouth, and Ben ended the conversation. I don't know what else I can say right now."

Her deep brown eyes went wide. "Holy shit! *Ben* did that?"

I glanced past my sister to see Avery charging down the hallway, hands in her hair. "Did something else happen?"

She quickly shook her head. "No, but... I've never seen Ben act like that. I mean, yes, I helped train the man, but that... He fucking snapped." Avery let out a tense breath as she shoved her hands through her hair again. "Lianne took over and sent me down."

Talia's attention bounced between us, her eyes wide. "Is Ben okay?"

"I think he will be fine once he cools down." She glanced over her shoulder and then looked at me again. "We should get in there before Lianne gets down here."

"I'll go get ready for whatever fallout comes from this." My sister handed Avery the first aid kit and then walked away.

Crossing my arms over my chest, I let out a sigh. "I didn't know he had that kind of fight in him."

Avery pressed her lips together and had a knowing look on her face. "It's the quiet ones you have to watch out for. Lianne is the same way. She may look sweet and kind, but there is a deadly weapon under that pretty exterior."

I considered her words and then nodded. "You make an excellent point." Lianne had shown up the entire team at the gun range more than once.

"I know. I didn't make it this far in life without learning a thing or two about identifying potential threats." Avery let out a deep sigh as she stormed into the interrogation room. "It's a damn good thing for you I respect the fuck out of my boss."

Liam jumped at her sudden appearance and narrowed his eyes warily. Well, as much as he could. His already swollen face impeded some of his efforts. "What's *that* supposed to mean?"

She took the first-aid kit and smacked him in the back of the head with it before dropping it on the table. "Like you don't fucking know."

I stared at her as she paced back and forth in front of Liam, seething. He also looked pissed as he reached for the kit. "What the hell are you doing picking fights with Ben, anyway?"

He ignored me and looked up at Avery. "Why did you tear Ben off me? Afraid he'd get hurt?"

The arrogance in that man's voice grated on my nerves. *Does he have a death wish?*

Avery stepped toward him, pulling her arm back, but froze when the door opened and barely stepped out of the way in time as Lianne stormed in and right up to Liam. "What the fuck is wrong with you?"

He tensed up, blinking in surprise. "Your husband attacked me. I was *defending* myself. Did you ask him why *he* lashed out?"

Before I could answer, Lianne punched Liam hard, his head snapping to the right from the impact, and nearly knocking him off the chair. "I did." When he righted himself, she leaned in so close their noses were practically touching. "You gonna call me weak and pathetic and punch me because I have the audacity to love people, too?"

The rage rolling off Lianne matched, if not surpassed what Ben had shown upstairs, and it actually scared me a little. Again, I'd only ever seen her composed, irritated, or deathly calm. This barely bridled anger was new to me. One glance at Liam and his wide-eyed look of terror told me I wasn't the only one. *Interesting.*

As she glared at the man, Avery edged closer to Lianne, readying herself. For what? I had no clue. *It's not like Liam can move far.*

Time slowed to a halt until Liam finally swallowed hard and shook his head. "No."

Lianne sneered as she stood straight and tugged at the bottom hem of her shirt. "Your protection is officially revoked. Next time you start shit with someone in this house, they can kill you for all I fucking care. I hope it was worth it." She turned on her heel and immediately left the room, slamming the door shut behind her.

I looked at Avery, who was also wide-eyed in shock. "Well, then." I shifted my attention to Liam and gestured to the first-aid kit. "I think you can handle this. Avery, a word?"

She nodded and followed me out of the interrogation room. I glanced up and down the hallway, and when I saw it empty, I grabbed her arm and pulled her into the observation side of the interrogation room.

Only to stop dead in my tracks when I saw Lynette standing there, staring at Liam through the window. Her face was eerily emotionless.

How long has she been in here? I thought she was in her office with Chloe.

"Your work with Ben paid off. Well done, Avery."

Avery cleared her throat and stood a little taller. "Thank you, ma'am."

We exchanged a glance, and the look in her eyes matched what I was feeling - completely out of my depth. *Now what?*

Lynette let out a tired-sounding breath. "I wondered how much more of his shit Lianne was going to tolerate." She paused and then shook her head. "And now it's the beginning of the end."

"Ma'am?"

Lynette looked to her right, staring at us both. "He just started the countdown to his death." She let out a sigh. "I have a meeting to get to."

We stepped out of her way as she left the room before staring at each other again.

Now what?

Chapter Twenty-Two

Lianne

After storming out of the interrogation room, I ducked into the war room and glanced around. Grateful to see it empty, I headed straight to the panic room attached to it, grabbed a pillow from one of the cots, held it to my face, and screamed as loud as I could.

I immediately knew how Ben felt when I walked into the kitchen.

I should have stayed professional.

I should have held it together.

I'm the fucking Don.

The door to the war room opened, and I froze.

"Lianne?"

Mom. Shit. I swallowed, took a deep breath, and walked out, hoping I looked calmer than I felt. "Hey."

She nodded and closed the distance before pulling me into a tight hug. "I love you so much."

"I love you, too, Mom." While grateful for the hug, I braced myself for a lecture.

"You did nothing wrong."

What? I couldn't help but chuckle, and when my mom leaned back and gave me a curious look, I shrugged. "I told Ben and Avery the same thing upstairs."

She smiled and rubbed my shoulders. "You aren't the first Agosti Don to punch that man."

My eyes went wide as my mouth dropped open. "Dad punched Liam?"

Mom nodded. "More than once, too."

Just when I thought I couldn't be surprised anymore. I sat on the nearest chair and let out a tense breath. "I'm going to need at least *part* of this story."

With a smug grin, she settled into the chair next to me, gently resting her elbow on the table. "One time was right before your wedding, after you and Quinn worked together so brilliantly to save Lukas. Before then, it was when Liam thought he could dictate to your father about how you should be handled when it came to working." Mom shook her head. "But the first time was after Adair got shot and disappeared. I'd never seen your father so angry. Ever."

"Well, shit." I slumped back into the chair and stared at the drop ceiling for a moment. It was comforting knowing Dad also had violent outbursts… Well, outside of regular mafia business.

She patted my knee before standing. "Try to give yourself the same grace you extended to Ben. I'm going to go back to my office and see what art Chloe has created since I left." Mom leaned over and kissed my forehead. "I'm proud of you, Lianne. Your father and uncle would be, too. You have done brilliantly since stepping up. The family is in good hands with you at the helm."

"Thanks, Mom."

I sat in silence for a minute after she left, letting my thoughts swirl around and my rage cool a bit more before heading back to the kitchen. Ben was standing by the windows, staring outside, holding the phone to his ear. When I walked in, he looked over and grinned. "I gotta let you go, Aaron. Thanks again for chatting. Love you."

I wrapped him in a tight hug. "Feel any better?"

He nodded and let out a sigh, resting his head on top of mine. "Yeah." After a moment, Ben leaned back and took my hands in his. He was about to kiss them when he glanced down and confusion filled his eyes. "Li, why is there blood on your hand?"

What? I glanced down and then pressed my lips into a tight line. "I *may* have punched Liam."

Ben shook his head and leaned in to kiss me. "Feel any better?"

"A little."

"Good. You still need to eat breakfast." His lips were still hovering over mine, and I felt the words as much as I heard them.

"Do I?"

He kissed me again and then shifted to whisper into my ear. "I promise to make it worth your while if you do."

Goosebumps erupted down my arms. "Only you could make eating breakfast sound like something scandalous."

Ben chuckled and kissed the side of my neck. "Whatever works."

Footsteps echoed in the foyer, and I let out a deep sigh, snuggling my head against his shoulder, not wanting to be needed for two minutes. I cherished these tiny moments where I was just Lianne.

No asshole brother.

No mafia.

No Don.

"Avery is holding the door for us."

I smirked. "I love that woman." Avery was truly one of my favorite people in our crew. She was fair, loyal, and lethal. She also had an uncanny ability to anticipate my needs almost better than Regina and Ben.

"I'm pretty fond of her, too." Ben let out a sigh and kissed the top of my head. "There's a plate with a bagel with cream cheese and jelly on the counter. I'm sure you have to get into a meeting after all that bullshit. Will you please take it with you?"

I looked up again into the blue eyes of the man I loved and married. "But we were supposed to eat breakfast together."

Love radiated from him as he stared at me. "I have forever with you, Li. Go be a badass. We'll have lunch together."

My heart fluttered. *He's the best thing to happen to me.* "Fine, but only if you pour a *very* large mug of coffee for me."

Ben grinned and kissed me again. "Deal."

Once I had my food and caffeine in hand, I headed out of the kitchen and glanced at Avery as I passed her. "In my office." I had a very good feeling I knew at least one reason why she was lingering in my vicinity.

The door to my office was barely closed when Avery broke her silence. "Is Ben okay?"

I nodded as I sat behind my desk. "For the moment. There's going to be a few extra baked goods by this afternoon. We'll see how he is after that." I paused, trying not to focus on how much rage had been vibrating through Ben's body when I held him earlier. "Thanks for letting him get a few hits in before pulling him away."

She shrugged. "I felt he deserved that much, especially with the shit Liam was saying." Avery glanced around and stepped closer. "It's not my place to question, and I'm not, but was it a scare tactic or an update to standing orders that you don't care if he dies?"

I sat quietly for a moment before responding. "A little of both. I need to have a meeting to settle something..." I trailed off and then looked at Avery. "How much do you know about the marriage contract between Liam and Adair?"

"Only what your mom and Adair have told me, which wasn't much. I was sworn to secrecy at the time. Why?"

I narrowed my eyes at her. "This goes nowhere, but *that* is the reason Liam has to stay alive for now. I'm working with Don Dallas to figure out what consequences we have to pay for breaking that contract. While we aren't the only party to violate the terms, I need to verify his death won't make things worse for the Agostis."

Avery bit down her smirk. "I think it would improve things, but you're the boss."

"Yeah." *Thanks, Liam.* I could have my dad right now, but no. If I had Dad, Liam would still be next in line to run this. *No. This is still better... somehow. Right?*

Sabrina

Lynette came back into the office looking lighter than when she left, and at the same time, more cautious. We'd heard Dante and Liam pass by, which was what prompted her to step out. I watched her, trying to glean any details I could, careful not to make it too obvious. "Everything okay?"

She let out a deep breath as she dropped down to sit next to Chloe. "It's better than before."

I left it at that. Lynette deserved her privacy, and so did everyone else here. It drove me a little crazy not to know everything right away, but this wasn't my family. I had very little, if any, sway here.

Chloe held up her drawing, cheeks pink with pride, for me to see before turning toward Lynette. "Gamma, look!"

She grinned at the blob-shaped yellow and purple cat. "That's wonderful! Should we put it on the kitchen fridge so everyone gets to see?" "Yea! We go now?" Lynette tucked a curl behind Chloe's ear and smiled. "Let's make a picture for Auntie Li first. Would you help me?" "Uh-huh!"Time passed in a flurry of sparkly stickers and crayon scribbles, and once Chloe was satisfied, Lynette carefully wrote 'For Auntie Li' at the top. As they headed to Lianne's office to deliver it, I went ahead to the kitchen ahead of them, letting them have their heartwarming moment.

When I walked into the kitchen, Ben was already measuring ingredients and dumping them into the bowl of the stand mixer. But what caught my attention was the bruise blooming on his cheek. *That wasn't there when Chloe and I left.* I took it in, then walked a little closer, voice low. "Are you okay?" Ben didn't look up, just stared at the bowl. "Yeah, why?" He must have known I'd noticed. I cleared my throat, standing close enough that the hum of the mixer was white noise between us. "I'd believe you more if you didn't have a split lip to go with that bruise." Ben laid his hands flat on the counter, jaw tight, and gave a short nod. "Fair enough."

We need to lighten this mood before Chloe gets in here.

"Could you use an adorable assistant?"

He tilted his head, a hint of a smile playing at the corner of his mouth. "You talking about you, or Chloe?""Chloe," I shot back, grinning, "but I'll take the compliment. Lynette is helping her deliver a picture to Auntie Li before they put another one of her masterpieces on the fridge."

His smile widened. "She's going to love that."

Right on cue, Lynette and Chloe came through the doorway.

"Unca Ben Ben! Look!" She held up her blob cat, and Ben immediately gushed over all the pretty colors and how much he loved it.

After putting it up on the fridge, Lynette snuck out, and I bent down to get eye-level with Chloe. "Want to help Uncle Ben Ben make cookies?"

"Yes, pease!"

Even with his split lip, he smiled and picked her up, carrying her to the pantry. When they emerged again, they both had aprons on, and I couldn't help but laugh a little at how the adult-sized apron swallowed Chloe whole. Ben sat her on the counter and painstakingly helped her scoop sugar, which promptly got dumped everywhere. Unwrapping the sticks of butter went marginally better. But when we got to the eggs, I was stunned he was able to keep shell pieces out of the dough.

These might actually be edible in the end.

Chloe was determined to add the flour all by herself, and to no one's surprise, all three of us ended up with it all over us. In a smart move, Ben had me help her measure out chocolate chips while he finished with the rest of the dry ingredients.

Laughter bubbled out of Chloe and Ben as she insisted on feeding him some of the chocolate, and I knew the sound was carrying out into the foyer and further into the house. It healed part of my jaded soul to be part of this loving and wholesome moment. Motion in my peripheral vision caught my attention, and when I glanced over, Lianne stood in the foyer, partly hidden in the shadows. Her expression was soft and a little sad. I tried to signal her to join us, tilting my head toward Ben and Chloe, but she shook her head and pulled out her phone.

Lianne: < He needs this more than I do. >

Lianne: < Honestly, just watching them brings me some peace. >

I could see it in the way her muscles relaxed as she leaned on the doorjamb. The joy and love in her eyes as she watched them. There was even a small smile at the corners of her lips. It wasn't long, though, before she let out a heavy sigh and headed back down the hall.

My heart felt full, almost too full to fit comfortably in my chest.

Once Chloe helped Ben scoop cookie dough onto two cookie sheets, I asked her if she wanted to go upstairs and read books while the cookies baked. Despite looking lighter and happier than when I first walked into the kitchen, I sensed Ben needed some alone time to further process his morning.

My pint-sized charge and I headed to her room, read several stories, and then made a fort out of pillows and blankets, where we colored and stacked blocks. About the third time Chloe asked if the cookies were ready, my phone buzzed.

Ben: < The cookies are done, and Avery and Connor are desperate to dive in. I told them my assistant gets first dibs. >

Ben: < I also made sugar cookies, if Chloe wants to decorate them. >

All it took was the mention of cookies, and she was pulling me out of the room, and going down the stairs far faster than I was comfortable with. When we walked into the kitchen, Connor and Avery were waiting, smiles on their faces, and joined in to help with the icing. Chloe's tongue was stuck out between her little pink lips as she concentrated solely on the one cookie she was decorating with extra care, studying it like it held the secret to happiness. When she was finally satisfied, she turned to Avery. "I give this to Dada." Avery let out a tense breath, set down the bag of frosting she'd been using, and wiped her hands. "He's busy right now, but how about we put it on a special plate and then bring it to him later, okay?"Chloe nodded, all business. "Okay!" She looked up at Ben. "Cookie for Li Li?"

He smiled and slid another plain sugar cookie her way. "Auntie Li would love a cookie."

Avery shook her head, still grinning as she started cleaning up some of the icing carnage. "That girl is going to rule the world someday."

Ben licked blue frosting off his thumb. "She already does. At least in this house."

I couldn't disagree.

After cleaning up, we delivered cookies to Ryan, Lianne, Lynette, and Gage, all of whom were very excited for the sugary snack. We even left some in the downstairs kitchen for whoever else was working today. And, of course, she had to sit in every chair available.

All the excitement and activity finally took its toll on Chloe. I could see the sleepiness in her eyes as she glanced up at me.

"Uppies?"

"Of course, Chloe." I bent down and scooped her up, swallowing down a surge of emotions when she immediately wrapped her arms around my neck and burrowed into my shoulder. I liked the feeling of her snuggled against me, all trust and drowsy affection. The way she melted into my hold and was sleepily playing with my hair made me feel needed in a way I couldn't explain to anyone who hadn't grown up in a house where safety and trust were not always guaranteed.

I climbed the steps and made my way past all the office doors again, slowly heading toward the stairs leading to the second floor. As I rounded the corner, careful not to jostle her too much, I almost ran straight into Dante.

He caught me before I could stumble, one strong hand on my bicep, the other automatically steadying the small of my back. Even now, he moved like a bodyguard, despite no visible threat in the hallway. His eyes went straight to Chloe, then back to me, softening a little the way they always did when we were close.

Dante dipped his head and gave me a quick kiss on the cheek. The kind you gave someone when you were glad to see them, but were too busy to make a production out of it. It was just a touch, but I felt it in my core. "You look amazing holding her." His voice was rough and low, and I could tell it wasn't some throwaway compliment. He meant it. He always did.

I wanted to roll my eyes, but I couldn't. The moment felt too precious. Almost sacred. "It helps that she's absolutely adorable."

He grinned. "Chloe almost out?"

I shifted her a little so he could see. "She's fighting it, but yeah. We made and then delivered cookies to everyone on the main floor." A smirk appeared on my face. "A few made it to the staff kitchen, and if you're lucky, there may still be one by the time you get down there." A heavy sigh came out. "She made a cookie especially for Liam. She said he's sad."

A dark expression flickered across his face before he glanced down the hall, then back at me. "I'm so glad she has the rest of us to pick up where her parents failed her." Dante rubbed his hand up my arm before brushing a thumb over my cheek. "You headed back to your room?"

I nodded. "I need to get her down for a nap, unless you need me for something."

Dante shook his head. "Not for anything we have time for. I just wanted to see you. That's all."

He kissed my forehead, brushed a thumb over Chloe's curls. It was a completely normal moment... if you ignored the fact we were in a fortress full of secrets and loaded guns behind locked doors.

Chloe stirred, blinking up at Dante. "Dada cookie."

He smiled at her, soft as can be. "You want me to take it to him?"

"Pease."

"You got it" His attention shifted to me, and he studied my face for a moment. "You sure you're okay?"

I nodded, a wave of exhaustion flowing over me. "Yeah. Just... you know. Doing my job."

He pressed his forehead to mine. "You do it better than anyone."

And for a second, I let myself believe it.

Chapter Twenty-Three

Sabrina

The next day started cheerfully and full of promise. Some of the new toys and activities Lynette purchased had arrived, and we'd spent almost the entire morning setting up and playing with the Chloe-sized kitchen.

And then the toy tea set arrived.

One thing led to another, and suddenly we were setting up for a full-out tea party in the dining room, with Lynette *insisting* we use her china.

"What good is it to have if you never use it?"

I had no good response, so Chloe was in the kitchen with Ben making 'tea' and putting the cookies from the day before on a pretty plate.

My phone buzzed as I smoothed out the tablecloth.

Lianne: < Dante checked in - Liam is going to join the tea party. >

Lianne: < Apparently he's remembered how to use his manners. >

My eyebrows shot up as I read the message. *How did he even find out?*

"Is everything okay, my dear?"

I glanced up at Lynette, who was in the process of pulling her tea set out of the china cabinet. The woman didn't miss a thing. "We're going to have another guest at our party."

She carefully set down the teapot. "Would it happen to be my oldest son?" When I nodded, she pressed her lips into a tight line before sighing. "Well, I need to make sure I have enough cups out for everyone."

Everyone? Now it was my turn to stare at her. "Who all are you expecting now?"

Lynette chuckled. "Do you really think Lianne and Gage *aren't* going to add a few more to the guest list after Liam's name? *Especially* when the Don Supreme is going to be in our home as well?"

"No, I suppose not." I paused for a moment as I processed her words. "Wait. Don Dallas is coming?"

"Yes. Lianne has a meeting with him."

I stared at her for a moment, trying to find a professional and respectful way to relay my thoughts. "Should Liam be upstairs at all right now?"

A wry smirk appeared on her face as her gaze hardened. "And deny another Don the pleasure of seeing how low he's fallen? Or deny Liam the opportunity to make his fate better or worse? Why would I do that?"

This was the mafia-hardened side of Lynette few ever saw. The cutthroat, seasoned businesswoman who was always several steps ahead of the rest of us.

I glanced in the direction of the kitchen, where Chloe was now sitting at the table with Lukas, working on making paper crowns for the party. "I suppose I should tell the art duo the update."

"Remind my favorite son to mind his manners."

The firm tone had me standing a little taller. "Yes, ma'am."

The kitchen table was an explosion of crayons, stickers, glue, craft pom-poms, and other crafting supplies when I walked in. "What, no glitter?"

Lukas half-glared at me. "Absolutely not. The sequins are more than enough."

I smirked as I sat across from Chloe. "Isn't that a significant part of your wife's job?"

He grimaced as he went back to helping his niece with the glue. "Yes, but it doesn't mean I'm going to opt in when I don't have to."

The image of Lukas's tactical gear covered with glitter popped into my mind, and I failed to bite back a snicker. "Fair enough." I paused before delivering my mixed news. "Your mother wanted me to remind you to mind your manners."

Lukas's attention snapped back to my face, wariness flickering in his eyes. "Why?"

"Your brother is joining us for tea."

"I see." The man gritted his teeth. "How delightful."

By the time the crowns were done, Ben had delivered the food and tea to the dining room. We had just put all the crowns on the table when Lianne's voice echoed into the foyer. Chloe took off running, and I was hot on her heels.

"Li Li! Uppies!"

Lianne chuckled as she picked up her niece and gave her a big hug.

Peter and Adair were there, too, and despite the calm expression on her face, the death grip on Peter's hand gave away her nerves.

Is she in on this meeting, too?

Suddenly, Ryan rushed out of his office and hurried past us. "They're here."

My eyes went wide as I looked at Lianne. "Do I need to make ourselves scarce?"

She narrowed her eyes and shook her head. "No. They know Chloe exists."

I nodded. "But what about me?"

Lianne gave me a pointed stare. "I'm allowed to have whoever I want in my home, including you *and* the Don Supreme. You are as welcome to be in this hallway as he and whoever comes with him is. I'll make it clear your presence here is to be kept quiet."

All I had time to do was let out a tense breath as two very familiar voices echoed in the foyer behind me.

"Good morning, Don Agosti, Ms. Vaux, Ms. Pennington, Mr. Grant." Dallas's attention landed on me, and his eyebrows rising ever so slightly was the only indication of any surprise at my presence.. "Ms. Rodriguez. Glad to see you made it home safe."

I gave him a tight smile. "Glad to be home safe, sir."

He nodded and then shifted his focus to Chloe. "And who do we have here?"

She tightened her hold around Lianne's neck as uncertainty washed over her face.

Lianne smiled. "Don Dallas, Mr. Maloy, this is Chloe, my beautiful niece." That earned a grin from the little girl. "Chloe, these are some very nice men I work with."

I glanced at the two men being discussed. Nice was not the first adjective I'd use to describe them.

The little girl looked at them and then at her auntie. "We have tea now?"

Lianne kissed the side of Choe's head. "No, sweetie. They are here for a meeting with me, but I'll have tea with you after I'm done, okay?"

She looked at Dallas wide-eyed, her bottom lip sticking out a little. "No tea?"

I froze in place. This was a situation I never thought I'd see. On one hand, Dallas could absolutely dismiss and ignore Chloe, but at risk of pissing off another Don. On the other hand, Liam was going to be upstairs soon, and I had no idea what *that* interaction would look like.

Dallas stepped forward, a warm smile appearing on his face. "Could we have tea another day? Then I can bring my favorite cake and share it with you."

An enormous smile appeared on Chloe's face. "Yes, pease." She looked at me. "Tea now?"

I nodded. "Yes, we can have tea now. I think Grandma is ready for us."

Chapter Twenty-Four

Lianne

I watched until Chloe and Sabrina turned the corner before looking at Peter and Regina. "We'll see you two after." Returning my attention to Dallas and Maloy again, I glanced at the doors to the lounge. "Shall we get started?"

Dallas glanced at Maloy, gave him a curt nod, and walked into the room. I smoothed out the front of my jacket, trying not to fixate on looking perfect. I'd met with Dallas before.

It's going to be fine.

Once Adair and I were inside and the door was closed, I gestured to the leather wingback chairs. "We might as well get comfortable. Would anyone like a drink?"

Dallas barely concealed his smirk. "Tequila, if you have it."

I nodded. "Done. Adair?"

She glanced at me, a mixture of nerves and determination in her eyes. "Whatever you're having."

I grabbed three crystal short glasses and poured two fingers of tequila in each. Before turning around, I glanced up at the portrait of my dad. *I hope I'm making you proud.*

When I turned, Don Dallas was studying me. Trying not to overthink why, I handed him his drink before giving Adair hers. There was a reassuring smile on his face now as he took a sip. "You didn't have to break out the fancy stuff for me, Lianne." His chuckle was light and airy, and it put me at ease.

I tried not to snicker. "It's what Lukas left on the cart." I took a sip, settled into my chair, and let out a tense breath. "Don Dallas, would you like to start?"

"Yes, however, Ms. Vaux—"

"Please, call me Adair."

With a small nod to her, he continued. "I am sorry for your Aunt Melanie's death and the surrounding circumstances." His gaze flicked to mine before I gave him a nod. "I'm not sure how many of the details you received, but she had cancer and hid it from your Uncle Kobe."

Adair nodded as she took a sip of her drink. "Lynette gave me the rundown. I have no hard feelings toward you for how it ended. If anything, I'm grateful Mrs. Dallas could step in, giving her the ability to leave on her own terms, gently and with dignity." She let out a long sigh as she toyed with the rim of her glass. "If Uncle Kobe had found out about the cancer, he would have burned down the city. Every doctor who touched Aunt Melanie would've ended up dead."

The words hung there, heavy, and Don Dallas watched her, holding the silence for a minute before moving on. "There isn't much of the house left, I'm afraid, not that he left much of it in great condition."

Adair shrugged. "Dante and Avery apologized for their part in that. Besides, actions have consequences, especially when you attack the Don Supreme."

Don Dallas gave a nod of agreement before turning back to the matter at hand. "As I told Lianne previously, the contract is the Agosti family repaying a debt to the Vaux family, and since one of the Agosti signees broke the terms, they are still on the hook to finish repaying the debt."

Adair nodded slowly. "She and Lynette mentioned that."

"Good. The Don would normally settle this, but the next Vaux Don hasn't been formally announced yet, creating a unique situation."

She tipped her head and narrowed her eyes in confusion. "Doesn't it default to you as Don Supreme?"

Dallas shook his head. "Not with the way the contract was written. Should you accept your lineage, it actually defaults to *you*."

My eyebrows shot up as Adair stared at him, wide-eyed. "*Me*, sir?"

"Yes, you. You and Susan are the last two adult Vaux family members alive. Because you are the oldest, you are next in line to be the next Don Vaux. If you decline the title and position, it goes to your sister and then her daughter." He calmly took a sip of his tequila before leaning back in his chair and crossing his legs. "Simple line of succession."

Adair took a deep breath, let it out slowly, and then downed what was left in her glass. "Well, then." When I reached over and rubbed her shoulder, hoping to give any comfort, her attention snapped to me. "How did you know stepping up was the right thing to do?"

There's a loaded question.

I took another sip of my tequila and put down the glass. "I didn't. All I knew is there was no way I could let my mom shoulder everything alone and still be able to look at myself in the mirror. She asked me to help her, but then Liam showed up... and in that moment of wanting to shut him up, I declared myself the Agosti Don. I didn't want Mom anywhere near him... I wanted to protect her... so I put myself in the only position that could guarantee that." I paused for a moment as memories of that conversation flickered in my mind. "I didn't realize then fully what I'd done,. Mom and I had a conversation or two about it later, the entire team declared their allegiance, and here we are." It was a wildly oversimplified version of the story, but this wasn't the time or place for all the details. "At the end of the day, you have to live with your decisions. I had a bumpy start, and it's not an easy job by any stretch, but I don't regret it." *Most of the time.*

She stared at me for a while before nodding. "Self-preservation is a bitch."

A stunned chuckle popped out. "Yeah it is."

Adair sighed and shifted to face Dallas again. "I don't have a team to take over or run the Vaux territory. There's not even a compound anymore... and I doubt if there are family assets to speak of to even start the process."

He took another sip and then nodded. "You are correct. After we leveled the house, we skimmed the liquid assets from all of the accounts, both state-side and international, moving them into funds dedicated into human trafficking support groups, rescue services, and re-establishment efforts. Any continued liquid cash coming in has been funneled that way as well. There are still those loyal to the Vaux name, who continue to work the businesses and manage properties held by the family. Those profits have been held in a trust, along with the properties that were designated for you and Susan. We have not liquidated those."

Adair leaned forward, rested her elbows on her knees, and nodded. "Okay. Good to know. Could we have some of those finances go to women's shelters or women's cancer research facilities? I'd like to honor my Aunt Melanie." I could see her mentally going through the list of businesses and properties that had been left to her in the trust. "If I take on the Vaux title, I want to keep the compound property. I don't know if it will ever get used again for mafia purposes, though. Maybe I'll build a shelter on it. Or a safe haven for those in need, especially those who've suffered from domestic violence."

Pride and relief showed in Dallas's eyes. "It's yours to do with as you see fit. If that is what you want, then we will make it happen."

Adair's eyebrows crunched together as she sat up with a start. "We? You've already done so much to take care of a territory that wasn't your responsibility."

Dallas leaned forward as well, eyes sharp but tone neutral. "That is part of the responsibility of the Don Supreme. I've been taking over some of the mafia business already to keep things running smoothly. Whatever needs to change hands, we can do it. I'll turn it all back over to you whenever you're ready, zero drama, zero questions."

She leaned back in her chair, and I recognized the beginning signs of her being overwhelmed. Her eyes were tight, she had a death grip on her glass, and her jaw was clenched. "The Susan and Liam drama needs to be squared away before I make anything official."

He nodded again. "I'll keep a lid on things in the territory while the Liam and Susan situation plays out, and will continue to do so while you pull your team together. We can also arrange to assist you with any startup costs, if that is a concern."

There was a touch of guilt in the man's eyes. This was such an unprecedented situation without any pre-established protocol, and we were all doing our best.

Adair shook her head. "Respectfully, sir, I want to cover the payroll for the new people and facilities. It's the honorable thing for a Don to do, and I want to do it. Honestly, with everything my dad and uncle left me, I have more than enough capital to get things started." She breathed out, not taking her eyes off him. "You did what you had to do to Uncle Kobe, his team, and his house. I respect that. And if you truly feel inclined to help fund or support any particular project for personal or professional reasons, I won't deny a donation to the cause."

Dallas nodded once, slow and deliberate. "I can accept those terms."

She sat up a little taller, looking proud and powerful.

The Don Supreme mirrored her posture. "Are you saying what I think you are?"

Adair nodded. "Don Dallas, I'd formally like to accept the title of Don Vaux." Before either of us could offer our congratulations, she continued. "Can I submit my line of succession to you now? I know formal paperwork will have to be filed, but I want this next piece of information as official as it can be in the meantime."

His eyebrows went up slightly. "Of course."

She sat up in her chair a little taller. "I want to appoint Chloe Agosti, my official heir. If something happens to me before Chloe is eighteen, the Agostis will rule in our stead. I never want Susan to have any chance of becoming a Don."

"As you will it, Don Vaux." Dallas glanced at me. "Do you accept the terms, Don Agosti?"

My chest tightened at the horrible prospect of protecting more than one territory. *That's not happening today. Calm down.* I nodded. "Yes. I'm more than willing to assist Don Adair Vaux." I couldn't keep the grin off my face. "The second female Don of Chicago. I love this so much."

"There will be at least one more in Chicago's future. Don Rodriguez's heir *is* currently under your roof."

I chuckled. "That, she is." I'd forgotten for a moment she was next in line.

I had barely absorbed that Adair was now a Don before she finished signing a few papers Dallas pulled from a leather portfolio before moving things along. "Now that the Vaux Don has been officially established, we can move forward with the discussion on contract retribution. As you know, Don Agosti, while both families were at fault in violating terms laid out, the largest grievances were made by the Agostis, specifically Liam."

Nothing I didn't already know. Whatever was coming our way, I'd take it. It was Adair's right to call for consequences. I caught Don Dallas' eye, and gave him a brief nod before chiming in. "As part of the contract, both families were to protect the other as if they were their own. Liam attempted to murder Adair Vaux, failed to stop her sister from attempting to murder her, and even though they had failed, they still married. If you go down the list of reasons either family could call in the debt, Liam broke just about every single one like they were a to-do list."

"Don Vaux... Adair." He corrected himself when she wrinkled her nose at the formality. "What do you wish to do about these infractions?"

Adair breathed out, slow and heavy, the same way I did when the weight of responsibility was too much. She stared at the glass in her hand, teeth biting the inside of her cheek.

I wondered what retribution she would call for. Would she call for Liam's death? Would she demand our territory? There really wasn't much, if anything, *not* on the table at this point.

She looked at Don Dallas again, searching, weighing. "After Liam and Susan tried to kill me, the Agostis did everything in their power to help me recover from what should have been life-ending injuries. They hid me. Protected me. Lost two safe houses in the process. And then, when Liam used his own daughter as a pawn against the Agostis, they brought someone in from the outside to solely protect her."

This was not the way I saw the conversation going, not that I was upset by it.

It's just a list of good things we've done. But will it be enough?

"Is that why I saw Ms. Rodriguez in the hall when I came in?" Don Dallas' smile was sly and knowing as he glanced at me. I couldn't quite read the meaning behind it.

I nodded. "It is. She is currently... assisting us in keeping Chloe, the now Vaux heir, safe and happy. Mutually beneficial for both families." He didn't need to know the rest of the details.

Dallas raised one hand, as if brushing away something. "I mean no disrespect, Don Agosti. I was just surprised to see her, as last I had heard, she was on an out-of-the-country assignment."

"She was." I kept it short. Let the silence settle. Even if I did know all the details, they weren't mine to divulge. Glancing back to Adair, concern flooded me when I saw her leaning forward, eyes darting back and forth. Her mind was clearly in overdrive. I didn't rush to move on in our conversation, and Dallas waited too, pouring the last of his tequila into his mouth like he had all the time in the world.

Finally, Adair straightened. "Can I have some time to think this over? I don't want my first major decision as Don to be a knee-jerk reaction."

His mouth curled into a real smile. "Take all the time you need. This is your decision to make on your timeline." Dallas stood up and shook Adair's hand. "Welcome to the family, Don Vaux." He turned, caught my eye, shook mine as well.

We all stood, and just as I opened the door, I was met with the angry voice of my brother. The one I detested.

"Why are you taking my daughter away?"

My eyes went wide as I locked eyes with Regina and then Maloy. They were both tense, poised, and ready to jump into action. *What happened now?*

"Clearly, you did or said something that made Sabrina consider you a threat. So, as it is her job to protect her, she removed Chloe from the situation."

My focus shifted to the section of the foyer I could see from the lounge door, where I saw the back of Liam, with Lukas facing him, glaring at him.

"Chloe is my daughter. I would never do anything to hurt her. She is my legacy." Liam scoffed. "She's also the only Agosti heir, since it seems I'm the only one interested *or able* to produce one."

You absolute sack of shit. I stormed out of the lounge, very much over Liam running his mouth. "What's *that* supposed to mean?"

He jumped at my sudden appearance, but then a malicious smirk appeared on his stupid face. "With all the *issues* caused by that gunshot wound a few years ago, are you even *able* to get pregnant?"

You fucking asshole. How the fuck does he know about this?

I balled my hands up into fists and took a deep breath, letting it out slowly.

Liam glanced around the room, the smug arrogance growing as he looked at me. "Why does everyone look surprised, Lianne? Have you been keeping secrets?"

Lukas chimed in before I could form a response. "First, my sister's choice or ability to have a kid is none of your damn business, asshole. Second, while I love my niece with all my heart, there is already an Agosti heir, and it's *not* her."

I froze as my eyes met my brother's, which were full of rage.

What heir is he talking about? Neither of us have any kids.

The two brothers were locked in an intense stare-down before Liam broke the silence. "Is that so?" He looked around again. "And where is this precious heir of yours?"

Lukas shook his head. His expression was now unreadable, even to me. "As far away from you as possible."

There was no way this wasn't going to end in more bloodshed. "Dante, get him the hell out of here."

"Can't take the heat, Li?" Liam's smug expression fell as his eyes went wide and all color drained from his face. "Don Dallas."

"Liam." The man's voice came from just behind me. "I'm surprised to see you alive, though I suspect that won't be for much longer."

I locked eyes with Dante and nodded my head toward the hall leading to the basement, and the man immediately shoved Liam forward, forcing him to move.

Maloy let out a derisive chuckle after the duo passed. "Oh, how the mighty have fallen. How did you break your face, Liam? Trip and fall over your ego?"

For all the anger coursing through me, I couldn't help but smile. *Thank you.*

Mom walked out of the dining room. "Lianne, is your meeting done, or was it interrupted?"

"We finished and were heading out right as Liam was running his mouth."

She nodded and then looked past me. "Emmett, I'm happy to walk you out, unless you have more business to attend to here?"

He shook his head. "I'm finished for today. I'd be honored to walk out with you, Lynette."

As my mom passed me, she gave my shoulders a squeeze. "Take your brother to your office. More than one conversation needs to happen."

I nodded. "Yes, Momma."

I vaguely heard her conversation with Dallas and Maloy as they walked out of the house. It wasn't until Lukas grabbed my hands that I realized I was still standing in the middle of the foyer, numb and overwhelmed. "Li?"

His touch snapped me back to the present. "Right. My office." Without waiting, I turned on my heel, half-dragging my brother with me as I walked. We were barely inside my office when I slammed the door shut and gave Lukas a hard shove. "What heir were you fucking talking about? I'm not pregnant! You would have fucking known if I was!"

If I even can. Fucking Liam!

"Think about it, Li." There was sorrow and apprehension in my brother's blue-grey eyes... and excitement?

It finally clicked. "Wait... Is Quinn pregnant?" He nodded as a proud smile appeared on his face. My brother was positively beaming now, and I pulled him in for a tight hug. Tears pricked the corners of my eyes as excitement chased my rage and hurt away. "I'm going to be an auntie again?"

There was a knock at the door. "It's me."

I smiled at hearing my sister-in-law's voice. "Come in."

Quinn's blue eyes were wide and filled with worry as she stepped into the room. "Is everything okay?"

Ryan and Regina were behind her, still in the hallway. They both looked concerned, not that I was surprised. "Ryan, get in here. Regina, can you get Ben for me?" When she stepped away and Ryan walked in, closing the door behind him, I returned my attention to Quinn and I nodded. "As much as it can be. Are *you* okay? How are you feeling?"

Quin blinked and then stared at me in confusion. "Fine. Why? What's going on?"

Lukas wrapped his arm around her shoulders and kissed the side of her head. "Cat's out of the bag, gorgeous. Lianne knows."

She let out a nervous laugh. "I'm not upset, but I *am* a bit surprised. *How* did this slip out exactly?"

Lukas let out a deep sigh. "Liam was running his mouth about heirs and the family legacy, and I had to shut him up."

Ryan crossed his arms over his chest and gave his best friend a curious look. "Not that I blame you, but it's not like you to drag your personal life into business."

My brother let out a deep sigh as he rubbed his face with his hand. "Yeah… I know. But when he attacked Li like that, rational thought left the building."

We stood there in silence for a moment.

"Lianne, what is Lukas talking about?" Quinn's question was hesitant, and I didn't blame her.

She doesn't know.

Most people didn't. It wasn't information I gave out freely. There wasn't a need to. Until today.

My office door flew open as Ben ran in and immediately wrapped me in a tight hug. "I'm so sorry, Li."

"Me too." I blinked back tears and swallowed down my emotions as I leaned into my husband's chest. I would have a good cry about this… again. But it had to wait. I needed to finish this conversation first. Leaning back, I nodded at Ben, mouthing the word 'later' before looking at Quinn again. "Several years ago on my birthday, there was a shootout in the parking lot as we left a restaurant. I caught a bullet in the side, and despite amazing medical care, there was quite a bit of damage, resulting in a lot of scar tissue. While I *should* be able to get pregnant, the likelihood of complications is high." I squeezed Ben's hand and took a deep breath, letting it out slowly.

There were tears in Quinn's eyes. "Lianne, I… I'm so sorry. I would have never—"

I surged forward and hugged her. "Please don't apologize. I am so fucking excited you are pregnant."

"Really?"

Leaning back, I nodded. "Absolutely. You are going to be such an amazing mom."

The tears in her eyes spilled over. "You want to know the best and most exciting part?"

"Yes!"

She grinned and looked at Lukas. "You want to tell her?"

"Tell Lianne what?"

I snickered as Mom breezed into the room.

Lukas's eyes glistened with more excited tears. "We're going to have twins."

Chapter Twenty-Five

Lianne

"Twins?" My eyes went wide with joy and excitement as I hugged them both tight. "Holy crap, now we really need to celebrate."

Lukas and Quinn's stunned expressions were almost comical. "What?"

"After all that bullshit, we need some joy in our lives. And this is definitely a joyful moment." I reached forward and took Quinn's free hand in mine. "Can we celebrate the babies? Please?"

She wrinkled her nose as her smile widened. "I would love nothing more than to tell everyone. Lukas and I were trying to figure out when to say something, but it never felt right... not with everything that kept popping up."

"I still have extra cookies from the tea party. It would be a shame for them to go to waste."

Mom chuckled as she looked at the man now holding me. "Ben, my dear, if you think for one second any of your delicious baking would go to waste in this house, you are sorely mistaken."

"I suppose you're right." He grinned and then looked at Quinn. "How are you feeling? Do you want any of your mint tea?"

She shook her head, but there was a smile on her face. "No, but everyone might have to fight me for the cookies. I'm so freaking hungry right now."

"There's been enough fighting. I'll happily hand you the cookie first."

Love and pride filled my heart as Ben, Mom, Lukas, and Quinn headed out of my office, leaving me and Ryan alone... until Regina walked in. She tilted her head to the side as she studied my face. "How you doing, boss?"

I chuckled. "Better than before. Thanks for getting Ben so quickly."

Regina nodded, smiling softly, understanding in her eyes. "It's who you needed." Nervousness flickered across her face as she glanced at Ryan and then me. "Who all knew about your... medical situation before Liam ran his mouth?"

A deep sigh came out as I sat on the front edge of my desk. "Mom, Ben, Lukas, Doc, and you."

Ryan shifted his weight from one foot to the other. "I want to be upset, but I get it. We all downplay our wounds."

"Well-spoken from the man who also likes to brush off *his* gunshot wound." I gave him a playful glare and then shrugged. "It's not that I was keeping it from you... or anyone... it's just that there was nothing to tell. There still isn't a reason for anyone to know. It's not a problem... yet. And the potential problem isn't life-threatening. I may or may not have issues having kids. If that's the worst thing to happen after being able to walk away from a gunshot wound, I'm doing a lot better than most people."

Silence hung heavy in the room as my thoughts went to my dad. The one who hadn't been able to walk away from his injuries. *All because of him.*

Ryan bumped his shoulder against mine as he stood next to me. "Don't get stuck in the past, Li. We owe it to the dead to live as fully as possible."

A sad smile crept onto my face as I nodded. I wasn't the only one who had lost someone. "You're right. Let's go celebrate life."

"Before we do, there's one more thing we need to discuss."

The sudden shift in Ryan's demeanor and tone had me on edge again. "What?"

He nodded toward my hip. "Check your phone."

I pulled it from my pocket, and my eyes went wide when I looked at the screen and saw two missed calls and a voicemail from Susan. "What the hell?"

Ryan let out a tense breath. "Yeah. I got a notification when she called you."

Of course you did. Honestly, I was grateful he knew. "Should we pull my mom and Gage in to listen to it?"

"I'd hold off on that for now."

My attention shifted from my phone to Regina. "Why is that?"

She glanced over her shoulder and then back at me. "Respectfully, I don't think I've seen her this happy... maybe ever. I think you should listen to it now before pulling her away from celebrating her future grandbabies. She needs to know, but it might not be a *right now* thing, if that makes sense."

"It does." The woman wasn't wrong. "Okay. We listen and then decide when to tell Mom." I pulled up the voicemail and played it, making sure it was on speakerphone.

"You are ruining everything Liam and I worked so hard to create. Stop playing pretend in your dad's office. Someone's going to get hurt... or worse."

Susan's bitter, grating voice made me roll my eyes. "Oh, look. More vague threats. I'm terrified." I looked up at Ryan, who was glaring at my phone. "Does Susan even have the manpower to back up any of this? Considering everything she's lost in the past month?"

He shrugged. "No clue, but we both know the more desperate a person is, the more wild and unpredictable they become."

"Fair." I glanced down at my phone again, knowing I couldn't just blow off my insane sister-in-law. "Now what?"

Ryan cleared his throat. "Now you let your team look into this and take a few minutes to celebrate with your family."

A smirk tugged at the corner of my mouth at the suggestion, and the smile widened when I clocked Regina nodding in agreement. "I suppose celebrating wouldn't be the worst way to take a break. You two should join me." Chuckling, I walked out of my office, pleased to hear two sets of soft footsteps following.

As I went to turn into the main hall leading to the foyer, I smiled at the sight of Peter and Adair walking toward us, hand in hand. After so much death and destruction in her life, the fact that she found the strength and bravery to open her heart to happiness again impressed me beyond everything. When she looked over and our eyes met, I couldn't help but chuckle again. "Who would have ever guessed you and I would be Dons... and at the same time?"

Adair shook her head. "I would have lost that bet, and soundly." She let out a tense breath as she stopped in front of me. "I'm still stunned... and overwhelmed by everything that's happened in the past month."

I gave her a sympathetic smile. "I know the feeling. Just remember, you don't have to figure it all out in one day."

"I know. I'm eternally grateful for that. It's a lot to digest." She looked past me, in the direction of the foyer living room where we could hear many excited voices, and narrowed her eyes curiously. "What's going on in there?"

My smile widened. "Something amazing. I'll let Lukas tell you."

My brother met us in the middle of the foyer, pulling Adair in for a hug. "*There* you are! I was wondering where you went after Dallas and Maloy left."

This is too perfect. I smirked. "Careful, that's a Don you're manhandling."

His eyes went comically wide as he looked between the two of us. "I'm sorry, *what*?"

You're not the only one with exciting news today.

Adair let out a nervous laugh and nodded. "Yeah... I got a new title... promotion... job... thing during the meeting."

He shot me a confused look, and I couldn't contain my amusement and pride as I nodded. "It is my honor to be the first to introduce the newest Don Vaux."

"I... Wow." Lukas blinked several times as he stared at her. "Congratulations, Adair."

She let out a deep, nervous-sounding sigh. "Thanks."

Ben clapped Peter on the shoulder, also shaking his head in disbelief as he took it all in. "As a fellow partner of a don, I feel like I need to take you under my wing like Lynette did for me." He let out a low laugh as his attention flicked to my brother for a second. "You technically outrank Lukas now... well, sort of. And not that it's the reason you should, but put a ring on it and you *definitely* will."

Adair's face went white and then pink as a dozen emotions flickered across it, the last being panic "Oh, my God. *Nothing* is changing right now. I took the title so Susan couldn't. Okay? I still need to figure out how I want to settle the contract, then deal with my sister, and *then* I have to figure out teams and crews and all that other Don stuff. I can only handle so many life-changing events right now, and I think I'm well over my quota for the year."

I feel that in the depths of my soul. My thoughts then shifted to Liam, his wife, and the damn voicemail she left for me. "Speaking of things that need handling. I should probably head downstairs." I smirked as I looked at Adair. "You have the energy and desire to potentially ruin someone's day?"

She furrowed her brow. "Who?"

I smirked. "A power-hungry pain in the ass."

Suddenly, her smile matched mine. "You know, I think I do."

Dante

Avery and I handcuffed Liam to the interrogation table before stepping outside the room for a moment. *This man must seriously have a death wish with the way he runs his damn mouth.* A deep sigh came out as I shook my head. “Liam making himself look like an ass in front of Don Dallas and Maloy was not something I expected to happen today.”

Avery snickered and shook her head. “Right? He couldn’t even play nice long enough to enjoy a tea party with his daughter. And then he had to shit-talk Lianne on top of it?” She leaned against the wall, crossing her arms over her chest. “I don’t know if I’ll ever understand that man.”

I glanced over at her, a little surprised. “Do you *want* to?”

She shrugged. “What can I say? Idiots fascinate me.”

There were few things my friend and co-worker liked more than getting information. “Speaking of idiots, I’m surprised Susan hasn’t done anything. We’ve had her husband and daughter here for several days now. You think she would have contacted someone here by now.”

“Right?” Avery let out a sigh. “I mean, she *could* have reached out, and we just haven't been told about it.” She narrowed her eyes at me. “Who has Liam’s phone?”

“I think Gage does. Why?”

She scowled. “Damn. I was hoping Ryan had it. While both men are vaults, I had a better chance of getting any morsel of information out of him.”

A chuckle came out. “You were going to utilize Ellen, weren’t you?”

Her shoulders raised slightly as she shrugged. “I learned long ago more than knives make people spill their guts.”

"Fair." We stood in silence for a moment before I looked at her again. “What do you think Lukas was talking about with the whole heir thing?”

Avery pursed her lips for a moment as she tilted her head to the side. "He could have been calling Liam's bluff or announcing that either Quinn or Lianne are pregnant. Time will tell." Voices echoed in the hall, and her eyebrows went up as she glanced to the right. "Incoming boss and entourage. Lianne looks way happier than earlier. Almost *too* happy, but not in a good way."

I looked over, confirming the too-wide smile on my boss's face. "That might be as scary as when she got in Liam's face after Ben beat the shit out of him."

Avery cleared her throat as she pushed herself off the wall. "How was your meeting with the Don Supreme? Were you able to get answers?"

Lianne nodded. "Don Dallas was most helpful. While we found solutions to several problems, there are still more details that need ironing out. I *cannot wait* to tell Liam."

The overly cheerful tone was a little off-putting and set me on edge. There was way more to this than she was letting on.

Lianne looked at Adair and Peter. "Would you initially like to watch from the observation side? You can decide if or when you want to join me."

Adair nodded. "Sounds perfect."

Once they were inside, Lianne looked at me and gestured to the door. "Shall we?"

Jumping into action, I pulled it open. Avery walked in first, immediately followed by Lianne.

"Just the asshole I wanted to see."

Liam narrowed his eyes at her warily. "Come to slap my hand for being honest with the family?"

She shook her head. "No. The fact that you intimidated more than one medical professional into violating HIPAA laws is the *least* of your concerns right now."

Arrogance now graced his features. "Then why are you down here, *Don Agosti*?"

The sarcastic and disrespectful tone somehow made her smile more. "Well, *Mr. Agosti*, I thought you'd be curious about the results from my meeting with the Don Supreme... and how I met the new Vaux Don today." Her grin turned malevolent and sent chills down my spine. "It was an absolutely *delightful* meeting."

Liam leaned forward, eyes wide, mouth agape. "What? How is there a Vaux Don? They're all dead."

"Are they, though?" Lianne stared at him long enough that even I began to feel awkward. "Aren't you *married* to a Vaux?"

His face paled slightly. "No... It... It can't be."

"*What* can't be, sweetie?"

Lianne never took her eyes off Liam as horror spread across his face. I was doing my best to school my own expression. While I had no idea who Don Dallas would approve of taking over the Vaux territory, or if Lianne was bluffing, I fully supported her making him squirm.

Liam shook his head again. "There's no way... but he... and she said..."

Lianne arched an eyebrow and cocked her head slightly to the side. "Who said *what*, dear brother? If it's your wife you're worried about, Susan is *not* the new Don. She did, however, leave me a heartwarming voicemail. Well, if you call vague threats and whining heartwarming."

His eyes went wide, hope and fear flickering in them. "She called?"

"Yeah. Just a little bit ago." My boss nodded. "Curious, though. Your wife seemed more concerned about my actions than the well-being of her husband *and* her daughter." Lianne tapped her chin and tilted her head to the side. "It's like she doesn't even care that you're gone. That's got to suck."

He swallowed hard as his attention dropped to the table in front of him. I didn't miss the measured breathing, as if he was desperately trying to keep calm. *Why now, though?* We all stood there in silence until Lianne cleared her throat, regaining Liam's attention.

"While I'm in here, would you like to meet the new Don? I'd be more than happy to arrange an introduction. I'm sure they'd be interested in talking to you, especially with whom you're married to."

He took a deep breath before giving his sister a pointed look. "I would like to meet them. Maybe *they'll* hear me out, unlike *other* Dons."

Shit. Your almost three-year-old daughter whines less than you do.

Avery snickered. "Unlikely, but you keep dreaming, Liam. One day you might actually wake up from the land of delulu."

I shook my head, hiding my amusement.

Lianne's expression never wavered as she tipped her head up ever so slightly and glanced up at where I knew a microphone was. "Don Vaux, if you want to meet with this arrogant piece of shit, you're welcome to join us."

Liam's eyes went wide as he sat tall in his chair. "He's here?"

Arching her eyebrow, Lianne shot an annoyed glare at him. "Obviously. We still have unfinished business to discuss."

There was a knock on the door, and Peter poked his head in, a serious expression on his face. "Don Vaux says they would like to join you."

"Excellent. Let them in."

He pushed the heavy door open the rest of the way, and I almost missed Liam's reaction as none other than Adair Vaux walked into the room.

What?

There was a smug smirk on her face as she stared at him. "Hello, Liam."

"No. There's no way *you're* the new Don Vaux."

Adair opened the folder in her hands and pulled out one of the documents she and Dallas had signed earlier. "But you see, I have official paperwork stating just that."

Liam's face went pale before his cheeks went red. "No. No, this isn't happening."

She let out an annoyed-sounding sigh. "But it has, and once again, thanks to the actions of you and your wife, Don Agosti and I have more work to do." Adair shook her head. "Enjoy the time you have left while I figure out what retribution I'll require to resolve all the violations you made regarding a certain blood debt contract." Without waiting for a response, she turned and left the room, with Lianne right behind her.

Chapter Twenty-Six

Sabrina

I gathered up the coloring books and crayons, listening as Lukas kept making Chloe giggle with the silly voice he used while reading. Quinn was there as well, making two of the stuffed animals act like they were also listening to the story, but mostly making them hop up all over Lukas and Chloe. The heart-warming moment between a niece and her uncle almost brought tears to my eyes. It was so much like my early childhood, and despite the circumstances that brought Chloe here, I loved that she could have moments like this with her aunts and uncles.

Once Lukas finished the book, he turned toward me, face hopeful. "So, the weather's actually nice today. Would you be okay if we took Chloe for the afternoon? Let her get out for a bit and maybe run around at the playground."

I paused and gave him a sly grin as I put the coloring supplies into their bin. "You two practicing for the twins already?"

Quinn didn't even hesitate, even going so far as to match my sass. "Is that such a terrible thing?" She glanced at Lukas. "Hey, do you think Adair could come too? She'd probably love to spend time with Chloe."

Lukas nodded, but then sadness flickered in his eyes. "Maybe. I wish I could pull Lianne out of the house for a bit, too." He checked his phone and then smirked.

Before I could ask him about it, there was a knock at the door before it opened, revealing Connor, smiling widely. "Excuse me, but Don Rodriguez is downstairs with Ms. Lupe Rodriguez, and they are wondering if Sabrina is available for visitors."

My body went still as my heart raced with hope and excitement. "My mama's here?"

Connor's grin grew broader as he nodded. "She brought a surprise for you, too."

As I turned toward Lukas again, he waved me off. "Go. Chloe's more than safe with us."

I barely missed crashing into Connor as I rushed out of the room and bolted for the stairs. My heart leaped with every step, and it was a miracle mixed with all my training that kept me from falling down the stairs I landed on the main floor with a loud thump, the impact jolting my knees. In the foyer, Mom stood with Uncle Ceaser, embracing Dante. For a second, time stopped as joy filled every ounce of me. *She's really here.* As Dante stepped aside, I ran forward and nearly knocked her over with the force of my hug. "I missed you, Mama."

"Missed you too, *Mija*." Her breathing hitched as she held me tight, and I had flashbacks of times as a child. It was the same reaction after I'd been away for even a day or two spending time with Uncle Ceaser or *Abuelita* and *Abuelo*.

I didn't let go, even when Dante and Ceaser exchanged greetings behind us, both of them laughing like old friends. I finally had my mama again. She was the only one I'd missed more than Dante. Inhaling deeply, I expected to smell her favorite floral perfume, but instead I was met with fried dough, well-seasoned beef, garlic and onions. *What?* I looked around and saw Zee standing near the door, smiling, tears in their eyes, holding a tray of empanadas that glistened under the plastic wrap. *No. Way!*

"You brought Zee *and* empanadas?" Pulling back from my mom, the joy all over her face was radiant.

She took my face in her hands and kissed my forehead. "You are my one and only brilliant and amazing daughter, and you thought I *wasn't* going to bring your favorite food?"

"I love you so much!" In a flash, I turned and pointed a finger at Dante, barely able to keep a straight face. "You *cannot* and *will not* eat them all. I don't care how much I love you."

Dante snorted. "I have manners. I also know it's in my best interest to let you have one or two first."

Rolling my eyes, I hugged Uncle Ceaser, once again grateful for everything he'd done for me. "Thank you, *Tio*."

A pleased hum resonated in his chest. "Anything for you, *Mija*."

Lynette's voice echoed in the foyer. "I thought I heard trouble out here."

"Lynette, you've been trouble since the day you met George."

I turned in time to see her arch an eyebrow and give my uncle a pointed look. Anyone else making that comment would have been knocked onto their ass. The sharp expression quickly dissolved into a grin and low chuckle. "Oh, I was trouble *long* before then, my friend. I'm *still* not entirely sure my George knew what he was getting into with me."

My uncle smiled proudly. "He got one hell of an amazing woman, I can tell you that."

"I second that, respectfully, ma'am."

Lynette nodded at Dante's comment before smiling at me. "Thank you both very much. Now, how about we head into the kitchen and at least *pretend* we're going to be civilized with this tray of empanadas?"

Once we'd filed into the kitchen and Zee set the food on the counter, my mom gave everyone a hard look. "I don't care if you're a Don, second to a Don, or dating my daughter, Sabrina has been away for two years and gets first crack at what I fried up today."

Dante nodded solemnly, as did my uncle. It was entertaining as hell to see those two put in their place. Lynette just grinned, and I didn't miss the glimmer of amusement in her eyes. She was loving this as much as I was.

I immediately pulled the plastic away and grabbed an empanada, letting out a moan of delight after the first bite. It was everything I'd been missing and more. It was perfect.

It was then the woman glanced at the far wall where Zee was hovering. "You're joining us for at least one, yes?"

They paused for a moment, but then nodded. "I would be honored."

I rolled my eyes before gesturing for them to join me. "You pulled shrapnel out of me, stitched me up, and dealt with my whining. You've more than earned an empanada."

Zee shook their head, chuckling. "I won't argue with that logic."

There was a sudden stillness in the room, and I noticed the wide-eyed stares Mama and Dante were giving me. "What?"

"Shrapnel, Kitten?"

Why does he look so shocked? Ignoring Dante's use of his nickname for me, I looked at my uncle, wide-eyed. "You never told them?"

He stared at me, his expression cool and unreadable. "I had to keep you safe."

"And not telling them I got hurt was going to accomplish this, *how*, exactly?"

"We knew you got hurt, *Mija*, just none of the details." My mama let out a tense breath and grabbed Uncle Ceaser by the ear. "Don or not, she's my daughter. You should have told me she'd been shot." All he did was give her a curt nod, and she released him.

Lynette cleared her throat and moved on to another conversation topic. "So, Ceasar, how is Callie doing?"

My eyebrows pinched together as I ran through the list of people my uncle employed. There was no one with that name. I gave him a pointed look. "Who's Callie?"

"Ceaser Alejandro Hernandez Rodriguez." My eyes went wide at my mama's stern voice. *Holy shit. She pulled out the full name.* "You haven't told Sabrina, your niece and *heir*, about Callie?"

He shook his head, suddenly looking nervous. An expression I was *not* used to seeing on his face. "There hasn't been time to get into that." My uncle shifted in his seat and then looked at me. "I met Callie Dawson while helping Emmett with a Vaux problem a few months ago. She was in a shipping container on the docks. We are still dealing with some of *that* drama as well as the *La Muerta Rubí* issue. She's..." He ran his hand through his dark hair with silver at the temples. "Important."

My gaze met Dante's, who had a knowing glint in his eyes, and I nodded as I looked at my uncle again, a smirk tugging at my lips. We knew what that meant. "I can't wait to meet the woman who thawed your heart, *Tio*."

He glared at me, but there was no heat behind it. If anything, there was an excited sparkle I hadn't seen there in a very long time. It brought me joy seeing it.

"Speaking of thawed hearts." Mama shifted her attention and fixed a shrewd look on Dante. "When are you going to make an honest woman of my daughter?"

I tried to swallow, but ended up inhaling and half-choking on my own saliva. "Mama! I haven't even been back for a week!"

She arched an eyebrow; her knowing brown eyes pinning me where I sat. "And?"

It took most of my training to keep my jaw from dropping and my temper in check. Mama was one of two, maybe three people who could throw that attitude without consequence.

Dante set his glass down and let out a tense breath. "With all due respect, ma'am, she's been back five days, and I've maybe seen her for twenty-four hours total."

I forced in a calming breath as Lynette and Ceaser exchanged smirks while Dante and my mom stared each other down. And then my Auntie 'Nette, ever the peacemaker, stepped in. "Lupe, as much as we can't wait for their marriage, it's true, they've barely had a moment together."

Mama nodded, like she already knew what the answer would be, and then raised both eyebrows, giving Dante a pointed look. It was one I recognized. She wanted an answer to an unasked question. *But what?*

He gave a little shake of his head, something tightening in his expression. "I'm working on it, but things have been... busy around here."

Her focus and expression didn't budge. "Too busy to marry the love of your life?"

Dante didn't crack, either. "Did you miss the part where I've also not seen her for two years and have barely had a moment alone with her since she literally appeared out of thin air a few days ago? It will happen. I promise."

For a heartbeat, everything hung suspended as my mama and the man I loved stared at each other. The moment was bright with possibility mixed with a little bit of chaos. I wasn't sure if I wanted to laugh or hide, but as much as I hated the unpredictability of this conversation, I didn't want it to end. Dante was right. Busy was not the right word for what was going on here, but it was good enough for the discussion.

As quickly as my mom had gone sharp to extract her answers, she relaxed, leaning against the back of the chair, and glanced at Lynette. "I think we could use some tequila after all that, don't you?"

My honorary aunt chuckled and nodded. "Absolutely. Do you want the pretense of tea, or are we just diving in?"

"Why dilute it if it's good?"

Lynette made short work of pouring everyone a drink, and once the conversation turned to Quinn and Lukas, Ceaser caught my gaze and gave a tiny, precise jerk of his head. It was a silent order as clear as any barked command: up, now, and follow. His body language had very much shifted from a relaxed uncle spending a casual afternoon with the family to a sharp and lethal Don. I stood and obeyed, feeling the eyes of the room follow me.

Ceaser led me out of the kitchen into the dining room, walking all the way up to the french doors at the end. His back was to the foyer, and I leaned against the doorjamb. For a moment, neither of us spoke. He studied me with a predator's patience, eyes narrowed, hands clasped thoughtfully behind his back.

I braced myself, let my posture go military for a second to reflect his, but then softened it. "What's going on?"

He inhaled, dragging his gaze away from me to the glass panes in the door as a deep sigh came out. "We need to talk Rodriguez business. Specifically, your safety." He glanced back, and for a fleeting instant, I saw something like regret. "I know you hate being handled, but you know why you're here."

I nodded. "Aside from helping out Lynette, there aren't many places safer than this house."

Ceaser continued to study me. "Do you feel safe even with Liam here?"

"Liam isn't a threat to me." A small smirk tugged at the corner of my mouth. "He doesn't seem to like that I have authority over his daughter, but he's no threat. If he goes after anyone, I won't be the first person."

"Good." His voice dropped, not in volume, but in intensity. "*La Muerta Rubí* has been relatively quiet... aside from moving more men to the States, mostly in Florida. As far as I can tell, Chicago's not on their itinerary. Yet."

I waited, letting the silence stretch, because that was how Uncle Ceaser worked. He let the other person fill the gap, then pounced on what they revealed. But I'd learned that lesson already, so I just stared back and waited him out.

He relented first, but only a bit. "You know what bothers me about holes in coverage? It means somebody's paying for silence.

Part of me is still used to the old way—guns, threats, the occasional dead canary in a mailbox. But business isn't done the old way anymore. These people have money, leverage, entire networks of people and computers built for a single purpose: to make us think we're safe. Until we're not."

I felt a chill chase up my spine, but I didn't let it show. "You think they're building something here?"

He gave a short laugh, brittle and cold. "They could be, and if they are, you'll be the first target." He paused. "I don't say that to scare you. I say it because you need to know."

I nodded, absorbing it. "Do I need to lock down even more?"

"No. No. You should get out. Go on dates with Dante, take Chloe to the park, whatever Don Agosti and her team approve, just be diligent and safe about it. Make sure you guys have coverage. In any super public place, I want Zee with you."

That surprised me a little, but I didn't comment on it. "Noted. Will you clear that with Lianne and Lynette?"

"I'll make sure they are both aware."

Going for forgiveness and not permission, I see. Perks of being best friends with another Mafia family. I cleared my throat. "How are things in Argentina?"

His hard expression thawed a little. "Better than expected. Crops are secured. Only one incident—a brush with someone trying for the opium shipment." He let the words hang, testing me. I didn't bite. "You put in good work. I'm sorry it dragged out and kept you away from Dante for so long. It was never supposed to be two years."

I shrugged. "The job takes as long as it needs to."

He looked away, lips pressed into a tight line. "I mean it. Two years was a lot. For all of us." For the first time in my life, he seemed less than invincible—a man who truly felt responsible for what happened to the people he cared about. I hadn't seen this kind of vulnerability since my aunt died.

He gestured vaguely toward my shoulder. "How're you healing up?"

"Fine." I meant it, too. "Still get the occasional twinge. Mostly just working up to full strength again."

His smile was quick and wry. "You've been back on the range?"

"Not yet. A certain assignment has taken precedence."

Uncle Ceaser didn't seem to like that answer as he clenched his jaw. "I'll talk to Lynette and see what can be arranged." He reached out, clapped my shoulder, then hesitated and squeezed for a second, before withdrawing. "I'm proud of you."

I nodded. I knew my uncle was, but this was coming from my Don. "Thanks."

Uncle Ceaser had my best interests in mind and tried with everything he had to balance that with the best interests of the family. After giving me a hug, we headed back to the kitchen, where Mama and Lynette sat laughing about something. Zee was posted in the doorway, facing the foyer, and stood a little taller as we approached them.

He nodded toward me. "Keep tabs on her. If she leaves the compound, you're with her."

Zee glanced between us. "You got it, sir. I'll take the bullet for her if needed."

"You better not have to." Uncle Ceaser tensed slightly before passing them.

The second I entered, Mom opened her arms and patted the open seat next to her. I didn't hesitate and snuggled up against her side, head on her shoulder like I used to do when I was ten and the world was simple. She kissed the top of my head, and I let myself melt into her.

Lynette steered the conversation to one of Uncle Ceasar's recent trips, and he gave us the sanitized version without blood or bullet holes. But he let enough of the edge slip through that I could tell there was more to the story than he was letting on. She then started telling a story about the last time Ben cooked for the house and prepared that five-course meal that had everyone fighting over seconds.

"There were so many of us sneaking into the main kitchen in the middle of the night for leftovers. It was *that* good." Dante nodded when I gave him a curious look. "Seriously, Ben is a goddamn wizard in the kitchen. I'm convinced he could make cardboard taste like filet mignon."

"He really is something," Lynette said, pride evident in her voice. "The Agosti kitchen is his domain. You should see what he can bake when he's excited and not stressed out. Masterpieces!"

I'd spent two years thinking about this. About coming home. About sitting here with the people I loved, about hearing their voices and feeling their arms around me. I'd tried to forget how much I missed it, because the missing had been a hollow, gnawing ache that made everything harder. But now, right now, there was no ache. Just joy. I never wanted the moment to end.

Mom stroked my hair for a long time as the conversation drifted, and I let it wash over me as I relaxed at her touch, only catching bits and pieces.

Dante was silent, but his presence filled the room. I felt it. Every so often, my eyes would find his, and we'd hold the gaze that both said nothing and everything about how much we meant to each other. I wanted to move across the room and crawl into his lap, but I could wait. This was enough.

At one point, Mama whispered, "You love him, don't you?" Her breath was warm against my ear.

I nodded, not bothering to try denying it. "With everything I have."

She hugged me tighter, and I wondered if she was going to start crying. She didn't. She was strong, always.

Eventually, Lynette and Uncle Ceaser drifted out, and Mom and I sat there in silence, my head on her shoulder, her hands running over my scalp. Dante watched us from his chair, one arm thrown over the back of another one, eyes so dark and steady it made my chest ache.

I closed my eyes, just soaking it all in until my mom nudged my shoulder gently. "*Mija*. Are you still hungry?"

I groaned as I sat up and rubbed my eyes. "For your food? Always."

She nudged me again. "Go get your boyfriend and have some more to eat. I don't like how thin you've gotten."

I didn't want to move, but the promise of more of my mama's cooking and the chance to be alone with Dante, even for five minutes, was enough to get me moving. I stood, stretched, and glanced over to where he was now standing, talking to Zee.

They slid the tray my way as I walked up to the kitchen island and winked. "Didn't eat them all. See? I can be responsible."

I snorted, grabbed two, and shoved a bite in my mouth before I even sat down. The flavor hit me so hard I nearly moaned again. "God, these are so good. I love when Mom puts extra garlic in the filling."

Dante sat down next to me, so close our knees touched. He watched me eat for a moment, eyes dark and focused.

"You're staring," I mumbled, mouth full.

He shrugged. "You're beautiful when you're happy. Not to mention, you're making sounds usually only I can pull out of you."

The words went straight to my core. I stared at him, torn between wanting to glare at him for saying something that scandalous outside of our bedroom and trying to figure out how I got so fucking lucky. "You're such a sap."

I watched as his demeanor shifted from 'work Dante' to my Wolf as he leaned in, voice low. "And you're the only one who gets to see it."

My heart skipped a beat at the intensity of his stare. I wanted to kiss him right here, but I forced myself to take another bite instead.

"If you keep looking at me like that, I'm going to do something regrettable in front of the empanadas."

He smirked. "Promise?"

I shoved him, but he didn't budge. "Asshole."

But he smiled for real now, and the way he looked at me was like I was the only thing in the world that mattered. Zee rolled their eyes, muttering something about us getting a room. I flipped them off, but they grinned and walked in the same direction Mama had gone. Dante and I ate in silence for a bit, just the two of us at the island. Every bite was like a piece of home I didn't know I'd been missing.

He finished his empanada and leaned back, eyes never leaving my face. "You really okay? After all that?"

I knew what he meant. Cuba. The shootings. The separation. All of it. We still hadn't taken the time to get into *that* particular discussion.

I nodded. "Yeah. Honestly, right now, this is all I ever wanted. Hell, dreaming about this moment is what got me through some tough days."

He reached over, took my hand, and squeezed. "I hated being apart from you."

My chest went tight at the declaration. For a second, I thought I was going to cry, but I fought it back. "Me too. But I'm here now."

He kissed my knuckles so softly it made my skin tingle. "And you're not going anywhere."

There was promise in his voice, and it sent a jolt through me.

"I love you," I said, barely more than a whisper. I didn't care if Zee or anyone else heard. I wanted it out there, in the air between us.

"I love you, too."

There was so much emotion in the room, I almost couldn't breathe. I wanted, no, *needed* to touch him. To have him. So, I leaned in and kissed him.

Chapter Twenty-Seven

Sabrina

I'd been here almost a week, and while the adrenaline from the unexpected re-entry into my old life, the start of a new and wildly different assignment, and living in another Don's home was coming down, I didn't know if I was ever going to get used to living under the same roof as Dante.

We were settling into a routine, but I still felt a certain level of restlessness living so close to him, yet not being able to spend a lot of time with him. I craved him, the heat of his hand at the small of my back, the certainty of his presence, the way my heart skipped a beat and then calmed at hearing his voice. But there hadn't been time for us, and it left me with a deep ache that affected every other sensation. In some ways, it was almost worse than when I'd been hidden away in Cuba.

I couldn't let it show, especially with Chloe constantly in tow. The child was a perfect little sensor, picking up on the tiniest changes in mood in the adults above her. More than once I noticed how she shrank away if someone came off angry, and I only ever wanted to feel like a safe place to her.

From the minute she woke up until she fell asleep, Chloe was my little shadow, never wanting to leave my side, and today was no exception. We were alone in her room upstairs. I'd bribed her with juice and cartoons, and for a brief, golden ten minutes, she was snuggled in my lap, sitting still.

My phone vibrated on the dresser, and the illusion of peace shattered when I checked the screen, surprised to see Lianne's name on it.

Why is she calling me? She always texts.

I took it on the third ring.

"Sabrina, please keep Chloe upstairs for a while. In the room. I... We need her out of sight."

My eyes went wide. "Of course. She's watching one of her favorite shows right now. The letter of the day is E, by the way."

Lianne let out a weak chuckle. "Okay, and thanks."

The call ended, and I let out a sigh. While I wanted to know more, it was above my pay grade for the moment. Lianne clearly wanted her niece safely tucked away from the rooms downstairs, a conversation, or some kind of evidence of what we all were and what we all did for a living. I respected that she wanted to protect her niece from the world as much as possible.

So I did.

She watched me as I put down my phone, head tilted, like she could see every concern on my face. "Li Li sad?"

I swallowed. "I don't know if Auntie Li is sad."

Chloe narrowed her eyes and stared at me for a moment before standing up. "I hug Li Li."

Shaking my head, I gave her a hug. "In a bit, sweetheart. She's busy right now. That's why she called me."

"Hug her now!" Chloe was insistent.

A deep sigh came out as I maintained my calm demeanor. "No, we have to wait."

She glared at me in all her pint-sized fury, arms crossed. Chloe was impossible to reason with, even more so than some of the cartel people I'd dealt with. Sometimes I wondered if she'd inherited the stubborn gene straight from Liam. Needing to stop the impending tantrum before it blew up, I went straight to suggesting her favorite distraction, pointing to the corner where her stuffed animals were stacked.

"How about a tea party? We can have cookies."

Her blue eyes lit up with excitement as a huge smile crossed her face. "Yes, pease!"

Thank god that worked.

We dressed up all the animals and dolls. I even had to wear a crown. At this point, I would have done anything to keep her happy and in this room. Everything was going well, and all the 'guests' had enjoyed their 'tea', until I went to eat the last cookie.

"No, Bina! That's Li Li's cookie."

I whipped my hand away. "I'm so sorry."

Choe gave me a disapproving look that was a little too much like the aforementioned aunt, and then nodded. "Is okay."

"Should we clean up?"

My little charge jumped up. "And then we see Li Li?"

A deep sigh came out, and I checked the time on my phone. Miraculously, over an hour had passed. "Yes, Chloe, we can see Auntie Li *after* we clean up."

With the cheer she let out, you would have thought I told her we were going to have ice cream. The next several minutes passed in a blur, and to buy myself time to use the bathroom, I told Chloe she could wash her tea set in the sink. That girl loved playing in water almost as much as her tea parties.

I was barely sitting on the toilet when she glanced over. A flash of determination flared up in her eyes. "Chloe, no." My voice was low with warning. "You have to wait for me. Give me a minute." *I just need to pee.*

Dropping the teapot with a splash, Chloe jumped down from her stool and raced out of the room.

"Chloe, no!" By the time I pulled my pants up and sprinted out of the bathroom, she was nowhere to be seen. *How?* Chloe also loved playing hide and seek, and after checking in the closet, behind the curtains, and under the bed, not finding her, I looked at the main bedroom door again. It wasn't fully shut.

Shit.

Running into the hallway, my heart dropped when there was no toddler in sight. I barely heard little footsteps from the direction of the stairs and headed that way. *How in the hell did she move that fast?* "Chloe?"

No answer. *Of course now she would stay quiet.*

I took the stairs two at a time, heart thudding so loudly I was sure everyone in the house could hear I hated this feeling—panic, loss of control, the sick lurch of old routines failing me. Downstairs, the kitchen was empty, and there was no sign of her in the foyer, the dining room, or the living room. I even checked the pantry, hoping Chloe might have been distracted by cookies.

Luck was not on my side.

She was gone.

I'd lost her.

How did she get so far already? Did she get out of the house?

Panic twisted in my chest. I was supposed to be hypervigilant, supposed to be better than this. I was supposed to keep her safe, and now I'd lost her on my watch. The Rodriguez family didn't tolerate mistakes, and neither did I.

She doesn't know where Lianne's office is. Does she? We've only been in Lynette's office.

I took off racing around the corner to check the office hallway and immediately slammed into someone.

"Holy shit. What happened? What's wrong?"

Dante. For a heartbeat, I stood there, pulse thundering. "I can't find her."

"Can't find *who*, Kitten? Look at me."

My eyes snapped to his. "Chloe. She wanted to see Lianne, got impatient, and made a break for it when I went to use the bathroom."

He pulled his phone out and sent a quick text before kissing me on the forehead. "The team's on it. We'll find her. In the meantime, go talk to Lianne. Let her know."

I focused on how Dante took my hands and held them tight as I took a breath and tried to steady my heart. It felt like walking to the edge of a cliff. Honorary cousin or not, she was a Don, and I was certain I was going to catch hell for asking whether Lianne had seen Chloe. I literally had one job - keep tabs on the toddler - and I'd messed up. Still, I forced my feet to move toward her office. The hallway was silent, heavy, and I forced myself to approach the door, each step a little harder than the last.

When I finally reached it, I raised my fist, hesitated for a second, then knocked. For a moment, nothing, then finally a faint, "Come in."

Please don't murder me for this.

Slowly opening the door, I stepped inside. "Don Agosti, I can—" I stopped mid-word when my focus dropped to a certain toe-headed toddler cuddling in her aunt's lap.

I nearly collapsed from the relief that crashed over me.

Lianne gave me a sympathetic smile. "She's fine. I promise."

Oh god. She's safe. She's right here. Words spilled out of me in a rush, apologizing every other breath, desperate not to insult anyone. "I'm so sorry. I never meant to let Chloe get away from me, and if you can't trust me after this, I understand, I really do, and I'll start packing right now if you want, I get it." My voice barely made it to the end. I took a breath and then explained further. "She saw you earlier. You looked..." I hesitated. "Upset. Anyway, Chloe noticed. And after we went upstairs, and you called, she said she wanted to give you a hug. I distracted her with a tea party, but when I went to the bathroom, she snuck out." I shrugged, a heavy exhale cutting through the silence between us.

"Are you done?"

I nodded slowly, my focus now on the carpet. *Here it comes.*

"Sabrina, please look at me."

It took some effort, but eventually I raised my chin and looked her in the eyes. I would accept my fate with professional dignity.

Lianne studied me for a moment before letting out a sigh. "I'm not going to fire or punish you."

"But—"

"But nothing, Sabrina. I'm the Don. I'm her auntie. For intents and purposes, I'm her legal guardian. I. Get. Final. Say. You aren't going anywhere."

"Yes, ma'am."

Lianne kissed the top of her niece's head. "You're amazing with her, Sabrina, truly. Also, you're allowed to use the bathroom. It's not your fault this little one was bound and determined to get to me. Do you know what Chloe said when she came running into the kitchen, practically crashing into me?" I shook my head. "She said, 'Bina said wait... but I hug Li Li now.' I couldn't say no to that, so I picked her up and brought her to my office. I was about to call you when Dante's text came in."

I let out a sigh, proud of Chloe for knowing exactly what her auntie needed.

Lianne's eyes went glassy for a moment before she took a deep breath, let it out slowly, and kissed Chloe's head once more. "Looks like some of the good Agosti genes made it to you."

I stood there, trying not to fidget, but unsure as to what I should do next. "I... I can take her upstairs if you need to get some work done."

She shook her head. "Chloe isn't bothering me any. She can lay on me as long as she wants. If she falls asleep, then so be it."

"Is she reminding you there's still something good in this world?"

A tense, dark expression flickered in Lianne's eyes as she glanced down, but then a smile crept onto her face. "Something like that."

"Would you like me to stay here or..." I trailed off, unsure for once in my life about what to do.

Lianne shook her head. "Take a breath and a break, Sabrina. You've been going full speed since you walked into this house. I promise we'll find you when we need you."

Letting out a tense breath, I nodded. "I'll be in the kitchen prepping some snacks for her." When she arched her eyebrow and gave me a pointed look, I continued. "And maybe I'll also grab a cup of coffee and sit for a few minutes and not work?"

"Thank you."

Nodding my head in respect, I turned and headed out. When I saw the hallway was empty, I sent a text to update Dante and the rest of the crew before unlocking the door leading to the backyard, walking outside, and sinking onto one of the patio chairs. I needed peace and quiet for two minutes to pull my shit together. All I focused on was the cold temperature and taking deep breaths, letting them out slowly to hold off the impending anxiety attack.

I'd messed up so badly today. Keeping tabs on Chloe, the only Agosti grandchild *and* heir, was my entire job. It was a miracle nothing bad happened to her... or me. Several dozen breaths later, I heard a door open and nearly silent footsteps approach.

"Kitten?" My attention snapped to Dante upon hearing his voice, and I watched as he walked over and squatted in front of me. "Did you get in trouble?"

"No. Chloe found Lianne in the kitchen and is currently curled up in her lap. It was exactly what Lianne needed. Not that it makes me feel any better knowing Chloe got away from me in the first place."

Dante pulled me into a full hug, holding me tight against his very muscular chest. I wrapped my legs around him as he scooted me to the edge of the chair. Resting my head on his shoulder, I sniffed as he ran his hands up and down my back. "Oh, Kitten. No one is mad at you. Do you think any of us would have let her get out of this house?"

"She got past me, Dante. It's literally my job to know where she is at all times, and I didn't for at least three minutes. Do you know how far she could have gotten? What could have happened?"

"Do you know what Ryan and Lukas did the second we even thought Liam would bring Chloe here?" I shook my head, and he leaned back enough to push my chin up gently with his finger. His dark eyes bored into mine. "They ordered and installed special locks to make it so that even if she got her hand on the doorknob and turned it, she wouldn't be able to open the door."

I shook my head, feeling slightly ridiculous, especially since I'd needed to unlock the door to get out here.

"What are you doing now that you know your charge is safe?"

I shrugged. "Lianne told me to take a break. When I told her I was going to work on some stuff for Chloe, she glared at me."

He chuckled, and I loved how it sounded and felt. "That sounds like Lianne. Well, if it helps, I'm about to have some lunch. Would you like to join me?"

"I'd love to."

~~~~

Dante

It threw me off more than I would have admitted, seeing Sabrina so pale and shaken. The woman was a machine—relentless, unflinching, able to run for days on nothing but adrenaline and spite. I knew she'd once taken a bullet, stitched the wound herself, and then barked orders at a half-dozen of her men without missing a beat. I'd also watched her break a guy's nose and calmly sip her espresso before he hit the ground. Sabrina didn't do frazzled. Yet, when she
~~~~

barreled around the corner and crashed into me, her whole body drawn tight as a piano wire, I almost didn't recognize her.

It took a minute to unwrap her from around me, but once I did, I led her down to the kitchen and pulled out a chair at the battered table; the one riddled with knife nicks and gouges from years of wear and tear. "Please sit down before you fall down."

"I'm fine." The words were not at all convincing.

I rolled my eyes. "Says the woman who had less color than a ghost a few minutes ago? Yeah, not buying it. Sit down." Sabrina glared at me, but to her credit, she sat. Sort of. She perched on the edge of the seat like she was poised to jump up and defend herself at a moment's notice. I took a glass from the cabinet, filled it with cold water, and set it down in front of her. "Drink."

"I'm not a child, Dante." Even shaken, the edge was still there.

The pushback challenged the Dom side of me, but while we were alone, we were still in a semi-public area, not the privacy of our bedroom. This was not the time or place for me to fully step into that role. That didn't mean I wasn't going to take care of my woman.

"Then drink your water like a good girl." I let my voice drop an octave, the words coming out as a low command rather than a suggestion, and then watched as her pupils dilated in response. Her cheeks darkened with a flush running from the tips of her ears to the base of her neck, and I didn't miss how her breath hitched a little. Without hesitation, she picked up the glass and took a measured sip, eyes fixed on me over the rim. "You okay, Kitten?" I asked, my tone as neutral as I could manage, trying to walk the line between concern and command.

She cleared her throat, looking a little self-conscious, and set the glass down with a quiet thunk. "I... Uh... Yeah. I'm fine."

I kept my face neutral, but inside I cataloged her reaction. Sabrina Rodriguez—the woman who'd once dislocated a man's jaw for touching her shoulder without permission—yielded to me. Her breathing settled and her shoulders relaxed and dropped more as

I maintained eye contact, that telltale submission response we'd established between us years ago. I knew better than to acknowledge it here, though. Our dynamic was private. Sacred. Never something that should have ever happened while at work. She made me promise, and I had.

I need to tread lightly.

Breaking eye contact, I turned to the refrigerator, making my movements deliberate and slow as I gathered ingredients. While Sabrina was less worked up than before, she was by no means calm. I arranged everything with precision she'd appreciate—the knife perfectly parallel to the cutting board, condiments in a neat row. From my peripheral vision, I caught her watching my hands with a particular intensity she only showed when she was slipping into her submissive headspace.

"Turkey and cheese sandwich okay?" I asked, keeping my back to her. I was desperately trying to keep my actions professional. We were already in some very grey area.

She hesitated, which was unusual for her. "Yes, please."

I got to work, hands moving on autopilot as I pulled two plates from the cupboard.

"I'm more than capable of making my own lunch, Dante. You don't have to do that." The words came out a little sharper than I expected, but it also didn't surprise me. Sabrina was likely at war with herself, both over what happened with Chloe and the fact I'd Dom-ed her at work.

Keep it light. "Yeah, and? We both need to eat, and I am more than capable of making two sandwiches." I assembled the bread and slices of pickles, cheese, and meat, keeping things efficient but not rushed. I needed her to know I'd take care of her, that she could lean on me if she ever wanted to. Not that she'd ever ask for it out loud.

Sabrina shifted in her chair, restless, tapping her fingers once against the tabletop before tucking her hands beneath her thighs. I set the mustard down, turned to face her, and leaned a hip against the counter. "It's a sandwich, not a life debt. You are my partner, Kitten. Can you please let me do something nice because I want to?"

There was a pause, like she was running the whole conversation through a threat matrix in her brain, looking for the angle, the hidden meaning, the trap. I watched as her eyes glossed over, and the twitches on her face all told me she was spiraling out. In two strides, I was standing in front of her, one hand on her neck and the other in her hair.

"Kitten, breathe." I held her gaze, but the fact that she couldn't maintain eye contact for more than a fraction of a second told me she was mentally circling the drain. I squeezed her neck a little tighter, and there was a quick burst of clarity that shone as I lowered my voice to that octave that always had her listening. "Breathe."

She did, and slowly, after taking a few more deep breaths, I watched reason come back to light.

"Good?"

She nodded, and I let her go, giving her a soft kiss on the lips before releasing her neck.

"Thank you." Her lips were soft against mine. I gave her a quick nod and turned, quickly double checking no one else was around. The room was still empty. *Good.* Aside from the fact she would have been mortified if anyone had seen her like that, Sabrina had made it abundantly clear she didn't want me doming her in the house. I understood and respected why, but this had been an extenuating circumstance. I needed to shut her brain off for a moment, get it to stop spinning, and settle her. I had to take care of her.

Convinced she was okay for the moment, I went back to the counter, opened the cookie jar, pulled out two oatmeal chocolate chip cookies, and placed them on her plate with the sandwich. When I set it in front of her and joined her at the table, she stared at the plate for a moment, like she wasn't sure if it was a test or a trick.

I rested my hand on hers, giving it a gentle squeeze, lifting it to my lips. "You are amazing, and I love you."

"I love you too." Her focus hadn't left the food in front of her, and I had to keep reminding myself that it had nothing to do with me, and everything to do with her trauma and the mental state she was in.

"I don't know what you're used to, but here we work together and have each other's backs."

"I'm seeing that." Her head popped up. "It's not that my uncle's team doesn't work together, because they do, it's that... well..."

"You're a woman in what is traditionally a man's world, and a lot of people are still sexist as shit?"

Sabrina let out a tight laugh. "Yeah. Something like that." She then finally picked up a cookie, broke it in half, and popped a bit in her mouth as if to prove she could decide for herself. I didn't care *how* she ate her lunch, just as long as she did.

Chapter Twenty-Eight

Lianne

It had been one of those weeks where every hour felt like a game of emotional Jenga, and I was one wrong push from collapsing. I needed so much more than a good night's sleep, but that was the best I could hope for at this point. For the first time in days, the house was quiet. No one knocking on my door for a last-minute signature. No one was bitching at me about Liam, who had been on surprisingly good behavior lately. No one was bleeding, getting blown up, had been shot, or was missing.

I sent Regina home around dinner time, Ellen had pulled Ryan from his office an hour ago, Gage was out spending time with Sunny, Mom was with Adair in the lounge, Lukas was having a movie night with Quinn, and Ben was upstairs in our room, hopefully asleep.

A deep sigh came out as I finally left my office and headed upstairs. I was tired. It was more than that, though. Exhaustion didn't quite cover it, either. There was a heaviness on my soul that never seemed to get any lighter.

As I passed through the kitchen, I grabbed one of the cookies Ben and Chloe had made earlier, smiling at how adorable they were together. He was so much lighter with her. They all were. Once at the top of the stairs, my focus lingered on the door to what was now Chloe's room, and I immediately felt love and unease in my chest.

There was no way I could have ever predicted the sequence of events that brought us to the point of her living in this house.

Am I doing the right thing?

Letting out a sigh, I turned down the short hall that led to my room. The door was cracked open, spilling a narrow triangle of warm light onto the rug in the hallway, and I could hear faint scratching as I pushed the door open and stepped inside. Ben was cross-legged on the bed, hunched over his battered sketchbook, the end of a charcoal stick pressed between his thumb and forefinger. My adorable orange cat was curled up and sleeping on my side of the bed.

I hesitated just inside the threshold, watching him to see if he noticed me, but he always knew when I was nearby. It was a sixth sense for him, like how he could tell if something in the kitchen was burning from two rooms away, or how he could always spot a lie before it finished sliding off someone's tongue.

"Why are you still awake?" My voice was quiet as I took another step.

Ben didn't look up as he dragged the charcoal across the paper again. "Couldn't sleep." The image on the page was already emerging, all bold lines and dramatic shading. He kept drawing as I made my way to the dresser, slipping out of my shirt and jeans and into an old university sweatshirt and leggings. In the mirror, I could see the tension in his jaw. He looked older than he had last year. Worn in, but not worn out. I wondered if the same was true of me, but didn't want to look in the mirror and see what the past few weeks had done to my face.

Nothing I can do about it right now.

Turning, I sat next to him on the bed. He typically angled the sketchbook away from me, not quite hiding it, but not offering it, either, and I couldn't help but smirk at his little ritual. Ben didn't like anyone seeing his art until it was finished. But tonight, he didn't seem to mind when I leaned over and watched his hands move. It was as much of an art form as the piece itself, and I hadn't realized how much I missed it until this moment.

"You haven't sketched in forever."

He shrugged. "Didn't have it in me for a while. Too much going on up here." He tapped his forehead with the charcoal.

Because of me, my family, and all our drama. "I'm sorry." A deep sigh came out as I rested my head on his shoulder.

Ben paused and kissed the top of my head. "I have no regrets, Li. I promise."

I watched as he filled in the space between two trees, layering the shadows so that the scene felt three-dimensional, even though it was just carbon smudged on paper. The path was narrow, the trees knotted and arching overhead, their branches tangled thickly. With a small surge of joy, I realized It was a forest path back in Colorado, the one we'd walked along before shit hit the fan with Lukas and Quinn. He'd loved it for the silence, and I'd loved how it made me feel briefly invisible. Like I could disappear there if I wanted.

"It's beautiful."

He stopped and gave me an incredulous grin when he glanced down at me. "You say that even when it's shit."

I sat up, arching an eyebrow at him. "Because it's never shit. I still think you should sell these."

Ben shook his head. "Still a no, Li. Lukas may want to share his art with the world, but this is for me." After adding a little more shading to the side of a tree, he set the sketchbook and charcoal on the nightstand, careful not to smudge anything, and then turned to face me fully. "You look tired. Still beautiful, but tired."

A weak laugh came out. "I *am* tired."

He reached out and tucked a strand of hair behind my ear, letting his hand rest on the side of my face. I leaned into the warmth, and for a while, neither of us said anything as we looked at each other. It was enough just to sit here with him in blissful silence. I was here with my Ben. I didn't need anything else.

Eventually, he broke the silence. "Did Adair say anything tonight?"

The warm and fuzzy moment faded as I shook my head. "No. I know she's talking to Peter and Mom about it, but I still don't have any idea of which way it's going to go." A shaky breath came out as I tried to keep my emotions in check. "I'm terrified she's going to take it all away. Everything my family has worked so hard to build could be gone in a snap. All because of my fucking brother."

Ben's eyes softened as he wiped a mutinous tear from my cheek. "She won't take it all away. She's not like that."

I love that you think that. "She *could*, though. It's her legal right as the Vaux Don. Aside from contract violations, she lost everything because of Liam: her family, Derek, her safety, and years of happiness." My voice cracked on the last word. I tried to swallow it down, but it was too much.

Ben pulled me closer, shifting us so I was sitting directly in front of him, wrapping his arms around my waist, anchoring me in place. "She's also alive because of the rest of your family. There was never a moment after Liam and Susan betrayed her where Adair wasn't being protected and cared for. She's not going to forget that. None of us are."

I blinked hard, trying to will my tears to stay inside. "I know. I just... I'm tired of fighting for peace that should be mine."

"What do you want her decision to be?"

That was the million-dollar question. "I don't know. I want to believe she won't take it from me, but I've never had to trust anyone with this much before. Her decision affects so much more than the Agostis. There's everyone who works for us, their families, the businesses we run, the neighborhoods we protect..." I trailed off, forcing myself to take a slow breath. Getting all worked up was not going to help things.

Ben squeezed me tighter. "You have to trust her, Lianne. Trust in just how much you and Adair mean to each other. Trust in how much Lynette is her mom, as much as she is yours. This family means the world to her, and she's not going to destroy it."

A weak chuckle bubbled out. "You just had to bring logic into this, didn't you?

He grinned and nodded. "I did. I know Liam has ruined so many things, but she is not him. She has courage, a brain, and a heart." Ben leaned in, kissing my forehead and then my lips. "You're not going to lose anything, Li. Not as long as I'm here."

The man in front of me, currently holding me together, had never once lied to me. Even if Adair took everything business-related, I'd still have him. I'd still have my family.

I love him so damn much.

Once again he shifted, this time pushing the blanket down and stretching out on his side, and then patted the open spot next to him. "Come here." I crawled up, burrowed under the blanket, and pressed my face against his chest, inhaling deeply. The smell of laundry detergent and lemon filled my nose, and I felt safe.

We lay like that for a while in comfortable silence as Ben traced shapes on my back, and I let my mind drift. One of my thoughts was of a future where this kind of quiet, cozy night was normal.

One day it will be.

It wasn't long before Ben's hand stopped moving, and his breathing deepened. Letting out a sigh of relief that he'd finally fallen asleep, I finally let myself do the same.

Chapter Twenty-Nine

Dante

I woke up early, fully expecting to see a text from my sister canceling on me. She went out the night before to a honkytonk she'd become obsessed with over the past few months to 'meet up with a friend,' and I assumed she was not going to be in any shape to work out.

I shook my head as I crawled out of bed and pulled on workout clothes. I knew who Talia hung out with. Whatever *friend* she was meeting up with was someone she was either trying to hide from her mafia life and/or some kind of hookup. And since my sister was kind enough not to poke at my personal life, I did the same for her.

For now.

Confident I was going to roll into an empty gym, I stopped dead in my tracks when I saw Talia already running on the treadmill. "How long have you been here?"

She glanced over, smirking. "Good morning, sleepyhead. Glad you could finally join me."

I narrowed my eyes at her as I walked over and rested my arms on the side of the treadmill. "Says the woman who bails on me on the regular because she wants to sleep?"

My sister half-glared at me before pressing a button to slow her treadmill. It was then I saw the timer. "You've already been running for twenty minutes? When did you get here?"

The faintest shade of red bloomed on her cheeks before she rolled her eyes. "Maybe a half hour ago or so. I woke up early and couldn't get back to sleep."

Anyone else would have bought the lie. But I knew Talia as well as I knew myself. I knew her tells. I knew where to look. "Want to try that again?"

The glare was real now. "I walked into the gym a half hour ago. Check the fucking cameras."

The heat coming off her words surprised me, but then I studied her face. "Have you slept at all?"

She arched her brow in a silent challenge. "Yes."

"In your own bed?"

A tense and angry sounding breath came out of my sister. "I'm allowed to sleep where I want, same as you. Do you want a workout buddy or not?"

"I don't know what's going on, but do we need to leave so you two can settle this without an audience?"

I spun around to see Ben and Ryan walking in, eyes wide. "Good morning. You're fine to be in here." Letting out a sigh, I glanced over my shoulder at Talia. "I'll stop. I'd still like a workout buddy."

After spending some time on the treadmill, Talia and I spotted for each other. I wasn't breaking any personal records, but that wasn't the point right now. I was working on rebuilding and maintaining the muscles I had. My leg was healing well, and it was close to being as strong as it was before I helped Don Dallas save his wife and his second in command.

Just in time to kick Liam's ass.

Once we had finished, I glanced at my sister as she grabbed her stuff to head out, immediately noticing she had her boots in hand. Not the usual ones she wore for work, but her cowboy boots with the red piping she wore when she went out. "Did you even stop by the apartment or our room on the way here?"

Talia let out a sigh. "I didn't want to be late, and I knew I didn't have enough time to go home first, so I just came straight here." She was tired. Still, I heard the laugh buried in her throat. "Now shush."

"Dante, can you spot for me?" Ben asked. "I'd ask Ryan, but I don't want to piss off Ellen or Doc."

A chuckle came out as I nodded. "Of course. Love how you put Ellen in front of Doc."

Ben shook his head, smirking. "Honestly, Ellen is scarier... Especially when it comes to Ryan."

"Can confirm." Ryan nodded. "She gives Jess a run for her money some days." He glanced at the door my sister had just walked out of and then looked at me. "Do you know where Talia was last night?"

I shrugged as I helped Ben load weights onto the bar. "Some honky-tonk she fell in love with. Why?"

"If you want, I can do some research and find information for you."

A small smirk tugged at the corner of my mouth. "As much as I appreciate the offer, I'm going to decline politely for now. If that changes, I'll let you know."

Ryan nodded. "Of course."

Moving to the bench press where Ben was, I was impressed with how much he'd improved in the last year. The man could lift almost as much as most of the crew now. That piece of information made me smile, partially because I appreciated weightlifting successes, but mostly because people assumed Ben was soft and nonthreatening.

Shaking my head, I couldn't keep the smile off my face. I had a feeling Liam wasn't going to be the only person to underestimate him, and I looked forward to Ben knocking more egos down a peg or two.

Chapter Thirty

Lianne

"Hi, Ryan!"

I smiled at my niece's voice. Even with the door closed, the sound still filtered into my office. I loved how comfortable she was getting with the people on my team. Sabrina had been making a point to visit everyone in the house with Chloe so she knew they were safe and not scary. Most of the time, the visit included a picture Chloe colored as a gift. It was the most adorable thing. The way they all bragged about them, you'd think it was some kind of award.

"Hey, Chloe. How can I help you?"

"I colored a pit-cher for you."

There was a light rustling of paper followed by the sound of an office chair rolling.

"This is beautiful. Where should I put it? On the door?"

Chloe giggled. "No. No tape on the door!"

I shook my head as I stared at the art very much taped to the back of my office door. *Who made that rule, I wonder?*

Their conversation continued, and about the time I was tuning it out, frantic typing caught my attention.

"I do it like this?"

"That's perfect, Chloe. Just remember to be gentle with the keyboard. You don't want to break it."

There's no way he's letting her touch his laptop. That man was overprotective and ridiculous when it came to his tech.

"I type like you!"

His chuckle was muffled through the door. "Yep. Keep practicing and you could type better than me."

There was no keeping a grin off my face. *She's really good for us.*

~~~~

I had just finished going through a report and approving modifications to one of our warehouses when there was a soft, deliberate knock on my office door. After I slid the papers back into their folder, I glanced up. "Come in."

The door swung open, and Adair stepped inside. Her hair was pulled back into a messy bun, her expression unreadable as she hovered just inside the doorway. Despite it being mid-morning, she looked as if she'd been up all night, if the bags under her bleary eyes were any indication. *Why does she look so tired?*

"Is everything okay?"

She gave me a weak smile. "Yeah. Do you have a few minutes?" Her voice was rough, like she'd been talking for hours.

"For you? Of course." I slid my mug of tea closer to me and gestured for her to sit.

She sank into the chair, hands in her lap, and didn't speak for a moment. I'd learned with Adair that initial silence usually meant she was still putting her thoughts together, and from the way she was wringing her hands, the woman was warring with something big. I took a sip as she stared at my desk for a moment, then let out a slow, careful breath. "I don't know how to do this."

"How to do *what*?" Her life had changed so drastically in the past month, that she could have been talking about anything.

Adair sat up, looking me in the eye. "How to choose someone as my second. I was trained to be the *wife* of a Don, not *the* Don. I went from being the supportive soon-to-be spouse, to on the run for my life, to the one who makes all the decisions... and ones that will affect so many people." She shifted nervously, clenching and relaxing her hands. "It's been so long since I've had people around me, and now
~~~~

I'm surrounded by them, which is great, but on top of wrapping my head around being the newest Vaux Don, I have to choose someone I can trust above everything to help me run everything."

I set my cup down and nodded sympathetically. Being overwhelmed felt like a constant state at this point. "That's the hardest part, though, isn't it? Not so much the press of people, but trusting those people."

Adair let out a deep sigh, jaw clenched. "It is."

I watched her for a moment before continuing on. "Do you have any thoughts on who you might want as your second?"

Her response was immediate. "I want Peter. He's... I trust him. He's good. Patient. Understanding. But..." She hesitated, and then her next words tumbled out unguarded and desperate. "We're... kind of together, and he's also on Agosti payroll, and I don't know if wanting him as my second... well, if that's allowed."

I nearly smiled, not at her dilemma, but at the naked honesty of it. "Picking a second is no small feat, but at the end of the day, there aren't really any hard and fast rules about who you can and can't pick. I fell into mine with my mom." A weak laugh came out. "She had asked me to be *her* second initially, and I was absolutely good with that."

Adair narrowed her eyes and leaned forward. "Wait, so how *did* you become Don, then?"

A deep sigh came out, and I took another sip of tea. "It's like I said in the meeting with Dallas. Liam ran his mouth and decided to be a colossal pain in the ass about seeing the Don. Well, I didn't want him anywhere near my mom, especially so soon after we lost Dad, so I told him I was the Don and to start talking."

"What?" The way her eyes widened and mouth dropped open was almost comical.

I chuckled, shaking my head. "Yeah... I forgot there were cameras everywhere, and the entire team heard and saw the whole conversation. Mom, included. Honestly, I think it was her plan the entire time, and asking me to be her second was the gateway position."

Adair nodded, her focus fixed on me. "Did that automatically make her your second?"

"No." I pressed my lips together as I paused for a moment. "No, I could have chosen anyone, but I wanted and needed it to be her. She was Dad's right hand. She knew everything about the business. She still does." A proud smile spread across my face. Momma was the best and most lethal asset the Agosti family had. "If I didn't have her, I probably would have picked Lukas. I trust him above everyone else. He and Ryan, but Lukas is my twin. It's different... and Ryan has... well, he has tech skills no one else does, and I need him there more."

Adair relaxed a smidge, and I recognized the rawness of emotion in her eyes, something more than just fatigue. *Probably what I feel every day.* "That makes a lot of sense." She let the silence hang, and I waited for her to continue. "I don't have a default person, really, aside from Peter. Even if I do make him my second, I still need to pull together a team. Your family has generations of connections and loyalty. I'm not even sure if anyone still loyal to the Vaux family is alive... or if they'd still feel the same way about me."

I nodded again. "I felt the same way stepping up. Everyone loved and respected my dad, and had been anticipating Liam to take over, and then here I was, the youngest daughter popping up in the ranks. I thought it was going to be an uphill battle for respect."

"And?" Hope bloomed in her eyes.

"It was and wasn't. I had a few rounds with a person or two here, but Mom and I sorted that out. But outside of the house, apparently my work ethic preceded me. Well, that and the fact Don Dallas executed someone for disrespecting me, Ben, *and* making rude comments about how I ran my team."

Adair stared at me, once again mouth open, eyes wide in disbelief. "He did *what*?"

"Oh yeah." The memories flickered through my mind as if they had been a lifetime ago, and not just a few months. "He didn't do it until after I left, but Dallas personally called me that afternoon. Honestly, I think he was worried about my reaction."

She shook her head in disbelief. "No. There's no way *the Don Supreme* was worried about your reaction to some idiot running his mouth."

If only you knew how long it took for me to truly accept that same thought.

I leaned forward, resting my elbows on the edge of my desk. "Think about it, Adair. It was the first time I visited the Dallas compound as the Agosti Don. His people insulted me and mine. I could have declared war." I paused, searching for a way to help her understand. "How would your Uncle Kobe have reacted? Would he have brushed off your Aunt Melanie being disrespected? Or someone insulting your own mother, his sister?"

Her face went white. "Oh, shit. He would have killed someone." She gasped. "The attack on the Dallas compound!"

There ya go. "Precisely. While I did jam a gun into the neck of the idiot who ran his mouth, I didn't pull the trigger. At the time I said it was out of respect to Mrs. Dallas. The man *was* standing on a stunning white rug in the middle of her pristine foyer. But the reason I spared him was because I was still acknowledging *just* how much power I truly had." I took a sip of my tea. "If I was in that same position today? That rug would be the least of my worries, and I wouldn't have hesitated pulling the trigger. Just like you last week with William."

Adair sighed and nodded. "True. All very true. Okay. So, let's say I pick Peter for my second, what do I do about the rest of my team?"

That was a fantastic question.

I sighed and leaned back in my chair. "Well, I know there's a mole in Liam and Susan's house who has been helping us out for a while.

Maybe they can be on your team after the dust settles. Once properly vetted, obviously."

Adair blinked as she absorbed the information and then nodded. "I… Thank you for that." I caught the edge of relief she tried to hide with a roll of her shoulders. She was wary of owing favors, not that I blamed her. I also hated asking for help and owing people things. But I wanted her to feel less alone, especially when it came to being a Don. I knew the isolating feeling far too well.

We spent the next thirty minutes circling around logistics: new contracts she would need to create and enter into, how she was going to find her own team, ideas on how she wanted to do briefings, and reviewing the more illicit side of the Vaux businesses. She asked sharp, incisive questions, showing off all the training she mentioned earlier. *She's going to be an amazing Don.*

Eventually, she stood. "Thank you. I'm sorry for taking over your entire morning. "

I rounded my desk and gave her a hug. "You're always welcome here, Adair."

"Thank you." She let out a deep sigh as she leaned back. "I haven't made any decisions about the contract yet, but I wanted you to know I'm taking it seriously. I need to make sure the right person pays, and that it's the appropriate price."

Thank you for mentioning it so I didn't have to ask. "I know you are, Adair. It's not a decision that can be made lightly."

"Exactly." Adair gave me a tired smile, but there was respect in her eyes. "The Agostis have kept me safe and alive for seven years. I will never forget that." Then she left, shutting the door behind her with a soft click.

I sat down again and stared at the pile of paperwork on my desk, but my mind was elsewhere. I thought about Adair's careful loyalty, the way she guarded her feelings with the same intensity she guarded her secrets. Not at all unlike me. I thought about Peter, and whether he could truly be her second, or if love would always be a liability in this life. I thought about my oldest brother, currently in a holding cell on the floor below me.

Trust was a currency in rare supply, and it wasn't just Adair who was running short.

Chapter Thirty-One

Sabrina

Chloe fought her nap for almost an hour, but after reading what felt like every book in the child's library, she finally conked out. I sat there for another few minutes, listening to the deep, smooth breathing, making sure she was truly asleep before transferring her to her bed. When she let out a sleepy hum and hugged Bunny a little tighter after I tucked her in, I wanted to weep for joy.

Thank you. Now please stay asleep.

After closing the bedroom door behind me, I secured the baby gate in front of it in case she woke up during the five minutes I anticipated being gone. Smiling, I hurried downstairs, very much looking forward to lunch. I was starving after running around in the backyard and playing on the swing this morning, her insistence on learning how to do a somersault, and then pretending to swim like fishes. That was before a marathon coloring session. It felt like an eternity since I'd eaten my egg, bacon, and cheese bagel sandwich for breakfast, and the handful of fruit I'd snagged during snack time didn't do much to hold me over.

I had just peeled the banana and taken a bite while looking in the fridge for what I was going to have for lunch when hurried footsteps echoed through the foyer seconds before someone frantically pounded on the front door. A second passed before it was opened.

"Zee, can I help you?"

I froze in place as I processed what was going on. *That's Gage. Why is Zee here?* As much as I wanted to run out there, my training told me to hold tight until I had more information. Anything could be a setup.

"I need to see her. Now."

Their voice was strained and panicked. *What in the hell is going on?*

He let out a tense sigh, and then I heard the metallic click and then slide as the door was shut and locked. "And I'll help with that, but you have to calm the fuck down before I have to restrain you. I don't care if you're one of Don Rodriguez's favorites. Sabrina is most likely upstairs with Chloe, and I will *not* have you scaring her."

Now feeling more confident there wasn't an immediate threat, I raced out of the kitchen.

Zee locked eyes with me and then exhaled so hard their whole chest caved in. The next instant they were in my space, grabbing my shoulders, and holding me tight against them. The force nearly knocked the air out of me. "Are you okay?" Their voice was low and laced with terror.

"I'm fine. You don't have to crush me." I leaned back to look them in the eyes. "What happened?"

They wildly yet methodically scanned the foyer like they thought an enemy would come through one of the windows or doors. "Have you received any calls or messages?"

"Aside from expected, work-related ones, no. Why?"

They looked at Gage. "Has anything popped a red flag on your security sweeps?"

He shook his head, very much on edge now. "Not to my knowledge."

Zee let out another deep sigh of relief. "Good. Thank god."

I grabbed their shoulders and turned them to face me. "Talk to me, Zee. What happened?" My fight-or-flight response had been activated, and part of me wanted to race upstairs and shove Chloe in the safe room. *I need more information.*

"You got plans for the next few days? Any outings? Anywhere you're scheduled to be?"

I blinked. *Why aren't you answering my question?* "I had a thought about going to the aquarium or the zoo with Chloe, but nothing's set. Why?"

They took a step back, hands fisted at their sides. "They know you're not in Cuba."

"Who?" I straightened my back, prepping to move and defend at a moment's notice.

"*La Muerta Rubí.*"

My skin went cold as one of my worst fears came to life. There was a second, a full, silent second where it felt like the foyer dropped away and there was just me, the marble flooring, and the pounding in my ears. Memories of the bullets, the broken glass, the way Rod's eyes glazed over when he died, and hiding in Claudia's home immediately assaulted me. I shook my head and looked Zee in the eyes. *Pull it together.* "How sure are you?"

They didn't hesitate. "Absolutely certain. It's been confirmed from two sources: Rod's cousin on the inside and a tap on their comms. They're talking about you, specifically, and by name. They're pissed you got out of Cuba alive and in one piece."

Holy shit. It was one thing to have pissed off the cartel, but the fact they were discussing me by name was an entirely different level of terror. They didn't care about discretion. They wanted me dead even more. Gage staring at me intently reminded me in glaring technicolor where I was. "Do they know I'm in Chicago?" The last thing I wanted was to add to the Agosti's already full plate.

Zee shook their head. "We don't think so. There is movement all over Florida, and they are asking about you there, but they don't seem to have any indication you're home."

I grinned, looking forward to ending them once and for all. "Good. Let them try to find me."

They glared at me. "No, Sabrina. *Not* good. They know you. They know your patterns. They've already sorted out that you're in the States. It's only a matter of time before they figure out you came here." I opened my mouth to argue, but Zee cut me off. "Is there a private place where we can have a phone call with your uncle?"

I glanced at Gage. "Would Lianne mind if we used the lounge for a minute?"

He shook his head. "I can stay outside and hold the door, but then you have to talk to her."

"Of course and thank you." Grabbing Zee's hand, I half dragged them toward a room I'd only been in twice. Both had been official Rodriguez business; neither had been without my uncle. *Being on the phone with him counts, right?* Once the doors were shut, they pulled a burner phone out, tapped in a number, and put the call on speaker.

My uncle's voice sliced through the static two rings later, low and dangerous. "Report."

"*La Muerta Rubí* has confirmed Sabrina's no longer in Cuba and are already scouring Florida. They aren't prepping a hit yet, since they don't know her exact location. No other details have been confirmed."

He bit off a colorful swear. "And Sabrina?"

"I'm safe, sir." This wasn't uncle/niece territory. This was business.

"I speculate once the location is confirmed, they will use any and all tactics to flush her out, including attached family members."

Dante. Chloe. Lianne. Auntie 'Nette. My heart lurched. *No!*

"Sabrina?" His voice was pure steel and authority.

"Yes, sir?" I stared at the phone, willing it to give me any semblance of comfort.

"Remain inside the residence during daylight hours. Do not leave unless explicitly cleared by all involved Dons. I'll coordinate with them to arrange a second safehouse for you if it comes to that. Until then, no movement, no exposure." Even with a set of burner phones, I didn't miss how he refused to drop any information that could lead to my location. *He's as rattled as I am.*

I nodded, even though Uncle Ceaser couldn't see it. "Copy."

"Zee, stay close and keep her alive. I'll be in touch."

The call ended, and I let out a shaky breath as I sank into one of the leather chairs. They wanted me dead. Again. Still? It didn't surprise me as much as I wanted. I had made their life hell in Guatemala when I stopped a number of their attempts to take over our plantation. And then there were all the men I'd killed.

Before I could even try to process what the next twenty-four hours would look like, Zee squeezed my shoulder. "We need to talk to Don Agsoti."

"Right." When I opened the door, Gage turned to face me. "Is Lianne in a meeting right now?"

"No. Let's go."

We hit the office as a group. Gage knocked once and didn't wait for a response before opening the door. Lianne and Regina were both at her desk, reading something, and looked up the second we entered, eyebrows high. "What happened?"

Zee stood tall. "Rodriguez business."

My eyes were locked on Lianne, who was staring at me, brows furrowed. "Regina, hold the door until Gage or I come out."

"Yes, ma'am."

The second the door was closed again, Lianne sighed. "Talk."

I let out a tense breath. "Short version? A group I was associated with while away on assignment figured out I'm not there anymore and have made their way to the States. They don't know I'm *here*, but that clock is counting down. I'm under new orders from Don Rodriguez not to leave during the day unless agreed upon by the both of you. He also mentioned talking to you about arranging for a new safehouse for me if needed."

She nodded slowly. "Okay. What group?"

"*La Muerte Rubí*. The Red Death." I wrinkled my nose as the words left my mouth. It felt disrespectful to utter the name in this house.

Lianne's eyes went wide. "The cartel you had an unfortunate run-in with while in Cuba?"

She's been filled in, I see. "Yes, ma'am."

Zee cleared their throat. "We speculate once they find out where she is, that they will use anyone important to her as leverage or bait to draw her out."

Guilt slammed into me again. "I'm so sorry, Lianne. I thought it would be longer before they tracked me down.

Lianne let out a frustrated sigh. "We always think there's going to be more time." She tapped her nails on the desk, processing it all. "I'm sorry we have to lock you down."

Do I have a choice? I shrugged. "It's not much different from the past several months. And at least here, there is a lot more backup." Another deep sigh came out. "I prefer fighting over hiding, but I'm not dumb. It's smarter to hole up and pick my moment to attack than walk into a bullet. Not to mention, there is Chloe's safety to factor in."

"I feel the same way, and I agree." Lianne looked between us, then gave a sharp nod. "Zee, I have a feeling we are going to be seeing more of you in the near future. I'm glad Sabrina has you in her corner. Also, and I will relay this to Don Rodriguez, I will not retaliate if you have to take out a target within Agosti territory to protect Sabrina, and, by proxy, Chloe. If you spot a threat associated with *La Muerta Rubí*, eliminate it, no hesitation."

The definitive tone in her voice made my chest swell with love and pride.

Zee nodded. "Understood, ma'am."

"Thank you, Lianne." I swallowed down the surge of emotions.

She gave me a warm smile. "We're family, Sabrina. *This* is how it should work."

Zee joined me for a quick lunch and then hurried back to my uncle's compound. While their visit had started in chaos, it ended lighter and less frantic. And when I made my way back upstairs, I was delighted to see Chloe was still completely passed out, and that Lianne's cat, Frank, had somehow gotten into the room and curled up next to her.

Letting out a grateful breath, I stretched out on my bed and allowed myself a minute to let my thoughts run wild in the silence. I hated that *La Muerta Rubí* had figured out I was out of Cuba, but I wasn't entirely surprised. There was a reason all of Cuba feared them. Their connections were vast, and their wealth of knowledge was deep.

I didn't realize I'd fallen asleep until a sloppy kiss was pressed to my cheek.

"Bina, wake up."

A smile spread across my face as I opened my eyes to see Chloe leaning over me, Bunny in her clutches. "Hey, cupcake. Did you have a good nap?"

She nodded. "I pet the kitty!"

"Do you like Auntie Li's kitty?" Frank was single-handedly the most patient cat I'd ever met and let that little girl hold him and drag him around pretty much anywhere.

Chloe wiggled in excitement. "Uh huh. He's soft. Can we read kitty book?"

"Of course." I spent the next several minutes reading every cat book she pulled off the shelf and brought to me, smiling at how she snuggled in close for every story. It was like she knew I needed some extra cuddles.

Eventually, Chloe declared it was lunchtime but surprised me with an additional request.

"Dada have lunch, too?"

My eyes went wide. "Let me ask Dante if your dad is busy, but yes, we can have a snack."

We walked to the bathroom after she insisted on sitting on the 'Chloe potty', and I sent off a message to Dante.

Sabrina: < Chloe is requesting her dad's presence for lunch in the kitchen. Is today good? >

His response was almost instantaneous.

Dante: < I have to clear it with the boss ladies, but I'm in support of the visit. >

Sabrina: < Fantastic. Thank you. >

I helped Chloe wash her hands, and then we headed downstairs, where Avery was waiting for us.

"A-vee!" Chloe raced forward to her waiting arms. She scooped up the little girl and spun around in a circle, making excited squeals and laughter fill the room.

"Hey! Can I have lunch with you, too?"

The toddler's blue eyes lit up. "Yes, pease!" She looked at me. "We have fishies and cookies?"

I couldn't help but grin at Chloe's unfiltered excitement. "How about a peanut butter and jelly sandwich with fish crackers, blueberries, and strawberries? We can pretend the blueberries are bubbles in the ocean."

She gasped and clapped her hands. "Yes! And juice!"

It wasn't long before we were settled at the table with our food. Chloe's plastic tea pot made an appearance, and we filled it with water, 'just in case the fishies got thirsty.'

Footsteps echoed in the foyer, and I sat up a little taller as I watched the doorway. Seconds later, Liam walked in with Dante right behind him. There was tension in their body language, but they had smiles on their faces.

Chloe looked over and waved excitedly. "Hi, Dada! Want a fishie?"

"I'd love that. Can I join you?"

"Yes." He walked forward and went to sit on a chair, but then his daughter started yelling. "No! Not there!"

"Why not?" He immediately froze and looked around in confusion.

Interesting. Why doesn't she want her dad next to her?

Chloe stared at him and shook her head in disbelief. "The fishy princess is there, Dada. You squish her."

He let out a tense sigh but kept the smile on his face. "I'm sorry, sweetie. Where can I sit then?"

"By A-vee." She pointed to the open chair directly across the table from her.

Avery grinned as she pulled out the chair, patting the empty seat. "Come on, Liam. I won't bite if you won't."

I had to school my face to keep from snickering, but then Chloe added to my struggle when she gasped dramatically and pointed at Avery. "No bite. Biting is a bad choice."

The woman being reprimanded shifted her attention to the little girl and nodded very seriously. "You're right, Chloe. Biting *is* a bad choice. I promise to make good choices." She turned and shot Liam a pointed look. "Daddy is *also* going to make good choices, yes?"

Liam nodded nervously. "Of course."

"Good boy."

I didn't miss the flicker of anger in his eyes, but the man wisely kept his mouth shut as he took his seat. Chloe settled down and reached for the teapot and an empty cup.

"Would you like help pouring so you don't spill?"

Liam started to reach toward her, but she pulled back, looking mildly offended. "No, I do it."

The man bristled at the comment, but nodded. "Okay, sweetie."

Little did he know, Chloe was actually very good at carefully pouring water from her teapot into a cup.

I couldn't help but look at Liam for a moment and truly study him. The way he stared at her in wonder as she filled his cup made me question how much time he *actually* spent with his daughter during the day before coming here. Or if he and Susan consistently handed her off to a nanny. It gave a possible explanation for Chloe's growing obsession with cuddling and physical attention and made me want to hug her more.

"Dada like it?" Her question was quiet and laced with worry. She wasn't the only one who had clocked that he hadn't touched his beverage yet.

Avery elbowed him. "How's the tea, *Dada*?"

Liam quickly picked up his cup and took a sip. "It's delicious."

Chloe smiled proudly, but then collapsed into a fit of giggles when Avery noisily slurped her 'tea'. "A-vee you so silly!"

The woman grinned and nodded. "I *am* so silly! But I love your tea. It's so yummy."

During lunch, Chloe went on and on about fishies and 'pen-gins' and whales. I loved watching her face light up in excitement and wonder as she talked about each one. It was then I decided she had to go to the aquarium.

I just need to put together an approved plan that will keep her safe.

By the time we were done eating, her hands and face were a sticky mess. Liam stood and went to reach for her. "How about I help you wash up, sweetie?"

Chloe leaned away from him, almost looking offended. "No. Bina do it."

Hurt and frustration flickered across his face, and for the briefest moment I wanted to feel bad for him. It had to be painful for your child to choose someone else.

Like daughter, like father? No. She's better than her father.

Letting out a tiny sigh, I leaned in close to my favorite little girl. "I'm going to make sure your teapot stays safe. Can Daddy or Avery help you wash your hands?" If Liam wanted to try to be a good dad, I could give him a chance. It wasn't like there weren't two other incredibly well-trained and armed mafia members in here with us if he decided to be an idiot.

Chloe nodded. "A-vee do it." She gave Liam a wary look as her chosen adult walked over, helped her off the chair, and led her to the sink.

Oh shit. This is not going to end well.

My attention flicked to Dante, who had moved closer and was now within arm's reach of Liam. "I think snack time is over. Time for us to get back to your office."

"Dada work again?"

Liam clenched his teeth and tensed up for a moment before smiling at Chloe. "Yeah, sweetie. I have to get back to work. You be good for Sabrina, okay?"

She nodded. "I good for Bina. I love Bina."

My chest tightened at the declaration, and I sucked in a stunned breath. Chloe had never said that before. I'd never even prompted the use of the word... for anyone.

She loves me?

Liam stood, but when he went to step toward me, Dante clamped a hand on his shoulder and then looked at me. When I gave him a quick nod, he released his grip and Liam walked over to Chloe, kissing her gently on top of her head. "I love you too, sweetie. I'll see you soon, okay?"

Chloe nodded again. "Okay. Bye, Dada!"

Dante immediately escorted the man out of the room. I let out a sigh and took a few calming breaths. I truly disliked being in the same room as Liam, and I'd been in many rooms with all kinds of unsavory people. This was different, though. He put me on edge. Part of it was his unpredictability. Some days he was a loving, doting father; some days he was biting and rude; some days he was withdrawn and almost completely checked out; and some days he looked like a bomb about to explode.

One thing was absolutely certain. I was not going to let him hurt Chloe.

Chapter Thirty-Two

Dante

Sabrina: < Apparently I'm off duty after breakfast. Lianne and Ben are visiting his moms and are going to take Chloe with them. I think his nieces are going to be there too. >

Sabrina: < I wish you had this afternoon off. >

I had been cooking up a surprise for Sabrina for days now, and it was finally happening. Better yet, everything was going to plan, and a huge grin slid onto my face as I responded.

Dante: < Maybe I can bribe Avery to cover Liam for a couple hours. >

"You chatting up your girl?"

I glanced up, grinning at Avery, who was sitting across the table from me in the staff kitchen. "Yep. I just told her I'd try bribing you to cover Liam later."

"Did you now?" She wiggled her eyebrows at me. "I was going to cover out of the goodness of my heart, but to keep up with the story, if you clean up after one of my interrogations, you have a deal."

"Power wash the liquids down the drain? Done. I thought you were going to ask for a new knife or a silver platter for the next head you decapitate or something."

Avery let out a snort-laugh before drinking the rest of the coffee in her mug. "You know I'll never say no to a new knife. Also, you can power wash as long as you don't leave any wet spots behind you."

I feigned being wounded. “I’m far more of a gentleman than that.” Then I leaned in, smirking. “But isn’t a wet spot the sign of a job well done?”

“You dirty dog.” She punched me on the shoulder, laughing the entire time. “But, yeah. You’re not wrong.”

“You and I both know how to keep our partners happy.” Shaking my head, I stood up and walked over to the sink to clean up my dishes. “Thanks though, Avery.”

“Sure thing. And good luck later.”

I headed upstairs to my room, taking advantage of the temporary silence to go over my plans for the day one more time. The fact I was going to be able to spend most of the day with Sabrina was no small miracle. I had so many conversations with at least six different people, now owing two of them a favor, but she was worth it. There wasn’t much I wouldn't do to spend some uninterrupted time with my Kitten.

Smirking, I pulled out my phone and messaged my woman.

Dante: < Mission successful. When can I have you? >

Sabrina: < Really? Remind me to get something nice for her. >

I smirked.

Dante: < You know she loves sharp and pointy things. >

Sabrina: < I’ll meet you in your room once Lianne and crew roll out with Chloe. >

I let out a calming breath. All I had to do now was wait.

About twenty minutes later, I heard a quiet commotion from the hallway, and I opened my door a crack to listen in better. There were several excited voices talking. Chloe was the easiest to identify, but it didn’t take long to figure out the others were Lianne, Ben, Regina, Lukas, and Quinn.

That’s quite a family outing.

About the time I caught myself wondering why Quinn and Lukas were going with, I remembered Quinn was related to Ben’s nieces' mom. *Not that it matters. Lukas and Quinn can hang out with whomever they want.* Within a minute, the door to the garage opened and closed, taking the lively crew with them.

Sabrina should be down here any minute.

I leaned against the wall, arms crossed over my chest, tapping my fingers on my arm as I counted the seconds until we were together... and alone. A couple minutes later, there was a soft knock on my door before it was pushed open.

Sabrina stepped in, and the sight of her took my breath away. Even in jeans and a long-sleeved shirt, she was stunning. The woman was perfection to me.

"Hello, Kitten."

She gasped and then ran at me, wrapping her arms around my neck and pulling me in for a hard kiss. When I slid my hands down her back and under her ass, she hopped and wrapped her legs around my waist as I lifted her. Her lips never left mine as I walked across the room and sat on the edge of my bed, relishing how much of her I loved was pressed against me.

Eventually we came up for air, and Sabrina let out a breathy chuckle. "Hey."

I gently kissed her again. "That was quite a greeting."

She shrugged. "I didn't have to hold back." She then let out a happy hum and rested her head on my shoulder. "I love you."

My chest swelled with pride and love hearing those beautiful words leave her mouth. "I love you too, Kitten."

We sat like that for a while, simply enjoying being together without a time limit or worry of being interrupted.

A low chuckle shook my shoulders, and nerves shot through me as I remembered the plan for today. "As much as I love this, I really want to take you out for our date now."

Sabrina sat up with a start, eyes wide. "Wait. We're going out on a date?"

I nodded. "Surprise!"

She blinked several times while staring at me in awe. "What?"

There were so few moments when I truly surprised Sabrina, and I was soaking in every second of this. The sparkle in her brown eyes, the way her entire face lit up, and the wide smile on those perfectly plump peach lips. A few strands of hair had fallen from her ponytail, and I couldn't help but reach over and tuck behind her ear. "God, you're beautiful."

Her cheeks took on a pink tint as she shook her head. "Stop distracting me with flattery and tell me more about this date."

I leaned in and kissed her again, tightening my hold on her again so she was as close to me as possible. "I got permission from Lianne and your uncle. You and I are going to your favorite coffee shop, and then I have another surprise after that."

Sabrina sat up with a start, and I watched her struggle between reacting as my Kitten and the mafia heir she was. "You talked to Uncle Ceaser *and* Lianne about this?"

I nodded. "They know where we are going, the estimated timeline, and I confirmed that Zee will be shadowing from as discreet a distance as possible."

Tears gathered in her eyes. "We really get to go out? On a *real* date? With everything going on?"

"We do, Kitten."

She glanced down. "Do we have time for me to change into cuter clothes?"

A smirk tugged at the corner of my mouth. "You're beautiful right now."

An exasperated sigh rushed out. "Dante, it has been years since you and I have been out on a proper date. While I know my ass looks good no matter what pants I'm wearing, I want to put on something cuter. For me, if nothing else." Sabrina arched an eyebrow and gave me a pointed look. "And if you stop fighting it, I might even pick something *you'll* appreciate, too."

"How can I deny such a simple request?" After another quick kiss, I helped her crawl off my lap. "Please hurry. I don't want to waste a minute of today."

Sabrina snickered and rolled her eyes. "Like I know how to lollygag. I'll be changed and back down here in less than ten minutes." Winking at me, she turned and sauntered out the door, swinging her hips so I couldn't pay attention to anything other than the toned ass I loved to have my hands on.

True to her word, eight minutes later Sabrina was walking down the hallway toward me, and all I could do was stare.

Is she trying to kill me?

She'd changed into a dark red wrap dress that showed off all her curves that I wanted to trace with my hands. The V neckline dipped low enough to make me bite my knuckle, and then there were the black, knee-high heeled boots.

Sabrina smiled knowingly and reached out, closing my mouth with her finger. "Safe to assume you appreciate my wardrobe choices?"

I nodded and held her hand, lacing our fingers together. I wanted to say it was because I loved how alive I felt when any part of me was touching her, but it was mostly so I behaved myself.

There are too many parts in motion to stay home. I'll have all the time with her after.

We headed out to the garage, walking to the farthest spot, where I helped her into the passenger seat of a dark grey SUV. It was then I noticed the subtle makeup job. It was just enough to add a little color and sparkle to her face, and I was mesmerized. "You look absolutely stunning, Kitten. Enough to make this grown man drop to his knees and worship you."

A mischievous yet pleased expression filled her face. "You're very welcome to do that later, but I was promised a date."

After closing her door, I had to pause for a moment to collect myself before sliding into the driver's seat. I didn't know if I'd ever get used to how gorgeous Sabrina was. *And I hope I never do.*

It wasn't long before we were downtown and I was pulling into a parking garage and helping her out of the truck. "Ready?"

Her excitement matched mine as she pushed me against the side of the vehicle and leaned on me, giving me a scorching hot kiss that had me seriously considering tossing her into the back seat and escalating things.

"Kitten..." I closed my eyes as I said her nickname low and strained. "You are testing me." Her sultry laugh had me grabbing her hips, holding them tight against me, showing her *exactly* what that kiss had done.

"What? I can't kiss the man I love?"

I tipped my head forward so our foreheads were touching. "As much as I'd love to do nothing but kiss you, I don't want to have to explain to *two* Dons why the cops were called on us for public indecency. I promised them I'd behave and keep you safe." I glanced around, suddenly remembering we had a shadow. "Also, Zee is somewhere watching."

Sabrina snickered. "They can watch." When I gave her a pointed look, she let out a sigh and nodded. "Okay, I'll rein it in and behave... for now. I'm just really excited to be doing something so normal with you."

Grinning, I kissed her again, this one much shorter. "Me too. Come on. The coffee place is across the street."

Hand in hand, we left the parking garage and crossed Madison Street. I kept scanning the sidewalk, street, and passersby as we walked, keeping an eye out for anything amiss. The coffee shop entrance was between two skyscrapers, and once we were inside, I inhaled, smiling at the welcoming scent of hot coffee and freshly baked pastries.

Sabrina ordered the same oat milk vanilla latte with extra cinnamon she always did, and I ordered the same black espresso double shot I'd gotten since the day we met. We both got a bacon, egg, and cheese croissant, and having spent enough time around Ben, I also ordered a chocolate croissant and a cinnamon roll for the two of us to share.

Once we had our food and drinks in hand, I spotted a small round table with two light blue chairs near the window, and when I gestured to it, Sabrina took the seat facing the window. When she took the first sip of her latte, her eyes closed and the most blissful smile appeared on her face.

"Holy crap, this is delicious! I've missed good lattes." She glanced around. "I hope Zee gets something. They also deserve one of these lattes."

As we sat there, enjoying our brunch, Sabrina looked out the window and talked about Chloe's latest obsession with all things ocean and whether Lianne would approve of purchasing a fish tank and some fish. I watched her lips move and realized I would happily sit at this tiny table forever if it meant I could keep listening.

Sabrina let out an indecent moan when she took a bite of the chocolate croissant, and then stared at me in mild shock and betrayal when I told her Ben also makes them, and that they were as good, if not better. "You mean we could have these without having to leave the house?"

I nodded. "I don't think he'd mind making them, especially for you."

She chuckled. "Good to know."

It wasn't long before we'd finished eating, and after we headed outside again, Sabrina faced the wind for a moment, inhaling deeply. "God, I've missed this."

"The bracing winds of Chicago?"

She nodded as she linked her arm with mine. "Don't get me wrong, I definitely miss the smell of salt in the air and the ocean, but there is nothing like this city and Lake Michigan." When we didn't cross the street to head back to the parking garage, Sabrina glanced up at me. "Where are we going now?"

"To your surprise." She narrowed her eyes at me, but I held firm. "You'll see soon enough. If it makes you feel better, it's a seven-minute walk to where we're going." I saved the rest of my words, kept them balled up in my chest like a fist, because I wanted to get this right. It was too important. *Today* was too important, and I wanted to remember every single second.

When we reached the narrow, grey, and glass-covered building with a small yellow awning across the street from the Sears Tower, I thought my heart was going to break through my ribs, it was beating so hard. *Here we go.*

"What's in here?" Sabrina was eyeing the building curiously, but there was no signage to give our destination away.

"I need to pick up part of your surprise." I opened the single glass door and gestured toward the vestibule. "After you."

Once inside and in the elevator heading to the nineteenth floor, she grabbed the side of my coat and looked me in the eye, as if she stared hard enough she'd read my thoughts. My Kitten knew something was up. "Talk to me, Wolf. This is more than just some surprise."

The elevator doors opened, revealing a hallway, and I led her in the direction of our destination, stopping a few feet from our destination. Turning to face her, I didn't hesitate. I'd rehearsed it a thousand times in my head, all the ways I could say it, but none of them felt right. So I just told her the truth. "I want to get married. Today. Right now. We aren't promised tomorrow, and I love you too much not to do this. I want you to be mine. Always."

Sabrina stared at me, stunned, and the faintest flicker of uncertainty appeared on her face. Her lips parted, like she was trying to form a response, but nothing came out.

It was then my excitement slowly shifted to worry. *Does she not want to marry me?*

Suddenly she gasped, and tears formed in her eyes again. "Are you for real right now?"

I nodded, my heart pounding hard enough that I was sure she'd heard it. "I'm so for real, Kitten. I don't want to wait another minute, not with everything we both know could go wrong. We have this day, and I want it to be ours."

Sabrina looked down at where our hands were joined, and I rubbed my thumbs across her skin before she met my eyes again. "I never thought we'd get here."

"Me neither, but I wanted it. So I made it happen."

A huge smile appeared on her face. "What are we still doing standing here?"

I took a shaky breath. "I need your answer first. Sabrina Isabelle Rodriguez, will you marry me?"

She didn't look away. "I was ready to marry two years ago. My heart hasn't changed. Has yours?"

I shook my head. "Not for a single day."

Her grip was strong, and I was pretty sure the world could end right then and there and we'd still be standing, fused together, grinning like idiots. "Then yes, let's do it. Let's get married, Dante. I want every single minute."

I kissed her. Right there in the middle of the hallway. I didn't care if anyone saw us. All that mattered was that we were together, and she'd said yes.

Eventually she pulled her lips from mine and looked around. "Are you going to tell me where we are *now*?"

Smiling so wide it almost hurt, I pulled her toward the door. "A jewelry store... Of sorts."

Inside was a modern, almost sterile-looking studio. The white rectangular table in the middle had a few boxes on it. Ones I hope had rings in them.

Sabrina squeezed my hand tighter. "Dante. You don't have to get me some crazy expensive ring. I don't even wear jewelry."

I stopped in the middle of the room, tugged her around so she faced me. "I want you to have something you'll look at and know you're mine. Even when you're pissed at me, or even when you're halfway across the world, you'll see it and remember you belong to me."

Her breath stuttered before she regained her composure. "You always did have a possessive streak."

I grinned. "Yeah, and? You like it."

She bit her lip and grinned. "I fucking love it."

And just like that, I wanted to take her somewhere private. God, this woman would be the death of me.

The woman I'd made the appointment with was brilliant at her job. I'd given her some generic background information about my soon-to-be-wife, and the options she'd pulled were perfect. There were no statement pieces or pink stone or any of that frilly shit. Sabrina liked things simple. Strong. Dependable. I spotted a band set with a single, horizontal set, rectangle-cut sapphire, deep blue, almost black unless you caught the light. It was sleek and solid, and looked beautiful on her tan, small hand.

"Dante, it's perfect. And my size."

I pressed a kiss to her temple. "Almost like I planned it that way."

The matching band for me was a thick white gold ring, heavy and simple. The only 'fancy' element was it looked like it had been sandblasted. I was going to scratch it up at work anyway, so a polished surface felt impractical.

The woman did her spiel about warranties, resizing, and cleaning, but I was only half listening. Sabrina kept looking at me with a dazed, hungry look, like she was fighting herself not to pounce on me right there in public.

I was tempted to encourage her.

When the rings were boxed, I handed over my credit card, not blinking at the number. I couldn't put a price on this... or on her.

I put the rings in the inside pocket of my jacket, opposite my holster, smirking as I called for the elevator.

The second the doors opened, Sabrina pulled me inside and pressed my back to the wall, her hand firm on my chest. "You know what I want to do to you right now?" Her eyes were wild, and her voice was barely a whisper.

My blood pounded. "Tell me."

She came up on her tiptoes, and whispered in my ear, in graphic detail, *exactly* what she had in mind, and it took everything in me not to slam the emergency button to have her follow through on it. The growl that rolled out of my chest made her smile.

"Courthouse, Kitten." I was trying desperately to change her train of thought, just for a few hours, then she would for sure be following through on that promise. "We're less than fifteen minutes away. They do walk-ins; you just need ID. I checked."

Her mouth fell open, and then she snorted. "Of course you fucking checked."

I grabbed her hair, fisted it tight at the nape, and yanked her in for a desperate kiss. Her tongue was everywhere, and her breath came in little needy gasps. My other hand slid down her back to cup her ass, fingers digging in. I broke the kiss, chest heaving. "We need to stop, or we'll never make it to our wedding." My hand tightened in her hair. "Have some fucking discipline, Rodriguez."

"But, Wolf." I gave her a stern look at her playful whine before she sighed and grinned. "Admit it, you love that I want in your pants... Or want your pants on the floor of this elevator."

This woman. "I love everything about you. Even that mouth of yours."

Her eyes sparkled. "Especially my mouth."

I shook my head, both disappointed and relieved when the elevator doors opened. "Come on, we have a courthouse to get to."

Sabribna let me steer her back out to the street, and the whole time, she was humming to herself, swinging our joined hands between us like we were teenagers.

Chapter Thirty-Three

Sabrina

I walked into the courthouse hand-in-hand with Dante, and was immediately hit by that weird hush that hangs in government buildings, like even the walls were waiting for something significant to happen. Seeing the security checkpoint gave me pause. I knew for a fact Dante and I were packing. "Wolf?"

He gave my hand a squeeze. "I've got this." Walking up to one of the security guards, Dante leaned forward and spoke so quietly I couldn't make out most of what he was saying. The man nodded, pressed a button, opened a side gate, and gestured for us to follow him.

He guided us down a hallway that was way too quiet, and when we reached the judge's chambers, I stopped dead. This wasn't right. "Not the regular JP line?" I glanced between Dante and the heavy wooden door, half expecting someone to redirect us back to those uncomfortable plastic chairs where everyone else waited.

Dante just shook his head, that dangerous half-smile I knew too well appearing. "I *may* have called in a favor."

Before I could ask what the hell *that* meant, the security officer opened the door and ushered us inside. The judge's chamber was pretty much like I expected. Wood paneling, some slightly scuffed bookshelves, and a huge old wooden desk piled with papers and those stupid foam stress toys everyone pretends not to notice. I nearly stopped dead in my tracks when I locked in on Lynette and Gage standing there. And while Lynette was absolutely beaming, I didn't miss the small smile on Gage's face.

He smiles? Wait, is he holding a bouquet of flowers? Did they know?

Lynette broke the silence first. "Hello, my dear. You look absolutely beautiful today."

"I... Uh, hi, Auntie 'Nette. Thanks." I stared at her, stunned. "What are you doing here?"

She smiled and gestured to the man standing next to Gage. "Well, I wanted to catch up with Judge Garza, and you two need witnesses, so here we are." The woman made it sound like showing up for a courthouse wedding was as casual as grabbing coffee.

But isn't that what I was doing a half hour ago?

Dante's arm found my lower back, steadying me, and he leaned in, voice low, so only I could hear it. "You okay, Kitten?"

"I'm fantastic." I glanced up at him, seeing nothing but love in his deep brown eyes. "Truly."

His lips twitched just before a grin took over his face. "Me, too."

Lynette went back to chatting up the judge near his desk, trading inside jokes about some politician I'd never heard of.

Gage, who had been hovering by the bookshelf, walked up to us, shaking his head. "Seriously, Dante? A courthouse was the best you could do for the love of your life?"

"I didn't want to wait any longer." His voice was firm, but there was a playful tone to it. "Besides, I'm told the *real* party is the honeymoon."

I snorted before I could stop myself. "Let's actually get married before you start making plans to fuck me on the courthouse steps."

He smirked, pure heat in his eyes. "Don't tempt me."

Gage cleared his throat and held out a stunning bouquet of peach and white flowers. "I was told the bride needed flowers."

The bride. That's me. This is really happening.

"I... I guess I do. Thank you, Gage." My hands only shook slightly as I took them from him. They looked kind of like roses mixed with peonies, and when I brought the flowers to my face and inhaled, a light, sweet fragrance filled my nose. "These are beautiful. What are they?"

"Ranunculus. I couldn't get my hands on sunflowers with the short notice, but Dante thought you'd like these."

He couldn't get his hands on something? Wait. Did he arrange this? "They are perfect. Thank you."

The air in the room shifted as Uncle Ceaser, Mom, and Zee appeared in the doorway, slightly out of breath like they'd been racing against time. "Are we late?"

Lynette smiled at them with that perfect calm she always had. "No. You're right on time." And just like that, it felt settled. Like everyone was exactly where they were supposed to be, even if I hadn't known they would be there at all.

Uncle Ceaser quickly scanned the room, visibly relaxing when his eyes met mine, and raced over to hug me. "Hello, *Mija*." He squeezed me tighter for a second before leaning back. "I'm so proud of you, and I'm so happy for you and Dante."

I blinked back the tears quickly gathering in my eyes. "Thank you."

My mom shoved him out of the way. "You'd think you were her father the way you're carrying on. Move."

Uncle Ceaser bristled slightly at being gently shoved out of the way but then let out a sigh and kissed my mom on the top of her head. "I would never insult you or Ricardo's memory by claiming that. But *familia* aside, you know how important she is to me."

"*Sí, Sí.*" Mom waved him off as she took my face in her hands and stared at me, love and tears in her eyes. "My sweet, beautiful *Mija*. Your father and I love you so much. He would have loved Dante as much as I do." She glanced up at the man standing at my side. "You are a fantastic fit for my daughter."

"Thank you, ma'am."

Mama nodded. "Thank *you* for never giving up on her. I know the last two years weren't easy on you, either."

Dante looked down at me, love shining in his eyes. "I would have waited forever."

My heart pounded in my chest, and I couldn't tell if it was nerves, pure adrenaline, or some cocktail of both. Dante was standing so close to me that I could feel his body heat through my dress, and his presence calmed me, despite the air between us almost buzzing with a dozen emotions.

I tried to focus on the conversations happening around me, but my mind was spinning. I was really doing this. After everything, all the plans, all the years of being 'the reliable one' and keeping my shit locked down, all the times I had to put off my personal life. I was now about to get married on a Thursday with my uncle, mother, Zee, Auntie 'Nette, and Gage as witnesses. No big white dress. No bridal party. No elaborate security detail.

No fucking time to actually process it.

But for as chaotic as it was, it was par for the course and absolutely perfect.

Uncle Ceaser stepped toward where the judge and Lynette were standing. "Are we supposed to sit, or is this more of a stand-and-shuffle situation?" *Tío* was trying for a joke, but his voice wobbled at the edges. I hadn't heard that emotional waver since the day we buried my dad.

The judge finally turned from Lynette, with an easygoing smile on his face. "We'll keep it informal and gather in front of my desk."

Dante's hand never left my body as we walked over. I was grateful for it, even as I hated how shaky I felt. I'd faced down cartel hitmen in Havana bathrooms and barely flinched. *Why is this hitting so much harder?*

I couldn't stop looking at his hand, dark and broad against the burgundy of my dress. I'd chosen it in a rush, hoping it wasn't too tight, never once thinking I would be wearing it for a wedding. Red wasn't the color I should have been wearing. Not if I was going to adhere to any of the Cuban traditions. *Abuelita* would be so upset.

It's not like I knew.

"Oh! Wait! I almost forgot!" My mom rushed over to my side, pulling a carefully folded bag out of her purse. "You may not have had time to shop for a dress, but I had to bring this... in case you wanted to use it." She carefully unfolded it and pulled out a stunning white lace veil. "Your *Abuelita* wore it on her wedding day."

Tears sprang to my eyes as I picked up a piece of our family tradition. The delicate veil was covered with embroidered peach and white rosettes and pale green vines, and had white lace trim along the edges. I glanced down at the flowers in stunned wonder. *Did Gage know?* Swallowing hard, I lovingly caressed the sheer fabric. "I would be honored to wear it. Can you help me put it on?"

"Of course."

When Mom finished adjusting the comb in my hair, I wiped a tear from her face. "How do I look, Mama?"

"Like the most beautiful bride I've ever seen."

Dante took a step closer to Uncle Ceaser. "Did you bring the coins?"

He nodded and reached inside his coat, pulling out a small black velvet bag and handing it over.

I looked between the two men, thoroughly confused. "Coins? What coins?"

Mama sucked in a gasp. "Are there thirteen of them?" When Dante nodded, tears freely rolled down her cheeks. "You're keeping the *Arras* tradition?"

He nodded again, and Uncle Ceaser wrapped his arm around my mom's shoulders. "Some of the coins are from my wedding, some were given to me by Ricardo, and some are new, just for the kids."

As my mom pressed a delicate handkerchief to her eyes, I heard echoes of my *Abuelita* in my mind, telling me about all the old ways of our family. One of them had been how the groom gave thirteen coins to his bride during the wedding ceremony as part of his vow to support her. *How did he know?*

I didn't have long to think about it as the door to the office flew open, startling me. I wasn't the only one by the way Dante stepped in front of me, and Gage shoved Lynette behind him.

"Sorry! Did I miss it?"

I peeked around Dante to see his sister standing there, out of breath, with Raine behind her, shaking his head as he closed the door.

Dante let out an exasperated sigh. "No. You cut it real fucking close, though."

She glared at him, hands on her hips. "You think I was going to miss this? I would have been here sooner, but Connor took forever to get back with… his assignment."

She knew, too?

Talia rushed up to us, hugging her brother first and then me. "You look amazing." She took a step back and glanced around the gathered group. "Mrs. Agosti, Don Rodriguez, Ms. Rodriguez, Gage, Zee, sorry for the scare."

Lynette chuckled. "Raine wouldn't have let anyone else in without a heads up or a fight. It's all right, my dear." She looked back at the judge. "I believe we're all here now. Shall we begin?"

He cleared his throat, smiling at me like we were about to do something normal, like sign a lease or renew a passport. "Sabrina. Dante. Is it your wish to get married?"

I looked at Dante, and he met my gaze, and for a second the whole room shrank to just us. His eyes were so dark, so certain. I'd never seen him doubt anything, but I'd always wondered what it would feel like to be on the other end of that certainty. It was terrifying. It was addictive. It was mine. "Fuck, yes."

Dante didn't hesitate. "Absolutely."

The judge nodded, the corners of his mouth turning up. "Excellent. Now, before we get started, Sabrina, will you be taking his last name?"

Dante jumped in before I could respond. "No. I'll be changing mine to Rodriguez."

I whipped my head back to look at him, eyes wide. "What? Why?" It wasn't that I was against it, but we'd never gotten around to that particular discussion.

He reached up, his large warm hand cradling my cheek. "You are going to be Don eventually, Kitten."

"Yeah? And?"

Love shone in his eyes as he stared into mine. "I've known for a long time I'd be changing mine to yours. Just like Ben changed his from Mason to Agosti, I'm changing mine from Wilson to Rodriguez. It's our pride in being your partners."

I sucked in a stunned breath as I tried to process what was happening. "You talked to Ben about this?"

It was my Uncle Ceaser who spoke up next. "Actually, he talked to me about it. A while ago. I'm proud for him to become a Rodriguez."

I stared into Dante's eyes, warm, caring, and sparkling with tears of joy in them. "Me, too."

The judge cleared his throat. "Very well. We are gathered here today to witness the union of Sabrina Isabelle Rodriguez and Dante Theodore Wilson and to celebrate the love shared between these two people as they begin a new life together, founded in love, laughter, honesty, respect, and friendship. The promises you make to each other today should not be taken lightly. A marriage is more than a ceremony. It is a lasting and lifelong commitment."

My heart raced with excitement. This was really happening. I was getting married to my Dante. My Wolf.

The judge continued. "The future promises many happy days ahead, filled with unique opportunities, adventures, and challenges.

It is through trust, love, and the unfailing support of each other that you will meet these inevitable ups and downs." He paused and then looked at me. "Do you, Sabrina, take Dante, to be your lawfully wedded spouse, to live together in marriage, to love, honor, and cherish them, through joy and pain, sickness and health, for as long as you both shall live?"

I blinked back tears as I nodded, squeezing Dante's hands. "I do."

Shifting, the judge now faced the man I was marrying. "And do you, Dante, take Sabrina to be your lawfully wedded spouse, to live together in marriage, to love, honor, and cherish them, through joy and pain, sickness and health, for as long as you both shall live?"

He swallowed hard and grinned widely. "I do. Absolutely."

"If you have rings, please take them out now."

Dante pulled the boxes from the inside pocket of his jacket, opened them, and handed over the jewelry. Seeing them lying in the judge's hand, overlapping each other, made the moment so much more real.

"These rings are symbols of eternity and the unbroken circle of love. Love freely given has no beginning and no end. Today you have chosen to exchange rings, as a sign of your love for each other, and as a seal of the promises you make this day." The judge held his hand to me. "Sabrina, Dante, you may now exchange rings."

I took Dante's ring, appreciating the weight of the cool metal as I slid it on his finger. Once in place, I looked up into his eyes. "I love and respect you so much, and I'm so glad I get you for the rest of my life."

Tears glistened in his eyes as he took my ring and slid it onto my finger. "Sabrina, you are my love, my best friend, and the woman I am honored to share the rest of my days with." He then reached into his pocket and pulled out the small velvet bag of coins, placing it in my hand. "You will never want for anything, not while there is breath in my lungs."

My breath caught in my throat as I looked down at our joined hands.

This was it. I did it. I was his, and he was mine. After everything I had survived, everything I'd been forced to endure, this enormous slice of happiness was something that could never be taken from me.

The judge cleared his throat. "By the power vested in me, it is now my pleasure to pronounce you husband and wife. Dante, you may kiss your bride."

"With pleasure."

As sniffles and laughter filled the room, he wrapped one arm around my waist and slid the other hand up the back of my neck into my hair, pulling me close. The love, joy, and desire in his eyes took my breath away. "Finally, you are mine in every way."

I smiled. "I already was."

Dante leaned in and kissed me like he could finally breathe again. For a second, the whole world went black and silent except for his mouth on mine and the pounding in my chest. I kissed him back, desperate to let him know I was really here, I was in his corner, no matter what came next.

Someone cleared their throat. "You know, you don't technically have to consummate it in front of the witnesses, but I'm not judging."

Zee.

Dante didn't even break the kiss. "They can leave," he growled, low and quiet, so only I could hear.

I grinned against his mouth. "Let's at least pretend to be civilized for five more minutes?"

"Never liked pretending," he murmured, pulling back just enough to look me in the eye. His pupils were blown wide. "How am I supposed to drive home without showing my wife how much I love her?"

Home. Wife. The words tasted new. Heavy. Significant.

This is going to take a minute to get used to.

I blinked, fighting off the urge to cry. "Well, you're going to have to try. Or at least do your best so we don't get arrested in the parking garage."

"Technically, it's not all the way official until the papers are signed."

I looked over at the judge, who had moved behind his desk and was gesturing to the paperwork in front of him. "Right."

Lynette slid a pen across the desk with a flourish, like she'd done it a million times. "It was your Uncle George's pen. I know he would have loved to be here."

For the dozenth time, tears welled up in my eyes. "Thank you, Auntie 'Nette."

I took the pen and stared at it for a moment, taking in the details of the metal casing covered in intricate engraved filigree. I'd seen it before. It was one of the ones that was always on his desk. One he used to sign important things.

Even with the adrenaline and excitement coursing through me, my hand was as steady when I signed my name. My signature looked as confident as it ever had. I may have embellished a little on the 'z' at the end, but it was still very much me. Dante's signature was a bold scrawl. My uncle signed next, quickly and confidently, followed by Lynette's elegant script.

We gathered up the papers, sliding them into three large envelopes that Lynette and Uncle Ceaser took, each promising to make sure they were stored properly. The judge wished us luck, and we filed out into the chilly hallway, our steps echoing off all the hard surfaces. I kept looking at my hand, the ring, the flowers, as if the moment I looked away it would disappear.

Gage clapped Dante on the shoulder. "Congratulations. Guess you win the engagement to wedding speed run."

He laughed and nodded. "That wasn't the goal, but I don't mind being the man who wasted the least amount of time getting to the altar, so to speak. It's not *my* fault some of you insist on dragging your feet."

The man glared at him, but before a snarky comment could be made, Lynette stepped over and hugged me. She smelled of expensive perfume and something else I'd always found comforting. "You did well, sweetheart. He'll keep you on your toes."

"I know." The whispered words came out strained.

My uncle's hug was different. Fierce, protective, and loving. He pressed his lips to my hair, like I was still a kid and he could protect me from the world. "I'm proud of you." His voice was rough and quiet. "You deserve this. Even if he is a stubborn bastard."

Dante grinned at that. "That's why she likes me."

Then my mother stepped in, her face beaming with love and joy. "I love you so much, *Mija*." She kissed my cheek, and after doing the same to Dante's, she stepped back. "You take care of her."

Dante met her gaze, steady as stone. "Always."

Zee finally walked up to me, resting their hands on my shoulders. They stared at me for a few seconds before pulling in for a tight hug. "I'm so glad I pulled you out of that hole in Cuba. Make it count, Rodriguez."

My bodyguard turned best friend was never one for big emotions. I gave them a very pointed look. "I will if you will, Leveer."

"Fair enough." Zee chuckled and nodded as they leaned back. "I'm proud to serve at your side." They glanced at Dante. "I'm also proud to serve at your side."

Walking through the courthouse lobby felt even more surreal than entering the judge's chambers. People were coming and going, arguing about parking tickets and custody disputes, and I was standing there, a married woman, with a man who could kill with his bare hands.

Talia elbowed me as we walked out of the building. "So, how does this work? Do you get an extra bonus for marrying into the

Agosti family, do you have to pay Lianne something because you're stealing Dante, or is it just more headaches?"

I couldn't contain my laughter. "More headaches, likely. Also, if you thought your brother was an overprotective pain in the ass before, I think it's about to get worse."

She barked out a laugh. "Hardly. You've been his for years. The rings don't change anything."

Dante's hand found my hip again, pulling me flush against his side. Talia grinned, gave us a two-finger salute, and jogged off to catch up with Lynette.

Dante's voice was low in my ear. "You want to go home?"

I nodded. "Yeah, but I want you more."

His eyes darkened, and for a second I thought he might drag me into the nearest corner and make good on the silent, carnal promises he was making. I almost wished he would have.

But we had family obligations. Always.

Chapter Thirty-Four

Sabrina

The ride back to the Agosti compound felt like an unofficial parade. Zee was in front of us in their vehicle, and in the rearview, my uncle's black SUV trailed, carrying him, my mother, and Raine. I could see Lynette's SUV following as well, Gage driving with her silhouette bent over her phone. I could only imagine what conversation was happening there.

I had a strong feeling we were going to walk into some kind of celebration the second we rolled onto the property. My Auntie 'Nette loved celebrating accomplishments and milestones, and this was definitely both. In the meantime, I couldn't stop staring at Dante's profile. The sharp line of his jaw. The way his hand dwarfed mine. I felt safe. Protected. Which was almost laughable, considering what our families did for a living.

But this was us, the only thing I'd ever truly chosen, and I loved it.

"I can't believe you did all this." The words were half-whispered, half-laughed.

His hand squeezed mine a little tighter. "Why? I wanted you to be mine in every way possible, so I made it happen."

He said it as if it was the most obvious thing in the world. But then, it was.

Dante drove the rest of the way with one hand on my thigh, his thumb drawing lazy circles. We barely made it through the front gate before he threw the SUV in park, cut the engine, and leaned over the center console. His lips and hands were everywhere, frantic, like he needed to make sure I was really here, really his.

"Inside." His voice was raspy and strained. "We need to get inside. Now."

I gave him a quick kiss. "You going to make me walk or are you going to carry me over the threshold like a *proper* husband?"

He bared his teeth and gave me a wicked grin. "You want me to?"

"Try it... if you can." I was playing with fire with the dare, and was not at all surprised when he jumped out of the SUV, ran to my side, and practically ripped the door open.

My whole body tensed in surprise as he grabbed my waist and lifted me clean out of the truck, the world tilting as he tossed me over his shoulder. His arm locked across the backs of my thighs, keeping me in place while my dress rode up dangerously high.

Thank God I wore leggings.

Laugher erupted behind us, followed by a half-shocked gasp and the clicking of heels, but none of it mattered. All I could focus on was how solid Dante felt, how much I loved him, and the heat already pooling between my legs.

"Dante!" Lynette called after us. "You may want to put her down before you walk through those doors."

I felt the frustration in the breath he let out, but he set me down, pulled me close, and kissed me hard. A possessive growl rolled up his throat, reconfirming my husband was the sexiest thing alive.

My husband.

I was still laughing, half-drunk on adrenaline, half-drunk on pure joy when Dante pushed open the door to the Agosti house and dragged me inside. The hallway was surprisingly empty. His grip tightened on my waist as we passed the hall leading to his room, and for one hot second I thought he really was going to haul me off and consummate things.

Then I heard voices echoing from the foyer. Far more than usual for this time of day. "What's going on?"

"Surprise, my dear." Auntie 'Nette was beaming as she walked past us.

"Literally everyone knew about this except for me, didn't they?" The realization made me realize just how much Dante had done. The thought was overwhelming and somehow made me love him even more.

He rested his forehead against mine. "You think I could have pulled this off by myself, Kitten? If I've learned anything from working for the Agostis, it's that we're stronger and better as a team. How could I not pull in all the resources available to me to make this the most perfect day for you?"

"Bina here! Dante here!" Chloe's little voice broke the moment between us just before her footsteps echoed in the hallway, fast and chaotic.

"If they didn't already know we were here, they do now." Dante smirked. "Ready to celebrate with the rest of the family?"

I matched his smile. "We'd better get used to it, Rodriguez. It's our circus now." I could tell from the way his hand squeezed mine that he liked it.

We didn't make it three steps before Chloe came barreling around the corner, arms outstretched, flower crown on her head. She crashed into my legs, nearly knocking me over. "Bina marry Dante!"

Dante took the folder and my bouquet from me so I could scoop her up in a tight hug. "I did. I got married to Dante."

She blinked up at me, blue eyes sparkling with excitement. "You have cake?"

There was no way not to laugh, especially as I spotted frosting smeared on her cheek, with a couple of sprinkles stuck to it. "I hope so. Did you already have some?"

"Yes!" She giggled, then wriggled out of my arms and ran for the kitchen again, yelling, "They coming! Li Li, they coming!" The way she was bellowing was like we were rock stars and this was our red carpet entrance.

I looked at Dante, part mortified and part extremely touched. "I swear to god, there had better be some booze to go with these cupcakes."

He dropped his forehead to mine again, grinning. "I'll make it happen. We can even spike your cupcake, if you want."

I kissed him, quick and hard, just because I could.

The kitchen was packed. Lianne and Ben were there, him with his arm wrapped around her waist, resting his head against hers. Ryan leaned against the counter, cupcake in hand. Lynette was in the corner with a flute of champagne, looking like she was born for cocktail hour. My uncle was next to Lynette, my mom next to him, and all three of them were beaming.

Then I noticed the mountain of cupcakes on the kitchen island, arranged in a haphazard pyramid. At least a third of them were covered in so much rainbow confetti, it looked like a pinata exploded.

"You like my cakes?" Chloe grinned at me proudly. "I Ben Ben's little helper!"

I nodded. "I love your cupcakes. They are beautiful."

Ben stepped toward us. "A little birdie told me you like carrot cake with no raisins and an obscene amount of frosting." He gave the cupcakes a nervous glance before looking at me again. "I hope you like them."

"A little birdie, eh?" A chuckle bubbled out. "Did that same birdie mention his favorite was red velvet?"

Ben shook his head as his grin widened. "No, but the birdie's sister did. Don't worry, I made some of those, too." He reached for Chloe. "Would you like to help me give cupcakes to everyone?" After an earsplitting 'Yes!', I watched the duo hand work the room,

Chloe clutching a shaker of sprinkles and offering more sprinkles to every person.

Dante let out a low whistle as he looked around. "Holy shit. You guys didn't fuck around."

Lianne grinned, handing us each a glass of champagne. "It's the least we could do. Besides, Chloe said it wasn't a real wedding without cake. She insisted."

"*Chloe* insisted?" I shot her an incredulous look. "You want to try that again, Miss *I would eat pastries all day if I could*?"

She glared at me, but there was no heat behind it. "Fine. I *may* have suggested dessert. If it snowballed from there, what was I going to do about it? Stop my husband and niece from having a wonderful time in the kitchen? Absolutely not."

Lukas snatched two, stuffing one whole into his mouth. "This might be the best wedding reception I've ever been to."

"Careful, Lukas. I'm standing right here." Quinn's tone was teasing.

He leaned down and gave her a kiss. "Outside of ours, of course. Okay, and maybe Lianne and Ben's... Well... That was a hell of a weekend. No offense, Li, but this might better than yours. I hurt less, and I'm not covered in bruises."

She chuckled and nodded. "I mean, that's fair."

Uncle Ceaser raised his glass, voice rough. "To *famlia*, family, and to the poor man now officially stuck with my niece forever."

Dante lifted his glass too. "Wouldn't have it any other way, sir."

My mom just sipped her champagne, watching all of us over the rim, but there was a smile on her face I hadn't seen since I was a kid.

I accepted a cupcake from Ben, the frosting a good half-inch thick, and bit in. It was perfect. Moist, spiced, not too sweet, and *definitely* did not have a single raisin. I groaned. "God. That's almost better than sex."

Dante's eyes shot straight to mine. "Careful."

I licked a smear of frosting off my finger slowly and deliberately, just to tease him.

He tensed all over, and I could see exactly where his mind went.

Talia rolled her eyes. "Get a room, you two." She grimaced. "No, actually, you two go to the apartment. I'll stay here tonight. No one in this house needs to be subjected to your… shenanigans." Her face was all sisterly annoyance, but I could see happiness there, too.

Lianne chuckled. "I'm with Talia on this one. And to add to it, don't come back until tomorrow. Take a day, please."

I grinned, mouth full of cake. "You think one day is going to be enough?"

She glanced at her husband, smirked, and then looked at me again. "No, but maybe it will be enough that I won't have to spray you two down with the hose while the rest of us are trying to work." Then her expression turned serious. "You deserve this, Sabrina. Both of you do. Love like this in a world like ours is something you can't take for granted. You cling to it and never let it go."

I looked at the pile of sweets, then at people I'd kill and bleed for, and nodded. For a second, my surging emotions almost got the better of me. The urge to cry was right there, hot and sharp, but I swallowed it down. "Thank you."

No one gets to fuck this up for us. Not today. Not ever, if I have any say.

Nodding in return, she walked away, giving Dante and I the illusion of privacy.

I leaned into him, allowing myself a rare moment where I wasn't actively monitoring the room. "Tell me your wedding night plans," I whispered.

He didn't move, but his hand tightened on my hip. "I want to take you home, strip you out of that dress, and have my way with you until you can't say my name."

A grin spread across my face as my heart raced with excitement. "And if I can?"

He spun me around, pinning me to the edge of the counter. "Then I'll try again. And again. Until you can't."

I shivered and then arched an eyebrow, a little surprised at how forward he was being with everyone around. *I did ask, though.* "Sounds like a challenge."

Zee coughed, and when my attention flicked to them, I realized they'd heard every word. They grinned, raising their glass. "Off-site apartment or not, I give it an hour before we hear screaming."

Lukas popped the last bite of cupcake into his mouth and snickered. "I'll take the under on that."

Talia grimaced and plugged her ears. "La la la la. Things I don't want to hear about."

We all laughed, and for a second, the whole kitchen went soft and blurry around the edges. The cupcakes, the family, the love, the joy, and the ridiculous amount of sprinkles

I was married. To my Dante.

It was perfection.

Chapter Thirty-Five

Dante

It was fairly early in the morning still as I lounged in bed, reliving every glorious second of the day before when the first text came through, blinking on both my and Sabrina's lock screens.

Don Rodriguez: < Power down. No calls. No texts. You two are off until tomorrow morning. >

A slow grin spread across my face as I read it three times, making sure it wasn't a dream.

A minute later, my phone buzzed again.

Lianne: < Adjustment to your plans. You don't need to report back until tomorrow morning. >

I responded with a grateful 'thank you' and set the phone face down on the nightstand, smiling in disbelief at the gift we'd been given.

A whole day and another night.

Just us.

I stared out the window for a moment, trying to figure out the last time I had a full day off.

Not since Liam betrayed the family.

Sabrina's breathing changed slightly when I shifted. She was awake, just pretending not to be. I slid closer, pressing a kiss behind her ear. "We get to play hooky until tomorrow."

She cracked one eye open and stared at me like I was about to deliver the punchline to a bad joke. When I silently maintained eye contact, Sabrina rolled over and grabbed her phone. A stunned smirk appeared on her face as she stared at the screen. "Holy shit, we do!" Grinning, she put her phone back and laid down again, snuggling into my side.

We stayed tangled in the blankets while the city outside slipped into daylight. She reached for me, arm circling my waist, and for a while we just lay there, counting heartbeats, hers and mine. I could feel her pulse under my palm, steady and slow, a rhythm I never tired of. All the tension that usually ran through my body while working melted into something warm and peaceful. For once, we had time and permission just to be us. And I didn't want to waste a second of it.

Eventually I threw off the covers and padded to the kitchen after sliding on a pair of boxer briefs. I wasn't really a big breakfast guy, but this morning it was the first time Sabrina and I woke as husband and wife. I wanted to do this for her. Smiling at how I could take all the time I wanted, I made coffee and poured it into her favorite chipped mug, arranging toast and fruit on a plate. There was a ritual to the way I deliberately moved through the kitchen. One that brought me peace.

As I carried the tray back into the bedroom, nerves bloomed in my stomach, and as Sabrina sat up, her hair tussled from our night of consummating our marriage over and over again, I sat the tray down with the same carefulness as when I handled explosives. "Eat." My voice was still the low and gravelly octave that I took while her Dom, but I couldn't help it this morning. She was here. My Kitten was now my wife. I handed her the mug first, smiling when her fingers brushed mine, lingering a beat longer than necessary. I loved every time she touched me.

"Trying to kill me with kindness?"

I smiled at her. "No. You need food after last night."

Sabrina looked at me with a smug, hungry look as she sipped her coffee. "You know you don't have to serve me breakfast in bed just because I let you fuck every inch of me last night. Unless you're trying to make me soft, in which case, you're about thirty years too late."

I let my head drop back and laughed. I couldn't help it. I loved how amazing and normal this all felt. "Trust me, Kitten, my only goal this morning is to make sure you don't pass out from dehydration. Or low blood sugar. Since you barely touched your dinner last night and burned off every single calorie the second I got you out of that dress."

She just grinned, eyes dropping to my abs, and then dragged her thumb through the buttery toast before popping it into her mouth. "Well, keep bringing me fruit and caffeine and you can probably keep me vertical for a few more hours. *Maybe.*"

The way she said it, all teasing and soft, made me want to clear off the bed and have her all over again. It didn't even matter that we had more sex than sleep since stumbling into the apartment. I wanted more. It didn't matter that we were on our honeymoon; it was always like this with her.

I snagged a strawberry from the plate and brought it up to her lips. "Open."

She bit into it, slow, never breaking eye contact, and the look in her eyes set my entire body on fire.

It didn't take long before we were both naked. The bedding was a mess, shoved to the foot of the bed with the tray ending up somewhere on the carpet. I had her wrists pinned over her head, not even trying to be gentle, and the only reason I didn't have her screaming yet was that I wanted to hear every single gasp, every single little moan she made when I pushed inside her.

I'd always thought I was a quiet lover, at least until Sabrina. But with her, I wanted the entire building to know she was mine. Hell, I wanted the city to know. If it weren't for the soundproofing I'd added years ago, I was pretty sure the neighbors would have called the cops after the first round.

I gave her everything I had, not holding anything back, and after she fell over the edge, I finally let myself go, making sure she felt every single pulse of it. By the time it was over, we were both panting, dripping sweat, her hair a tangled mess. She didn't even bother to catch her breath first, just curled into me, palm pressed flat against my ribs like she needed to feel the heartbeat as much as hear it. I held her, kissing her forehead.

"Holy shit," she finally managed.

"Yeah." I laughed; that round had been rough and perfect. "Next time you challenge me, give me some warning."

She snorted. "I'll keep that in mind. Though I think the neighbors now know we fuck like animals."

"Soundproofing, remember?" I nipped her ear.

Sabrina shot me a look, still dazed. "Good. Otherwise, you'd owe the HOA about five grand in hush money."

I wanted to say something sweet, but it came out as another groan, because even now all I could think was how much I wanted to do it again.

After lying there for a few more minutes, simply enjoying holding each other, an errant thought popped out. "What do you think happens after Liam is dead and the dust settles."

She let out a long breath. "It has to slow down eventually, right? I've heard talk around the house. Not only are the Agostis going through their own personal war, but Don Dallas eradicated nearly all the Vaux family a few months ago. Adair is the new Vaux Don, which is going to bring so many changes in itself. Not to mention the fact *La Muerta Rubí* is trying to start or finish shit with us. The city has to calm down a little at some point."

I rubbed the top of my head with my hand as I thought about that and pulled her closer to me with the other arm. "Not to mention we don't even know what is really going on between San Augustine and Ivanov."

Sabrina lifted her head, eyebrows up in surprise. "They're bickering too?"

"That's the rumor. We don't know much about it right now." Then I smiled. "Did you know Don San Augustine had a daughter?"

She shook her head and narrowed her eyes. "I only know about Dominic."

"Yeah, we found that out around Christmas. It's Sunny. Gage's girl."

"No!" Her jaw dropped as she gasped the word. "Are you kidding me?"

"I'm not." I chuckled. "I mean, Chicago isn't a small city, but there are seven families with a piece of the pie. Is it really a surprise there is some crossover between families? We are pretty special, but it was bound to happen at some point."

"I suppose." Sabrina laid back down and went to tracing the lines on my chest and abs.

"Kitten. Careful."

"What? I can't touch my husband?" Her eyes were sparkling with mischief, but she settled into the crook of my arm, resting her head back on my chest. She was right where she was supposed to be.

We lay there for a while, watching the sun shift the shadows in my bedroom. When she excused herself to get up to go to the bathroom, I swung my legs off the bed and winced as I stood. Avery and Jess always joked about stretching and hydrating. They were typically talking about working out... but not always.

I definitely should have stretched.

Sometimes with too many repetitive movements, the knife wound in my thigh I had gotten during the Dallas extraction would twinge. I rubbed it with my hand before grabbing a clean pair of boxers from the drawer and slipping on a pair of sweats.

When Sabrina came into the main room in one of my T-shirts, I hummed in appreciation. I couldn't take my eyes off her as she went into the kitchen and poured another cup of coffee before looking up at me again. "Care for another cup?"

I let my gaze trail up and down her body as I shook my head. "Not really what I want right now."

"Horndog." Her eyes sparkled as she strode past me, opened the slider to our tiny patio, and jerked her head at me to follow.

You don't have to tell me twice.

"When my wife is this fucking sexy? You bet I am." I sat on the loveseat, and when she met my gaze, I patted my thigh.

Red bloomed across her cheeks, and I didn't fail to notice the catch in her breath. With both hands wrapped around her coffee like a lifeline, she came and sat down. Reaching back and lifting the top of the storage behind the couch, I pulled out an extra warm blanket and wrapped it around us. She settled in, sipping her coffee as I wrapped my arms around her and we gazed out over the city.

"I could get used to this." Sabrina took another sip and sighed. "Waking up next to you every day is going to be a dream. I'm looking forward to the days we can just sit and snuggle, letting the weight of the families off our shoulders for just a little while."

Same.

Thoughts of our future flickered through my mind. "Do you want to stay at the compound? Here? Somewhere else?"

We sat in silence for a moment. "I don't know. I didn't think that was something we'd need to sort out so quickly. We didn't really talk about it before." She chuckled softly before taking another sip. "What do you think?"

It wasn't something I'd dared to dream about either. "We could move into your place after the dust settles. You need to be close to the Rodriguez compound. Unless you want to look in Dallas territory?"

Sabrina snickered and shook her head. "No. That would be weird."

I nodded in agreement. "You're not wrong. I'd rather deal with your uncle than have that conversation with Don Dallas."

She shifted to face me, eyes wide with concern. "How would that even work though? You are still going to work for Lianne, right?"

Oh, Kitten. I reached up and caressed her face. "I am for the time being. However, once you become Don, I'm going to relinquish my position with the Agostis. Lynette and I talked extensively about that. It isn't going to be a problem with the Agostis if I stay working for them as long as their business and Rodriguez business stays separate."

Sabrina shook her head, smiling. "I can't believe how much you thought of and planned out. What about living around my guys, though?"

I shrugged again, but something flickered in his eyes. "Zee already loves me. Raine isn't a big deal. If I can deal with Avery, I can deal with him. Rob and Cobra don't have a problem, either. Rob seems to respect me more after working with me on George and Lynette's detail. If I have to report to your crazy family, I'll live."

She nodded. "When did you talk to Uncle Ceaser about the last-name thing?"

My eyebrows went up at the sudden subject shift. "Back when you were gone." I let out a tense breath. "I wasn't getting answers beyond 'she's alive', so I barged into the compound and demanded to know what was going on. Once he saw I was freaking out, he calmed me down and got me back on track. I wasn't handling it well, Kitten. Not at all." I reached over, gripped her chin with my thumb and forefinger, and turned her to face me before giving her a soft kiss. "After that, he apologized for not giving his blessing for us getting married sooner. Said it was obvious I loved you. He gave me his blessing to marry you and said Rodriguez-Agosti politics could wait. I don't remember who brought up the last name thing initially, but we hashed it out then. I told him I didn't care about changing mine if that's what it took. He said he'd be honored to have me as a nephew. So that was it. I would become a Rodriguez once we got married."

She stared at me, stunned. "Just when I thought I couldn't love you more, you've gone and proved me wrong."

Lianne

Chloe giggling nearby, and hushed voices filtered through my slightly open door, and I glanced up, curious.

That's way more than just Ben and Lukas.

Furrowing my brow, I walked out of my office in time to see a perfectly folded paper airplane fly past the end of the walkway.

"See, Chloe? That's how you throw it."

That's Connor. What is happening?

I glanced in Ryan's office, not at all surprised to see him completely immersed in something on his computer screen, and I couldn't help but smile at the collection of Chloe art scattered all over the front of his desk.

Another bout of giggles pulled me to the end of the hallway, and when I peeked around the corner, my heart immediately melted at the sight. There was a small pile of paper between Lukas and Gage, who were folding paper airplanes, and Ben and Connor were coaching Chloe on how to throw them. About a dozen planes in various states of being crumpled littered the length of the hallway.

"I was going to head into the kitchen to get more coffee, but I didn't want to disrupt them."

I glanced over my shoulder, grinning and shaking my head at the fact that my mother had snuck up on me yet again. "They're so adorable."

She smirked. "You *would* call four mafia men fully trained in death and destruction adorable."

"As another mafia person trained in death and destruction, I think *I'm* adorable. There's no reason they can't be too."

There was a slight scuff of a shoe against the carpet. "Ellen thinks I'm adorable."

Spinning around, I let out an amused chuckle at the sight of Ryan casually leaning against the casing of his office door. "As she should."

When I peeked around the corner into the hallway again, Lukas was looking right at me. "Enjoying your little spying game, Li?"

Rolling my eyes, I stepped out from my hiding place. "I was. So were Mom and Ryan."

At the mention of my mother, Gage practically jumped off the ground. "Did you need anything, Lynette?"

My mom chuckled and joined me. "You were keeping my granddaughter happy and safe. I have no complaints."

Connor chuckled as he leisurely stood up. "Sabrina makes this look easy." He glanced at Lukas, who was still sitting, holding Bunny. "You and Quinn have your work cut out for you."

He nodded. "Yes, we do. Good thing we've got Grandma in the house." Lukas winked at our mom, who chuckled.

"Good thing."

Chapter Thirty-Six

Dante

Sabrina and I were up early and out the door the next morning. As much as we loved the time alone, we were both anxious to get back to the house. We had important jobs to do. My leg was randomly being a pain again, but nothing a pain reliever didn't cure.

I really need to remember to stretch more after sex.

On the way back, we swung by a coffee place and picked up drinks for Avery, Ben, Lianne, and Lynette. It had been very kind of them to take on our responsibilities and let us stay an extra night. And that was on top of everything they had done to help me pull off the ultimate surprise.

When Sabrina and I walked in, Chloe was in the foyer with Ben, waiting for us with a small stack of pictures, all squiggled lines, stick figures, and smiles. After giving our favorite little girl all the hugs she wanted, Sabrina headed off with her, Chloe chatting away at a million miles an hour, leaving me and Ben standing there.

"I'm glad you had time away, but I'm glad you're back."

I smirked and nodded. "She and I feel the same way." I paused. "Is Lianne in her office?"

Ben's light mood dimmed slightly. "She is, and she wants to talk to you."

What happened now? "I was planning on talking to her before relieving Nash."

"Perfect. Thank you." Letting out a sigh, he slowly headed in the direction of the kitchen.

I watched him for a moment, noting the weight on his shoulders. *Will that be me when Sabrina steps up as Don?* Before heading toward Lianne's office, I made a mental note to sit down with Ben in the future and talk about what being married to a Don looked like.

Her office door was already open, so I tapped a knuckle against the doorjamb. Lianne didn't look up from her screen. "Come in." She finished typing up something before finally glancing over and spotting the to-go offering in my hand, and an amused expression played on her face. "Is that for me?"

I nodded. "Sabrina and I wanted to thank you again for letting us have extra time to be together."

She grinned. "You didn't need to bring a thank you gift, but I appreciate it all the same."

"Listen, I know how much better people are around here when they have their favorite caffeinated beverage." I set the cup on her desk. "I also know a vanilla chai latte is on your list of favorites."

Lianne reached over and wrapped both hands around it, gratitude plain as daylight on her face. "Won't argue with any of that." She took a sip and let out a happy hum. "Perfect."

It pleased me to see her happy. Sabrina and I had talked about this very thing on the drive over.

"Lianne is carrying a weight heavier than any of you realize. Hell, I'm the closest one to living the same situation, and I barely have a grasp on the magnitude of her role."

Clearing my throat, I moved on from my thoughts. "Ben mentioned you wanted to talk to me."

She gestured to the chair next to me. "I have a few things we need to talk about before you head down." Lianne let out a deep sigh and took a sip of her latte, as if she was bracing herself for something. "Mom and I discussed this at length. You're very welcome to sleep upstairs with Sabrina now. It feels completely unreasonable and downright cruel not to let you be with your wife at night. That being said, there are some ground rules." Lianne leaned forward, pinning me with a look so fierce I almost started sweating. "That is my niece in that room with you. At the end of the day, Sabrina is her main bodyguard and nanny. Chloe comes first."

"Of course. I would never compromise the safety of either of them."

I get to be with my Kitten at night.

The thought alone filled me with joy.

Lianne narrowed her eyes at me, immediately checking my excitement. "Sleeping and cuddling with your wife is absolutely fine, but you *will* keep any and all *extracurricular activities* out of that room. Do I need to spell this out?"

"No, ma'am. I understand and respect the rule." The fact that Chloe's bedroom was so close to all the Agosti bedrooms was all enough to make me toe the line on any affection I wanted to give Sabrina. It wasn't *our* space. Even if I was comfortable up there, she would never be able to check out of work long enough for anything to happen. There was also the old adage of not dipping your quill in the company ink.

Lianne relaxed slightly, but the intensity was still there. "I'm also aware of some elements of your relationship dynamic, and I'm not here to comment on it, but again, you will behave accordingly so as not to scandalize or traumatize my niece." She paused for a moment, the faintest twitch of frustration pulling at her mouth. "This entire Liam situation is so far outside of the realm of normal, and I'm trying to create protocol that works the best for everyone involved."

I nodded again. "It's extremely reasonable. I'm grateful I get to be with Sabrina at all."

A sad smile appeared. "I would hate being forced to sleep in a different bedroom than Ben. That's a special hell I don't want to inflict on anyone unnecessarily. There's no reason to keep you two separated. If something happens to change that, we'll have another conversation."

"Again, I appreciate that. I'm still beyond grateful for everything you did to help me propose to and marry Sabrina."

There was genuine joy on her face now. "I've known Sabrina almost my entire life, Dante. I see how happy you two make each other. I also know some of the hells she's walked through. If there is anyone in this world who deserves love and comfort, it's her."

"Thank you."

Lianne nodded, and just before she turned back to her laptop, a soft chuckle came out. "I can honestly say, I've done one thing better than Dad. I didn't hesitate in letting you marry your girl."

I pressed my lips into a tight line as I fought a smile. "I feel I should decline to comment."

"Fair enough. Have a good day, Dante."

With the conversation finished, I headed downstairs to find Nash and take over. He was going to Don San Augustine's to spend some time with Poppy, and when I stepped into the medical area, Avery was already there, chatting with him.

Nash grinned when he spotted me. "No need to step in. Looks like the newlywed remembered he had a job and actually showed up for it."

I rolled my eyes. "Don't you have a girlfriend to visit or something?"

He laughed and nodded. "Damn straight I do. And there's nothing to report. Liam was quiet and relatively well-behaved."

Avery smirked and shot a teasing look my way. "Happy to see you back. I'm a bit surprised at you, though."

I gave her a confused look. "Why?"

She snickered. "You look far too rested and are walking too easily. Should I ask Sabrina if she had a good wedding night?"

This woman. "We had a fantastic honeymoon, thank you very much." I reached for the cup on the table. "But if you're going to be a pain in the ass, I'll happily enjoy the latte I brought for you." Avery snatched it off the table, smirking and immediately taking a sip. I couldn't help but chuckle. "Don't you have some knives to sharpen or something? Or a partner of your own to harass?"

She sauntered out, and when I opened the door to Liam's holding cell, his gaze met mine. "Newlywed?"

"Yup. Married Sabrina two days ago."

Red rose up his neck as he stood up. "You married that Rodriguez tramp?"

I didn't even blink, but slapped handcuffs on him before escorting him to Avery's office. Though, I did find it interesting that someone who had grown up with Sabrina called her, of all people, a tramp.

"Sure did. That Rodriguez tramp is my wife now. You want to congratulate us, or should I go ahead and tell Sabrina you were talking shit so I can delight in watching her put you in your place?"

Liam rolled his eyes as I nearly shoved him into the room. "Can't even handle me yourself, Wilson?"

I'm under orders not to. For now. "That is Rodriguez to you. Now, you know as well as I do that I can take you in any fight you want to start. It's one of the reasons I have the honor of keeping you company down here instead of the family letting you rot like the piece of garbage you are."

He sneered, but I could see the way his jaw flexed as he fought for restraint. "You took *her* last name? What the hell? Are you trying to drag the Agosti name through the mud and make us look like we're crawling to the Rodriguez family for handouts?"

A snicker popped out. "If we're going to talk about trashing the Agosti name, I'm pretty sure *you* win that particular prize."

His fingers curled tight into fists on the table. "You think you're better than me now? You're not. You're just a fucking errand boy who got lucky."

I almost laughed. He was so bitter it made the air taste sour. "Liam, you want to come at me? Try to take your pound of flesh? Fine. But remember, *you're* the one sitting in this house with nothing to do. *I'm* the one trusted to keep the Don and her family alive. Maybe you should ask yourself why that is."

He stared at me, murder and rage burning bright in his eyes. I felt the urge to dig in, to keep poking, but Lianne had made it clear: keep things clean and don't escalate. None of us needed more drama. Though I was still a bit jealous that Ben landed a few good hits on him.

So I shrugged and grabbed my phone. "If you're done being jealous, I'll be next door working on my crossword puzzle. Let me know if you want to send us a wedding gift. Or an apology."

His eyes burned holes in me as I left the room. It didn't bother me any.

The rest of the shift was dead quiet. Not a single call, no motion outside, just the hum of the security system and the scraping of metal as Avery sharpened her knives in her office. I'd gotten through two crossword puzzles when I decided to check in on my wife.

Dante: < You good? >

Sabrina: < Chloe is in full arts and crafts mode today. Send help. >

Dante: < You're on your own, Rodriguez. I have a hostile at ten o'clock. >

Sabrina: < He causing problems? >

Dante: < Nothing worth getting worked up over. >

Sabrina: < Do I want to know? >

Dante: < He's just jealous and bitter that I've found happiness. >

Sabrina: < Oh, I want to know now. I can tag in Lukas for five minutes and come for a quick visit. ;) >

Dante: < Kitten, do not come down here. What we want takes more than five minutes, and I don't want to have to stop you from kicking his ass when he runs his mouth. >

Sabrina: < You're no fun. >

Dante: < That's not what you said this morning in the shower. >

I could practically see her rolling her eyes through the screen.

Avery came down around noon and told me to head upstairs to have lunch with Sabrina. Who was I to disobey that order?

When I walked into the family kitchen, Sabrina was trying to clean up Chloe who had glitter glue on both hands and a face like she'd just been crowned princess of the household.

When I kissed her cheek, she leaned into it, dropping her voice so only I could hear. "You okay?"

I nodded. "He tried to pick a fight. That's all."

She arched her brow. "Let me guess. He called me a t-r-a-m-p?"

"He did." I smirked at the fact she spelled it out, but the smile faded. "As much as I wanted to... discipline him, I refrained."

"He's not worth the effort."

Chloe piped up, "Dante, look! I made you pit-chur."

I looked down at the mess of marker, glue, and what might have been a drawing of me holding hands with Sabrina, crowned in gold crayon. It made my chest feel warm.

I cleared my throat. "That's amazing, Chloe. You're a real artist."

"I show Unca Ben Ben more pit-churs later."

About that time, Lynette came into the kitchen. "I thought I heard a precious cupcake. Can Grandma have lunch with you, too?"

"Gamma! Gamma!" She was so excited she started clapping, sending water splashing into Sabrina's face as the woman continued to scrub little hands.

"Chloe, you can have lunch with Grandma as soon as we get the rest of this glue off you."

She let out a big huff. "Okay, Bina."

Sabrina

I'd just coaxed Chloe to sleep, taking comfort in the soft rise and fall of her tiny chest when there was a gentle knock on the bedroom door. I immediately checked my phone to see if there were any messages I'd missed while reading to her, but there was nothing time sensitive.

Pulling myself off the floor, I walked across the room and quietly opened the door, stunned to see Lianne standing there. "Is everything okay?"

She nodded. "Oh yeah. I was actually heading off to relax for the first time in weeks, and I was hoping I could read a book to Chloe while in between meetings."

I hated that I was about to disappoint her. "She fell asleep less than five minutes ago, but you can still come in and sit with her."

Lianne let out a deep sigh but then nodded. "I'd like that."

I waited in the doorway as she quietly made her way over to the toddler bed, pressing a kiss to her forehead as she smoothed Chloe's blankets. The love she had for her niece would have been obvious to a blind man.

There was a smile on her face as she made her way back to where I was standing. "I can't tell you how much I've loved having her here. She brings so much happiness to this house. Even when everything is chaotic and going to shit."

I nodded, letting my eyes rest on Chloe's sleeping form. "She's a beacon of love, light, and hope. There's no denying that." Smiling, I bumped my shoulder against Lianne's. "A reminder that there's good in the world." We stood there for a moment, watching the adorable toddler sleep. "Hey, Li?"

"Yeah?"

"As you know, Chloe is absolutely obsessed with everything fish and ocean."

Lianne chuckled. "That she is. Ben and I were just talking about the serious aquatic themed book collection that little girl is amassing." She looked at me, eyes narrowed slightly. "What's up?"

"What would you think about taking her to the aquarium? The Shedd's indoors, so exposure risk is minimal. I get it if you don't think it's safe, but..." I trailed off. Chaotic mafia life or not, I wanted Chloe to have fun, 'normal' outings, like I'd had growing up.

"But Chloe deserves an adventure. And you deserve to see something besides these walls of this house."

I shrugged, letting out a laugh that barely made a sound. "I'm grateful to be alive to enjoy these walls, honestly. Plus, I have my Dante here." A smile appeared on my face as I thought about the fact he was now my husband. "Now, when it comes to seeing more than this house, I *was* just out for a day and a half."

Now Lianne snickered. "Yeah, for your *honeymoon*. You deserve more time out of here than that."

A smirk tugged at the corner of my mouth. "I'm grateful for the time we had. But what kind of coverage would we need to leave? I know it's going to have to be more than me and Zee."

"Uncle Ceaser informed me of Zee's required presence, regardless of your location." Lianne's deep sigh stretched into the silence before her gaze shifted to me. Most people would have squirmed under the weight of it, but I held my ground, waiting. She wasn't scrutinizing me, but considering the situation from multiple angles. I'd seen the same look on her face many times growing up. Finally she nodded. "Let me talk to Mom, Gage, and Ryan. If they can't give me actual, concrete reasons you can't go on a field trip... then you get to go."

For a second, my composure cracked and some of my excitement bled through. "Really?"

A slow grin crept onto Lianne's face. "I want to make it real for you, especially if it brings out *that* reaction."

I exhaled and felt my shoulders drop. "I'm assuming Dante can't come."

She pressed her lips into a thin line. "Let me battle it out with the boys. I'll see what I can do."

"Yes, ma'am."

Lianne rolled her eyes, but affection was there. She lingered for a heartbeat more, casting one final look at Chloe, smoothed the edge of the blanket with careful hands, and then slipped out.

Chapter Thirty-Seven

Sabrina

The next morning, Ben walked into the kitchen, much to Chloe's delight.

"Ben Ben!"

He grinned and gave her a tight hug. "How's my favorite cupcake today?"

"I good!" She handed him one of her fish crackers. "You want a fishie?"

"I'd love one." Ben happily accepted the snack and then glanced at me. "Lianne wants to chat with you. It's not an emergency."

My eyebrows went up. "Okay? Now?"

He nodded. "Part of the reason I'm here. I get to play messenger and see the cutest cupcake in the world!" He kissed the top of Chloe's head, putting an enormous smile on her face.

"You silly, Unca Ben Ben."

I crouched next to Chloe. "I'm going to talk to Auntie Li. You be good for Uncle Ben, okay?"

She nodded dutifully. "I be good. Love you, Bina."

"Love you, too." Smiling, I headed out of the kitchen and toward Lianne's office, hoping for good news. Her office door was closed when I walked up, and I knocked on it twice.

"Come in." When I pushed it open, she glanced up and smiled. "That was fast. I wasn't sure how quickly Ben was going to be able to get you down here."

I shrugged. "We were in the kitchen having fish snacks. His timing was perfect, honestly."

Lianne grinned. "Good. I'm glad. Well, have a seat. I have good news and bad news."

Letting out a sigh, I sank into the open chair, folding my hands in my lap. "Let's start with the bad."

"Dante's out for tomorrow. He can't go with you."

"As much as I'm disappointed, I'm not entirely surprised." I paused for a moment. *Wait.* "Is the good news that I can take Chloe to the aquarium?"

Lianne's grin could not have been wider. "Exactly. Mom thinks it's the best idea."

"How big of a detail are we getting for this little trip?" I asked, curiosity rising.

"Jess, Connor, and Zee." Lianne looked rather pleased. "The boys were being obstinate about you not going without a detail rivaling mine until we chatted with Uncle Ceaser. There was a lot of back-and-forth about how involved Zee would be. The final decision is for them to hang out at the aquarium in the general area you're in and keep in contact with Jess and Connor."

"But not with me directly?" I was mildly irritated about this. They were on my crew and always answered to me.

"Nope." Lianne shook her head. "Your only job is Chloe. She's going to keep you busy enough. You don't need the additional responsibility. Jess will be in charge of the diaper bag, and Connor will be on stroller duty. It may sound like overkill, but I'm not about to gamble with the safety of either of you. For what it's worth, the boys wanted twice the numbers and had even tossed around the idea of only letting you go before or after general admission hours."

I couldn't help the smirk that appeared on my face. "Would that be the case if you were going?"

She scoffed and rolled her eyes. "They'd try."

My smirk widened into a smile. "Fair enough. So, when's the field trip?"

"Tomorrow. We still need to finalize some of the logistics. Connor is taking care of a few things for me right now, but I'll fill him in when I get back."

"Oh! Where are you heading out to?"

Lianne's face lit up with joy. "I have a lunch date with my best friend."

As if on cue, Jess knocked on the door and sauntered into the office. "Hey, cuties. How's it going? You two plotting and planning to take over the world?"

Lianne let out a low chuckle and shook her head. "Nothing *quite* that nefarious or exciting. Just filling her in on the aquarium field trip tomorrow."

Jess plopped down. "I'm so stoked about this. Seeing Connor around otters is one of my absolute favorite things. He's so fucking adorable with that little grin."

I stared at her in disbelief. "Otters are his favorite?"

She nodded enthusiastically. "Oh yeah. The man melts."

A huge smile appeared on Lianne's face. "Can confirm. I was there."

I leaned back in the chair, shaking my head. "Connor has a favorite animal. Will wonders never cease?" It was in that moment I realized I didn't know what Dante's favorite animal was, or if he had one. Well, aside from his Kitten.

Jess shifted in her seat, bringing my attention back to our conversation. "So, the logistics? We can hash out the non-Connor specific ones before heading out."

Over the next several minutes, Lianne went over the timeline and procedure for the following day. Connor was going to drive the four of us in the newest SUV. Zee was going to meet us there, parking in the same parking lot, but not immediately next to us.

"Ryan will also be tracking you the entire time. Aside from your phones, there will be tags in the diaper bag, attached to the stroller, and on one of Chloe's shoes."

Jess shook her head again. "I pity his future children. He is going to be insufferable."

I shrugged. "A few tracking tags are the least of my worries. I'm grateful for the abundance of backup."

Lianne gave me a knowing look. "You're not on your own here."

~~~~~~

Lianne

Jess and I had the best time while out for lunch. We tried out a new molecular cuisine restaurant and picked up ice cream on the way home. My afternoon went smoothly, and now I was in the zone, headphones on, trying to finish reading through a report. I had two pages left when I barely heard a knock on my door in between songs. Letting out a sigh, I pulled the headphones off and looked up from the paperwork, my fingers still curled around the pen I'd been using to take notes. "Come in." The door opened, and when Adair walked in, I sat up a little taller.

She glanced at my desk and suddenly looked nervous. "If now's a bad time, I can come back."

The slight tremor in her voice had me immediately flipping the papers over. "Your timing is great. I actually needed a break." I would have stopped doing pretty much anything for her at this point. The fate of my family and our entire business was in her hands right now.

Is this it? Is this where everything starts... or ends?

Adair gently closed the door behind her and walked in, stopping just in front of my desk. There was determination in her eyes, but also several other emotions I didn't have time to identify.

"I made my decision about the contract, and I wanted to tell you first."
~~~~~~

The words hung in the air as time crawled to a stop. Ice cold fear sank into my chest, making it hard to breathe for a moment. For days I tried to push the thought of Adair's retribution for Liam's treachery to the furthest, darkest corner of my mind. Now, with the resolution at hand, every possibility tumbled to the surface. Would she demand my brother's life? The family's territory? Something more?

I forced myself to nod slowly, doubling my efforts to maintain my mask of composure. "And what have you decided?" I tried to hold her gaze, but my eyes kept catching on the smallest details, like the place where her sleeve was slightly frayed and how she was standing incredibly still. Anything to keep me from imagining the worst.

Adair took a breath and released it slowly before stepping closer to my desk. "I'm not starting a war. I'm not asking for any territory or businesses or anything else from you, Lianne. I refuse to make you, Lynette, or Lukas pay for the sins Liam committed. *He* broke the contract, so he alone will pay the price."

I stared at her as I processed the words, and relief hit so hard and fast that it nearly knocked me out of my chair. For a moment, I was so lightheaded I almost laughed.

I'm not going to lose it all.

It's not all going to disappear.

Mom and Dad's legacy will carry on.

Tears pricked the insides of my eyelids. I blinked wildly, refusing to let any spill, but my efforts were in vain.

Adair's expression softened as doubt flickered in her eyes. "Lianne? Are you okay?"

I nodded again, this time with a little more enthusiasm. "I am... I just..." I exhaled shakily, feeling the tightness in my shoulders relent as I managed a weak smile. "I thought you were going to... You could have demanded anything. You had every right."

A shadow of horror flickered across Adair's face. "Did you really think I was going to punish *you*?"

I tried to pull myself together, straightening my suit jacket and clearing my throat before answering, but my voice still came out strained. "It was well within your rights. The Agosti family did not comply with the terms of the contract."

Even now as she stared at me, stunned, I couldn't shake the sense of duty and obligation drilled into me by three generations of men who would have slit their own wrists before admitting fault, let alone surrendering to an enemy. I waited for her to counter, to correct me, to strip the pretense of honor I still clung to.

Instead, she rushed forward around my desk and pulled me into a hug so tight I nearly squeaked. "Lianne, no. This wasn't your fault. You, your mom, and your entire team have done nothing but try to keep me safe and alive. I want to be everything my Aunt Melanie was. Kind, fair, strong, and a complete badass. What kind of a Don would I be if I punished the people who literally saved my life?

I blinked, surprised at the suddenness of her affection, but then realized I was hugging her back just as fiercely. I let myself bask in it for a moment, then gently eased us apart, studying her face one last time for any sign of ulterior motive. There was none.

"You are going to do amazing things as a Don. And I am so here for it." I shifted in my seat. "That being said, what *have* you decided?"

She met my gaze, a new energy animating her. "How do you and Ben feel about becoming parents?"

I stared at her, stunned as the words bounced around my head several times before sinking in.

What?

Ben and I had discussed children. It was one of the many 'maybe someday after Liam' topics, usually brought up after a bit too much rum. But with Dad gone and the family in chaos, Ben and I had spent so much of the last year either bracing for or recovering from a disaster, it kept sliding down on the list of priorities. "I-I'm sorry, what?"

Adair lifted her chin and stared me in the eye. "I want to ensure Chloe has a loving, happy home for the rest of her life. That child is a the most perfect ray of sunshine and deserves more than the piece of shit parents she inherited. I want Liam and Susan to relinquish all parental rights of Chloe Lynette Agosti to Lianne and Benedict Agosti. Also, in regards to forfeiting territory or property... Anything with Liam's name on it, either solely or jointly or in trust, all accounts, trusts, bank accounts, etc. becomes Chloe's. I require a trust to be set up for her to inherit half at the age of eighteen, the other half at thirty, and a trust for the caretaker for the exclusive use of necessities for taking care of Chloe. If you and Ben accept, I want you to have the assistance if needed. I also want to make sure my niece has everything she needs."

I stared at her, shocked and slightly overwhelmed. I had anticipated blood, retribution, or a demand for property, but not this act of mercy. "Are... Are you sure?"

She smiled proudly. "I've never been more sure of anything."

My mind raced, cycling through the implications. Chloe would be ours, in every way that mattered. Safe, protected, maybe even happy, if we could figure out how to fix the damage that had already been done. The thought brought a strange, bittersweet ache to my chest.

Adair took a step back and dropped her voice to a hush, as if confessing a secret. "If Liam complies with this, he lives. If he doesn't, he dies. I want that to be very clear. And should he choose not to comply, and if you'll allow it, I would like to be the one to execute Liam."

The darkness in her eyes was chilling, and I recognized it as the same look I'd seen on her face two weeks ago, when she'd stood in the foyer, facing demons from her past, and refused to cry.

My heart was beating so fast it felt like it was going to burst out of my chest. I didn't trust myself to answer right away, so I stalled. "Have you spoken with Don Dallas?"

Adair shook her head. "No. I assumed you'd want to schedule an appointment for us to do that together."

Nodding, I studied her for a moment. "Is there anything else?" I needed to make sure this wasn't a trap. That this was truly everything she wanted.

"No, Don Agosti. Please let me know if the terms are acceptable to you."

A small, almost hysterical laugh came out. "I don't have the power to approve or deny. I *can't* approve or deny. All there is to do is accept. You have stated your retribution, and you will have it. I need to meet with Mom and Lukas to update them, and I have to talk to Ben about Chloe, but you know how much we adore her." I picked up my phone and sent a text to Ben asking him to come to my office. "I'll contact Mr. Greene to start pulling the paperwork together, and we'll meet with Liam as soon as it's done."

"Thank you."

When Adair opened the door to leave, Ben was just walking up, and a conspiratorial smile appeared on her face as she greeted him. He gave her an odd look before turning his attention to me. I extended my hand toward him, fingers trembling with adrenaline and an overwhelming amount of emotions, and he rushed toward me, taking it without hesitation as he wrapped me in a hug. "What's wrong?"

Leaning against Ben, I let the steady beat of his heart ground and calm me as I took a deep breath, letting it out slowly. "Adair just gave me the list of what the Agosti's retribution will be."

He gently rubbed my back and kissed the side of my head. "Is there... Is it as bad as you thought?"

"No." A sob snuck out as I shook my head. "She's not taking anything from us."

Ben slid his hands up to hold my face, forcing me to look him in the eyes. "That's amazing, Li. See? I told you it was going to be okay."

I nodded, tears rolling down my cheeks. "You did."

He narrowed his eyes as he studied my face. "What are her demands then? You're still too worked up about this."

"It's not blood or property. Not exactly. It's Chloe." My throat constricted on the last syllable, and I looked into the eyes of the man I loved. "Adair is calling for Liam and Susan to sign over all parental rights. She wants Chloe to be ours."

Ben blinked slowly as he stared at me. It was almost comical the way his face went from confusion to shock to awe, each emotion taking a full second to bloom. "Ours?"

When I nodded, his eyes went glassy with tears. Not the showy kind that people conjure for sympathy or attention. These were different. Raw. Real.

"We get to be her parents?" His voice cracked in the middle, turning the question into a benediction.

"We do."

For once in this office, I didn't need to mask my emotions or play strong. I let the tears fall, and Ben pulled me close and kissed me so hard I nearly lost my breath.

"I never thought… I thought she'd be gone, or sent to some boarding school, or—" I cut him off with another kiss, this one slower. When I pulled away, he rested his forehead against mine and held me close. "I love you so much, Li."

"We have to protect her, Ben. *Really* protect her. She's been through so much shit, and she needs…" My voice broke again, but I forced myself to finish. "She needs good, loving parents. She needs us."

He nodded, and when I saw the intensity in his eyes, I knew I'd never have to worry about him wavering. "She'll have the best. I swear it. She'll never grow up wondering where her next meal is coming from or if she's safe or if she's loved. She'll have everything."

I believed him.

Not because I thought we deserved a happy ending, but because Ben was the kind of man who would bulldoze every obstacle in his path to make something possible. He'd had a wild, unpredictable, and at times, violent childhood, and I knew he would do everything in his power to make sure she never lived through anything even remotely close to what he did.

For the first time since everything went to hell, I felt something like hope.

In the silence, I started to let myself imagine it: birthday parties with kids running around everywhere, trips to the park, tiny furrowed brows over math homework, the sound of her laughter ringing down the hall, decorating for Christmas. I let myself picture her running toward me in the yard, hair streaming, shrieking with the wild, unselfconscious joy that every kid should get to have.

Ben must have seen it in my face, because he grinned. "She's going to love growing up with my nieces... and my brother and moms will spoil her rotten." He paused. "She's going to have her cousins, too."

I smiled as more happy tears ran down my face. "You planning on being the fun parent or the scary parent?"

He raised a brow. "You terrify most grown men, Li. I think we both know how this is going to go." He paused, and the expression on his face softened. "I always wanted a daughter."

It was my turn to be stunned again, caught off guard by the admission. "You never told me that."

"I didn't want to jinx it. But I did." He smiled, resting his head on mine again. "I do."

We just stood there for a while, leaning into the new shape of our lives, until my phone buzzed.

Adair: < Totally stayed in the hall to eavesdrop... Sorry, not sorry. Can I assume from the excitement that Ben's on board? >

A chuckle shook my shoulders just before Ben kissed my cheek and turned to open the door. Adair stood there, phone in her hands, tears in her eyes. He closed the distance between them and wrapped her in a hug. "I am one million percent on board."

When we finally managed to compose ourselves, the three of us pulled Mom and Lukas in for a meeting. Once they realized this was real, they each fell apart in their own ways. Lukas sobbed openly, clinging to me like we were kids again. Mom smiled through her tears and immediately began to fret about preschools and whether Chloe would like ballet, art, or karate classes.

It was chaos, but the good kind. The kind that families are supposed to have, not the kind that leaves bodies in rivers.

Today was a good day.

Chapter Thirty-Eight

Sabrina

Chloe was so excited the next morning, she could barely eat her breakfast. And when Liam joined us, food was completely forgotten about.

"Dada! I see fishies today!"

Liam gave her a stunned smile. "Really? That's great, Chloe." He gave me a pointed look. "Is it safe to take her there? That's my only child you're gallivanting about with."

I nodded, not taking the bait. *He's not worth the fight.* "It is. There's an entire plan to ensure it, expanded security detail and all."

I watched as he tried to help Chloe eat her breakfast, growing more agitated the more curt he became with her. *Maybe solitary confinement is finally getting to him. I hope Lianne and Adair get to the bottom of the contract stuff soon.* While I didn't think he would do anything to hurt his daughter, I couldn't dismiss the feeling he might lose his temper and lash out at her unnecessarily. When his tone went sharp and her eyes went wide with fear, I stepped in between them, facing Chloe. "You want to put on your shoes and leave for the aquarium now?"

Joy reappeared in her eyes as she shouted, "Fishies!"

Scooping her out of her high chair, I got her away from Liam as quickly as possible. As soon as we were out of the kitchen, Dante was in front of me. "I know we're working, but check in, Kitten."

My focus snapped to his face. "I'm at a yellow with your charge because of how he was treating his daughter."

He nodded and then gave me a quick kiss. "I've got him. You take care of Chloe and have all the fun, okay?"

"Okay."

"Bye, Dante!"

He smiled at the toddler. "Bye, Chloe. Be good for Sabrina." Dante then looked at me again. "I love you, Sabrina."

"I love you, too."

Chloe chatted nonstop the entire way to the aquarium. It was adorable, and her excitement was infectious. By the time we pulled into the parking lot, she'd almost infused enough of her energy to override my anxiety and apprehension about being in such a public place. Almost, but not quite.

Jess gently bumped my shoulder after I secured Chloe in the stroller. "We've got this."

I nodded and let out a tense breath as I scanned the street and the sidewalk for potential threats. "I know."

She glanced at me. "Zee is here already, if that makes you feel better."

Smirking, I huffed out a quiet laugh. "It does a little. Not that you and Connor aren't capable."

Jess shook her head knowingly. "I understand feeling more comfortable with certain people. This one up here"—she nodded toward Connor—"I trust implicitly. Now, that's not to say I don't trust Gage or Avery, but he and I have made it through some pretty bad shit together. There's a deeper connection."

My smirk widened into a full smile. "There's also the small detail of how you're married to him."

She snickered. "Touché, but that connection was there before. Kind of like you and Dante."

"Fair enough."

Once we were inside, I felt marginally better. We were less exposed, and I'd spotted Zee on the opposite side of the room. The next hour or so was full of Chloe staring wide-eyed in wonder at the different exhibits.

"Bina! They so boo-ty-ful!" She pressed her little finger against the glass of the lionfish tank.

Connor chuckled. "She *would* love a venomous fish that can cause temporary paralysis."

And then there was the excited squeal that flew from her mouth when we walked into the massive room where the entire wall was curved glass, showcasing sharks, schools of fish, and a coral reef. Chloe dragged me across the room, practically plastering her face to the front of the tank. She jumped back only a little when one of the zebra sharks swam right past us, but then clapped and loudly declared it pretty.

Jess let out an amused hum. "Is there *anything* this girl is afraid of?"

I shook my head and tightened my hold on Chloe, smiling when she let out a content sigh and snuggled against me. "Who knows?" I loved how carefree and happy she was. *Maybe she'll be okay in the long run.*

As predicted, Connor became almost a different person when showing Chloe the otters, and Jess showed the exact same level of animation when we saw the penguins. It was wild seeing mafia bodyguards acting so... normal. I glanced around, locking eyes with Zee for a second. The slight smile on their face told me I wasn't the only one amused by this.

But then we rounded the corner, and Chloe raced to the observation window, sucking in the most dramatic gasp as she flattened both her hands on the thick glass. "Bina, what this?"

"These are Beluga whales."

I swear little hearts appeared in her eyes as she watched one swim by. "I love 'luga whales, Bina." The pure joy all over her face was so raw and wholesome, it made my chest tighten up. The smile didn't falter for one moment the entire time, and I knew this would be a core memory for her. When a momma whale and her calf swam by, Chloe danced in place. "Bina! A little 'luga! It little like me!"

A chuckle came out. "That's a baby beluga. And it is little like you, but both of you are going to grow up to be big and strong."

She nodded seriously and then spent the next fifteen minutes trying to imitate the whales' movements. Chloe squealed and bounced when one of the whales came and stopped right in front of her and had a smile on its face.

"Ner! 'Luga smile at me!" She tugged at his jacket, and the love and admiration in his eyes warmed my heart.

We moved into a small observation room with a bench, where I sat and she stood, leaning against the window, never taking her eyes off them.

"Chloe, do you want to play in the submarine? You get to drive it."

The little girl shook her head. "No. I want 'lugas."

Connor leaned in. "If you're good with me stepping away for a minute, I'm going to buy that little girl a Beluga whale stuffed animal. I thought Jess was obsessed with her penguins, but she's got nothing on Chloe."

I nodded. "Jess, Zee, and I can hold down the fort for a few. I don't see us leaving this window for a while."

Once Connor returned, we convinced Chloe to go upstairs, but only because we told her she could see more Belugas.

She immediately wanted to join the trainers who were feeding and taking care of the whales, and couldn't stop giggling every time they tossed fish into their mouths. There was more excited squealing and clapping every time she saw the baby, and especially when any of the Belugas came up for air and sprayed a little water.

I'm totally paying for a behind the scenes encounter when she's older.

It wasn't long before Chloe asked for 'uppies,' and rested her head on my shoulder. When she hadn't moved for a while, I turned to face Jess. "Is she passed out?"

A little smile appeared on her face as she nodded. "She's out cold."

Letting out a sigh, I nodded. "Now might be a good time to head out. We can tell her the whales needed a nap, too."

"Works for me. Let's go."

We wrapped Chloe's coat around her as best as we could before leaving the building. It wasn't too cold, but the wind coming off the lake was chilly.

Something caught my attention as we made our way off the property, and when I glanced to my right, a man caught my attention. There wasn't anything about his general appearance that initially sent up any red flags, until a wicked, terrifying smirk teased the corner of his mouth. Malice flared up in his eyes, and my heart rate took off.

Please don't be who I think you are.

"Jess, you want to check in with Zee?"

She was already on her phone when I shifted my attention to her. "You two must be psychically linked. They just messaged that we need to keep moving."

Not wanting to draw attention to ourselves, or broadcast the fact we spotted a threat, we kept our pace the same. It was then that Chloe woke up.

"Bina, I no leave 'lugas! I want to go back."

I kissed the side of her head as I hugged her. "They needed to finish their lunch and take a nap, just like we do."

She scrunched up her face unhappily. "I want 'lugas, Bina."

Jess cleared her throat. "Fido, we need to roll."

Fido?

It was then I noticed the man I'd clocked earlier was trailing us... and he wasn't alone.

Shit.

Connor's response was quiet and practiced as he turned toward me, his focus tight and clear. "Chloe, do you want to fly to the truck?"

Her entire demeanor brightened as she started to wiggle in excitement. "Yes, pease!"

Connor stepped close, hands steady as he lifted her from my side. "You and Jess keep carrying on as normal. I'll get her to the truck and then out of here."

I nodded, keeping a cheery smile on my face. "Be good for Uncle Connor."

"Okay, Bina!" She then started chanting, "Fly Ner. Fly!"

"You got it, cupcake." He lifted her over his head and then with a whoosh, they weaved playfully along the sidewalk, Chloe's bright giggle floating through the air. I would have loved to watch her, soaking in the pure joy on her face, but we had company. People I didn't want within a mile of that sweet little girl.

"Oh, Jess! We never took our skyline selfie!" She gave me a curious look, but I glanced around, clocking at least three more men who weren't walking like any other tourist. "No cars coming. Quick. Let's take it."

She wrapped her arm around me as I lifted my phone and took the photo, making sure to get at least two of the guys in the frame. I let out a breath of relief when I also saw Zee nearby.

"Perfect! We should get to the car before Connor leaves us behind."

I let out a laugh. "He would never."

Please don't go after him and Chloe.

We made our way toward the parking lot slowly, giving Connor time to get Chloe into the SUV, buckled in, and if necessary, the hell out of here. I took the opportunity to send the picture to Uncle Ceaser.

Sabrina: < We have company. >

I had barely hit send before one of them called out, accent thick. "Señorita Rodriguez, I'm surprised and impressed to see you made it out of Cuba alive."

When I turned, I saw one of the assholes who had killed Rod. "I'm not sure why you're surprised."

"How's your fake husband these days?"

You fucker. I saw red, pulled my knife nestled in my cleavage, expertly flipped it open, and charged.

"Shit." Zee bit off the curse as they also pulled out their knife. "That was the *wrong* move, buddy."

Chapter Thirty-Nine

Lianne

The phone vibrated across the table as I was trying, for the third time, to take a bite of the turkey and cheese sandwich Ben made for me. I glanced up, an apology already forming, but Ben offered his small, knowing smile and nodded toward the phone. Glancing at the screen, my heart rate took off when I saw Connor's name.

Please be calling to ask if I want coffee or ice cream.

"Hey, Connor."

He didn't even bother with a greeting. "I've got Chloe. She's safe. We're both fine."

There was a small, bright giggle in the background. "I fly with Ner, Li Li!"

I simultaneously let out a sigh of relief while sitting up with a start. "Hi, Chloe. Did you have fun?"

Ben tipped his head slightly to the side, watching me warily.

"I love 'luga whales, Li Li!"

Her cheerful, excited voice did nothing to calm the panic building in my chest. "I'm so glad to hear that, sweetie. Um, Connor, where's the rest of the crew?"

"We caught a tail. Jess, Zee, and Sabrina stayed behind to handle it. I got Chloe out."

Time paused. The words ricocheted around my brain, immediately splintering in a dozen directions, each one blooming into an uglier scenario. "Connor, are *you* safe?" I said, feeling the words click together too slowly.

"Yeah. We're about ten minutes out."

I was immediately on my feet and heading toward my office. "Do you know anything else?"

"No, ma'am. I'm sure the ladies aren't far behind us, but wanted to give you a heads up when they weren't with me and Chloe when we arrived." He was silent for a moment. "I've got a bad feeling about this, Li. The three of them are more than capable, but..." He hesitated. "The way these guys closed ranks, it felt like a test. Or a message. These were not amateurs."

My heart sank as I passed my door and walked into my mom's office. "Take Chloe straight to her room when you get back. I'll have Mom and Ben in there to take over."

"Yes, ma'am."

The call ended, and I stood there for a moment before looking at Momma, who was now already walking around her desk, toward me.

"What happened, Lianne?"

More bullshit we didn't need. "Connor is on his way with Chloe. Sabrina, Jess, and Zee ran into a snag."

She let out a tense breath and nodded. "And you need me for Grandma duty?"

"Yeah. I don't know when or in what condition the ladies are going to return, and if there's anyone who can distract that little girl, it's you and Ben."

Mom gave me a quick hug before walking toward the door, pausing as she reached for the handle. "You might want to give Dante a heads up."

I nodded. "Yeah. I'll be in my office until I know more."

As I walked into my office, Ben, Regina, and Ryan were already there waiting for me. My bodyguard spoke up first. "Trouble?"

I nodded again. "Yeah."

Over the next few minutes, I filled them in and they sprang into action as I rapidly issued orders. Mom and Ben were prepping lunch for Chloe, to be followed by a bath and anything else that would keep her occupied upstairs. Ryan dove into pulling any security and surveillance footage he could get his hands on in and around the aquarium and nearby parking lots and streets so we could identify the threat. Regina went to update Doc and assist in any prep work.

Gage: < Connor and Chloe are here. She's none the wiser about the situation. >

I let out a relieved breath reading the message.

Two home. Three to go.

After finding Avery, I took on the task of updating Dante. I needed to do it in a way that didn't send him storming out of the house with a gun in his waistband and murder on his mind.

He was on his feet when I walked into the medical area. "What's happening? Regina is refusing to talk."

I glanced at Avery. "Move Liam to your office."

She gave me a curt nod. "Yes, ma'am."

Returning my attention to Dante, I nodded toward the door. "War room. Now." He followed me out, and I closed the door behind me once we were inside. "Sabrina, Jess, and Zee are going to be a bit delayed. Connor just rolled in with Chloe. I don't have any other information to give."

Every muscle in his body went tense as he took a breath. "Is she okay?"

"She was when Connor saw her last."

My phone rang, and I wasn't at all surprised to see Don Rodriguez's name on the screen. "Uncle Ceaser."

"Lianne, do you have any updates on what's going on? Sabrina sent me a photo of the men who were following them."

Men? As in multiple people? Shit. "Can you send it to Ryan? Connor and Chloe made it back, but I haven't heard from the ladies yet."

"I can't reach Sabrina." His tone was full of worry. "Raine and Ricky should be there by now. If for nothing than to help with cleanup."

My phone buzzed again.

Ryan: < They're here - alive - going straight to Doc. >

I gasped as I pulled the war room door open and stepped into the hallway just as Sabrina and Jess walked into the medical area. "They just walked in alive and moving under their own power."

"Thank you." I could hear the flood of relief.

"You're welcome, Uncle Ceaser. I promise to call you after I debrief them."

"Again, thank you. We both know she's more than capable of taking care of herself; I'm just a worried old man."

I couldn't help but chuckle as I leaned against the wall, taking a moment to appreciate the much lighter banter. "Well, you *are* ancient, Uncle Ceaser."

"Hey, fifty-three isn't ancient."

"I know better than to argue with my elders." There was no keeping a grin off my face when he snickered. "I'll call you back." After shoving my phone into my pocket, I hurried into the infirmary where Jess and Sabrina sat side by side on one of the exam tables, battered but still alive, with Doc already fussing over them. There was blood on their sleeves and bruises blooming, but they were upright.

They'd made it back.

They were okay.

Jess met my gaze and let out a low whistle as she shook her head in amazement. "You should have seen her, Li. I mean, the guys were huge and fast, but Sabrina fucking went at them. The one in the yellow jacket? He's never walking again. She broke his fucking neck with her bare hands."

My gaze flicked to Sabrina, expecting some kind of reaction. She just rolled her shoulder, face impassive, and didn't meet my gaze, keeping her focus on the floor. There was blood on the side of her hand, drying brown in the creases of her knuckles and cuticles, and her jaw was clenched so tight I worried she might shatter her a tooth. I recognized the posture. It was one I'd seen many times after shit went sideways on a mission.

What is going through your head right now?

Dante rushed in and stopped right behind me. His breathing was a notch too slow, controlled, like he was ready for something to jump out of the darkness.

Jess wrapped her arm around Sabrina's shoulders. "No, seriously, I've been in some ugly scrapes, but she and Zee went through these guys like a damn blender. It was fucking awe-inspiring. I'd have her on speed dial for the next time you need someone's head ripped clean off."

Sabrina shrugged. "It was luck and good timing. They weren't expecting that much of a fight. Not from all three of us."

"They likely didn't expect to leave in body bags, either." Jess let out a stunned laugh.

I was used to my best friend deflecting with humor, but I needed definitive answers. "Are you two okay?"

Jess nodded as Sabrina rolled her shoulder again. "I'll be sore. You know how it is after a fight, but yeah, I'm fine. Connor had Chloe out before anything happened, so I don't think she saw anything."

I let out another tense breath as I stared at the duo, watching Doc tend to some of the bigger scrapes. "Tell me what happened after Connor left. He couldn't give me much."

Jess started. "We clocked at least one of them as we headed out, and when Zee noticed two more and how they were closing in, she called in code red. That's when we had Connor 'fly' Chloe to the truck. The three of us stayed back to give him time to get away. We were almost to the parking lot before the one guy called out for Sabrina. He ran his mouth, and then all hell broke loose."

Sabrina was still pointedly not looking at anyone. The haunted and angry look in her eyes was one I recognized and understood. She was reliving every second, every muscle twitch, every breath of that fight. Something in all this had gotten to her more than she wanted, and if she was still anything like me, the second she met Dante's gaze she was going to break.

Jess snorted before continuing. "The guy with the neck tattoo that called her out? She put him on his knees and twisted his head until something snapped. No hesitation."

I raised my eyebrows. "Sabrina, you want to add anything?"

She shrugged, finally looking up at me, and I saw a shadow of fear and determination that passed over that gaze. "He would have shot me. He had a gun under his coat, but his draw was slow. Letting him live wasn't an option."

"You recognized them?"

She nodded. "Two of them were at the Nacional Hotel the night everything went to hell. There was no missing the tattoos or how they moved." Her teeth ground together as she continued. "I killed the guy who took out Rod, though." She hesitated and let out a long breath. "I'm sorry Rodriguez business followed me here, Lianne. I really didn't think they would find me so quickly."

I nodded, not surprised at her guilt. "It wasn't on purpose. Also, we knew the risk when we brought you in. I have no regrets."

Tears tried to gather in her eyes, but she blinked them away. "But now I've brought more problems to your front door."

Letting out a tense breath, I stepped in front of Sabrina and gently took her hands in mine, holding eye contact. "They are well-connected, but so are we. Mafia families aren't exactly known for peaceful encounters."

The tiniest hint of a smirk appeared on her face for a moment. "Yeah, and the cartel isn't really known for being subtle. Everything they do in South America is with a statement. There is a reason they are feared."

That tracks with the information Ryan and Uncle Ceaser gave me. "Do you think this was a scouting mission or an actual hit?"

Sabrina's answer was instant as she scoffed. "Scouting for sure. If they wanted us dead, they'd have brought more and used more firepower. This was a message."

"The message being?" I tilted my head.

"We know where you are. You can't hide. And we don't care who sees us."

A chill shot down my back. The arrogance of it was almost impressive. Glancing over my shoulder, Dante hadn't taken his eyes off Sabrina. There was something in his expression that made me pause. It wasn't just concern. It was the kind of raw, burning protectiveness that didn't leave room for much else. He was barely holding himself in check.

Is that what Ben and I look like sometimes?

"I'm almost done, Dante, and then she's all yours for a few."

He nodded. "Thank you."

"Have you heard from Zee?"

I looked at Sabrina again, shaking my head. "No."

Her jaw clenched again. "They tossed their keys at Jess, screaming for her to get me out of there. Jess was a bit of a bitch getting me into the truck..." She glanced at the woman in question. "Sorry about that."

Jess shrugged. "I've literally been in your shoes before. Connor had to shove me into the back seat of a truck before, and I wanted to kick his ass... until the gunshots started. Then I stopped fighting."

Sabrina nodded. "Yeah. Something about the back window of the vehicle you're in being blown out will check your attitude real fast." Her breathing picked up as her eyes locked onto mine. "If something happened to them..."

I gave her hand another squeeze. "I'll see what I can find out. I promised to call Uncle Ceaser back after I chatted with you." It was at that moment Connor came racing into the room, and I looked at him. "Perfect timing. Please take Jess into one of the patient rooms and finish cleaning her up and bandaging her."

He looked around the room and then nodded, as if he'd put together what I was doing. "Come on, Renegade. Let's keep your bestie and boss happy."

Once they were behind a closed door, I looked at Dante. "Take care of our girl."

"Yes, ma'am."

With that, I headed back upstairs and straight into Ryan's office, hoping he had an update.

Chapter Forty

Dante

I barely held it together while Sabrina reported to Lianne. She had been truthful with Lianne, but her eyes told the rest of the story and couldn't hide how rattled she was. She never once looked in my direction, and I got it; I really did. My Kitten was desperately trying to maintain her tough, professional exterior.

Locking my hands behind my back to keep myself from pulling her into me, I stood off to the side and waited. It didn't stop me from noticing the way she flinched as Doc checked over her ribs. Every cell in my body wanted to shove him out of the way and do it myself, but I forced myself to stand still. It was not my place, and I was outranked by almost everyone in the room. When I moved forward after Sabrina flinched, Doc glanced back at me with a look that screamed, 'pull it together or get the hell out.'

I exhaled through my nose and took inventory of her injuries as he finished doing his thing.

A bruised rib.

Old shoulder injury acting up after Cuba.

Some scrapes.

Sabrina was physically fine. It was all surface level injuries, nothing she hadn't survived before. *But she's still struggling.*

Doc stood straight as he pulled off the examination gloves. "I suggest you don't carry Chloe for a few days to give your muscles some time to heal, but that's it. I'm done poking at you." Doc turned my way. "Be gentle with her, please."

Sabrina snorted, her bravado a weak shield for everything swirling inside her. "No promises on that one, Doc, but I'll do my best to keep him in check."

He nodded at her and walked into his office, closing the door behind, and I was in motion before she could say a word. My arms wrapped around her, and for a second I worried I'd squeezed her too tight. Instead of tensing up from the pain, she instantly melted, leaning into me in a way that made the rest of the world slip for just a heartbeat.

Then reality crashed back in, hard and cold. I stepped away, gently holding her face in my hands. "Fuck, Kitten, are you okay?"

"You heard Doc. I'll be fine." Her voice was steady, but her hands trembled.

I leveled her with a stare that cut through the mental static, and had we been in the bedroom, would have had her submitting in an instant. "We're in some grey area, and I'm trying really hard not to turn into Wolf right now." Sabrina looked me in the eye and opened her mouth to respond, but nothing came out. Tears sprang up, and I cursed, wiping them away with my thumbs, helpless frustration burning through me. "Kitten..."

She swallowed hard and took a deep breath, as if steeling herself. "When he smirked at me, it was like I was in Cuba all over again. I saw Rod die, over and over. His last words kept echoing in my head." Her breath hitched, and a tear slipped out and rolled down her cheek. "And while I was fighting off the first guy, I saw the other one go straight for Zee. I wasn't going to let another member of my team die for me. I couldn't stand by and let that happen again." Her words came out quiet, strained, and so much smaller than before.

I kissed the top of her head, trying to press every shattered piece of her back together. "It's okay, Kitten. I got you."

She was shaking now, barely holding it together. "I need to know Zee is okay, Wolf." Her eyes met mine, full of panic and raw fear, and I wanted to tear it all out of her. "I have to hear their voice."

She needed the answers, and I was going to find them. Without a word, I grabbed my phone, dialed, and put it on speaker. Two rings later, he answered the call.

"Dante, we're en route to the Agosti house."

I nodded. *Good.* "Ricky, where's Zee?"

"They—"

"I'm right here, Dante, driving our asses back to your place. Take a breath." Zee cut off Ricky, sounding frustrated.

Sabrina sagged against me, letting out a barely audible, "Thank God."

I glanced down at the phone. "Wait, Zee's driving?"

Ricky let out an irritated-sounding breath. "Yeah, they wouldn't let me drive even though I'm *not* the one bleeding down my leg or with a dislocated shoulder."

I grimaced, remembering the last time I was in a vehicle with blood trailing down my leg.

"Oh, my God, you two. I'm fine! We're almost there. Everyone needs to chill the hell out."

I shook my head at Zee's stubbornness, but then Sabrina sat up with a start and grabbed my phone.

"You're driving with a wounded leg and a dislocated shoulder? I swear to God, you get your ass here so I can kick it myself." She angrily ended the call, and I wasn't sure if she was going to throw my phone or not. "I am going to kill them... or maybe I'll have Raine do it instead." She slid off the table and instantly winced when her feet hit the floor.

"Kitten, let me carry you up."

Sabrina arched her eyebrow defiantly. "Look, I'm barely holding it together right now. Let me pretend I'm fine long enough to bitch Zee out, make sure they're really okay, and *then* we can go to the room and I—" She cut herself off, voice breaking, eyes pleading with me to understand.

I nodded and kissed her, slow and soft until some of the tension in her body released. "You can't clock out until the job is done and everyone is back. I respect that." I rested my forehead against hers and held her tight. "I got you, Kitten. Wolf's here, and no one's getting through."

"Thank you." The words came out as a faint whisper.

About the time we were standing up to leave, Ricky burst into the medical area, frustrated and a little bloody. "They are a menace, but damn are they good at what they do."

Zee followed, less dramatically, arm in a sling cobbled together from their jacket, a deep gash above their brow, and a limp that suggested their leg was a mess. Still, they flashed me a bloody-toothed smile as Doc led them to one of the examination tables. "Don't look so worried, Sabrina. You should've seen the other guys. Raine made one of them look like they went through a wood chipper."

Sabrina tried to laugh, but it was half-hearted at best as she grabbed the hand not in the sling. "Are you *actually* okay, though? You saved my ass back there."

Zee shrugged, then hissed at the pain. "You'd have done the same. Ricky and Raine found us just after you and Jess left. We had it in the bag."

"That's not the point, and you know it." Sabrina spat the words through clenched teeth. This was her team, her responsibility, and I recognized the angst we all felt when anyone got hurt while on an assignment. She and Zee exchanged a look, and something silent passed between them. "Retribution and revenge were mine to take."

"But if it's between that and keeping you alive, I'm picking your life every fucking time." Zee tipped her chin up and caught my eye, quickly glancing at Sabrina and then back at me. "Take care of our girl while Doc takes care of me."

"You don't have to tell me twice." I wrapped my arm around Sabrina's shoulders and escorted her out of the medical area and up the back stairs that led to the garage. It was technically closer to my room, and I needed to get her alone and horizontal as quickly as possible, and for completely wholesome reasons this time.

Once inside my room, she was holding me so tight I thought something might break. We stood there, unmoving, until I felt the quake in her breath.

"I got you, Kitten." I scooped her up, cradling her against my chest, and brought her to my bed, where I stripped her bloody shirt and jeans off gently, then did the same for myself. "Lay down."

She never stopped watching me, those eyes holding on for dear life. It was a lifeline, and I wasn't letting go. Once we were under the blankets, curled around each other, the dam broke, and she sobbed, hard and ugly.

"I fucked up so bad... We put Chloe at risk... *La Muerta Rubí* wasn't supposed to find me yet... we weren't supposed to endanger the Agostis... How will Lianne ever forgive me?"

"Shh. It's okay, baby. No one is mad. Everyone made it home safe. That's what matters."

"But it could have gone so wrong," she gasped between tears. "I could have lost Chloe. Connor and Jess could have gotten hurt. They even went after Zee. All to break me... to get to me. They could have done it, Wolf. So easy."

Wolf. Her shield. Hers.

"But they didn't." I kissed the top of her head, trying to ground her any way I could. My phone vibrated, more than once, and as much as I wanted to ignore it, there were too many people who would come busting into this room if I didn't. I reached for it, thumb flying across the screen as I unlocked it and opened the messaging app.

Tal: < Is Sabrina okay? I saw the state of the vehicles coming in and have been on glass cleanup duty. >

Tal: < Do you need anything? >

Lianne: < Glad Zee and Ricky are back and okay. Noticed Sabrina wasn't in there anymore. Is everything okay? >

I answered Lianne first.

Dante: < I'm with Sabrina. She's okay physically... just needs a minute. >

Lianne: < Not surprised. Don Rodriguez wants her to call him. >

Dante: < I'll let her know once she decompresses. It might be a while. >

Was I supposed to tell my Don that Sabrina wouldn't be calling hers right away? Should I have pushed back? It didn't matter. Sabrina was my everything. She was always first. I had plans. Our future, mapped out and waiting for us. I'd been building it for years, and I wasn't about to let some South American cartel walk in and smash it to dust. Now that Sabrina was home? Nothing was stopping me.

Lianne: < Take care of her, Dante. We'll talk more later. >

Dante: < Yes, ma'am. Thank you. >

Letting out a relieved sigh that Lianne didn't take my head off, I responded to my sister.

Dante: < I've got Sabrina. She'll be okay. I'll let you know if we need anything. Love you, Tal. >

I silenced the phone, slid it aside, and wrapped both arms tight around Sabrina's sleeping form. I breathed her in, my heart rate steadying with every inhale. She was a force on her own, but nobody touched what was mine. Nobody destroyed what was mine.

If *La Muerta Rubí* wanted war, I'd be right beside her as she burned them to ash. Whatever it took. Wherever they ran. They would end long before we did.

Chapter Forty-One

Lianne

After a wild afternoon, the night went rather smoothly. The following morning started early with a meeting with Don Dallas and Don Rodriguez, recapping the events and new information regarding *La Muerta Rubi*. I had just gotten off the call when a text popped in.

Ben: < You should come to the kitchen if you can. Your best friend is hilarious. >

Lord. Now what did she do?

I didn't have anything super pressing to finish that very second, and I could use a reason to smile, so I pushed back from my desk and headed out of my office.

There was a small party in process as I walked into the kitchen. Chloe was standing on her step stool at the island, giggling with Jess, Quinn, and Ben. Jess locked eyes with me and grinned. "Chloe, you need to show Auntie Lianne your new shirt."

My niece looked over at me and gasped in excitement. "Li Li!" She jumped off her stool and raced toward me.

I had just enough time to squat down before she slammed into my chest. "Hey, Chloe." When she gave me a tight hug, my heart swelled with so much joy, I thought it was going to burst.

After a moment, she leaned back, pride and excitement sparkling in her eyes. "I have a new shirt, Li Li! See?"

I reached out and held the bottom of it, pulling it straight so I could see what was on it. It was a blue short-sleeved shirt with a crescent moon and several aquatic animals scattered across it, but it was the text that had me shaking my head. I glanced up at Jess, who looked far too pleased with herself. "Really? You got Chloe a shirt that says 'I slept with the fishes'?"

She dissolved into laughter as she nodded. "Oh, come on, Li, it's hilarious, and you know it."

"You like my shirt?" The uncertainty swirling in Chloe's eyes had me checking my reaction.

"I love it. I think the jellyfish is my favorite part."

She beamed at me with a brilliant smile. "I have a 'luga whale. Wanna see?" In a flash, the little girl dashed across the kitchen, snatched the small white stuffed animal off a chair, and ran back to me. "I love my 'luga!" She gave it a hug, kissed it, and then looked at me again. "I show Dada?"

I didn't miss how all the adults in the room locked up, but I never took my eyes off hers. "Let me talk to your dada and see if he's busy."

Chloe nodded dutifully. "Dada work a lot."

"Yeah. He does." I leaned forward and kissed the top of her head. "I'll be back in a little bit okay?"

"Okay. Love you, Li Li."

I grinned as my heart filled with joy. "Love you too, cupcake." *More than you'll ever know.*

After standing, I turned and walked out of the kitchen, and was almost immediately stopped by Ben.

"Li, can I ask why you're letting our little girl visit *him*?"

Oh, love. His overprotective side was out with a vengeance, and I took his hands in mine. "Aside from the fact that Liam is still her father, Chloe asked. There's no reason not to let the visit happen."

Not that he knew, but it was going to be his last visit as her legal guardian, and I couldn't help but wonder if it was going to be his last visit with her, ever.

One thing at a time.

Chapter Forty-Two

Dante

My heart swelled with love and joy when I spotted Sabrina walking in hand-in-hand with Chloe.

That's my wife.

Had I seen her a couple hours ago? Yes, but I was so in love with her, it didn't matter. Sabrina always made me feel this way.

Lianne, also holding one of Chloe's hands, was dressed in one of what she called her 'power suits,' looking every bit the part of Don. Seeing her smiling and so light with how she was interacting with Chloe was such a wild contrast from the strong, fierce, and determined woman she was when running the family.

That was the power Chloe had over us all.

She looked at Sabrina. "I need you two to stay here for a second while I make sure Liam is ready."

Sabrina nodded and crouched down next to Chloe and started talking to her. I didn't have a chance to pay attention to it as Lianne walked up, stopping right in front of me. "How is he today?"

"Grumpy, but non-aggressive at the moment."

She nodded and then stepped into the medical area, staring at the door to the holding cell Liam had called home for the past two weeks. After a few moments, she let out a deep sigh. "I can't believe it's come down to this."

I wasn't entirely sure what she was talking about. "Ma'am?"

Lianne shook her head and let out a small sigh. "This will all be over soon enough. Open the door."

A million questions sprang into my mind, but I shoved them aside. If and when my Don wanted me to know more, she would tell me. "Yes, ma'am." I unlocked the door and pushed it open. "Good morning, Liam. You've got company."

He glanced up immediately, furrowing his brow when he spotted his sister. "Oh, *Don Agosti* has deigned to grace me with her presence. To what do I owe *this* pleasure?"

She arched her eyebrow as a ghost of a smirk appeared on her face. "Chloe wants to see you and tell you all about her trip to the aquarium. I came to see if you were available. If you don't want to see her, all you have to do is say that. You don't have to be a raging asshole to prove your point."

Rage flared up in his eyes for a split second before his entire demeanor softened. "*Of course* I want to see my daughter."

"Then fucking behave." She spat the words through clenched teeth.

Several emotions flickered across the man's face before he gave her a forced smile. "Fine."

"Good. If that changes, I will remove her." After taking a step back, Lianne's expression transformed from rage to joy before she glanced out the open medical area door. "Chloe, your dada is ready to see you."

An excited squeal echoed in the hallway, followed by frantic footsteps. The pint-sized Agosti raced into the room, and when Lianne gestured toward the door, Chloe ran up to it.

"Dada! Hi!"

A far more genuine smile appeared on his face as he rushed toward her and scooped her up for a hug. "How are you, sweetie?"

Chloe rambled on excitedly about her trip to the 'fishy house', and while Liam was invested in everything she had to say, there was a sadness to his expression. After she handed him her 'luga whale to see, he held it like it was the most precious thing, keeping his attention fixed on his daughter like she was the center of his universe.

Doed he actually love her? Does he regret his choices? Or is he just sad he missed the time with her?

I almost felt bad for the man, but when I glanced at Lianne, there was now something sharp and a little too poised about her expression and body language that shoved the fleeting thought aside and reminded me why the man was being held in solitary confinement in the first place.

Even monsters can pretend to love. That's what makes them extra dangerous.

It wasn't long before Chloe asked Sabrina to go upstairs to play with her toy kitchen. The little girl gave her dad a hug and a kiss on his cheek and then ran out of the room.

Lianne watched the door after they left and waited until we could no longer hear Chloe's adorable voice before she let out a deep sigh and looked at Liam again. "Don Vaux has decided on the retribution for the contract you breached. She's waiting for you upstairs to spell out the consequences. Don't keep her waiting." Without another word, Lianne turned and headed out of the medical area.

Liam immediately turned into a grumbling pain in the ass again. "Are you fucking kidding me? Consequences? Really? Who the fuck does she think she is?"

Which woman are you talking about? "A Don with business to attend to. Now get your ass moving. Or do you require assistance?" I glared at the man, holding his gaze until he stood up.

By the time we made it upstairs, Regina, Gage, and Peter were lined up along the wall across from the door to the conference room, and Lianne stood just past the door, arms crossed over her chest. No one looked particularly pleased.

What happened out here?

Leading Liam into the conference room, I wasn't surprised to see Lukas and Adair already sitting at the table, both wearing suits and serious expressions.

"Good morning, Dante, Liam."

I nodded at Adair as I showed Liam to his chair, not missing how she'd mentioned me before my charge. "Good morning, Don Vaux."

Pride flashed in her eyes as she returned the nod.

Lianne entered next, glancing around the room, her attention briefly stopping on each person before she stood behind her chair. "Mom's finishing up something with Mr. Greene and will be in shortly."

Liam leaned forward, brows furrowed. "Why is our lawyer here?"

"Because we asked him to be." Lukas looked at his brother like the man was an idiot. "You violated several terms and conditions of a contract and new ones had to be drafted because of it. Who the fuck do you think we'd bring in?"

Lynette walked in then, closing the door and facing it for a moment before taking her seat at the head of the table. Once settled, she leaned forward, resting her folded hands on the polished surface. "Don Vaux, the floor is yours."

Adair cleared her throat. "Liam Douglas Agosti, you have been found guilty of knowingly and intentionally breaching the blood debt contract between the Vaux and Agosti families. As stated in section six point two, breaches include, but are not limited to, betrayal of spouse/soon-to-be spouse, failure to honor family obligations, breaking of omerta, and collaboration with the enemies of either family." She looked up from the paper and stared Liam in the eye. "Actions to support these breaches include having an intimate relationship with Susan Vaux once the engagement to Victoria Vaux was official, allowing Susan Vaux to shoot Victoria with the intent to kill, marrying Susan Vaux despite no tangible proof Victoria was dead, working with Rodrigo Barlowe against the wishes of the former Don Agosti, aiding in the murder of the former Don Agosti, attacking and attempting to murder the current Don Agosti, as well as members of her staff and family, and finally endangering your child, an Agosti heir, to undermine and spy on Don Agosti and her family. Do you deny these actions?"

Liam stared at her for a moment. "Are you serious right now?"

Lukas sighed. "Answer the question, Liam. Or don't. The result will be the same."

He rolled his eyes. "Fine. I did everything you said. I'm a fucking monster. Is that what you want to hear?"

To Lianne and Lukas's credit, neither of them even blinked at Liam's biting response. Not that I expected them to. This wasn't the first Liam tantrum any of us had witnessed.

"Thank you." Adair picked up a pen and wrote something on the paper before looking at him again. "Which brings me to the consequences."

Liam arched his eyebrow. "I've read the contract, Adair. I hardly think you're going to declare war on my family."

Her eyes narrowed. "I would never declare war on the Agostis, not when the current Don, her second, and their entire team have worked tirelessly to keep me safe and alive. No. They aren't the problem here. *You* are. You and Susan."

He scoffed. "What, are you going to declare war on *us*, then? You and what army? You've been Don for ten minutes. Anyone loyal to Vaux is dead."

Adair took a deep breath and let it out slowly, the calm expression on her face never flickering. "I don't need an army, and I don't need to declare war. The Don Supreme signed off on my decision, and Mr. Greene has all the paperwork ready to go to implement it."

Liam scoffed, but there was a noticeable tensing of his posture. "Oh, and what *terrifying* fate do you have in store for me?"

It baffled me just a little how nonchalant and downright disrespectful this man was while facing two mafia Dons. I knew he still had a chip on his shoulder about so many things, but Liam had been raised in this world. He had been trained on the importance of following contracts, as well as seeing or doling out the consequences.

There were clearly things I was never going to understand about him.

"Aside from taking every penny and piece of property attached to your name? I'm removing Chloe from a dangerous situation before she becomes another casualty the dangerous game you insist on playing."

He narrowed his eyes at her warily. "What the fuck is *that* supposed to mean?"

In a smooth move, Adair slid a folder across the table toward him. "You're never going to see or endanger your daughter ever again."

"You... You *cannot* be serious." When all she did was gesture to the folder, Liam let out a tense breath, leaned forward, and started reading. He shifted in his seat and then shifted his attention to Lynette. "Mom, this is your granddaughter. You're just *letting* this happen?"

She gave him a cool, even stare. "This is out of my hands and above my pay grade, Liam. Don Vaux was benevolent enough to choose *not* to take away everything your father, grandfather, and great grandfather worked their entire lives for, even though she had every legal right. I'm stunned and grateful for her choices."

His eyes went wide, but then a snarl appeared on his face as his attention snapped to his sister. "Lianne, *you're* okay with her ripping apart my family?"

Liam's rage was slowly slipping into hysteria, and it made me uneasy, so I shifted closer to him. *Don't do anything stupid.*

Her stone-cold expression didn't waver. "Like Mom said, we didn't have any say in this decision, but even if we did, why are you so upset? You had no problem ripping apart *my* family. Also, hearing about you *willingly and knowingly* letting Susan shoot your fiance with the intent to kill, taking out Ross, taking out Dad, watching you shoot Ryan, and then enduring you berate and blackmail me." Lianne glared at the man. "You've earned so much worse than losing parental privileges to my niece."

He reached over and grabbed Lynette's wrist. "Mom, you have to see reason. You have to stop her."

I moved to restrain him, but Lynette gave me a sharp look and shook her head before returning her focus to Liam. "I *do* see reason, Liam. Reason to respect and listen to Don Vaux. Reason to follow the letter of the law as written in that blood debt contract you signed. Reason to allow the actions of your consequences to play out." Lynette paused, gripping her son's hand a little tighter. "I also see reason to fill you in on one last secret, Liam Douglas *Vaux*."

My jaw dropped slightly. *Holy shit. She took away his last name.*

Despite the fact Liam physically recoiled at her words, the snarl stayed on his face, and he also tightened his grip. "And what would *that* be, Mother?"

Lynette's expression remained composed. "Your father and I knew all about your side projects. Even the secret ones you thought you were so clever at hiding. I know all about how you were never going to honor the contract you and Adair signed. I know Susan came to you in a complete panic when Adair was nowhere to be found after you let her shoot her. I know it was always your plan not only to take over the Agosti family, but also to take as much territory from neighboring families. I knew you were already buying properties just outside of the Agosti territory to start the process. I know you wanted to ally with Vaux to threaten and blackmail other families into joining your mission to take out the Dallas family and steal the Don Supreme's throne. I even knew you and Susan always planned to use Chloe against us in some childish, desperate, half-thought attempt at getting more from us." She shook her head in disappointment. "I'm so glad your father and uncle aren't here to see your disgrace."

Liam opened and shut his mouth twice before. "Momma, I—"

"I also knew you were *never* going to be Don." Lynette spoke in a bitter, disgusted tone I'd never heard before. "Your father *ensured* it."

What? Glancing around the room, I clocked several other stunned expressions. This was apparently news to all of us.

Liam stared at his mother in shock. "No. I *was* next in line to be the Don, Momma."

Lynette shook her head. "Did you ever once see a single piece of paper with *anything* in writing about you taking your father's place?"

"Well, no, but he told me I was going to be his replacement."

A wicked smirk spread across her face. "You of all people should know there needed to be more than a gentleman's agreement to solidify or confirm your place as Don. Did you even read all of your father's will?"

He narrowed his eyes at her. "Mr. Greene read it after the funeral. We were all in there."

Lynette closed her eyes and let out a frustrated sigh. "Did. You. Read. It?"

"I… No. Why?"

The woman then smiled in a way that made a chill run down my spine. "You were *never* going to be Don. It was spelled out clear at day."

His nostrils flared as he clenched his teeth. "What? That's ridiculous. If it wasn't me, who was it, then?"

"Me."

Liam shook his head, his hand now shaking. "No. *I* was his second. I was next in line."

Lynette let out a dry, humorless laugh. "Yes, you were second to *him*, and then were going to be second to *me*. George and I saw what your soul was like. I would have signed everything over to Gage, Ryan, or Ceaser before *you* if both of your dear siblings had passed on it." Lynette stared at her oldest for a moment and then shook her head before glancing at Adair. "It's been a joy and an honor spending time with you in person the past few weeks, my dear. I'm so proud of the woman you've become and the Don you're growing into."

Adair narrowed her eyes in confusion. "Thank you?"

Lynette nodded, giving her a tight smile, and then shifted her attention to me. "Dante, it's also been an honor seeing you flourish with us. You make sure my grandbaby and Sabrina stay safe, happy, and healthy, okay?"

I swallowed hard and nodded. "Yes, ma'am." *Why is she thanking us?*

Liam narrowed his eyes, looking freaked out by the exchange. "Why are you talking like that?"

Lynette arched an eyebrow, her demeanor cooling significantly as she addressed her son. "Talking like *what*, Liam?"

He stared at her, studying her face, as if trying to figure out a puzzle. "You... You're talking like you're not going to make it out of this meeting."

Lynette scoffed and gestured around the room. "Was it *ever* your plan to let to walk away from this? Hasn't it *always* been your plan to take me out and make it look like an accident? Or if I didn't die, you'd make it look like you saved me to ingratiate yourselves to your sister?" Liam opened his mouth, but she silenced him with a glare. "I know you and Susan have an unofficial hit out on me. Your team and my allies have been *most* informative."

My jaw dropped, as did Liam's.

What the fuck?

"Momma! I'd never—"

Lynette reached over and slapped him hard across the face with her free hand. "Do *not* insult me by lying to my face, Liam Douglas. Your siblings and their teams *might* have believed a fraction of this goodwill act you've had since you showed up with Chloe, but I've always seen it for what it is. A fucking act. Nolan and William's appearance was a test. We all know how well *that* turned out."

My heart rate took off with how the conversation was escalating. I'd never seen Lynette lash out at anyone like this before. Physically or verbally. And by the looks on everyone else's faces, they hadn't either.

The stunned expression on Liam's face slipped just long enough to show the rage simmering just below the surface. "You ruined everything!" He spat the words out through clenched teeth.

My eyes went wide, but Lynette's professional mask never faltered. If anything, she almost looked bored. Or was it sad?

What else does she know?

Lianne

"I've ruined nothing, Liam. You did that all on your own."

In a swift move I didn't see coming, Liam ripped his hand off Momma, stood, and hit Dante in the side of the head. The man immediately dropped to the ground.

What? How?

Time slowed to a painful crawl as I realized there was a gun in Liam's hand.

Where in the fuck did he get that?

As Lukas and Adair jumped up and drew their guns, Liam pulled the trigger twice in quick succession as two shots went off next to me right before they both disappeared from my peripheral vision.

Shit! Please be okay.

"No!" I aimed my gun at Liam, but hesitated when I saw he was behind Momma, arm wrapped around her, with his gun pressed against her head. *How the fuck was he that fast?* "Get your hands off my mom!"

Time went back to normal as a wicked grin appeared on his face, one that widened when there was pounding on the conference room door. One that didn't open. *What? Why can't they get in?* I couldn't take my attention off the nightmare scene unfolding in front of me to check.

"You pull the trigger, I will, too. What's the plan, *Don Agosti*?"

I paused for a moment, trying to figure out if there was any way to get Momma out of this alive.

He sneered. "You really should have cleared the room of guns, *Don Agosti*. Didn't dear old dad ever tell you about the ones hidden in here?" Liam let out a smug little hum as his other hand moved at Mom's waist... right where her holster was. "Now, unless you want Mom's blood on your hands, call off your guard dogs *and* this bullshit paperwork."

Why aren't Lukas or Adair shooting?

Gunshots went off outside the door, and for the first time ever, I hated the upgraded doors we had in the house. Bullets weren't going to get through them. My focus shifted to the woman being held hostage. "Momma?"

She gave me a tight, determined smile. "Lianne, it's fine. Remember what I taught you."

Tears threatened to fill my eyes as my thoughts went to one of the first conversations Mom and I had after I became Don.

"When the time comes that someone uses me as a pawn in their sick game, choose the greater good over me. I've lived a long life. Don't waste your time on an old woman like me."

I'd hated having the conversation, and I hated it even more that she was right.

Swallowing hard, I nodded at her and then glared at my brother. *I hate you so much.*

Mom went limp and started to drop, forcing Liam to tighten his hold on her to keep her from hitting the ground.

Again, two shots went off, but only one of them was mine.

I was the only one standing.

Horror washed over me.

No.

Time slowed to a crawl again as Liam sank to the ground, shoulder bleeding.

When another gunshot went off, a stunned expression appeared on his face at the same time his shoulder jerked back and a hole appeared in his chest.

"Apologize to your mother before I fucking end you!"

I wanted to weep in relief at hearing Gage roar at Liam.

Wait. When did they get the door open?

Liam immediately looked down, looking stunned and horrified. "I... I'm sorry, Momma."

She let out a resigned breath and shook her head. "I wish you were, my dear. I also wish I could have saved you from your fatal attraction to *her*, but here we are."

Two more shots rang out, and another hole appeared in Liam's chest, while crimson erupted from the shoulder of his shooting arm. More blood poured out, and Lynette shuddered.

"Cease fire. This job is mine. Gage, get my mom the hell away from Liam. I need him to stand up and pay his debt like the man he fucking pretends to be."

Gage vaulted over the conference table and pulled Momma from Liam's hold, protectively cradling her in his arms as he backed away. Regina rushed past, checking over Dante, and there was motion behind me, but nothing pulled my focus from him as he struggled to stand and stay upright.

I took a steadying breath. "Agostis never forget, Liam Douglas, and I will forever cherish the memory of watching the light leave your eyes."

He narrowed his eyes at me. "She will seek revenge."

"She has to live that long." I pulled the trigger, and a final shot rang out as a hole appeared in Liam's forehead, the back of his skull immediately exploding and splattering against the wall. “Good riddance.”

Silence filled the room, and for a second, no one moved. I could barely breathe.

Holy shit.

I stared into the blank eyes of my brother’s corpse.

I killed Liam. I killed my brother.

For a moment, I had flashbacks of him pushing me on the swing in the backyard when I was little, him intimidating my date for my first dance, the two of us celebrating Chloe's birth, him hugging me at my wedding. As tears threatened to overwhelm me, my memories shifted to Liam with a gun trained on Jess as we ran into her dad’s office, how he threatened me and Mom in front of the house, him aiming a gun at Lukas and Ryan, how he used his daughter as a pawn to spy on his family, how he held a gun to our mother’s head...

For all the good things he’d done, he’d done twice as many bad.

Actions have consequences.

A strained cough pulled me back to the nightmare scene in the conference room. “Mom?”

She gave me a tight smile. “I’m still up.”

“Lianne... we have a problem.” Gage held up his hand. It was coated with blood.

Panic surged through me. *Please don’t belong to her.* “Who’s is it?”

“Mine, my dear.”

Mom? No!

Chapter Forty-Three

Sabrina

Two faint but definitive cracks cut through the air, immediately freezing me in place. It was a sound I knew all too well. *Those were gunshots. Inside the house. Shit.*

As my heart rate took off and adrenaline flooded my body, instincts and training took over. I jumped off the bed, putting myself between the door and Chloe's bed, where my pint-sized charge was peacefully napping. My hand was already wrapped tight around my weapon, safety off, finger on the trigger. I kept the barrel locked steady on that threshold, just in case the next person who tried to enter wasn't on our side.

Chloe's soft snore was all I could hear in the room for a moment, and while I was grateful, I also prayed she stayed asleep.

Hard and fast footsteps echoed in the hallway on the other side of the door, and I braced myself for whatever happened next. A soft, patterned knock sounded on the wood. One. Three. Two. Most of the team had specific knocks, and I knew this one was Avery's.

Please actually be her.

The door opened, and Avery barreled through. Her eyes were wild with panic for one raw second, then when she saw me, gun drawn, that fear blew out and she let out a low, fierce laugh that was almost a sigh. "I knew I liked you." She sounded way too calm for just having run up at least one flight of stairs after hearing gunfire. The woman wasn't even out of breath.

I kept my weapon up, refusing to let down my guard. "What happened?"

"Shots. Conference room. More than two. We need to get you two to the safe room. Now." Avery's words came out fast and low.

Nodding, I jammed my Glock back into the holster on my waistband and grabbed the go bag I'd put together for Chloe before rushing to her bed. My shoulder and side screamed in pain as I scooped up the sleeping toddler and held her tight to my chest while racing out of the room. A little pain was a price I was willing to pay to ensure her safety.

"Move, move, move!" Ben's voice rolled down the hallway in a deep, tight growl. He was at the top of the stairs, weapon up, stance rock-solid. Avery jerked her chin and fell in ahead of me, leading me toward the upstairs safe room. I'd walked the route a hundred times in my head and didn't even have to think about where I was going. Down the hall, into Lynette's room and straight to the bookcase.

I held Chloe tighter, mumbling into her hair. "Hold Bunny and your whale tight and close your eyes. I have you, cupcake. You're safe. I promise."

She squeezed her stuffed animals hard and did exactly what I asked, and I was so stinking proud of her I could have cried. All I wanted was to keep her from seeing the guns, the rage and intensity that filled Ben and Avery's faces, and the way everything felt dangerous.

But when Chloe lost her grip on Bunny and it tumbled to the floor, her cry nearly broke me. Ben or Avery must have scooped it up, because when we made it into the safe room, someone pressed it right back into her hands.

Thank you.

Inside was nothing like the steel saferooms I grew up with. I stared at my surroundings for a moment as I caught my breath. The Agosti's version was all polished wood paneling and even had a throw rug. There was a fold-out table with board games stacked on the shelf next to it, bunk beds, a couch I'd bet hid a mattress inside, and a kitchenette. Then there was the wall of screens locked onto every angle of the house. I shook my head. The Rodriguez compound needed an upgrade after seeing this.

Quinn and Jess were already there, intensely staring at the screens. Ben surged inside right before Avery, who slammed the door behind us, locking the world out.

Avery raced up to the screens and was thinking out loud as she ran calculations. "Two shooters, maybe three. No sign of Lianne, Lynette, Lukas, Dante, Regina, or Liam. What in the hell happened?"

I zeroed in on the monitors. Cameras covered the outside doors, the hallways, and the foyer, where Regina, Gage, and Peter were pressed up against the door, trying everything to get through. "No cameras in the conference room?"

"There's supposed to be." She pointed to one part of the screen that showed a black rectangle instead of a camera feed. Avery reached to flip the sound on, but Ben stopped her with a shake of his head, eyes flicking toward Chloe.

"Little ears present."

I loved that he also didn't want her hearing any more than she had to.

"Bina?" Chloe's voice was tiny and trembling.

When I looked down at her, her eyes were wide as she clung to Bunny and her Beluga whale. *Oh, Mija.* "Remember how we practice being safe?" She nodded, and I kissed the top of her head. "We are practicing being safe. The grownups needed to practice too, so we're using Grandma's secret fort to do it." I kept my voice soft and steady, hoping at least Quinn would join me in this lie.

As if she had heard my thoughts, Quinn turned and walked over. "Hey, Chloe. Can I sit by you and Sabrina?" When the little girl nodded, she smiled. "Would you like to color with me? Is that something we can do while practicing being safe?

Chloe nodded again, now looking a little less worried. "Yes. We color. We have snacks. We play with Bunny. We have to be quiet and follow 'truck-shuns'."

Quinn smirked. "I can do that. How about we sit at the table and color while Sabrina gets snacks for us."

"Okay!"

Once I had the duo settled in with coloring supplies I had packed into the go bag, backs to the wall of screens, I walked over to Ben, Jess, and Avery, two of whom were texting.

"Should I let my uncle know… in case we need backup?"

Avery hesitated. I could see her weighing the options, considering the ramifications before she answered. "I want to say no, but I don't know the full extent of the situation downstairs. I also can't tell you not to contact your uncle."

"Contact him." Ben's answer was immediate, and there was no room for argument in his voice.

Don't have to tell me twice. Nodding, I opened the encrypted app and messaged Uncle Ceaser.

S: < SOS. Come ASAP. >

I hesitated, then sent another message.

S: < I'm fine. C is fine. >

I watched the outgoing status, begging it to change to 'sent'. While waiting, I forced my focus back to the screens and the small world inside this reinforced room. Outside, the situation was evolving in real time. Gage, Regina, and Peter had finally gotten the door to the conference room open, but with the angle of the camera, we couldn't see inside.

This is not your priority.

As much as it hurt to walk away, I moved back to where Chloe was and crouched next to her, gently stroking her hair and whispering the lullabies my mother used to hum in Spanish. I didn't know I'd even remembered them until I was halfway through the first verse. It was pure muscle memory, something that bypassed my conscious mind and went straight to the part of me that still believed in luck.

My phone buzzed.

Tio: < How hot is it? >

It was such a mundane question, so perfectly him, that I almost laughed. My hands shook only a little as I replied.

S: < Someone burned themselves at least twice, but I'm cool. >

A familiar metallic sliding sound pulled my attention, and I glanced up to see Avery was checking the magazine. In the background, the security feeds were still bright on the wall. The sound was on, but very low, so as not to scare Chloe, who was blissfully coloring and eating blueberries with Quinn.

Avery caught my eye and gave a grim little nod, the kind fellow soldiers or officers give each other when there's nothing left to say.

"Ceaser knows." I didn't bother to hide the relief. "We'll see who he brings with him."

We all froze when a burst of gunshots cut through the silence.

Chapter Forty-Four

Lianne

I stared at the blood on Gage's hand in horror.

"Momma! No! Where did he get you?" I knew damn sure my shot hadn't hit her.

Ryan burst into the room. "I have an ambulance on the way."

My mom shook her head. "No need. My time here is done."

"No, it's not!" I ran to her side and took her hand.

Gage swallowed hard. "No, Lynette. It can't be. I—"

"It's a gut wound. I know my fate. This isn't something I can bounce back from." She struggled to take a shaky breath. "I'm not long for this world. Thank you for being here with me, my friend."

Tears fell from Gage's eyes. "Is there nothing else I can do?" His voice cracked on the last word.

A proud smile appeared on my mom's face. "Keep an eye on my little girl. She's brilliant and more than competent, but you know how parents worry."

"Momma, no." I sniffled. "Stop talking like this. You're going to be fine."

"It will be my honor, Lynette." He took her hand in his and held it to his chest. "It has been my absolute honor to serve you, your husband, and your daughter. I know this is part of the game we play, but... George married the best woman."

A sob shook my entire body. "Momma... You... You're going to be fine."

"Shhh, Lianne...There..." She reached up and gently touched my cheek. "There was no stopping Liam. Tell Lukas I love him," she struggled to take another breath, "and that I'm proud of both of you."

"Tell him yourself." My voice was so thick with emotion, I could barely get the words out. "You can't leave yet. I need you, Momma. We all do."

Lynette looked up and tears filled her eyes as a smile spread across her face. "My George is here..." Her voice trailed off before she looked at me again. "It's time for me to go.... He..." Her smile grew wider. "He wants you to know he's proud of you." She took a shallow, gurgly breath. "End this, Lianne. Make my death worth it. I love you." She let out a whisper of a breath, and I stared as the life faded from her beautiful blue-grey eyes.

"No! Momma!" I choked on the words as another sob shook me.

This isn't happening.

She's not dead.

She'll be fine.

This is a nightmare.

I just need to wake up.

Tears rolled down my cheeks as I clutched her hand and stared at her in disbelief for what felt like forever. It could have been minutes, seconds, days. I had no idea.

A pained groan pulled me back to the present as Dante shifted. "What happened?"

I just stared at him, unable to speak.

"Lianne?"

Ryan's panicked voice had me spinning around. He was kneeling next to Lukas, who was flat on his back... eyes closed... head bleeding.

Fuck. No!

"Lukas!" My scream tore through my throat. Not giving a damn about anything other than getting to my brother's side, I crawled under the table and would have shoved Ryan out of the way if he hadn't moved. I took Lukas's face in my hands, tears still falling down my face. "Lukas, no. You have to be okay. You can't leave me, too. I can't do this without both of you." I leaned down, touching my forehead to his chest to listen for breathing when he let out a strained cough. Sitting up with a start, I stared at him, daring to hope he was okay.

He coughed again and grimaced. "Fuck, that hurt."

"Holy shit, you're okay." I collapsed in relief onto his chest and sobbed even harder. "How are you okay?"

Lukas wrapped his arms around me as best as he could. "I'm good, Li. I wore the bulletproof vest." We stayed that way for a moment before he shifted. "What the fuck happened?"

I sat up again and stared at him. "I... He... I tried so hard to save her."

"What?" Lukas's attention shifted past me and then realization hit. "No!" His eyes filled with rage as every muscle in his body tensed up. "You fucking asshole!" My brother grabbed his gun off the ground, aimed, and squeezed the trigger. Again. And again. Not stopping even after he'd emptied the magazine into Liam's body.

Hands shaking, I pried the gun from him and took his face in my hands, making him look at me. "He's dead, Lukas. He can't hurt us anymore."

Tears spilled from his eyes and rolled down his cheeks. "He took Mom *and* Dad from us. It's always going to fucking hurt, Li."

A wry smile appeared on my face as a thought popped into my mind.

He sniffled and gave me an odd look. "How in the hell can you smile at a time like this?"

"Mom, Dad, and Uncle Douglas are probably kicking Liam's ass right now."

Lukas glared at me as if I was the devil himself. "Mom and Dad did *not* go to hell, Lianne Emelie."

I returned the angry look and shoved him. "Of course not. Mom *easily* convinced someone to give the three of them a one-time hall pass."

Lukas shook his head as he wiped tears from his face. "You know, I can't even argue with that."

I looked around the room, taking in the death and devastation, my vision quickly blurring as I processed the fact my world was falling apart. "Lu, I really need another hug."

He practically launched at me, wrapping me in the tightest hug ever. "I got ya, Li."

My heart broke again as he held me. "How are we going to get through this... again?"

Gage cleared his throat, and when I glanced his way, tears were also streaming down his face. "You do what your mom told you to do, Lianne. You end it. For good."

Chapter Forty-Five

Sabrina

Avery looked at her phone and then at me. "We need to go downstairs. They need us. Now."

"All of us? Is it safe? What about Chloe?"

Jess rested her hand on my shoulder. "I've got her covered. Go."

Trusting the team around me, I raced down the stairs and through the foyer. Connor stood there, waiting for us. He locked eyes with me first. "Dante's downstairs with Doc. Go. Jess, give me Chloe; Ryan needs you in his office."

Nodding my thanks, I turned the corner and hurried down the hallway, noting the acrid scent of blood, death, and gunpowder as I passed the conference room, the door no longer on the hinges.

What the hell happened?

I didn't slow down to investigate, but ran downstairs, to the medical area, and up to the man I married, taking his hand in mine. I hated the fact he was stretched out on one of the examination tables with a bandage around his head. "Dante? Love, talk to me."

His eyes fluttered open, and tears formed. "Hey, Kitten."

I sniffled. "Are you okay?"

He let out a shaky breath. "Yeah. I'm good. A little banged up, but nothing one of Chloe's cartoon bandages won't fix."

A laugh mixed with a sob snuck out as I leaned forward and kissed him. "I'll make sure Doc uses them next time." Hard sobs from Lianne grabbed my attention, reminding me there were other people in the room, and when I looked over my shoulder, the rage and pain in Ben's eyes as tears rolled down his cheeks had me on high alert again. "What happened?" *How many times am I going to have to ask?* I glanced at Adair, who looked shell-shocked, tears also steadily running down her face.

Where is Lynette?

Uncle Ceaser ran in at that moment, looked at me, and let out a sigh of relief as he rushed to my side, wrapped me in a tight hug, and kissed the top of my head. "I'm so glad you're okay, *Mija*."

I leaned into his warmth and strength for just a moment, letting it ground and settle me. "Me too, *Tio*."

He kissed the top of my head again before releasing his hold, and I watched as he walked over to Lianne. "Where's your mom?"

Lianne opened her mouth and looked out the door and then back at him, grief all over her face. "I... She..."

His posture stiffened. "Tell me Lynette is going to walk through that door."

She swallowed hard and then shook her head. "I can't. She... She's not..."

Uncle Ceaser moved to stand in front of Lianne and took her hands in his own. "Lynette died, didn't she?" When she nodded and fresh tears fell from her eyes, he pulled her in for a hug. "I'm so sorry, Lianne."

They stayed that way until she let out a sigh and sat up again. "Thank you."

"And what of Liam?"

She pressed her lips together, and a flurry of emotions flicked across her face. "He's dead, too."

Uncle Ceaser nodded and swallowed hard. "With your permission, I'll take care of Liam and make sure everything else is covered while you take care of your mother."

Chapter Forty-Six

Sabrina

"I want Gamma."

My throat was thick with emotion as I sat her down. "Grandma can't come up here right now."

"But Gamma read fishy stories." Her little blue eyes filled with tears, and I reached over to give her Bunny and her Beluga whale, a poor substitute for the woman she requested. I knew Chloe was overtired and in need of her nap, and while she didn't usually demand to see Lynette, today was apparently the day to start.

It broke my heart to see her like this. Lynette was never going to hold her, tickle her, read her books, or give her little kisses on her cheeks again. Liam, horrible human as he was, was never going to hug her again.

"I'll read fishie stories for now, okay?"

"In Bina's bed?"

If that will make you stop asking about your grandma, we can sit in the bathtub and read every book in the world for all I care. "Of course!"

She let out a whiny sigh before nodding. "Okay. Bina read stories."

I had just finished the eighth book when there was a soft knock on the door, and Dante walked in. His cheeks were tear-stained, and he came over, sat next to me, and wrapped his arm around my waist. "I see she finally fell asleep."

I nodded. "She passed out two books ago, but I just kept reading. I couldn't stop."

"You wanted to cling to something normal. I don't blame you." He kissed the top of my head, and I glanced up into his beautiful, bloodshot eyes.

"I know Li is going to tell her, but having to explain to a two-year-old that Grandma is busy all the time now...knowing she's never going to be in this room again... It makes the pain of losing my Auntie 'Nette even worse." I swallowed hard, blinking back tears that formed every time I thought about my favorite aunt. "The Agostis never deserved all this pain, death, and destruction, Wolf. Mafia or not, they didn't deserve this."

"I know, Kitten."

I swallowed hard, trying to wrangle my emotions. "Don't get me wrong, Li has done an amazing job stepping into Uncle George's shoes, but it's not fair. There are so many burdens she should never have been forced to deal with."

He let out a long breath. "I was just telling Ryan the same thing. They've endured so much loss. We all have. We lost Kevin and almost lost Ryan and Adair. I can't even begin to guess how Gage is doing right now. Fuck." Dante shook his head. "And then there's all the attacks and betrayals. The last year has been brutal."

"I've grown up in this world. I know death is part of this life. My own father fell victim to it, but the Agostis haven't been gunned down by some outside rival or gang. No, their own fucking son destroyed it. Why? Because he's greedy? Because his wife is a selfish whore?" I met his gaze and felt the fire that burned within them. "I *will* help Li however she needs it. I have no doubt *Tío* will too. I'll talk to him. See what we can do to help."

A proud smile filled his face. "You know Lianne is going to claim it as Agosti business."

I nodded. "And I will vehemently remind her it's also my family business. And as her fucking cousin, I'm here to help however she needs it."

Dante broke through my thoughts as he pulled me closer and kissed my temple again. "I'll be right beside you to do it. Family is family. It doesn't start or end in blood, and we protect our own. The Agostis never forget."

"Or forgive." My voice was more hostile than it had been in a long time. No one fucked with my family, and I would be there when *the* Don Lianne Agosti took justice in to her own hands.

We sat there for about ten minutes, his presence slowly curbing the rage, before I got up and put Chloe in her bed. Once she was tucked in, and I had the baby gate set up at the door and stepped outside the room, Dante pulled me close. I pressed my face into his chest, letting the tears fall from my eyes.

My phone rang with the dedicated tone I had for my uncle, bringing me out of my stupor. "Hola, *Tio*."

"Sabrina." His voice comes through tight, clipped. "We have confirmation from Alvarez, Menendez, and the Brooklyn crew that *La Muerta Rubí* has plans to take you out at the funeral."

"What?"

"They'll be watching the cemetery," he continued. "Every entrance, every tree line."

I close my eyes, picturing the rows of black cars, the flower arrangements, the dark suits. Lynette's casket. "And?" I gripped the phone harder as I walked into the otter office; my knuckles went white.

"Just got off the phone with Lianne. Made her aware of the situation." He paused for a moment. "I'll represent the family while you stay at the house."

The room suddenly felt too hot, too small. "What? No! Auntie 'Nette braided my hair for my first communion. She taught me how to load a Beretta." My voice cracked. "You can't—"

"You're my heir." His tone dropped an octave, the way it did when he was speaking as Don Rodriguez, not my uncle. "Protocol exists for a reason."

I slammed my palm against the wall. "Dallas will bring Backnoff. San Augustine will be bringing Dominic. Every other family will ignore your precious fucking protocol. If I'd been here for Uncle George, would you have locked me away then, too?"

The silence stretched.

I could hear him breathing, the ice shifting in his glass again.

"That's what I fucking thought, *Tio*."

"It's not safe, *Mija*." Uncle Ceasar's voice held a finality only he could achieve. "Even for you."

I narrowed my eyes and glared, as if he would materialize in front of me. Anyone else would have let the argument end there. But I wasn't just anyone. "I don't see you hiding, *Tío*." I hated how snippy and desperate I sounded, but part of me didn't give a damn. "Lynette was my family as much as she was yours. I can't... I won't let her get put in the ground without saying goodbye."

"You can and you will." I could practically see him, closing his eyes and rubbing his forehead as he prepared to out-stubborn his only niece. "This isn't negotiable, Sabrina. You're my heir. You're the only one that matters."

Fuck that! "Uncle Ceasar—"

"No." He cut me off. "La Muette Rubí will expect us to be together. They'll be waiting. They want you, but if they have the chance to take both of us out, they will. If anything happened to you..." He trailed off, clearly not wanting to talk about my death.

My temper rose, and something in me snapped. "So we just let them scare us into hiding away? Let them dictate who mourns family and who doesn't? I can take care of myself, *Tio*. I've been doing it since I was twelve."

"Not like this, you haven't. Not with this kind of exposure. I need to bring you up to date on everything that's happened since you got home, but now is not the time. You are currently their sole target." He let out a tense breath. "If you were thinking straight, you'd agree with me. I know you're hurting, *Mija*, but I won't gamble your life for tradition or pride. I lost Fatima and Vanesa. I won't lose you,too. Not while I am still breathing."

I stared at the wall, hot tears breaking through. He was right, but that didn't soften the ache. If anything, it made it worse. Every Rodriguez was raised to keep the family safe first, to do the necessary thing even when it hurt. But this— *this* wasn't some mission or asset recovery. This was Lynette Agosti. My Auntie 'Nette. The one person who'd never once asked me to be less than I was.

"You don't trust me to handle it," I finally said. "You think I'll make it worse."

"Not at all." This time the edge was gone, replaced by something more gentle. "I trust you more than anyone alive, but I won't let your grief get you killed. I need you here. The family needs you here. Dante needs you here." His voice, so rarely soft, came close to breaking. "This is the only way."

I couldn't speak. Couldn't breathe for a second. I just sat there, phone pressed to my ear, my heart pounding against the inside of my ribs. Uncle Ceaser waited, silent and patient, knowing he'd already won.

Dante stepped into the room and wrapped his arms around me. The moment stretched until I finally muttered, "Fine." I hung up before I could hear his relief.

I leaned forward, falling against my husband's chest, hands clenched so tight in his shirt that my knuckles ached. The helplessness settled like a stone in my stomach, heavy and cold. For the first time since I could remember, I was being benched, sidelined by my own blood for my own protection. It made me want to scream, or break something, or run until I couldn't feel any of it.

What hurt worse was that I was being shut out of saying this one last goodbye.

After her nap, Chloe grabbed Bunny and turned to look at me. "We see Li Li?"

I nodded. "Yes, I'm sure Auntie Li would love to see you." Hand in hand, we slowly made our way downstairs, through the foyer, and stopped in front of her office door. "Chloe, would you like to knock?"

She smiled and nodded, immediately knocking on the door. "Li Li!"

I grinned at the bellowed greeting.

Please be in there.

Suddenly the door opened and Lianne was crouched down, eye-level with her niece. "Hello, cupcake."

"Li Li!" Chloe rushed forward and hugged her auntie, and hit her with enough force that Lianne landed on her butt and pulled her niece into her lap. The two cuddled for a moment before Chloe reached up and wiped something off Lianne's face. "Li Li sad?"

She nodded. "Yeah. Auntie Li is sad today. Could I have an extra hug to feel better?"

"Yes!" Chloe squeezed tight, and once she finally released Lianne, she held out her Bunny. "Here."

Lianne gave her a confused smile. "For me?"

"Yes. You hug." Chloe nodded and then looked up at me. "Nack, pease?"

I nodded, swallowing down the surge of emotions that came up as I watched the two Agosti ladies. "Yeah, we can have a snack."

"Li Li, nack too?"

Lianne glanced at me and nodded. "I'd love a snack, sweetie. Maybe Uncle Ben is in the kitchen."

Chloe let out an excited squeal. "Unca Ben Ben!" She hopped out of Lianne's lap and grabbed her hand. "We go now."

"Yes, ma'am."

It was absolutely adorable watching Chloe 'drag' Lianne to the kitchen, complaining when 'Li Li' was being too slow.

Ben walked in the same time we did and grinned when he spotted his niece. "Who's in my kitchen?"

Chloe cheered in delight. "Me, Unca Ben Ben!"

She rushed forward, and he scooped her up in a huge hug, spinning her around in a circle, making her squeal and laugh.

"That makes things suck a little less."

Lianne let out a shaky sigh. "Yeah. I'm all about grabbing onto whatever happiness I can right now."

"Including the man you married?"

Her expression softened, and a tiny smile appeared. "Yes. I'm keeping him *very* close right now."

I couldn't keep the grin off my face. "Would the two of you like some time with Chloe?"

Lianne let out a sigh. "You know? I think we would. I like how light she makes things."

Ben, with Chloe still in his arms, walked over to us. "Chloe thinks we need to make marshmallow rice treats and watch the fish movie. What do you think, Li?"

She smiled and nodded. "I think that sounds perfect."

My heart hurt a little less watching the trio move around the kitchen. That little girl may have lost her father, but she would never want for love and affection.

Chapter Forty-Seven

Lianne

It was bad enough to watch my father's casket get lowered into the ground almost seven months ago. The fact I was standing at his grave site, watching my mother join him was a new and special level of hell. I knew I was going to lose them at some point, but not this fast... or this close together. *Or both at the hands of my oldest brother.*

"Li?" Ben squeezed my hand. "I think Don Dallas would like a word."

I nodded and took a deep breath, taking a moment to shove down the rawest and sharpest feelings. There was no hiding the tears silently running down my face or my red eyes, but I wanted to at least appear marginally pulled together. Turning, I gave him, Backnoff, Beth, and Maloy a nod. "Thank you all for being here."

The barely concealed rage and pain in Dallas's eyes matched mine. "There's no place we'd rather be, Don Agosti." He stepped forward and lowered his voice. "I'm truly sorry for your loss, Lianne. I held both your parents in the highest regard, as I do you. I understand it's Agosti business, but if there is anything we can do for you, it's my responsibility," he paused. "No, it is my *honor* to help."

As I stared at Dallas, I heard echoes of what had been said at Mom and Dad's funeral. The offers for help. The desire to take out the enemy responsible. How no one knew the person responsible for Dad's death. We'd kept everything close to the chest then.

But now everything has changed. There's no reason to hide a dead man.

I raised my chin and nodded. "I appreciate your generous offer, Don Dallas. And while it is Agosti business, I don't mind telling one of our closest allies that Mom's death has already been avenged. The traitorous murderer is no longer with us."

His eyebrows went up slightly. "A silver lining to a dark day."

I nodded again. "I don't know if I'll ever fully recover from the depths of his betrayal, but I at least guaranteed he can't hurt us anymore."

Dallas cleared his throat. "Lianne, who killed your mother?"

More tears fell, and I blinked them away. "The same poor excuse of a man who took away my father. The same man who used his daughter as a pawn in a game she is far too young and innocent to be part of." Ben tightened his hold on my waist, and I rested one of my hands on his, giving it a squeeze.

Don Dallas's posture stiffened as he inhaled sharply. "It's really most unfortunate Liam turned out the way he did. I know George and Lynette did not raise him to act the way he did. I'm sorry the Vaux line struck yet again."

I nodded, pleased he'd figured it out. "Mom certainly had a final lecture for him." I then glanced at Adair, and a small smile teased my lips. "But not *all* of the Vaux line has fallen victim to greed and destruction."

He nodded. "I stand corrected. I apologize and meant no disrespect to the new Don Vaux and her chosen family."

The formality of this conversation was too much. "We both know you weren't talking about Adair. And in regard to your offer, I'll call when we need backup."

Dallas reached out and took my hand in his. "Your father would be so incredibly proud of you, if not more than how proud your mother was. It truly is an honor to work side by side with you."

I swallowed hard, caught off-guard by the depth of his compliment. "Thank you, sir."

Beth shifted and stepped forward, holding her arms out. "May I?"

A hug.

"Yes, please."

She immediately wrapped her arms around me and held tight. "Mrs. Dallas was very upset she couldn't be here. She wanted me to tell you that she's proud of you, that you are doing the impossible today, and that you are doing it so much better than you think. And personally, as someone who's lost close family as well, I understand some of the pain. You're not alone in this." Beth leaned back and let out a tense breath. "I know I'm not mafia like you, and I know you have your people, but if you need a friendly ear, I'm happy to come over. Say the word and I'll make Wes or Jensen bring me."

A small chuckle snuck out. "You'd *make* them?"

Beth glanced over her shoulder, and Backnoff narrowed his eyes at her in confusion before she looked at me again, nodding. "Yeah. Especially if it's for you. Us mafia ladies need to stick together. The guys can't have all the secret meetings."

Dallas shook his head, but I saw the flicker of a smirk before Backnoff walked up. "Darling, I think we need to let Don Agosti get on with her day."

Beth gave my shoulders one last squeeze. "You've got this. I'll see you soon."

After finishing my farewells, the Dallas crew slowly made their way to their vehicle. The second they were out of earshot, Ben leaned in. "I like Beth. She reminds me of another badass woman... one I love very much."

I glanced at him, unable to keep a small grin off my face. "Me, too."

It wasn't long before most of the funeral guests had cleared out and I stood next to Ceaser, staring at the open grave. "I guess it's time to go home without her now."

He nodded. "Lynette's body may be here, but you're never truly without her, Lianne. She and your dad both live on in you. In your work. In the love you show your family and crew. In the love your family and crew show you. That was their legacy. That is *your* legacy."

A tiny smile crept onto my face. "That's a legacy I'm proud to carry on." I glanced to my right, overwhelmed with love and support at the sight of Ben, Regina, and Gage lined up, keeping watch, with Talia and Avery at the SUVs. After wiping more tears from my face, a deep sigh came out. "I suppose I should keep up Mom's tradition of going home and having a cannoli."

"I think she'd like that."

As we turned to head back to our respective vehicles, I spotted a large white van winding through the cemetery, approaching our location.

"Li, get in the truck. Now."

I glanced at Gage, a little stunned by his tense order. "We're all heading there right now."

He shook his head and then looked at me, tension and guilt flickering in his eyes. "I don't like it, Lianne. I need you safe."

Ben rushed me along a little faster toward the SUV Avery was next to, his left hand on the small of my back. We were maybe twenty or thirty feet away from the vehicles when the panel door of the van slid open and four men jumped out and ran toward us.

Chaos immediately erupted.

Gage grabbed me in a bear hug grip and raced me toward the open door of the SUV. I tripped and almost fell, but he held firm, never slowing a step.

"Ben!" I tried to glance back, but Gage's hold was too tight for me to move enough to see.

"I've got him."

Regina! "Keep him safe!"

Shots went off as I was shoved into the back seat the same time one of the side windows shattered, sending glass pieces flying everywhere.

Shit!

When I went to pull my gun and fire back, Gage forced my head down against the dark leather, leaning over me as he returned fire before slamming the door shut. "Get us the hell out of here!"

"No! We need to help them!"

The engine started, and we were immediately moving.

I tried sitting up again, only to have Gage fight against me. "No, stay down, Lianne. You're not catching a fucking bullet."

My gut was screaming for us to go back. I needed to be there. "I'm not leaving without Ben."

"Avery and Raine have him."

In a rage, I shoved Gage off me and sat up. "Why are we leaving them? We have to help them. We have to—"

He grabbed my shoulders and made me face him. "Our priority was getting you the hell out of there and in one piece. Which we did."

The wild desperation and fear all over his face was not what I was used to seeing. "I'm fine. I promise."

"But you're not." Gage shook his head, and I didn't miss how his hand trembled slightly as he pulled a handkerchief from his pocket and dabbed the side of my face.

I hissed at the unexpected sting, and when he pulled the thin fabric away, there was blood on it. "It's just a scratch."

"I can't lose you too, Lianne."

The man who rarely showed an emotion other than irritation or serious focus was tearing up and trembling. In a moment of insanity, I threw my arms around him and pulled him for a tight hug. "I'm right here, Gage. I promise I'm fine. You did your job perfectly." He took a shaky breath and nodded.

I didn't know what was more jarring. The fact I hugged Gage like a mother would a child, or the fact he let me. When I glanced at Regina in the rear view mirror. Her eyes were locked on the road in front of her, but there was no missing the tension in her face, or how she was clutching the steering wheel.

It wasn't long before we pulled into the driveway. Lukas was waiting for us in the garage, and the engine wasn't even off before my brother ripped the door open and let out a relieved breath so deep, I thought he was going to collapse.

Tears were in his eyes, and he pulled me into his chest. "I'm so fucking glad you're okay." After he leaned back, he looked between me and Gage. "What in the hell happened? Where did that white van come from? Who in the hell attacked us?"

"I have no idea. Wait." I narrowed my eyes at Lukas. "How do you know what happened already?"

Regina walked over, touched her ear, and pulled out an earpiece. "Because of these. Avery, Gage, and I all wore them today."

My brother nodded. "Nash was in the war room, listening the entire time. He called me the second shit went sideways."

"Oh." That was a fucking brilliant move. "Where's the rest of the crew?"

"I don't know, Li. I was focused on you. Ryan should have that info. He's downstairs."

"Considering he has trackers on everything under the sun when it comes to vehicles and people, I certainly fucking hope so." I raced down the garage steps to the other basement entrance and then into the war room. "Where are Ben, Avery, and Talia? Are they okay?"

Ryan looked stressed as his focus was locked onto his computer screen. "The truck is en route to the house, but we lost signal to the earpieces. None of them have answered their phones."

He clicked a few more things, followed by more frantic typing. There was a desperation to his actions that set me even more on edge. "What aren't you telling me?"

"I lost connection to Ben's phone."

My blood ran cold. "What?"

Ryan shook his head as he glared at his computer screen, still typing and clicking away. "I can't get a location on Ben's phone. I have Avery and Talia's locations, same as the truck, but not his."

I sat on the chair next to him before I collapsed. *This cannot be happening right now.* "Could his phone be off? Or super damaged? And that's why you can't track it?"

He nodded. "We'll know in a minute. The truck's almost here."

Jumping to my feet, I sprinted down the hallway and back up into the garage.

Please be in the truck.

Please be okay.

I can't do this without you.

Lukas caught up with me and pulled me back as the garage door opened, but when I spotted two of the windows shot out, I broke out of his hold and ran up to the SUV. Avery was in the front passenger seat, with blood smeared across her face, busted lip, looking absolutely pissed.

"Avery?"

She clenched her jaw and locked eyes with me. Hers were bloodshot and bright with anger. "I did everything I could."

My heart stopped. *No. Not again.* "What are you talking about?"

Talia walked around the front of the truck, looking as roughed up and bloody as Avery. I didn't miss the field dressing on her arm, or that there was blood seeping through it. "There were too many of them. We fought like hell, but when Raine got hurt..."

I looked between the two of them as anger and panic surged through my veins. "Where is Ben?"

The two women glanced at each other. "Lianne... I... We..."

"Where. Is. My. Husband?"

To be continued in Fatal Consequences...

Up next for the Gorgeous, Armed, and Dangerous series:

Fatal Consequences

Coming late 2026

About the Author

Elisabeth Garner is a master of suspense romance, blending heart-pounding tension with witty banter and powerhouse characters.

As an author, she crafts stories that linger long after the last page. As an editor, she helps authors polish their works into something even more magnificent.
As a graphic designer, she transforms the author's vision into a piece of art.

When she's not lost in her writing and designing, she's a dedicated wife and mom, fueled by tea and lattes. A D&D enthusiast and DIY aficionado, Elisabeth embraces creativity in every aspect of her life. Unapologetically chaotic, she invites readers into her thrilling world.

www.emgarner.net

Facebook, Instagram, Threads, TikTok – @ booksbyemgarner

www.ingramcontent.com/pod-product-compliance
Lightning Source LLC
LaVergne TN
LVHW010631110826
845149LV00014B/2824

* 9 7 8 1 9 6 0 4 8 9 1 5 9 *